STRANGER IN THE NIGHT

Center Point
Large Print

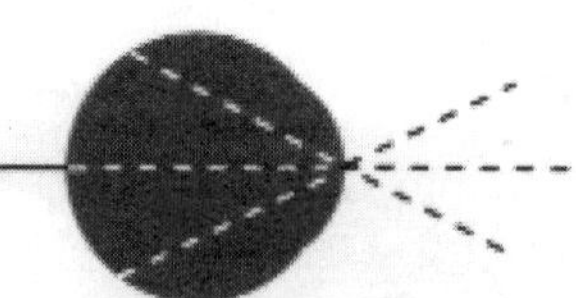

This Large Print Book carries the
Seal of Approval of N.A.V.H.

STRANGER IN THE NIGHT

A HAVEN NOVEL

CATHERINE PALMER

CENTER POINT PUBLISHING
THORNDIKE, MAINE

This Center Point Large Print edition
is published in the year 2009 by arrangement with
Harlequin Books S.A.

The text of this Large Print edition is unabridged.
In other aspects, this book may vary
from the original edition.
Printed in the United States of America.
Set in 16-point Times New Roman type.

ISBN: 978-1-60285-510-6

Library of Congress Cataloging-in-Publication Data

Palmer, Catherine, 1956-
Stranger in the night / Catherine Palmer.
p. cm.
ISBN 978-1-60285-510-6 (library binding : alk. paper)
1. Saint Louis (Mo.)--Fiction. 2. Large type books. I. Title. II. Series.

PS3566.A495S77 2009
813'.54--dc22

2009014831

To the refugees in Clarkston, Georgia,
who have brought such joy into my life.

Acknowledgments

Many thanks to those who shared stories of their work with refugees. In particular, I'm grateful to Tim Cummins, Terry Earl, Bennett Ekandem, Kim Kimbrell and all the caseworkers and other staff at World Relief. May God bless each of you. As always, my gratitude to my husband is boundless. Thank you for reading every word—sometimes more than once. I love you, Tim.

"When a stranger sojourns with you in your land,
you shall not do him wrong.
The stranger who sojourns with you
shall be to you as the native among you,
and you shall love him as yourself . . .
I am the Lord your God."
—*Leviticus* 19:33–34

"Come, you who are blessed by the Father,
inherit the Kingdom prepared for you
from the foundation of the world.
For . . . I was a stranger,
and you took me in."
—*Jesus Christ*
Matthew 25:34–35

Chapter One

Sweat dampening the wrinkled sheet beneath him, Joshua Duff counted the spurts of AK-47 bullets hitting the front door. The first round slipped into his nightmare—house check on a nameless street in Kabul. A search for insurgents. Dread crawled through him like a snake, twining around his neck, suffocating him as he crept forward in the heat. Faces stared at him, brown eyes luminous beneath long, fringed black lashes. Mouths smiled, lips parting over missing teeth. Hands reached out, fingers extended.

Friend? Or enemy?

The second round of staccato hammering woke Joshua from the troubled dream. The strangled breaths were his own. Jerking upright, he reached for a gun that wasn't there. The smell of gym shoes, basketballs, dusty concrete caught in his nostrils. This was not his barracks.

Or was it?

His eyes searched the darkness. Confusion tore through his brain as he worked to decipher data. A form lay on a bed across from him. The mound of muscled shoulder was motionless. Another man sprawled on a mattress near the door.

Comrade or civilian?

Asleep or dead?

A single window filled the only visible wall.

Somewhere nearby, an animal snuffled.

Death still stalking him, perspiration beading his bare chest, Joshua gripped the rounded aluminum frame of his cot. He licked his lips, expecting grit. Its absence surprised him. The tendon in his jaw flickered as he tried to force reality into his brain.

Of all the adversaries he'd faced in his thirty years, this was the most wily. This doubt and hesitation, this inability to decode the truth, eluded him like a Taliban sniper in the Hindu Kush Mountains. He tensed, waiting for an imam's voice to drift from a distant minaret, the morning melody of Islam. The start of another day.

The hammering rang out a third time. Not a machine gun, it was fist against metal.

"Devil take 'em." Sam Hawke's familiar voice was drowsy in the stifling room. Hawke was a fellow Marine. Reconnaissance. They had patrolled the streets together too many times to count.

The other man unfolded now, a hiss groaning through the air mattress beneath him. "Where's Duke? Come here, boy."

A German shepherd's low-throated growl answered. Joshua recognized it. He had seen the dog before. But where? Toenails clicked across the cement floor as Duke paced. The edges of Joshua's nightmare began to sift away like desert sand.

"I'll get the door," Sam said, rising. He glanced at Joshua. "Duff, you stay put. Let's go, Terell."

Terell Roberts—the third man's name. He stood and stretched. His dark skin shimmered with perspiration.

Duke tensed, waiting for one of them to open the door. The dog anticipated each movement the men made. He knew this routine.

Sam flipped on a lamp and Joshua scanned the room, distinguishing a heap of jeans and T-shirts awaiting detergent and a dryer. He noted a clipboard near his cot, the list of activities Sam had planned for the coming day. Joshua recalled his friend handing it to him, explaining what he'd written—basketball practice, homework and tutoring, woodworking, computer skills, ballet lessons, crochet, arts and crafts.

Hardly the business of their Marine Corps reconnaissance unit.

He spotted his wallet and keys on a low table. That wallet held U.S. tens, twenties, fifties. More than a month had passed since he'd carried colorful paper *afghanis* with their detailed etchings of mosques, and handfuls of jingling *puls* in his uniform pockets. He had rented a civilian car at the airport. He recalled parking the black Cadillac near the building's front door the evening before.

This was what they called post-combat disorder. Post-traumatic stress syndrome . . .

A fourth round of hammering broke his focus.

"Persistent booger," Sam muttered.

Shaking off his confusion, Joshua got to his feet. "What's up, Hawke?"

"Nothing. We get this every night. Homeless folks in search of a bed, a drink, another fix bang on Haven's door. Some think it says Heaven."

"Yeah, and they're ready." Terell chuckled ruefully as he stepped into a pair of flip-flops.

Joshua recalled the old building now. *Haven,* the sign over the entrance read. This was Sam Hawke's place, the youth center he and Terell Roberts had opened about a year ago. While deployed together, Sam had told Joshua about playing basketball in college. He had spoken of Terell, the consummate athlete, destined for the history books. Last night, Joshua learned that Terell had spent a few years in the pros before bottoming out. Sam had come to his rescue, and with the last of Terell's NBA savings, they had started Haven.

Sam Hawke was loyal, a man who never forgot a friend. Joshua hadn't been home in Amarillo for a full day before Sam called and invited his friend to St. Louis.

"Come see what I've got cooking, Duff," Sam had urged. "Your old man is planning to slip those velvet handcuffs around your wrists any day now. Get over here and pay me a visit while you can."

The idea of spending time at a youth center in the run-down inner city didn't appeal to Joshua. He had invested more than enough of himself in the poverty and danger of Afghanistan. His parents' rambling adobe house with its swimming pool and tennis court looked pretty good. He would enjoy riding out on one of the Arabians his father bred. There would be dinners with friends and family, flying over the spread in the Cessna, heading into town for a . . .

Come to think of it, Joshua couldn't figure out what he'd want to do in Amarillo. The ranch certainly wasn't going anywhere. His father's oil business and the executive position could wait, too. With his parents both protesting, he had grabbed his duffel bag and headed back to the airport.

In St. Louis, he had rented the Cadillac. Then he drove into the city. Though it was late when Joshua arrived at Haven, he, Sam and Terell had stayed up talking for hours. When his head hit the pillow, Joshua had expected to sleep at least until the sun came up. But it seemed the two directors of the youth center were accustomed to regular interruptions of their night's rest.

"Armed?" Sam asked Terell as they stood in the half-light of the large room.

Expecting the men to reach for handguns, Joshua was surprised when Terell picked up a can of pepper spray. Defensive weapon. Strange choice, he thought.

Sam reached for a box he kept under his bed. He offered it to his friend.

Gleaming steel knives. Joshua glanced up in confusion. Sam and he were both expert marksmen.

"We keep a low profile around here," Sam said with a shrug.

Fingers closing around a slender stiletto, razor sharp, Joshua considered his friend's arsenal. A knife was an offensive weapon. That fit with what he knew of Sam Hawke. Highly trained leaders, the men were still very much alike.

The German shepherd led the way out of the humid room, across a dank landing to a flight of chipped concrete steps.

"Male," Terell said as they began the descent.

"Agreed." Sam's voice was husky. "White."

"Nah, black. A kid. Scared."

Joshua realized this must be a nightly guessing game.

"Middle-aged," Sam offered. "Drunk."

"Bleeding."

"Probably." Sam picked up a first-aid kit near the stairwell. "Knife wound."

"Gunshot."

None of it sounded good to Joshua.

The three men crossed the cavernous gym, the site of Haven's single basketball court, two foursquare layouts, and just enough room for a gaggle of jump-ropers. Duke huffed with anticipation as he padded ahead. Yet another round of knocking began as they arrived at the front door.

“Whatcha need?” Terell called.

“Open the door. Please open.”

At the pleading voice outside, Sam and Terell looked at each other, blue eyes meeting brown.

“Illegal alien,” Sam said. “Adult male. Lost.”

“Bet he got kicked out of his apartment,” Terell muttered, reaching for the bar that secured the door.

Joshua weighed the stiletto in his palm. Earlier that evening, Sam had told him that African-American kids were a consistent majority at Haven. Latin Americans were part of the mix, too—most poor, persecuted, living on the brink. Unable to obtain visas or achieve refugee status, their parents had spent all they had and risked their lives to enter the U.S. illegally.

But the composition of the neighborhood had begun to change in recent months. Charitable foundations were resettling refugees by the score in St. Louis. An influx of immigrants from Burma, Somalia, Sudan, Congo, Bosnia and other war-torn countries led to new youngsters stepping timidly through the metal detector at Haven’s front door.

Long ago, Sam and Terell had decided to take a “don’t ask, don’t tell” policy regarding legal documentation, they told Joshua. Haven was about the business of God’s work. And the Lord had laid out a clear mandate for His people to welcome the alien.

"You ready?" Sam asked, flicking a glance at Joshua.

He gave a brief nod as he sized up Terell. Tall and massively built, the man held up his slender can of pepper spray while Sam lifted the bar and drew back the bolt.

At the slide and click of metal against metal, wisps of Joshua's nightmare floated across his mind. He gritted his teeth. The door swung open.

Liz Wallace turned a page in her scrapbook and ran a fingertip over the photograph of her parents waving goodbye at St. Louis's Lambert Airport. They had no clue that within three days, their precious child would be sitting down to a meal of roasted bush rat.

In fact, they never found out the whole story. You couldn't just fire off an e-mail that read, Hi Mom and Dad. Ate monkey meat and fried termites for dinner today.

This was not the kind of thing that would boost their enthusiasm for Liz's dreams of becoming a foreign aid worker. Of course, her brief trip to the Democratic Republic of Congo hadn't exactly been about transforming the plight of a Third World nation. She and her college teammates went to help rebuild a primary school that had been hit too many times by mortar fire. They put up a few walls and hurried home.

But that trip, more than a year before, had

changed Liz's life. The moment she graduated from college, she took a job with Refugee Hope, a resettlement agency in St. Louis. Her goal: to learn Swahili, enter a training program and move to Africa to work for the United Nations in refugee camps.

On this stifling night, unable to sleep after long hours toting supplies to incoming families from Burma and Bosnia, Liz couldn't sleep. Not unusual. Most days she was so exhausted she could hardly stand up. But after arriving home to her studio apartment, eating a quick bite of dinner and checking her schedule for the next day, she felt her second wind kick in. Wide-awake and unable to turn off her brain by 2:00 a.m., she made a cup of decaf tea and settled on her sofa with the scrapbook.

Liz turned the page and studied the faces gazing back at her, impassive and worn. She had briefly considered decorating the page in the colors of the Congo flag and placing stickers of wild animals here and there. But why distract from the beauty of the Congolese people with their buttery chocolate skin and deep eyes?

Yet what suffering the people had endured. Until that trip, Liz had never heard of such horrors. She understood now that Rwanda's civil war had sent nearly a million refugees pouring over the border into Congolese camps. When those refugees began to build power to retake their homeland, they enlisted the help of men in Congo's government. That brought resistance.

War began in Congo in the fall of 1996, complete with genocide, looting and genital mutilation. In some areas, soldiers raped more than half the women. Almost fifty thousand children were kidnapped and forced into combat, slave labor, sexual servitude.

Not long after a cease-fire was signed in 1999, insurgent groups led a second uprising. Yet another peace treaty was signed in 2003. By the time Liz arrived in Kinshasa, more than four million people had died. Some were killed in the conflict, but most perished from disease and starvation.

Three million were homeless. Houses, hospitals and schools lay in rubble. Fields and food supplies were burned. People hovered on the brink of starvation.

Under the umbrella organization of Refugee Hope, Liz cared for many of those woeful survivors who arrived in St. Louis. She wasn't doing much to help, though. Her job was mostly desk work. Filing government forms.

She wondered if anyone could prevent genocide. Probably not.

Four sets of dark eyes stared back at Joshua. He had seen this before—a man, a woman, two children, a plea for help written on earnest faces.

Their innocence could belie a body strapped with explosives. In battle, Joshua had learned not to trust any expression of virtue. But this wasn't warfare—not the combat kind, anyway.

With a tired smile, Sam stepped into the open doorway of Haven. "Hey, there," he greeted them. "What can we do for you tonight?"

The man gave an awkward little bow. Skin of polished ebony glowed in the streetlight. His gray shirt was too big, made of cotton, short-sleeved and wrinkled. Khaki trousers sagged at the ankles. Shoes, cracked patent leather with frayed laces, had parted at the seams to reveal threadbare socks.

"Good evening, sir," he said, clutching a battered suitcase. A faint British accent, Joshua noticed. "I am Stephen Rudi. If you please, may I present my wife, Mary. And here is my daughter, Charity, and my son, Virtue. We come from Paganda."

"What are you folks doing on the street at this time of night?" Sam asked. "This is a dangerous area."

"Yeah, and it's after two in the morning." Terell was peering at his Rolex, evidently a vestige of his once-lucrative basketball career. "Mr. Rudi, your children ought to be in bed."

"Indeed, sir. But we have had a most unfortunate day. Please, may I explain? You see, we had recently arrived in Atlanta when we received a letter from my wife's brother. This man is our only family member to escape the recent unrest in Paganda. He invited us to join him here, where we could live with him and find better jobs. We traveled to St. Louis by bus, arriving this morning. But we searched all day, and we could not find him."

"Aha." Terell stifled a yawn. "So, you're from where? South Africa?"

"Paganda, sir. It is in East Africa, near Lake Victoria."

Joshua could see that neither Sam nor Terell recognized the country. He didn't recall much about it himself. Former British colony. Few natural resources. Tribal conflict—humanity's constantly failing effort to eradicate enemies. Sunnis and Shiites. Kurds and Iraqis. Hindus and Muslims. Nazis and Jews. Spaniards and Aztecs. Settlers and Natives. Boers and British.

Extermination never worked, but people forgot that. Again and again they attempted the wholesale slaughter of their foes. Genocide wouldn't end until trumpets rang out in the eastern sky to announce the end of time.

"You still got that letter?" Terell asked, focusing on the man's wife. "Uh . . . what was the name?"

"Mary." Stephen Rudi spoke for her. He fished in his pocket and then unfolded a tattered sheet of notebook paper. Holding it out to Terell, he tapped a place near the end of the page. "This is the address, sir, but my wife's brother is not to be found. Our search revealed nothing, not even the correct street."

While Terell and Sam studied the letter, Joshua appraised the Pagandan woman who stood beside her husband. Tiny and thin-boned, she wore large round spectacles that all but masked the distinguishing features of her face. She kept her eyes downcast and her fingers woven together, as if determined to draw no attention to herself. Joshua had seen this attempt at self-preservation in Afghani women and children. An effort to hide in plain sight.

A scarf, elaborately knotted, covered her head. Her dress, threadbare pink gingham with eyelet lace at the neck, was mostly covered by a length of ethnic-patterned fabric. She had wrapped it in a sort of African sarong. The woman had the look of a frightened bird.

Turning his assessment to the two children, Joshua saw exhaustion weighing on them. They gazed up at their father in a mixture of respect and concern. Charity's hair was braided in messy cornrows. Her bright almond eyes glowed with intelligence. She had white teeth, a pug nose, round cheeks. She would do well in school, Joshua thought.

The boy was a mirror image of his older sister—minus the cornrows and several teeth. How did so many five-year-olds manage to lose their two front teeth not long before Christmas? he wondered. The old song "All I Want for Christmas is My Two Front Teeth" wouldn't be meaningful without a few toothless kids belting it out.

"I don't think that street exists," Terell commented. He passed the letter to Sam. "You ever heard of this place?"

Joshua eyed the document as his friend read it. Pulled from a college-ruled notebook, the page had been handled so much it was about to fall apart. Messy pencil marks were smudged, hard to read. A grease spot had blurred the signature. In the upper-right corner, a water ring muddied the blue lines. The letter was written in an African language, but the address at the end was clear enough.

Sam returned the precious page to its owner. "You sure this is in St. Louis, Mr. Rudi?"

"Indeed, sir." Stephen glanced at his wife, suddenly hesitant. He spoke to her in their mother tongue for a moment. Head low, she uttered a couple of barely distinguishable words in response.

Stephen nodded. "If you please, sir. My wife is quite certain her brother lives in St. Louis."

Terell and Sam eyed each other for a moment. Finally Sam spoke up. "I'm sorry, but Haven is not a homeless shelter. Our mission statement prohibits taking in strangers. We have a rule."

Joshua couldn't believe what he was hearing. He nudged his friend's elbow. "Sam, can I talk to you for a second?" They stepped back into the building. "Since when did you abide by rules?"

"If we let these folks in," Sam replied in a low voice, "we can't turn anyone else away."

"Come on, man. We can't leave those kids on the street."

Sam gave him a long look and shrugged. "I'll probably regret this, but okay."

As they emerged onto the sidewalk, Joshua reached for the children's hands. "Come on, you two. The sooner you're settled, the sooner we can all get some sleep."

Sam let out a breath. "We'll put you up for the night, Mr. Rudi. No longer than a week, though."

"That's our max, so don't try to argue us out of it." Terell spoke as firmly as he could, which wasn't saying much. "Do you understand?"

Terell Roberts looked as if he could tear a man's head off. But his gentle tone led Joshua to believe the guy was a bona fide teddy bear—compliant, impossibly kind, generous. How would he respond in a conflict situation?

"We would never wish to impose upon your kindness," Stephen vowed to his benefactors as Sam bolted the door behind them. "Indeed, we are sincerely grateful."

The Rudi family accompanied Terell across the basketball court toward the stairwell. Sam followed with Joshua.

"They'll beg for more time," Sam said under his

breath. "They always do. The homeless, hungry, sick, battered, dying—they come to Haven hoping for a solution to their problems."

"Do they ever find one?"

"Temporarily. We let them stay a night or two until they find other quarters. Relief agencies, shelters, food kitchens fill the gap. But it's never enough."

"Doesn't the constant need drag you down?"

"Nah. It's like the war. You focus on the good, the hopeful."

"Your fiancée?"

Sam smiled. "Ana helps."

The woman who had walked into Sam's life that summer brought him to life again, he had told Joshua. He felt almost human for the first time since his military discharge. Sam said Ana's intensity matched his own. She could be difficult and definitely stubborn. But with Ana, he could let down his guard.

Joshua was happy for his friend. He'd been too long without a woman in his own life, and he didn't see much prospect for that changing anytime soon. Most of the girls at home were provincial. They believed everything they heard on television. Few had set foot outside the U.S. Some had never left Texas.

One or two women had caught Joshua's eye while in Afghanistan, but a military romance was not for him. He enjoyed a lady who knew how the world functioned, but he didn't want the separation or anxiety of such a relationship. He wouldn't like to worry about safety. If he ever found love, he couldn't risk losing it. So he had kept himself distant, focused on the task at hand.

"Ana's not the only good thing in my life," Sam said as they approached the stairwell. "We've got a lot to be thankful for around here. Lead paint abatement crews just finished stripping and recoating our walls. Ana wrote an article about the paint problem, and a surge of donations poured in. We formed a nonprofit organization—complete with a board of directors and grant writers. The bathrooms are finally working. The ramps, exits and stairwells meet code. It's been a long haul."

"The place looks good," Joshua agreed.

"We've got new volunteers, too. Plus, the vet gave Duke an all-clear this morning. Hip dysplasia forced him out of police K-9 service too early, but he's been God's gift to us."

"And this Pagandan family. Thanks to Haven, they'll sleep safely tonight."

"You're the one who made that happen," Sam said. "We've turned away people a lot more pitiful."

"I'd never let a kid sleep on the streets. You wouldn't, either, Hawke. You know it."

As they began to climb the steps to the second floor, Charity and Virtue stretched tiny hands to pat the big dog. Joshua guessed the canine had been trained to sniff out drugs and could take down a grown man, but these small children sensed he wouldn't harm them.

When Virtue sagged against the stairwell wall, Joshua lifted the tired boy into his arms. Sam scooped up the little girl.

"So Paganda has some big cities?" Terell was asking their father.

"One," Stephen said. "But we come from a small village beside Lake Victoria. Our people were fishermen."

"Were?" Terell frowned. "You mean they stopped?"

"Sir, the village was burned. My people . . . are not there now."

Joshua silently prayed that Terell would take the hint. But subtlety was not the man's strong suit.

"Headed for refugee camps, I'll bet. Good thing you got your family out."

"My children and I are three of only nine people who survived from my village." Stephen paused in the stairwell, his voice growing low. "When my wife learned that the rebel army was coming, she placed these two—the youngest except for our baby—inside a metal water drum. There were only a few liters remaining inside it, and she put a padlock on the top. Because of rust, the drum had small holes. Through these, the air could come. When I returned to my house, I saw that the roof and walls had burned. Rebels had looted the furnishings. But God protected the drum. Inside it, I found my two children."

As Stephen spoke the final words, a chill crawled up Joshua's spine. The drowsy little boy whose head lolled against his shoulder had survived the destruction of his village because his mother had hidden him in a water drum? At their young ages, the kids might have drowned. The burning house could have caved in on top of them. They might have been discovered and killed. The child was a miracle.

"But where were you the whole time?" Terell asked Stephen as the group walked down a hall.

His grunt was bitter. "I was attending a pastors' meeting in another town. When I heard news of the rebel attack, I rode my bicycle as fast as I could. But I arrived at my village too late."

"So your baby? What . . . I mean . . . Where's the baby?"

Shaking his head, Joshua realized that Tyrell had never seen the shell-shocked faces of civilians whose lives were destroyed by war and death. His own inability to shrug off nightmares and block memories of events he had witnessed showed how difficult it could be to recover from such trauma.

"My son, Justice, was killed," Stephen said, the words muffled. "Also my first wife, Priscilla, and my other children, Purity, Hope, Fidelity and Honor. I would thank you, please, that we not discuss this subject further tonight, sir. By God's grace, I still have Charity and Virtue. I must protect them from the memories of what they heard and saw."

"Oh, yeah, my brother. We can drop that topic forever." Terell looked shaken.

The group stepped into a small room outfitted with several beds and a table. Despite its rules, Haven had made provisions for just such an emergency as this.

"You've got clean sheets there," Sam said. "We keep crackers and power bars on that shelf. Towels and soap are in the bathroom, along with paper drinking cups."

"I could run out for some milk," Terell offered. "I'd be glad to do it."

"Water is most acceptable for us." Stephen faced his benefactors. "May God bless you for your kindness."

Joshua bent and gently laid the sleeping Virtue on one of the beds. He pulled a sheet and thin blanket over the child. Thumb thrust into his mouth, Virtue barely stirred. Charity, too, was sound asleep.

When he straightened, Joshua noted that Sam and Terell had left the room. Stephen was murmuring to his wife. It was time to leave the family in peace. Yet Joshua needed to speak.

"Excuse me," he said. The two Pagandans fell silent as Joshua addressed Stephen. "You're a pastor, then. A Christian."

"I am, sir."

Joshua hesitated a moment. "The pain and the loss you feel. The fear, too. I've known some of that. God takes care of it after a while. He uses it to make you better. Trust Him."

Stephen swallowed, unable to meet the other man's eyes. He nodded slightly, but did not otherwise respond.

"Good night," Joshua said finally. "We'll see you in the morning."

He closed the door and started after Terell, who was questioning Sam as they walked to their shared room. "Did you hear what that guy said? Rebels killed his baby. His baby! That is just wrong. Those other names—were those his kids, too?"

"Yeah, and his wife," Joshua said, catching up to them.

Sam frowned. "But his wife is with him."

"Mary must be someone new. He said Priscilla was the mother of his children."

Terell groaned. "Aw, man, the first wife must have gotten killed by the rebels. Sam, those two kids were locked in a barrel. They could have starved."

"Or been slaughtered like their brothers and sisters. But they're alive—that's the important thing."

Joshua nodded. "Now the family has to figure out a way to move ahead without the past dragging them down. Like all of us."

He could feel Terell's eyes on him as they entered the room. "You think the kids heard their mama being murdered?"

"Maybe. They know she's dead."

"That's terrible, yo. If anybody went after my mama, I'd kill him."

"Good job. You just described the basic recipe for genocide." Joshua stretched out on the cot. "Revenge never did anyone a bit of good."

Sam dropped down onto his bed. "Let it go, Terell."

"You dudes don't have any feelings. I can't hear a story like that and then let it go. Those are *my* people."

Sam gave a snort as he switched off the lamp. "They're not your people any more than they're mine."

"They're black. Africans are my ancestors."

"And my great-great-grandfather was a Scottish laird. You don't see me playing bagpipes and dancing a jig."

Joshua knew he should let the two men hash it out, but he couldn't resist offering his thoughts. "We're all connected. Forget skin color and bloodlines. God doesn't see that. Neither should we."

"Haven may not have room for everyone," Sam said. "But we're here to help the Rudi family. If his wife's killers walked in here, we'd probably help them, too. Get over yourself, Terell."

"Me? You're both loony tunes. The sand in your heads rusted out your brains. Go find a couple of camels, yo. Get on back to the desert where you belong."

Joshua could hear Sam chuckling. A comforting sound. In a moment, both men began to snore.

Joshua stroked the warm steel blade in his palm. Turning onto his stomach, he slipped the knife under his pillow. It might just come in handy.

Chapter Two

Liz locked her purse inside the drawer under her desk and switched on the computer. She was tired. Too tired to be at work this early in the morning. But the day wouldn't wait.

Before meeting a Somali family at the airport at ten, she had to fill out status reports on two groups of Burmese immigrants brought in by Refugee Hope. They had landed in St. Louis the week before. Ragged, little more than skin and bones, they had stared at her with gaunt faces and milky eyes. At the sight of an energetic white woman with a mass of brunette curls, the children clung to each other. Their parents couldn't quite muster a smile at having finally arrived in America, the land of their dreams.

With a sigh, Liz shook her head.

"Incoming!" Her closest friend at the agency

breezed past the small cubicle. Molly stuck a thumb behind her to indicate the cluster of people headed Liz's way. "They're all yours!"

Molly loved mornings.

Liz groaned and reached for her flask of hot tea. Before work, she always steeped a pot of the strongest black tea on the market. The first cup opened her eyes. The second turned on her brain. With the third, she usually had the gumption to say—

"No." Holding up a palm, Liz rose from her chair before the newcomers could step into her cubicle. "I don't know who sent you here, but you have the wrong office."

"No?" A tall man with close-cropped brown hair stepped around the collection of bewildered Africans. His dark eyebrows narrowed. "Did you say no?"

"I'm sorry, but this is not one of my families." She met his blue eyes. Deep navy with white flecks, they stared straight into her.

Why hadn't she started that third cup on the drive to work?

"I know my own people," she informed him. "This group doesn't belong to me. If you'll go back to the front office—"

"The front office sent us to you." Gaze unwavering, he stuck out a hand. "Sergeant Joshua Duff, U.S. Marine Corps. And you are?"

"Liz." She grasped the hand. His warm fingers

curled around her palm, crushing her knuckles together. She caught her breath. "Liz Wallace."

"A Scot. I'm Irish."

"American, actually." She pulled her hand away and stuck it in the pocket of her slacks. "So, Semper Fi and all that. I appreciate the interest you've taken in these people, Sergeant, but Refugee Hope is accountable only for the families we relocate. If you're responsible for this group, you'll have to—"

"Semper Fi and all that?" He leaned forward, as if he weren't sure he heard her correctly.

Oh, great, Liz thought. She picked up her flask, unscrewed the lid and poured the third cup. Praying he couldn't see her hand trembling, she lifted the mug to her lips. The tea slid down her throat.

This was not what she needed a few minutes after eight in the morning. Not an overwhelming, overbearing, overly handsome sergeant with a death grip. And certainly not a pair of striking blue eyes that never seemed to blink.

"Sergeant Duff." She found a smile and hoped it looked sincere. "Please forgive my lack of courtesy. I have a large number of families in my caseload. An overwhelming number. This group isn't among them."

With effort, she dragged her focus from the man's sculpted cheekbones and clean-shaven square jaw. The group huddled under his protection shrank into each other as she assessed them. A man, midforties, she guessed. His wife, hard to tell her age behind those big glasses, clearly traumatized. Two children. The girl, about seven, needing new clothes. The boy, probably five, missing several front teeth.

"This is Reverend Stephen Rudi," Sergeant Duff said, clamping his big hand on the man's shoulder. "His wife, Mary. Their children, Charity and Virtue. They're from Paganda."

Paganda. Images flashed into Liz's mind. Photographs she'd seen. Villages burning. Mass graves. Boy soldiers toting machine guns. She thought of the people she had met in Congo. They spoke of Paganda in hushed tones. Even worse than most places, they said. Genocide. A bloodbath.

Liz shuddered and sized up the little family more closely. Who knew what these people had endured? Too often these days, she caught herself regarding the refugees as line items on one of her many lists. Family from Burundi: mother, father, eight children. Family from Bosnia: mother, her brother, four children. Family from Ivory Coast: mother (pregnant), father, six children.

When had they ceased to be human beings?

"Reverend Rudi, good morning." Liz offered her welcome in the African way—right hand extended, left hand placed on the opposite arm near the crook of the elbow. A demonstration of honor, as if to say, “I will not greet you with one hand and stab you with the other.”

The man stepped forward, shook her hand and made a little bow. “Good morning, madam. Thank you very much for your time. My family is in great need of assistance.”

How often had she heard these words, Liz wondered. The need was a pit, bottomless and gaping. A hungry mouth, never sated.

“Which agency brought you to St. Louis?” she asked him. It was a relief to turn her attention from Sergeant Duff. Like a male lion poised to spring, the man didn’t budge. His presence filled the cubicle with a sort of expectant energy Liz could hardly ignore.

Reverend Rudi’s voice was strained but warm, carrying familiar ministerial overtones. “Madam, Global Care brought my family from a refugee camp in Kenya. We traveled by airplane from Nairobi to Atlanta. My wife’s brother invited us to St. Louis.”

“Global Care doesn’t have an office here,” Duff inserted. “The Rudis will need your help.”

Liz returned her focus to his face. The man had moved closer to her desk now, his fingertips touching her stack of files, his shoulder tilted in her direction.

“I’m sorry, Sergeant. As I said before, if Refugee Hope didn’t bring this family to the States, we won’t be able to provide assistance.

The Rudis need to contact Global Care in Atlanta and make arrangements."

"But as you see, they're here now. So what can you do for them?"

"Nothing. I'm authorized to work only with my families. Those brought in by Refugee Hope."

"So transfer them."

She studied the blue eyes. He really did expect her to obey. He thought she would capitulate right on the spot. The man was used to giving orders, and to having them followed.

Liz had never done well with authority figures. She simply didn't buckle.

"If Global Care wants to make provisions for this family," she informed him, "you will need to speak to someone at their headquarters in Atlanta. Refugee Hope is based in Washington, D.C. St. Louis is a resettlement point. We follow our agency's rules."

Joshua Duff straightened. His eyes narrowed. Then he turned to the family. "Pastor Stephen, how about you go find a snack machine and get the kids something to eat."

He fished a wallet from his pocket. Liz tried not to gawk at an accordion of cash that unfolded when he opened it. He removed several bills and held them out. The African minister took the money with some reluctance. Duff misunderstood.

"Snack machine." He motioned as if he were

pushing buttons with his index finger. “Food. Candy bars. Crackers.”

With a nod, Reverend Rudi shepherded his little flock out of the cubicle. The moment they were out of sight, Duff leaned into her desk.

“Listen, ma’am, I came across this family last night. I agreed to help them. You work for a refugee agency, right? These are refugees. So do your job.”

Liz stepped around her desk. “This is not the Marine Corps, Sergeant. But we do have a protocol and you’re asking me to violate it. I will not do that.”

The dark eyebrows lifted. “All right, I understand. So, what do we have to do to make this happen?”

“I’ve told you. Call Global Care and turn the family over to them.”

“And where is that pitiful bunch supposed to go while the agency figures out what to do with them?”

“You could put them on a bus and send them back to Atlanta.”

“They don’t want to live in Atlanta. They want to stay here and look for the lady’s brother.” He set one hip on her desk, bringing himself down to her eye level. “Ms. Wallace, you wouldn’t be working for this agency if you didn’t have compassion. These folks need a place to stay, decent jobs, a way to get around. That’s what you do, isn't it? Why don't you just help them out of the goodness of your heart?"

"Why don't *you?*"

"Because I live in Texas."

He looked away, the muscle in his jaw flickering. Liz could see the man was struggling for control. Good. She had a full day of work ahead, and she didn't like being pushed around.

In a moment, he faced her again. "Look, I've just spent seven months hunting insurgents in the Afghan mountains. My third deployment. I'm tired. My patience—never a strong suit—is wearing real thin right now. I came to St. Louis to visit a friend for a couple of days, and this morning he sent me out on a little mercy mission on behalf of Reverend Rudi and his family. Now, they're nice folks, and they've been through an ordeal worse than most. I believe you know exactly how to arrange a happy American life for them, ma'am. Am I wrong about that?"

"I know how to resettle refugees, yes. But as I said, I'm not allowed to work with families who aren't on my list. If you're so worried, you help them. It's time-consuming but not all that complicated. I'll tell you what to do step by step. How does that sound?"

He bent his head and chuckled. "Well, well, well. You know something, Liz Wallace? You're more trouble than a couple of Pashtuns haggling over the price of a camel. I can handle them. I can track a sniper across five miles of bare rock. I can even talk a sheikh into turning loose a few goats to feed some hungry beggars. But I can't seem to get a social worker to help a family of refugees. Did I catch you on a bad day, or are you always this mean?"

Liz rolled her eyes. "Move. You've got your *Duff* on my files, Sergeant."

With a laugh of disbelief, he stood. Liz scooped up her paperwork and flipped open the first file.

"You see this family?" she said, covering the name with her thumb. The photographs of four Somalis were lined up along one side. They looked like criminals posing for mug shots.

"This mother was raped by guerrilla soldiers. Seven of them. In front of her husband and children. They killed the father, the baby and the other two youngest of her five kids. Chopped them up with machetes. They took the oldest girl, raped her, tied her legs and arms together and then threw her into the back of their truck. They took the oldest boy as a slave. Then they drove away."

She paused and glanced at Duff. His grim expression told Liz she was getting through.

"The mother never saw her children again," she continued. "She was left with one daughter, a thirteen-year-old who had been fetching water from a stream when the rebels attacked. This woman and her daughter walked more than a hundred miles across the Somali desert into

Kenya. They lived in a mud hut inside a United Nations refugee camp for five years. They ate gruel and got water from a spigot that served twenty other families. Both gave birth to sons. This mother, her daughter, son and grandson are here now. In St. Louis. Are you with me, Sergeant?"

"All the way."

"Shall I continue?"

"Go ahead." His face had grown solemn, but his eyes were not focused on the photographs. He was looking at Liz.

Disconcerted, she closed the file and set it back on her desk before speaking again.

"Two weeks ago, I greeted this woman and her family at the airport, Sergeant Duff. I took them to a run-down apartment in a high-rise not far from here. Refugee Hope has prepaid their rent for three months. Within those three months, it's my job to make sure this mother learns how to use public transportation, goes to English language classes and attends job training. I have three months to enroll the daughter in a school where no one speaks her language and yet see that she's able to cope. Three months to ensure that the two babies are brought back to health and provided with adequate day care. I have three months' worth of funds with which to buy food and clothing. If this family isn't successfully working, attending school, living independently and eating with proper nutrition in three months, I haven't done my duty, Sergeant Duff. They'll be cut loose from Refugee Hope, and no one will follow me to pick up the pieces."

She looked into his eyes. The bluster was gone, and in its place, she saw a deep sympathy. A warmth. So unexpected she felt her heart stumble.

"How many families do you have, ma'am?"

"Twenty-three current groups. If I don't get some work done at my desk this morning, I'll be late to pick up family number twenty-four at Lambert. And you can call me Liz."

"Liz." He was silent for a moment. "I live in Amarillo, Liz. That's a long way off."

"But see, the Rudi family is here now." She repeated what he had said to her earlier. "So what can you do for them?"

"You're good. You've trapped me."

"I can't track a sniper over bare rock, but I'm not stupid. You wouldn't have brought those people here if you didn't have a compassionate streak. We're alike in that way. Let me tell you how to help them, Sergeant."

"You can call me Joshua."

"You'll enjoy lending a hand, Joshua. Lots more fun than dealing with squabbling sheikhs."

He opened his mouth to answer, but the return of Reverend Rudi and his family silenced the Marine.

Charity and Virtue, it became evident, had discovered Cheetos. Their lips and fingers coated with orange dust, the two children sidled into the cubicle. Liz struggled not to laugh and scoop them up into her arms, as she so often did with the precious little ones who came under her wings of care. But she couldn't afford to melt. Not now.

Sergeant Duff needed to take responsibility for this family. His wad of cash would surely buy bus tickets back to Atlanta. He was a good man, kind and concerned. But he had just returned from the war, and his home was in Texas. The last thing he would want to do was take on a group of Pagandans.

"What've you got there?" he asked, hunkering down in front of Virtue. "Let me see those fingers, kiddo."

The child glanced up at his father. Pastor Stephen said something in their native tongue, and Virtue held out his hands. When he noticed his orange fingers, the boy gasped and then burst into a gale of giggles. His sister looked at her hands and started laughing, too.

"Cheetos," Duff informed the pair. "Puffed or fried, can't beat 'em. My favorite."

He rubbed his stomach and made smacking sounds. The kids joined in, rubbing and smacking, clearly enjoying a moment of silliness in the midst of such a solemn day. Pastor Stephen held up the empty cellophane bag.

"The food is very . . . pink," he told Liz. "Pardon me . . . orange. Yes, orange. Can it be washed?"

"Certainly," she told him. "There's a bathroom down the hall. You can stop by on your way out. I believe Sergeant Duff is going to help you contact Global Care and make sure you're safely on your way back to Atlanta."

"Am I?" Joshua stood, again filling the cubicle in a manner that seemed to dwarf everyone else in the tiny space. "I don't remember telling you that, Ms. Wallace."

"Liz. And I told you I couldn't help them."

"But you said you'd help *me.* You'll tell me the steps, and I'll settle the family here. Right?"

She couldn't believe she had heard the man correctly. People didn't do this. Volunteers might take a few hours out of their lives to assist refugees. A church might adopt a family or two. But no one dropped everything. No one single person simply gave up the weeks and months it took to acclimate an entire group. Liz was paid, and even she had to rely on other aid workers and volunteer helpers.

"You told me you live in Texas," she said.

"Texas can wait. I'll stick around here for a while." He set his large palm on Virtue's round head. "We'll go to the airport with you and meet family number twenty-four. You can explain your system to me on the way."

Liz bent her head and rubbed her eyes. This was absolutely not the way her morning should go. She had files to sort. Forms to fill out. A plane to meet. Clothing and food to deliver. A refugee patient to visit in the hospital. She did not need a U.S. Marine and four Pagandans following her around like a flock of lost sheep.

Unable to bring herself to speak, she held up her hand. Instantly, Joshua's fingers closed around hers. As she lifted her head, he tucked her hand under his arm, splaying her fingers against his biceps.

"I don't want to hear your favorite word, Liz," he murmured, leaning close. "*No* isn't good. *Yes* is much better. Say *yes* to the Rudi family, Liz. If you say it, I will, too. And then we'll make a difference together."

Everything inside Liz begged to differ. But how could she keep arguing? The man refused to hear any of her very plausible reasons why his scenario wouldn't work.

"Fine," she said, pulling her hand from the warm crook of his elbow. "Step one. Take the Rudi family back where you found them. Make sure they have a decent place to live with running water, flushing toilets and enough beds. Drive them to the grocery store and buy a week's supply of staples and a few perishables. Then go to a thrift shop and see if you can find several outfits for each person. And look for coats. Winter's coming."

She picked up a couple of business cards and handed one to Joshua and the other to Pastor Stephen. "Here's my number. Call me if you need me."

Before either man could protest, Liz pushed past Joshua and headed for Molly's cubicle, leaving the five wayfarers standing inside her own. If this was going to be a good day, she needed fortification. Her best friend would be happy to accompany her to the coffee shop down the street for a couple of lattes.

A few hours later, Joshua pulled his Cadillac into a parking space in front of the large brick edifice and switched off the engine. He knew he shouldn't do this. If he were at all smart, right this moment he'd be on his way back to Amarillo. After a couple of easy days on the road, he would drive out to the ranch. As a matter of fact, nothing would feel better than to strip off his jeans and T-shirt, dive into the Texas-shaped pool and swim a few laps.

No doubt Magdalena would put on the dog for him—enchiladas, chile rellenos, carne adovada, homemade tortillas and a big serving of flan for dessert. The cook had been with the Duff family for years, almost a second mother to Joshua and his four brothers. During each of his deployments, she faithfully e-mailed him once a week to let him know the menu of every meal he had missed. Exquisite torture.

After Magdalena's home-cooked dinner, he would sleep well in his big, clean, nonsandy bed. Then the following day . . .

As always, Joshua's thoughts came to a screeching halt at the idea of driving into town and stepping into the Duff-Flannigan Oil building. He could almost hear his boots squeaking down the long waxed hallway. His voice would echo as he greeted his father. The large corner office would still be waiting—as it had all these years.

Business. The oil business. That's what we do, son. It's a Duff thing. Your daddy did it. Your grandpas did it—both sides. And your great-grandpas. That's why we sent you off to college to get that petroleum engineering degree. You'd be doing it right now if 9/11 hadn't happened and made you want to serve your country. We're proud that you did, but now it's time to take your place here. Your big brother will be CEO one day. You're our president of field operations. Duff-Flannigan Oil is counting on you.

Hadn't Joshua just been fighting a war some said was based on a gluttonous thirst for foreign oil? Or had it been about terrorists and the need to quash insurgent cells? Was it about politics—or changing people's lives for the better? Things could get confusing up in the high arid desert of Afghanistan.

There.

The object of Joshua's latest quest pushed open the door of Refugee Hope and stepped out onto the sidewalk. At the sight of Ms. Liz Wallace, something slid right down his spine and settled into the base of his stomach. And this was why he should be headed for Texas.

Sam was right about his friend. Joshua had been too long without a woman. He needed to get home, find a couple of pretty gals, and . . .

What? He hardly knew how to go on an old-fashioned date anymore. Did people even do that these days?

He was thirty. Thirty and battle weary. And Liz Wallace looked so good he had almost dropped to his knees the moment he laid eyes on her.

Instead, he had bullied his way into her office and annoyed her to the point that she ran him off. Worse, he had hog-tied himself to the Rudi family. Not only did he feel obligated to help the dignified Reverend Stephen and his traumatized little wife, but Joshua was positively smitten with Charity and Virtue.

Sighing, he unlatched his door and pushed it open. Liz glanced his way. Her face . . . for an unguarded moment . . . said exactly what he needed to know. She had felt it, too. That *something.* A palpable pull. The irresistible beckoning toward what was probably a huge mistake.

"Liz." He called her name as she approached on the sidewalk. "Thought you'd take me up on my offer to drive you to the airport. Get a little more information from you about how to manage my new best friends."

She swallowed. Her brown eyes went depthless

for a moment as she met his gaze. Then she focused on his car. "Too small. I'm bringing back a family of five. Thanks, but I always take the agency van to the airport."

"Good. Where's it parked?"

"Listen, I appreciate your interest in refugees, Sergeant."

"Joshua."

"I don't need your help picking up this family, and I can't take the time to explain our system to you right now. It's very complicated. I have a lot on my mind."

"I'll drive while you think." He imitated her frown. "You're not going to use your favorite word again are you, Liz?"

Letting out a breath, she shrugged. "Oh, come on, then. But I'll do the driving. Agency policy."

"You sure? You look tired."

"Thanks."

"Beautiful but tired."

At the expression of surprise on her face, Joshua mentally chastised himself. *Bad form, Duff. You don't tell a woman she's beautiful right off the bat.*

On the other hand, Liz Wallace was gorgeous. Slim and not too tall, she had the sort of understated figure he liked. Nothing demure about that hair, though. Big, glossy brown curls crowned her head, settled onto her shoulders and trickled down her back. Her skin was pale, almost milky. Those melted-chocolate eyes stirred something deep inside him. But it was her lips that drew his focus every time she spoke.

"We have twenty minutes to make it to the airport." She pushed back her hair as they approached a mammoth white van sprinkled with rust spots. "When we get there, we'll be going to the area where international flights arrive."

"Been through those gates a few times myself." He smiled as yet another look of surprise crossed Liz's face.

"I've seen the Army grunts at Lambert," she said. "In and out of Fort Leonard Wood for basic training. I didn't think the Marine Corps used the airport."

"You might be surprised at what Marines do."

She opened the van's door and with some effort clambered into the driver's seat. Joshua had all he could do to keep from picking her up and depositing her in place. But he knew better than to manhandle Liz Wallace. She might be small and delicate, but the woman had a razor-sharp streak he didn't want to mess around with.

"I've flown out of Lambert, too," she said as Joshua settled into the passenger's seat. Starting the engine, she added, "I left the international area on my way to the DRC."

At that, she glanced his way. The slightest smirk tilted those sumptuous lips. Clearly this was a test she hoped he would fail. A little global one-upmanship.

He fastened his seat belt and tried to relax. It wasn't easy. Liz had on a khaki skirt that had seemed more than modest in the agency building. But in the van, it formed to the curve of her hip and revealed just enough leg to mesmerize him. He slipped his sunglasses from his pocket and put them on.

Concentrate on the conversation, Duff.

"So, did you land in Kinshasa?" he asked. "Or maybe you were headed for the eastern part of the country. A lot of people fly into Kampala and travel across the border from there, don't they?"

She laughed easily. "Okay, you've been around. My group landed in Kinshasa. Have you ever visited Congo?"

"You mean the DRC?" He returned her smirk. "Nah. North Africa mostly. How'd you like it?"

"Interesting. It changed me. I'm planning to spend the rest of my life working with refugees in Africa."

"Africa?" He frowned at the thought of settlements plagued with disease, hunger, violence. "You're doing a good thing right here, Liz."

"The people who make it to St. Louis are the lucky ones. All I do is mop up. Try to repair what's already been broken. I'd prefer to go into the UN camps where I can really make a difference."

"You're making a difference now."

The brown eyes slid his way for an instant. "How do you know?"

"I saw what you do."

"Not what I *want* to do. My job is too much about lists and quotas. It's all red tape and documents and files."

"It's people."

"It was once. In the beginning, I thought I was really helping. But there are so many people, and the needs are overwhelming. I don't speak anyone's language well enough to communicate the important things I want to say."

"What is it you want to say?"

Again she glanced at him. "Were you an interrogator?"

"Tracker." That left out a lot, but he didn't want to drag his military service into the open. "I did a little interviewing."

She nodded, her attention on the traffic again. "What I want to say is . . . meaningful things. But I can't. My Swahili is horrible. I'm doing well to meet my refugees' basic needs. I don't have time to follow through with schools to make sure the kids are adjusting. I can't teach the mothers how to provide good nutrition. Most don't know the simplest things about life here."

"Like what?"

"That eggs and milk go in the refrigerator. How to use hangers in a closet. Where to put a lamp. How to microwave popcorn or make brownies from a mix. What to do with credit card offers that pour in through the mail. A lot of them don't realize children need to wear shoes in America. Especially in the winter. But it goes beyond that."

Joshua held his breath as she swung the van into four-lane traffic. Interstate 70 at midmorning was a free-flowing river of passenger cars and 18-wheelers. The van nestled in behind a semi, then darted out to take a spot vacated by a cab. Liz drove as he did, fearlessly. Maybe recklessly.

"I don't know the subtext," she was saying. "So many people groups come through Refugee Hope, and I've only learned a few things. Each culture is different. If I were to ask about your family in Texas, you'd give me the names of your closest relatives, right?"

"Maybe."

"Of course you would. But a Somali would recite twenty generations back to the name of his clan father. In Somalia, men and women don't touch each other in greeting. Elders—even total strangers—are addressed as aunt or uncle. And babies aren't diapered. Now, that's been interesting in St. Louis."

"I'll bet."

"The Burmese—people from Myanmar—have complicated customs that involve naming a baby by the day of the week he's born on, and his age and gender. And the name changes according to who's talking to them. In Somalia, it's polite to give gifts to a mother before her baby is born, like in the U.S. But you'd never do that in Burma. It would bring misfortune on the child. And you don't give scissors or knives or anything black—to anyone. Trust and honesty are important to the Burmese. Inconsistency and vagueness are considered good manners in Somalia. It's a positive thing to be crafty, even sly and devious."

"The tip of the cultural iceberg."

"A society's rules are subtle. You were where? Afghanistan? I'm sure you learned their ways."

"Oh, yeah." He leaned back in the seat and verbally checked off some of the idiosyncrasies he'd been taught. "The people may seem to be standing too close, but don't step back. It's their way. Men walk arm in arm or hold hands—it means they're friends and nothing more. Never point with one finger. Greet male friends with a handshake and a pat on the back. Belch in appreciation of a good meal. Never drink alcohol or eat pork in front of an Afghan. Don't wink, blow your nose in public, eat with your left hand or sit with the soles of your feet showing."

"Well done, Sergeant Duff," she said. "Then you know that until you begin to understand people, you can't help them much."

"And you're all about helping."

She pulled the van into a space in the short-term parking area at Lambert. "So are you, Sergeant. We've just chosen different ways to go about it."

Before he could unbuckle his seat belt, Liz hopped out of the van and started for the terminal.

Joshua had never considered tracking insurgents a mercy mission. He was a huntsman. A sniper. A warrior who set out on a mission and didn't stop until he'd accomplished it.

Watching Liz stride purposefully through the sliding-glass door, Joshua realized she might be right about him. Maybe they had more in common than he knew.

Chapter Three

Liz sat at her desk, staring. The stack of files blurred as her eyes lost focus. The sounds of people talking in cubicles nearby faded. Unnoticed, the hand on the clock ticked toward five. Even the candy bar in her desk drawer ceased its demand, its chocolate-caramel siren song ebbing.

"Wakey-wakey, Sleeping Beauty!" Molly breezed into the cubicle. "Time for your happy news report from the Fairy Godmother."

Settling on the edge of a chair, her favorite perch, the reed-thin woman waved a sheaf of stapled pages. Molly's exuberance and generally cheerful outlook belied the fact that she had battled an eating disorder most of her adult life. Only Liz knew, and the two made it a matter of prayer each evening before they left the office.

"More trouble in Africa," Molly began, reading from their weekly headquarters update. "Sudanese refugees are still flooding south. Tribal tension continues to flare in Eastern and Central Africa. The Kenyan camps are full to overflowing. Really? Surprise me some more. Congo and Burundi are still unstable. Rwanda isn't much better. And on to Asia! Hostility has increased toward the Karen people group in Burma/Myanmar. Refugees are heading for Thailand in record numbers. People are still fleeing Vietnam and North Korea. Yeah—when they can get out. Europe is pretty quiet, but the Middle East is tumultuous. This could've been last week's report."

Liz had closed her eyes and was trying to pull out any important information between Molly's running commentary. Sarcasm bordering on outright derision was the woman's stock in trade.

"Now for our weekly federal government refugee resettlement averages," Molly continued. "Currently in St. Louis there are 2,500 Somalis, more than 1,000 Ethiopians, 700 from ex-Soviet states, 700 Liberians, 500 Sudanese, 300 each from Bosnia, Vietnam, Iran and Afghanistan. The Turks and Burmese are passing the 100 mark, and Ivory Coast, Sierra Leone, Burundi and Eritrea are catching up fast."

"Just give me next week's airport list, Molly." Liz held out a hand. "I can't process this stuff right now."

"What's going on? Have you been staying

awake all night again—plotting your own refugee flight into darkest Africa?"

"No, it's not that. I've had a hard day."

"The Marine."

Liz looked up. "You remember him?"

"Who could forget? Every woman in the building—married and single—watched you drive off with the guy this morning, Liz. I'd have been in here sooner but I had to pick up some sardines and Spam to welcome my latest batch of Burmese."

They laughed together at these favorite foods of the silent, polite and terribly modest people group. It was hard to know what would strike the fancy of a given batch of refugees. A few local stores had started carrying live bullfrogs and eels, packaged duck heads and various other items too pungent even for Liz—who considered herself brave compared to many in the agency.

Molly set her elbows on Liz's desk and rested her chin on her palms. "What's his name, where's he from and how long do you get to keep him?"

"I don't want him." Liz let out a low growl. "Men like that should not exist. They complicate everything."

"But they're oh, so nice to look at."

"I can't argue there. You could drown in his eyes. Seriously, though, this guy is a pain. Very demanding. When he's not chasing insurgents in Afghanistan, he lives in Texas. He's visiting a friend here, and somehow he got tangled up with a family of Pagandans."

"Ooh. Paganda is not a nice place."

"No, and Joshua's people have been through the wringer. Global Care brought them in from Kenya, but they're on their own now. Except for Sergeant Duff, USMC. Their story won him over. The two children hid inside a metal drum while rebels massacred their mother and siblings. Their house burned down around them, but they survived."

"Wow." Molly fell silent—for once.

"Joshua met these people last night, and now he's determined to help them through the entire resettlement process. I told him that was crazy. It's too complicated and time-consuming for one person, but he wouldn't budge."

"Is he aware of the cost? Without an agency supporting the family, that could get expensive."

Liz paused, weighing whether to tell Molly what she had learned about Joshua's family. Finally, she spoke. "Okay, the guy is filthy rich."

"Mmm. Even better. Let's see. Joshua is rich. Joshua is handsome. Joshua is tenderhearted toward the poor and needy. What's not to like about Joshua?"

"He doesn't take no for an answer, he's domineering, he's forceful, he's way too self-assured and . . . and . . ." Liz clenched her fists. "I don't want to like him, Molly!"

"Why not?"

"Because I'm going to Africa. As soon as I become fluent in Swahili and get enough experience for the UN to want to hire me, I'm out of here. I don't have time for complications. I can't let myself think about Joshua Duff, and I hope I never see him again."

Liz shook her head. "No, that's not true. I can't think about anything else, and it's driving me nuts. You know what I went through with Taylor. It took me forever to figure out how wrong we were."

"I could have told you in two seconds."

"And you did."

"Liz, you need a man with backbone. Taylor was idealistic and friendly and good-hearted, but what a pancake. Flat. Boring. Wimpy. Pass the syrup."

"Molly, please. He wasn't that bad."

"Have I been married twice, Liz? Do I know the good ones from the bums?"

"Apparently not. Case in point—Joel."

Molly stood. "Yes, but I'm not marrying Joel. He's a friend."

"You're sleeping with your friend, Molly. That's a dumb thing to do. Have I told you that before?"

"Two thousand times. It's in my DNA to do dumb things with men."

Liz stood and picked up her purse. "Molly, please stop living this way. You don't need Joel. You don't need men who are bad for you. Why do you do that to yourself?"

"For the same reason you dated Taylor. He was there, you were lonely and it felt good at the time."

"I didn't *sleep* with Taylor. When I figured out he wasn't right for me, I got out pretty easily. You're tangled up all over again, Molly."

"And you can't stop thinking about Sergeant Joshua Duff. We're the same." She tossed the refugee update on Liz's desk. "Let's hurry up and pray, because I need to get some time on my treadmill before Joel comes over."

"All right, all right. I'll start."

The women had been friends for a couple of years. Liz had talked Molly into going to church not long after they'd met at the refugee agency. Now they prayed together at the end of every workday.

But Molly's life didn't change. She kept plunging from one mistake into another. As Liz took her friend's hands and bowed her head, she had to wonder how different they really were.

"Gangs." Sam Hawke tossed Joshua a white T-shirt from a stack on the desk in the front office. "Get used to it. This is the Haven uniform. We don't allow gang colors in here."

Joshua unfolded the cheap cotton garment. He had spent most of the afternoon under an oak tree in Forest Park, using his laptop to search out jobs and apartments for the Rudi family. It was high time to complete this assignment and move on to the next, he had decided.

The Marines had kept Joshua busy and in the thick of action for nearly a decade. Reflection and contemplation didn't sit well with him—especially when his own thoughts were so troubling. The pitiful condition of the Somali family he and Liz Wallace had met at the airport disturbed him. Liz disturbed him more.

But Sam's mention of gang activity piqued his interest. Maybe his military skills could be useful in St. Louis.

"Which gangs are causing you problems?" he asked, recalling the two he knew. "Crips and Bloods?"

"Around here, Crips are usually called Locs. Bloods are Dogs. We've got Murder Mob, Sets, Your Hood, Homies, Peoples, Cousins, Kinfolks, Dogs. Girls' gangs are called Sole Survivers and Hood Rats. The Disciples and the 51 MOB are unique to St. Louis. Hispanics have 'em, too—mainly the Latin Kings, but Florencia 13 is making inroads."

Joshua frowned. The St. Louis gangs sounded as complex as the factions he had encountered in Afghanistan and Iraq. Those sects had been founded on religious differences, but their current enmity went far beyond matters of faith.

"What's the gangs' focus?" he asked. "Territory? Violence?"

"Those are part of it. Arms and drugs play a big role. Just like everywhere, gangbangers worship the idols of the modern world—money, power and sex."

Sam leaned against the edge of Terell's old steel desk and studied the youngsters playing basketball on the large court just beyond the office window. "Our black gangs deal in crack and powder cocaine, marijuana, black tar heroin, powder heroin and heroin capsules. The Hispanics used to handle mostly commercial-grade marijuana. When Missouri clamped down on local methamphetamine producers, Mexican ice exploded. We're doing all we can to keep tabs on what's moving through the city."

"Who's *we?*"

"Haven. But there are others." He held up a hand and began ticking off the groups. "The St. Louis County Gang Task Force. The Metropolitan Police Department Gang/Drug Division's gang unit. GREAT, the Gang Resistance Education and Training program set up by the mayor, works in elementary and middle schools. REJIS is an agency that notifies parents of a child's gang affiliation. CeaseFire is a coalition of law enforcement, school and government officials, clergy and crime prevention specialists. We've got citizens' groups, too—INTERACT, African-American Churches in Dialogue, the St. Louis Gang Outreach Program, you name it. But no one's winning this war."

Leaning one shoulder against a post, Joshua unfolded the T-shirt. "African-Americans, Latinos—sounds like the gangs run along racial lines."

"Typically. A new gang showed up this summer, though. Hypes. They're unusual—racially mixed."

"So what binds them?"

"As near as we can figure, it's their leader. Fellow goes by the name Mo Ded."

"Sounds more like the definition of a cult to me—a group focused around a single charismatic person."

"Maybe, but they operate like a gang. Nothing religious about them. We're guessing Mo Ded is a newcomer to St. Louis. He was smart enough to pull together all the 'losers'—the gang rejects. You don't find anyone more loyal than the disenfranchised."

"Exactly how cults get started."

"Cult, gang, whatever. Mo Ded has been recruiting, organizing and training people all summer, carving out his turf and building his weapons cache."

"What race is this guy?"

Sam shrugged. "Anyone's guess. He's not black or white. But he's not Hispanic, either. Some say he's got Oriental eyes, but I hear they're a weird green color. Definitely not Asian."

"You haven't met him?" Joshua's recon experience had fine-tuned his ability to sniff out bad guys, and he knew Sam had similar training. "Don't you want to know who's sharing your territory?"

"Nobody *shares* turf, Duff. This block, including our building, belonged to the 51 MOB. Terell and I knew that when we bought it. We had to push them out and set up defenses."

"Like when we took streets in Baghdad or Mosul."

"This is war, man. Same thing—only without the manpower or arms on our side. Haven has a dog, a metal detector and Raydell and his crew to guard the door."

"You sure Raydell is clean?"

"When I first met the kid, he had a baby Uzi tucked in his pants and a juvie record that would have put an older man inside the walls—exactly where Raydell's father is right now. But our boy is working on his GED and planning to join the police force."

"Big change."

"One of Haven's few success stories. If a kid wants to spend time here, he's got to pull up his britches, leave his do-rag and grill at home, cover his gang tattoos, go through the metal detector and let Duke give him a sniff. The police keep a close watch on our place. We even have a few snitches. Terell and I realized we could let Haven become a staging area—a place where gangs congregate for retaliation and violence. Or we could essentially become gang leaders ourselves and make Haven our turf."

"Haven's homeboys. Does your woman know about this?"

"Ana knows and worries. But I remind her I've got unseen forces on my side. You may have noticed that sign in my office—If God is for us, who can be against us? God is really the leader of Haven. No one stronger than Him. The gangs know our focus on faith, and that helps some. But they've learned we'll do whatever it takes to protect our kids. We had to earn their respect, and we did."

Joshua was impressed. On first sight, the old building didn't look like much. Now he understood it was hard-won property.

"How about the 51 MOB?" he asked as he stripped off the shirt he had worn all day. "Did they ever surrender Haven?"

"Yeah, but it took a while. Haven used to get marked with graffiti all the time. I would paint over it, knowing that targeted me for death. You don't strip gang signs without getting killed. They'd spray my name on a wall and X it out. Essentially, that meant I was dead. They came after me a few times, but we worked it out."

"What about Terell?"

"He's an ex-offender. That gives him a lot of street cred. They know he can take care of himself. He uses his past to relate to the kids, but he doesn't want to get mixed up in the gang thing. I've got the military training, so I mostly handle it."

"Do the Hypes respect you, too?"

"Mo Ded doesn't give a rip about *anyone.* He's had his people loitering right outside Haven, inviting some of my best boys to jump off the porch."

"Join up?"

"That's right. Most gangs require a kid to join by beating in—walking between two lines or standing inside a circle of gang members who beat him to a pulp. But to get into the Hypes, you have to go on a mission."

"Military term."

"Worse. Mo Ded's favorite technique—he makes a boy put a blue rag on his head, dress all in blue and walk through a Blood neighborhood. Or wear red and walk through Crips turf. If the kid survives, he's a Hype."

"What age are we talking about?" Joshua asked.

"Around here, any boy over twelve either owns or shares a gun. Mo Ded starts them out at eleven."

Joshua shook his head as he unfolded the white T-shirt Sam had given him. "Reminds me of child soldiers in Africa. Sudan and Rwanda."

"Don't forget Paganda. As bad as he's had it, Pastor Stephen thanks God his sons weren't forced to fight for the rebels."

"The ones who were killed?"

"They end up dead either way. At least with a massacre, the suffering is short. In these African countries or in the kind of war you and I fought against terrorists, the only way to win is to eliminate the enemy. That or be eliminated yourself. You know what I'm saying, Duff. There's no middle ground. It's the same here in St. Louis. According to gang code, the only way to get rid of another gang is to kill all the members."

"That's genocide."

"Welcome to my world."

Joshua let out a breath. "Hatred. It's a grown man's game. Why are these gangs recruiting kids so young?"

"Same reason al-Qaeda straps explosives to children and sends them into marketplaces on suicide missions. Talk to your new friend at the refugee agency about child soldiers in Africa."

Uncomfortable at the mention of the woman, Joshua began putting on the T-shirt. He tried to work his arms through the sleeves. "Do you know Liz?"

"Pastor Stephen told me about your encounter at Refugee Hope. He and I had a long talk this afternoon. Stephen Rudi may be Pagandan, but he understands St. Louis."

"Yo, Hawke. This shirt's too small."

"One size fits all." Sam studied his friend for a moment. "Still got the six-pack abs, I see. I'd better not let you get too close to Ana."

"When am I going to meet this fiancée of yours, anyway?" Joshua said, wincing at the tight fit around his shoulders. He rolled the shirt down over his chest, but he knew the thing would never stay tucked into his jeans. Slouch time for the ol' Marine sergeant. He would have to get used to it.

"She'll be around," Sam told him. "Ana teaches a creative writing class on Saturdays, but I've stopped encouraging her to come over here much. Too dangerous. I go to her place if we want time alone. We cook dinner, watch a little TV. It's a nice break from the smell of sweat socks and dirty sneakers."

"What about Terell? Does he have a woman?"

"His church hired a new youth director last month—lovely lady named Joette. She doesn't know it yet, but she's got a former NBA star in her future. And you? Anyone out there in the battle zone catch your attention?"

"Plenty. But you know me. Careful." He decided it was time to change the subject. "Let's go catch some of the action."

Sam indicated the door, and the two men stepped out of the office. The basketball court swarmed with players. Whistles blew, the buttery aroma of popcorn drifted in the air, kids shouted. A toddler wandered out of one of the small classrooms. Smeared with blue paint, he looked around, lost. His face wrinkled into the start of a wail. Just then, a teenage girl sailed out of the room, snagged the child with one long arm and hauled him back to safety.

Too many kiddos, Joshua realized. This place could make a real impact, but not without more space. Sam had mentioned an idea to turn the parking lot outside into a basketball court and playground. Good plan if the gangs would leave them alone.

"No girlfriend?" Sam wasn't going to let it drop. "Come on, Duff. You're not getting any younger. Doesn't daddy want his boy back in Amarillo pumping oil and raising heirs?"

"He'd like nothing better than to see me build a house right down the road, get married and do the whole Duff-Flannigan Oil thing just like my big brother. No doubt the younger Duff boys will fall in line. I've been the black sheep."

"The lone ranger." Sam clapped Joshua on the shoulder. "Well, you've got your hands full right now. Those Pagandans are quite a bunch. I like Stephen Rudi. You won't believe what he wants to do in St. Louis."

Joshua glanced at his friend. He hadn't had time to look in on the family since returning from his trip to the airport with Liz. Her wariness about his undertaking had put him on guard.

"Reverend Rudi had better be happy to work for minimum wage," he told Sam. "That's all I can find for him around here. The wife doesn't speak a word—English or anything else—that I can see.

She's a walking shell. No telling what the woman went through before they got together. The little girl will have to go to school. Maybe the boy, too. What did Stephen tell you?"

"He wants to start a church."

Joshua scowled. "No way."

"He's dead serious. He believes God spared the family from genocide, brought them to the States and plans to use them to further the Kingdom right here in St. Louis. The man practically had Terell and me on our knees this afternoon right in the middle of a basketball game. He's pretty magnetic."

"Magnetism won't pay bills." Joshua studied the busy room. "Listen, Sam, I want to get the family hooked into the system here as fast as I can. I admire what you're doing at Haven, but it's not for me. I need to get on with my life. Got any idea how I can plug Pastor Stephen into a job?"

"We can find him work, but what about you, Duff? You don't want to sit behind a desk and count money for the rest of your life."

"Nothing wrong with money as long as it's used right. I don't know about that desk, though. You know me—I'm a hands-on man. I like getting down and gritty with people, working to change lives."

"Sounds like what we do at Haven. Why are you on the run?"

"Not sure. I have a few things to figure out."

Joshua ran a finger around the neck of the T-shirt. "I'm no social worker, that's for sure."

"You're not Recon anymore, either. I doubt you'll bust up any al-Qaeda cells in Amarillo. Why not stick around here? We've got Mo Ded and his brand of terrorists right outside these doors to keep things interesting. There's a lot more to Haven than social work, and we could use another man the kids can look up to. I'm starting to think we need a liaison with the refugee community, too. Maybe that could be you."

"Nah. The social worker at Refugee Hope showed me the error of my well-meaning ways. The things that go into resettling these people—it's more than one guy can do."

"Come on, Duff. I know you too well. You'd take on a challenge like that any day." Sam assessed his friend. "What's up with you? You've done a one-eighty since this morning."

Joshua focused on a group of youngsters carrying stacks of freshly laundered and folded white T-shirts toward the office. The last thing he wanted to admit was the way Liz had affected him. Five minutes, and she'd had him in overdrive. Not just her looks, either. They had clicked big-time. She knew it, too.

But it wouldn't work. She was headed to Africa. He was expected in Texas.

"I shouldn't have come," he said finally. "This place is messing with my mind."

"It's not St. Louis. The war did a number on your brain. If you're like me, you've still got one foot in the sand."

Joshua recalled his nightmare. "I need to take care of the Rudis and move on."

"You can't escape it, man. What else is bothering you?"

"Want the truth?" He chuckled. "*Women*—the only way I can think to get my head out of combat mode."

"Ana's got friends. Or how about that caseworker? Pastor Stephen said you looked at her like you planned to marry her."

"*Marry* her? Are you kidding me?"

"Like I said, the man is . . . insightful. *Intense* might be a better word. So what's the lady's name?"

"Liz Wallace. Gorgeous but on her way to some UN job in Africa. All day I've either been avoiding imaginary land mines or trying to figure out how to get that woman into my arms. Neither one good. I need to focus on the Rudis—find that missing brother, get Pastor Stephen a job, enroll the kids in school, locate an apartment and get them set up. All without letting myself get tangled in a pretty missionary's curls."

"Now there's an assignment worthy of the Sergeant Duff I met on a dusty base in Iraq."

"I'd rather hunt terrorists."

As Sam laughed, Joshua decided it was time to

cut the chitchat. He needed to find the little minister and his wife. Sam beat him to the punch.

"Pastor Stephen is in one of the classrooms. Said he wanted to start teaching Bible stories to the children. He's that way."

Joshua set off in the direction Sam had indicated. He definitely did not want to marry Liz Wallace—or any other woman. Not soon, anyway. He'd have to set the Rev. Stephen Rudi straight on that point. As well as a few others.

Chapter Four

Liz pulled her car to a stop in front of Haven and gathered up the stack of documents in the passenger seat. A shiver prickled down her spine as she focused on the young man slouched against the wall at the building's entrance. Compact, taut with gleaming dark muscles, he wore a white T-shirt, baggy jeans and an expression that dared anyone to mess with him.

The task could have been saved for another time, Liz realized, and maybe she should have waited. The streets were dangerous at this hour. Her headache had worsened throughout the day. With her patience stretched to the limit, all she wanted to do was curl up in her bed and sleep.

Please, Lord, let me sleep!

Why did He choose to answer this prayer so rarely? Liz shook her head as she pushed open the car door. Insomnia had become her demon, haunting her days and lying in wait to sabotage her nights. She ached for sleep yet dreaded the moment she would switch off her lamp each night. Her bed had become her worst enemy.

"Good evening." The young man's polite greeting surprised Liz so much she stopped walking. He straightened and stepped toward her. "Welcome to Haven, ma'am. I'm Raydell Watson, on door duty here. You'll want to give me those papers, your purse and anything that might set off our metal detector."

Belatedly, Liz noted the electronic apparatus just inside the door. Beyond it she spotted a dog. A large German shepherd, ears perked forward, tail raised.

"That's Duke," Raydell told her. "He's our drug canine. He won't do nothing to you—unless you're carrying."

"No. Of course not." Liz handed over the sheaf of paperwork. "You know, maybe you could just deliver these for me. They go to a man named Joshua Duff. I really don't need to talk to him."

"You'll want to go on in. We like for every visitor to take a look at our place." Raydell smiled, and now Liz noted the single gold tooth. "We're real proud of Haven. Just sign our register on my clipboard here." He glanced at her signature. "Thanks, Ms. Wallace. Now hand over your purse, and I'll let you through the door."

With some reluctance, Liz gave the young man her bag. "I work for Refugee Hope." She felt an odd need to explain. "Sergeant Duff is helping a Pagandan family with the resettlement process."

"Right through this door," Raydell said. He bellowed over her, "Visitor, Shauntay!"

As Liz stepped through the metal detector, she saw a young woman motion to the German shepherd. Wearing a white T-shirt and tight-fitting tan slacks, Shauntay gave Raydell a knowing smile as she took the registry. Then she picked up the dog's leash and led him toward Liz.

"Don't worry, Ms. Wallace. Duke don't bite unless we give the command." She walked the dog around Liz as she spoke. Satisfied, she handed back the purse. "You lookin' for Uncle Sam or T-Rex?"

Liz frowned. Who were Uncle Sam and T-Rex?

"Actually," she said, "I need to talk to Joshua Duff. I understand he's staying at Haven."

"That big dude? Over there shootin' hoops." Shauntay gestured with her chin. "He come in yesterday. Friend of Uncle Sam. They was soldiers together over in Iraq. He movin' in here."

"To Haven? No, I'm sure he plans to go home to Texas soon. He told me so this morning."

"Texas? What he gonna do there?"

"Oil, I think." Liz took a moment to study the young woman at her side. Tall and slender with a long graceful neck, Shauntay had the gentle beauty of a gazelle. Her almond eyes were dark brown and framed with long lashes. She could be a model on a magazine cover.

"Oil like what you fry chicken with? Or oil like you put in a car engine? Or hair oil?"

"The kind they make into gasoline. I believe Sergeant Duff's family is in the oil drilling business." Liz smiled. "What about you, Shauntay? What do you plan to do with your life?"

"Me?" She touched her chest as if the question surprised her. "I always wanted to have a hair place and do braids and weaves and twists and locs, you know? But I got two babies already, and I ain't even finished school yet. T-Rex say I could have a hair place if I want to. If I try hard and get my GED and all that."

"T-Rex?"

"Terell. The man. Him—over there with all the kids crawling on him." Shauntay laughed. "T-Rex. He funny, you know? We like him. He make us believe, because we see how he done his life—comin' up out of the hood and into the NBA, gettin' rich, then losin' everything to bein' a pipe head. And then he come here to help us do better. Him and Uncle Sam. I think that big guy gonna stick around, too. He done fightin' in Iraq, and he good friends with Uncle Sam. You seen his tats? *Dog.*"

"Tats?"

Shauntay pointed out the tattoos that marked her

arms and knuckles. "I used to be a 51 MOB queen, you know. A Hood Rat. They had me slangin' keys and runnin' from the 5-0 and everything else. The homeboys used to jump on us queens. They said we couldn't get out once we was in. They'd kill us. But I got out and got both my babies out, too. Now I spend my time at Haven. I worked my way up through KP and laundry all the way to Duke duty. One of these days, I really might get my GED and start me a hair place."

Liz tried to assimilate the information. Shauntay used a slang she didn't know and spoke English with an accent almost as unfamiliar as that of the refugees who passed through her cubicle every day. Though she had merely stepped from a St. Louis street into a St. Louis building, Liz felt much as she had the first day she got off an airplane in the Democratic Republic of Congo.

Haven was another country. Another world.

"I'm glad you spend your time here," Liz told Shauntay. "You're a beautiful young lady. I hope you do get your degree and start your own business. I'd be your first customer."

"You?" At this, Shauntay laughed so hard that Liz began to wish she hadn't said anything. Even Duke appeared unnerved as he paced back and forth on his leash. Shauntay shook her head. "Lady, you *white!*"

"So? I have hair, don't I?"

"You got hair, but . . ." The young woman took a step closer. "Lemme see you."

Liz tilted her head to one side. Shauntay gently dipped her fingertips into the mass of loose brown curls. For a moment, she murmured unintelligible comments, as if assessing something completely foreign. Then she made a sound like a cat purring.

"Yo, Ms. Wallace, I bet I could do you a goddess braid." The pronouncement was definitive. "I got two or three ideas in mind already."

Liz felt strangely happy. She took Shauntay's hand. "Deal. But not tonight. I have to give these papers to the sergeant over there and head home. I'm exhausted."

"When you gonna come back?"

"Come back . . ." The implications of her offer sank in. "Later. Maybe this weekend."

"Okay, Saturday. What time?"

Liz glanced across the room and noted that Joshua Duff had stopped shooting baskets. He was staring at her.

"I'm not sure about Saturday," she said. "I'll need to check my calendar."

"You got it in your bag?"

"Um . . ." Now he was walking toward her. "Listen, Shauntay, I'll be back soon. I promise. Would you give these papers to Sergeant Duff? I need to get going."

"You ain't comin' back. I met people like you before. Make promises and don't do nothin'."

"No, I *will* be back." Liz focused on the young woman's mahogany eyes. "All right, Saturday. Two o'clock. You can do a braid for me."

She made an attempt to pass off the paperwork. Shauntay shrugged one shoulder and turned away. "We'll see. C'mon, Duke. Let's go talk to Raydell. Probably some Hypes out there on the street tryin' to move in on our set."

"Wait. Please." Liz wrapped her arms around the sheaf of documents as she watched Shauntay saunter away and Joshua Duff approach. This had been a mistake. She would get it over with as quickly as possible.

"Liz Wallace." His damp white T-shirt clung to his chest. Through the thin fabric, the tattoos were visible, marking his biceps. She dragged her focus to his face. White-flecked navy-blue eyes pinned her. "You're here."

"As you see." She made an effort to copy Shauntay's gesture of indifference. "I thought I'd drop off a copy of my agency's handbook and some of the other information I mentioned on the way to the airport this morning. Lists of supplies your family will need. Community resources. Government assistance programs. Here you go." She held out the documents.

He stood motionless. "Why did you come?"

"The paperwork." Again, she pushed it at him.

"But I didn't intend to see you again."

"You didn't?" His statement confused her.

"You're still planning to resettle the refugee family from Paganda, aren't you?"

He appeared perplexed for a moment. Then he nodded. "Oh, yeah. I worked on it this afternoon."

"These will help you."

This time he took the paperwork. "You caught me off guard. I've been shooting hoops."

She tried not to look at his chest. "Yes. Well, I hope you're having fun. This is a nice place for the kids. Your friend has done a good job."

"Do you want to meet Sam?"

"No. I mean, I just swung by to drop off the copies. I'm on my way home. Please greet the Rudi family for me."

Before he could respond, she turned toward the door.

"Hang on." He caught her arm, pulled her closer. "Liz, wait."

"Really, I have to go. I'm tired."

"Let me introduce you to Sam and Terell." His hand cupping her elbow, he maneuvered her onto the basketball court. "Sam agreed to help me find Pastor Stephen a job. The guy wants to start a church, but—"

"He does?" Joy washed through her. "We desperately need local churches for the refugees. Pastor Stephen speaks Swahili, right? It's a common language in eastern Paganda, and many of our people pick it up while they're living in refugee camps in Kenya or Tanzania. I've been hoping to start a Bible study for Swahili speakers at my apartment."

"You know Swahili?"

"Not well. I learned a little while I was in the DRC, and I've been taking classes at the community center. It's part of my preparation for the UN job."

He stopped walking. "Africa. You're going to Africa."

"Lord willing."

For a moment, they looked at each other. Liz sensed the activity around them, kids running by, balls bouncing, a child crying, whistles blowing. But all she saw was the desire in Joshua Duff's eyes. Desire for her.

He wanted her.

She felt his hunger wrap around her chest and tighten her heart. Her own response caught in her throat, taking her breath away. She couldn't move. Couldn't speak.

"Who's this?"

A deep voice broke the invisible shell that had surrounded them. Liz glanced up to see the towering T-Rex, the impression of height increased by a golden-haired child perched on his shoulders.

"You got a lady friend, Duff? Why didn't you tell us she was coming over? Welcome to Haven." He stuck out a large hand. "I'm Terell Roberts. This is Brandy, up here. She's my sidekick."

Liz shook Terell's hand and focused on the

child. The angelic illusion of pink cheeks and blond curls faded beneath the reality of the little girl's runny nose, matted hair and grimy face.

"Hi, Brandy. My name is Liz Wallace." She returned to Terell. "And you must be T-Rex. Shauntay pointed you out. I work for Refugee Hope."

"Liz Wallace—you're the lady who . . ." His eyes darted to Joshua for an instant and then back, looking her up and down. "I heard about you. Yeah, you live up to your billing."

At that, Joshua sobered. "Terell, can you introduce Liz to Sam? I remembered something I need to tell Pastor Stephen. Thanks for the paperwork, Liz. I'll put this to good use."

Before she could reply, he strode away, leaving her alone with Terell and Brandy.

"Sergeant Duff and I don't get along, you see," she said. "We got off to a bad start this morning at Refugee Hope. The Rudi family came to the States through a different agency, and I didn't feel I could help them. So we had a bit of conflict."

"You did?" Terell studied Joshua, who was going into one of the small rooms that lined one side of the basketball court.

"That's not what Duff told Sam and me at supper. The way I hear it, you're the prettiest thing he's laid eyes on in years. Said you're making him crazy."

Liz knotted her fingers together. "I'm sure he

meant crazy in a negative way. Anyway, it's been nice to meet you—and you, too, Brandy."

The little girl waved down from her perch. "Bye-bye!"

"Hold on now—you need to meet Sam," Terell said. "We've got refugees starting to come to Haven, and we need help figuring out how to handle them. Nobody on staff speaks Spanish or Swahili or any of that, and some of those kids talk like lightning in the strangest gobbledygook I've ever heard. Sam's in the office. C'mon, Liz. Follow me."

Despite her urgency to get away, Liz could do nothing but accompany Terell to the youth center's office with its long windows overlooking the main room. A striking man wearing Haven's requisite white T-shirt rose from behind a desk as they entered.

"Sam, meet Liz Wallace. Duff's lady." Terell lifted Brandy off his shoulders and set her on the floor. "Liz, this is Sam Hawke. We run Haven."

"Us and a slew of volunteers. So you're the woman." Sam smiled in a way that made Liz even more uncomfortable. "Duff was right."

"That's what I told her," Terell confirmed.

"I'm glad you're filling our resident Marine sergeant in on the refugee situation," Sam continued. "We hope he'll stick around and help us out. The refugees are starting to trickle in here, and I have a feeling we're going to be inundated before long."

"I wouldn't be surprised. Several resettlement agencies have contracts with apartment managers in this area. Refugee Hope placed families from Burundi and Congo right around the corner. We're negotiating with a manager to place some incoming Somali immigrants in a building down the street. Terell mentioned that Reverend Rudi is interested in planting a church in the area. I hope you'll encourage that."

"A church where they talk *Swahili.*" Terell enunciated the word.

Liz smiled. "Refugee Hope has learned that children from our African families assimilate to city street culture very quickly. It's a way of coping that often leads them into gangs—and then into a lot of trouble. As a faith-based agency, we do all we can to help our immigrants build a stable lifestyle. Any intervention you could provide at Haven would be great."

"Your visit here tonight can't be an accident, Liz." Sam crossed his arms. "The Rudi family must be the tip of an iceberg we've just begun to notice. If families are moving into the area at the rate you're describing, we need to let Haven's board of directors know about it and put some strategies in place."

"You have a board?"

The corporate sound of the word contrasted with the pile of dirty white T-shirts in one corner of the room and the row of ancient computers on a long table near the desk. Broken trophies littered a shelf. A large metal barrel labeled Lost & Found overflowed with jackets, caps, mittens and flip-flops.

"Thanks to the legal help of one of our sponsors, Haven went nonprofit a few weeks ago," Sam explained. "We're all set up now. We have a grant writer, too."

"We're a 501(c)(3) charitable organization," Terell clarified. "You can get grants even if you're faith-based, which we are."

"Sounds like Haven and Refugee Hope have similar goals." Liz reached into her purse and pulled out a business card for each man. "Call me if you run into any problems. I've given Sergeant Duff a stack of information about our agency and the people we resettle. We have a lot of resources at our fingertips. And please support Pastor Stephen in his effort to start a church. It's the best thing that could happen to this neighborhood."

"We'll do everything we can," Sam said. "Thanks again for coming by, Liz. You're welcome anytime."

"I'll be back on Saturday. I promised to let Shauntay braid my hair."

His grin broadened. "Good—you'll get to meet my fiancée. Ana teaches a writing class on Saturdays."

Dreading the thought of any deeper involvement with Joshua's friends, Liz gave the men a nod of farewell and turned to go. “You aren’t planning to walk to your car by yourself, are you?” Terell accompanied her out of the office, Brandy clutching his hand. “Did you park nearby?”

“Not far. Your door guard—Raydell?—will keep an eye on me.”

“Naw, that’s no good. We got Hypes casing our set day and night. They’re looking for trouble. You’ll be a sitting duck out there. Let’s find Duff.”

“No, really it’s—”

Too late. Terell lifted the whistle that hung by a lanyard from his neck and gave an ear-piercing blow. Joshua—who had been hunkered down talking to some kids at the far end of the room—turned to look. So did everyone else.

“Yo, Duff! Your lady!” Terell’s long arm snaked overhead, his index finger pointing down at Liz as he yelled. “Walk her out!”

Mortified, she ducked her head and started for the door. She hadn’t made it halfway there when Joshua fell in alongside her.

“I thought you’d gone,” he said.

“You’re the one who walked away.” She focused on the metal detector. “I’ve been talking to your buddies.”

“Sam and Terell? Listen, Liz—don’t pay any attention to what they say.”

“They said a refugee church led by Pastor Stephen would be a good idea. I’m sure you’ll encourage him, too. Right?”

A low groan rumbled deep in Joshua's chest. "My goal is to find that guy a real job, an apartment and some kind of transportation. I've got to head back to Texas. If he wants to start a church, he'll need to do it on his own time."

"I didn't realize you were a janitor, like me. Mopping up the mess left by genocide—but not getting deeply involved with the people. Finding them employment, a place to live. That's about all I've been able to do at Refugee Hope. The name is a little ironic."

"You give them hope, Liz. Meeting the basic needs of a family is important."

"I want to do more. When I met you this morning, I thought you did, too." They had arrived at the door. Shauntay and the dog were nowhere in sight. "I'll let myself out, Sergeant Duff. I work in these neighborhoods. I'm not afraid."

He was two steps ahead of her. "I'll see you to your car."

"Don't. Please." She shook her head. "I'm not comfortable with you."

"Because of what Terell said." Blocking her path, he pushed through the one-way swinging door. He glanced up and down the street, then beckoned her through. "Terell jumped to conclusions. I barely mentioned you."

Liz held her breath as she walked past him. She could not allow herself to look, to smell, to touch. Dreams and goals lay clearly ahead of her. A sweaty ex-Marine on his way home to Texas was not among them.

The streetlights were inadequate, she saw at once. Darkness hovered in doorways and alleys. A muffled, pumping drumbeat pulsed from open windows. The scent of cigarette smoke and urine mingled in the humid air. A woman laughed. A man shouted. A bottle broke.

Liz gripped her keys in one hand—the long car key jutting between index and middle fingers to serve as a weapon if the need arose. Her small canister of pepper spray dangled from the key ring. A class she'd taken in self-defense had prepared her for this. She mentally reviewed the weak points on an attacker's body, reminded herself to check her car—front and back seats—before getting in, scanning her surroundings.

Of course, it didn't hurt to have Joshua Duff at her side. The sudden realization of his military training flooded Liz. Fear slunk away. Wariness eased. She let herself drift closer to him as they crossed the street.

"That's my car." She pointed out the American-made compact. "Thank you. I guess . . . all right, I *am* grateful you came with me. I thought Raydell would be out here."

"The kid with the gold tooth?" Joshua frowned. "He's been on door duty all day. Sam said someone is always supposed to be standing guard . . . . Uh-oh."

Liz turned in the direction of his gaze. Two figures were pressed against a wall a hundred feet from Haven's door. She recognized Shauntay's tall, slender shape. The other had to be Raydell.

"Where's the dog?" Joshua tensed. His arm stretched out in front of Liz as she backed against her car. "The kids have gone AWOL. Someone's taken the dog."

"Duke. That's his name," Liz whispered. "Do you see anyone?"

"Get into your car, Liz. Drive. I'll take care of this."

She spotted three silhouettes under the awning of the shuttered building beside Haven. "There," she whispered, stepping close. "To the left."

"I've got 'em." He bent slightly. Something small and shiny materialized in his hand. A glint of silver. "Liz, get into the car."

When she didn't obey, his voice hardened. "Do it now."

"This is America, Sergeant." She slipped her cell phone from her bag and pressed a single, preprogrammed key. "And by the way, I don't take orders well."

As she spoke, the three stepped out of the shadows, the dog at their side. Young men. In the light, she saw their white T-shirts. Haven garb? One held Duke's leash. The canine whimpered. Were these good kids? Or Hypes?

A glance at the entwined pair in the distance

gave her little hope. They'd be no help. Raydell and Shauntay had other things on their minds.

"They've got the dog," Joshua said. "They want us to know that. It's a first step. They'll try to take you next."

"They don't want me. I'm sure there's a reasonable explanation for this."

Sensing a transformation in Joshua that frightened her, Liz touched his shoulder. "The police are on the way—I just called. Relax. We'll find out what's going on."

She heard him breathing. Sensed the strain of muscle against fabric. Saw the knife in his hand.

This man would erupt, she understood suddenly. He would kill.

Before he could move, she stepped around him. At that moment, the dog leaped.

Chapter Five

Chaos. The kind of pandemonium Joshua knew well enveloped the street. As the dog yelped, straining against his leash, adrenaline surged into Joshua's veins. His mind snapped into combat mode.

Enemy contact.

Prepare to engage.

His body tensed and his heart hammered. Gripping his weapon, he assessed the situation.

Night. Three humans approaching. Two more at

a distance. One dog. Business district—storefronts, sidewalk, street. He sorted priorities. His own safety. The safety of those in his charge.

Those in his charge?

There was just one—the woman beside him, too small, out of uniform, unarmed. She didn't fit his paradigm, and the reality tripped him up.

"Duke! Duke!" A teenage girl ran toward the dog.

"Stop, Shauntay! Come back!"

"Break yourself, Raydell," she screamed. "Break yourself!"

Shouts, shrieks. The dog tore free. White teeth bared, fur bristling.

The enemy materialized, then faded. People pushing, shoving, struggling for position. Joshua saw his opportunity and moved into the action—blocked, protected, surged into offense mode. He knew these moves.

Yet there were no guns. No explosions.

Why not? Again—unexpected.

The knife in his hand flashed. Why couldn't he see better? He reached for his night-vision goggles. Gone. How had he lost them?

"Joshua! No—stop!"

Small bare hands gripped his arm. The woman's voice called his name again. *Joshua!*

He halted, fighting for breath. Blinking back sweat. Trying to focus.

Two vehicles swung onto the street, lights flashing, sirens wailing. *Police.*

He read the word and shook his head. That wasn't right. It should be written in Arabic, a language he knew almost as well as English. Something had gone wrong.

The police cars stopped, doors opened. The enemy fled.

Joshua rubbed his hand over his face, wiping away perspiration as he tried to make sense of it. Where was he? Was this the nightmare again?

"What's going on here?" The voice spoke in English, and he saw the face. The order came at him. "Drop the knife! Drop the knife!"

Who was this man? He couldn't move.

"Joshua? Joshua, are you all right? Please talk to me."

He recognized the eyes, the lips. "Liz?"

"Give me the knife, Joshua."

He knew her. This was Liz Wallace, and he was not in Baghdad. He handed her the weapon.

"Ma'am, I'll take that. Do you know this man? Is that your dog over there?"

In the light of the cars' headlamps, Joshua saw the dog lying on its side in the street. He tensed. Dead dogs often hid explosive devices—IEDs. Didn't these people know that? Why were they kneeling around the animal, touching it?

Others, mostly children, streamed from a nearby building. Haven.

"Duff—hey, man. What's going on? What happened?" Sam Hawke laid a firm hand on his shoulder, stepped close. His voice was low. "Time to let your guard down, Duff. Relax. This is St. Louis."

Joshua blinked. St. Louis. Of course it was. He knew that.

Sam's voice again. "It's all right, Officer. This man is my guest."

Hawke edged Joshua off the street and onto the sidewalk. "Okay, listen to me. I've been through this drill before, Duff. You'll get used to it after a while—the constant triggers. The spurts. It's confusing, takes you back into the conflict. But you're with me now. Let me handle things, okay?"

"Yes." It was all he could manage.

Standing on the sidewalk, Joshua watched his friend return to the cluster of people in the street. Still breathing hard, he tried to force his brain to reconfigure. He wanted to believe Hawke.

St. Louis.

But how? The situation had been identical to what he'd encountered countless times in the alleys and roadways of Iraq and Afghanistan. Street patrol, confusion, insurgents, dogs, children, the innocent mingled with the enemy.

Yet, this was different. English signs, police cars, street lingo. A white woman, no uniform, head uncovered. Soft curly hair framing her pretty face. She approached him now.

"Joshua?" Her voice was soft, lyrical as she said his name. "Are you hurt?"

How could he answer that? Of course he was hurt. Everything hurt. His head, his body, his conscience, his heart. Could he ever explain what the years had done to him?

"I need to re-up," he said. The words came from someplace deep inside. "I don't know how to exist outside it."

She stepped closer, leaning into him. Her shoulder was warm against his. Tension ebbed at once. Clarity returned.

"The dog . . . Did I—"

"No, it wasn't you. One of the others had a knife, too."

Joshua bent his head, massaged his brow. If his focus had been off, he might just as easily have been the perpetrator. This was bad. Sam Hawke's guard dog—now one of Haven's few defense systems—lay dead in the street.

"I need to talk to Hawke." He started forward, but Liz slipped her arm around his.

"Stay with me." She looked at him, her eyes deep. "Let Sam and Terell deal with the police. They know what to do."

She was silent for a moment before speaking again. "You scared me."

Joshua lifted his focus, searching for stars. He saw none. "I'm sorry. I don't know what else to say."

"Well . . . tell me what just happened."

"You saw what happened."

"Look, Joshua, in my work with refugees . . . I've studied trauma and terror. The constant presence of death. I know what those things do to people. I understand PTSD."

Joshua couldn't hold in a groan. Post-traumatic stress disorder. He'd listened to endless lectures about PTSD—before he deployed, amid the conflict and when he got back. He knew the symptoms. Knew he had them, too.

So what? Everyone who had been deployed had at least a little PTSD. Troops who hadn't seen a second of combat had heard incoming fire, mortars exploding, A10 tank killers and Apache helicopters cutting the air overhead. Everyone had seen things, heard things, done things they didn't like to remember. Joshua had always believed that those who couldn't transition were pathetic.

He was not a weak man.

Besides, he didn't like the cure for PTSD. *Talk,* the experts said. Talk to someone—a counselor, a minister, a loved one. Tell your wife. Tell your girlfriend. Spill your guts.

Exactly what he didn't want to do. Why talk about something you'd just as soon forget? Why relive the close calls? No man in his right mind wanted to explain how it felt to be shot at, to handle the dead body of a close friend, to kill an enemy combatant. Joshua didn't want to admit his fear, his grief or his guilt. Who would?

The way he'd always handled it was to hunker down and try to forget. When he couldn't forget—which he finally understood he never would—he focused forward to the next deployment. Back in the saddle with others who understood. In his youth, he drank too much in an effort to manage the pain. Now, anger sometimes masked it. But rage and alcohol were not solutions. Control held the answers, he believed. Self-control and constant prayer.

"I know it's not easy to talk," Liz Wallace said, snapping him back to reality. "But I'd be willing to listen."

"No thanks. I know how to handle a transition. Been through the process many times. There's always an adjustment period. Doesn't last long."

"Meanwhile dogs die."

Joshua stiffened. He could see people loading the animal into the back of a car. Through shards of light, he distinguished Sam and Terell amid the throng. Others—teens and kids—swarmed the street. Terell was calling out, trying to regain control. Sam focused on the dog. Raydell paced, anger and frustration in every step.

And now Stephen Rudi approached.

"My friend!" he cried, holding out a hand. "Are you well?"

"No problems here." Joshua shook the hand. "Your family okay? The kids?"

"My children are inside. Of course—upstairs.

But you? I was told men attacked you. Here! In St. Louis, America!"

"America, Paganda, Iraq. Every nation has its problems, Pastor."

"My family—we did not expect to find such a situation here. My wife's brother said nothing of this in his letter. These gangs. This is what we saw in Paganda too many times. Thuggery. Looting. Riots and killing. It is very bad."

"Calm down, my friend. I'm working to move you and the wife and kids to your own place. We'll find your brother-in-law and get you a job. Your wife can work, too. The kids will go to school. You won't have to live with violence."

"But why is it here? This is America! This is the United States of America! How many years did we wait in that refugee camp in Kenya, praying to find salvation in the land of our hope? Now what? Has the hostility followed us?"

"It was here long before you arrived," Liz told him. "Poverty, greed, empty promises. These always breed problems. America isn't exempt, Pastor Stephen."

He shook his head. *"Nimeshangaa."*

"Say what?" Joshua glanced at Liz.

"*Shangaa.* It's a Swahili word. Means to astonish, overwhelm."

"Even to defeat," Pastor Stephen added. "I am amazed by this news. Greatly discouraged."

Liz touched the man's shoulder. "We're all discouraged by the problems in the inner cities of America. Just like in Paganda, there are no easy answers here."

"I cannot bring my children from one place of terror to another! How can this be? Here they even kill the dog!"

"Dog ain't dead." Raydell shouldered his way through the crowd and stepped onto the sidewalk with the others. "Sam's takin' Duke to the emergency vet. This is all my fault. Sergeant Duff, man, I'm sorry. I let everyone down. I was supposed to guard the door, and I got tempted away."

"Shauntay," Liz said. "Is she in a gang?"

"Naw, ma'am, I don't think she's a hood rat. But I can't be sure. She's gone now, yo. Took off runnin' and didn't look back."

"Any idea the affiliation of those three guys?" Joshua asked. "Dogs, Locs, Disciples?"

An expression of respect transformed Raydell's face. "You know this turf? Uncle Sam been talkin'."

"I've been listening."

"Those were Hypes, yo. You see their do-rags?" He tapped his forehead. "Purple—for royalty, they say. Hypes brag they gonna rule the streets. Mo Ded, he's their man. He's got kids jumpin' off the porch every day. They want this street."

"They want Haven." Joshua watched Sam's car pull away. He looked down a moment, thinking of the dog. Had his knife cut the animal? Could he have been responsible for such a thing?

"Yo, Sam told me you a soldier." Raydell's dark brown eyes searched his face. "You know this drill?"

"A little."

The young man spat on the sidewalk. "Hypes. They'll do all they can to take us down. We need you at Haven, man. You better stick around."

Joshua couldn't keep from glancing at Liz. Then at Pastor Stephen. He shook his head.

"I'm expected in Texas."

Raydell nodded. "Didn't think you'd stay. Nobody does if they can get out. Except Sam and Terell. How about you, ma'am? You leavin' us, too?"

"I plan to go to Africa." Her voice sounded small. "To work in refugee camps."

"You ain't got enough war here—you got to go to Africa to find one?" He snorted. "You headin' out, too, I guess, Pastor Stephen."

"I must protect my children."

"Ain't no fathers around here to protect *them* kids—nobody but Uncle Sam and T-Rex." He focused on Terell, who was herding the children back into Haven. "Mothers, yeah. You only get one mother, and if somebody kills your mama, you got to kill him back. But fathers? Shoot, naw. They might act like they care, but they just want a cut of your money. Nobody thinks twice if his father gets killed. No remorse, yo. My dad—he's in the big house. The walls. I don't never see that guy."

Before anyone could respond, Raydell gave an exaggerated shrug. "Sam and Terell are the only father I ever had. Anyhow, I gotta go. I messed up bad tonight. I ain't gonna do that no more. Count on it."

The trace of a swagger affected the young man's gait as he crossed the street. Joshua cleared his throat. "There's only so much anyone can do. The kid's too young to know that. Liz, if you'll hand me those keys, I'll open your car door."

"He is not too young to have seen the truth." Pastor Stephen's voice was low. "This boy's words have cut me. In Africa, we love and respect our fathers. The father is the leader of the family. Yet he says that here in America, these children have no fathers?"

"More *shangaa,*" Joshua said. "This is a harsh place, Pastor. But I've promised to move your family out, and I will. Now again—Liz—why don't we get you into this car and make sure you're safely on your way home?"

She brushed a curl from her cheek. Without answering, she opened the door and slipped into the driver's seat. In a moment, the engine fired and the car eased out of the parking space. Liz pulled away without even a final look at him.

"We shall not see her again," Pastor Stephen declared. "She is troubled."

"Things got rough out here for a few minutes. Anyone would have been shaken up."

"It is not the attack that alarmed her." The African's eyes settled on Joshua. "It is you."

"It's not him. It's me." Liz curled her toes inside her kitten-heeled pumps as she spoke. She took a deep drink of steaming tea—milk-laced and well sugared. The thick liquid slid into her stomach, lending it a comfort she felt nowhere else. Though autumn had been trying to encroach on St. Louis for several weeks, the air whipping leaves around the sidewalk of the outdoor café was muggy. Even so, she welcomed the hot tea on this Friday afternoon.

"No, it's not you," Molly countered. "It's definitely the Marine. He's the biggest problem you've got. Last night made you want him more than ever. Admit it."

Molly had ordered a cinnamon roll, picked the almond slivers off the top and eaten them. Now she poked at the roll with her fork, turned it one way and another on the plate but didn't take a bite.

"You're wrong about that," Liz insisted. "What happened last night was a clear message to run. Run as fast as I can from any guy as messed up as Joshua Duff. Did I tell you about the knife?"

"At least three times."

"It appeared in his hand like magic, Moll. I can't imagine where he'd been keeping it. The minute those gangbangers got close, he turned into a machine. He could have killed one of them, you know. Probably all three."

She shuddered. The event had shaken her so much she was unable to sleep all night. She sipped her tea again.

"What's not to like about a man who can defend himself?" Molly asked. "And defend you? Come on, Liz. You went over there to see him. You liked what you saw, and now you can't stop thinking about him."

"The man I can't stop thinking about is Stephen Rudi."

"The Pagandan preacher?"

"You should have seen his expression under the streetlight. Heartbreaking. He was devastated when he found out America can be as violent as his homeland. He loves his children, and he thought he was bringing them to the land of opportunity. But there was something else about the guy that got to me, Moll. Pastor Stephen was repulsed and frightened by the brutality, sure. But he was truly concerned. When he learned that most gang members have no fathers, he got very upset. I have the oddest feeling God is going to use him here—despite his stilted English and Pagandan heritage."

"And this relates to our handsome Marine in what way?"

"Would you stop with Joshua Duff already? I'm serious here. All night I kept thinking about the expression on Pastor Stephen's face. He actually believes things are worse *here* than in Paganda."

"No way. Have you heard the stuff that's been going on over there? The machete killings, the burning of churches, the forced circumcisions? Rape so brutal women need surgery to repair the damage? The gang stuff is nasty, but it's not *that* bad."

"I didn't know about the circumcisions," Liz said. "What's the deal with that?"

Part of Molly's job was to keep up with world events—essentially to stay abreast of political and economic developments in the countries from which Refugee Hope brought people. As she unwound a thin strip from the side of her cinnamon roll, she shook her head.

"For centuries, one tribe has used circumcision as a rite of passage—an initiation into manhood. The opposing tribe uses a different rite—they knock out six back teeth. Tribe A says they'll never submit to the authority of an uncircumcised male. It would be like surrendering to a child. So, the men of Tribe A are taking on the job of surgically altering every male they can capture from Tribe B."

"Surgery? We both know any forced sexual activity in wartime is a form of terrorism."

"Of course."

The women sat in silence for a moment, Molly turning her plate in circles, Liz clutching her warm mug. Though Molly had never said a word about her own past, Liz wondered if some form of sexual assault had contributed to her eating disorder.

How could there be such pain and suffering in this world? Liz asked herself for the umpteenth time. Wasn't God supposed to be all about love? Hadn't His compassion for mankind led Him to send Christ as Savior? *For God so loved the world that He sent His only begotten Son . . .* She had learned *John* 3:16 as a child and had believed every word.

So why the gangs of St. Louis and the tribal violence of Paganda? She knew the answer, of course. Despite God's gift of love, sin still ran rampant in the world. Satan was a prowling lion, seeking whom he might devour.

"So, did he put his arm around you or anything?" Molly must have found another almond sliver. She was chewing when Liz looked up in surprise at the question. When it registered, she couldn't hold back a frown.

"If you're so obsessed with the guy, Molly, why don't you go after him?"

"Me? I'm with Joel. Besides, I know you too well, Liz. Come on, admit it. He fascinates you."

"I don't mind admitting that. I like his intensity. I felt . . . I don't know . . . safe, I guess. Is that the right word? Because Joshua is definitely *not* safe. He draws trouble like honey draws bees."

"Ooh, honey."

Liz rolled her eyes. "The oddest thing though . . .

he did make me feel protected and secure. He has some kind of strange presence. Strength emanates from him."

She shook off the chill that crept up her spine at the memory of Joshua's massive form stepping between her and the three troublemakers. There was a power in him she hadn't anticipated. It soothed and disturbed her, all at the same time.

"Anyway, the real issue isn't Joshua Duff," Liz went on. "I've been trying to tell you—it's me. What am I going to do, Molly? Ever since my trip to Congo, I knew I was meant to go to Africa. But last night when I saw Pastor Stephen's face . . . when I reflected on his concern for the young people *here* . . . it reinforced these doubts that have started creeping in. Maybe I'm not supposed to go. Maybe I should stay here. Is there more for me to do here than there? And how am I supposed to know?"

"Your problem is obvious, girlfriend. You want to go wherever you can find the most trouble. You've got this messiah complex. Like you can save the world all by yourself. Well, here's some news—you can't. You'll come, you'll go, and after you're dead the world is going to be in just as sorry a state as it was before. No one can change anything. So where are you going to do your bit in this lifetime God gave you? I don't know about you, but I'm happy living right here in the Lou, where I can drink a latte and go home at night to the arms of my latest romantic conquest."

With that, Molly threw a paper napkin over her cinnamon roll and rose from the table. "My own meaningless charity work is calling," she said. "I've gotta get back to my dear little cubicle and crunch some numbers for the suits in the home office. I refuse to take a pile of paperwork home with me tonight like I did last weekend. Coming?"

Liz pushed back her chair and stood. "I don't intend to spend my life doing meaningless charity. I intend to make a difference. And I don't have a messiah complex, by the way. I care about people."

"Right." Molly dumped the remains of her cinnamon roll into the trash. "You're different from the rest of us somehow. Your work is actually going to rescue mankind from sin, disease, poverty and eternal damnation. If I were you, honey, I'd stick with the handsome Marine."

Chapter Six

Joshua set the shovel tip in the dry grass, put his foot on the blade and pushed. The spade sank two inches into the ground and hit concrete. He moved the implement to the left and tried again.

Clank.

"Yo, Sarge, this used to be a hardware store." Raydell strode across the empty lot beside Haven. "Right here. I mean, right on this spot there was a four-story brick building. You ain't gonna get down there with a shovel. No way, dude. You need a jackhammer."

"We don't have a jackhammer."

"We don't have a lot of things, but that doesn't stop us," Sam said. Standing in the center of the open area, he unrolled a large sheet of paper.

While Terell kept the Saturday-morning activities going inside the building, several of the strongest young men among Haven's regulars had joined Sam, Joshua and Raydell outside. Their mission: stake out and start building a recreation area on an empty lot the youth center owned. A few curious onlookers, including Pastor Stephen, observed from the sidewalk. Joshua noted that Stephen's wife, Mary, stood near the door, her large glasses reflecting the afternoon light. Her bright scarf made a stronger statement than the woman herself had uttered since the family had arrived.

Sam had tacked a rough sketch of the new basketball court, playground and picnic pavilion to a telephone pole. Those drawings were amateur, but he now carefully unrolled a brittle-looking blueprint.

"This is the plan for the old store built here in the mid-1800s. Got my hands on it when we purchased the lot. That building was demolished years ago, but its foundation still exists beneath our feet. We've got to figure out where we can dig without running into concrete."

"Or gravel." Joshua picked up a handful of pebbles he had managed to scoop up from the ground. "I'm guessing this became a parking lot after the hardware store went down."

"How could I forget?" Raydell clapped his hand on his forehead. "Yo, Uncle Sam, people used to park cars here when I was a kid. Six dollars a day or twenty bucks for five days. A Chinese guy ran the lot. This was all covered with little rocks, dude."

"Gravel." Sam groaned. "Just what we need."

Joshua scanned the blueprint. "I've dug through worse ground than this. It may be an advantage to have a solid foundation here. The basketball court won't be hard to pave. If we can set the legs of the gym equipment and the pavilion deep enough and cement them in, they'll stand for years."

Sam grunted. "There you go, Raydell. That's the military mind at work. Never say never."

As Sam began to point out areas where the group might hammer in stakes and begin carving out holes, Joshua laid a hand on Raydell's shoulder. He kept his voice low. "Did you ever find out what happened to Shauntay last night? Is she all right?"

"That queen?" The young man spat. "She's fine. Whole thing was a setup, yo. The Hypes got to her. She'd been after me for days—ever since T-Rex assigned her to Duke duty—and I finally gave in. The minute I stopped paying attention to the entryway, she made sure they got their hands on the dog. They would have disabled the door and gone into the building if they hadn't run into you, man. I can't believe I fell for it."

Joshua's blood ran cold. "You're saying the girl worked her way into a position of responsibility at Haven on gang orders?"

"She used to be in the 51 MOB, but she said she got out. Forgot to tell me she jumped the porch right into the Hypes."

"You mean Shauntay got herself assigned to the drug canine and then flirted with you—all to pave the way for the Hypes to move against Haven?"

"Why you so surprised, man? You ain't never seen somebody do a thing like that? Give theirself away just so they can feel like they belong?"

Reflecting on the terrorist cells he had tracked for years, Joshua realized he understood it all too well. "I've seen it. But I didn't expect that level of loyalty among gang members. They're intent on taking Haven's turf, aren't they?"

"F'sure."

"What is Shauntay getting out of the deal?"

"Huh." Raydell gave a sardonic laugh. "What you think, yo? Mo Ded takes care of his homeys. A place to stay. Food. Protection. Respect. That girl's got two kids, y'know. She's gonna do everything she can to survive and keep them babies alive. I should have seen it. Man, I fell like a ton of bricks."

Sam had walked over during the explanation, and now he nodded. "You sure did, Raydell. Listen, I've been talking to T-Rex. We don't think we can keep you at the door."

"What? No way, man! I always do the door!"

"You've been compromised. The Hypes got to you. Duke is down, and the vet isn't sure he'll make it. Haven's security system has been breached. We've still got the metal detector, but they took you and the dog out of commission in about five minutes flat."

"Excuse me, please." Pastor Stephen touched Joshua's arm. "See there, on the corner."

Joshua noted the collection of young men gathering at the far end of the block across the street from Haven. "Uh-oh. Looks like we've got company."

The teens slowly merged into a sizable group and started down the sidewalk, a distinct aura of purple drifting with them. Purple do-rags, purple armbands, purple T-shirts. One wore purple slouch socks.

Leaning on the shovel, Joshua analyzed the opposing force. Eleven of them, but as Sam had told him, this group had nothing obvious holding it together. Certainly not race. They were a mixed bunch, varying hues and undeterminable origins. None appeared to have much going on in the way of size or build. In fact, they looked downright scrawny.

"Hypes," Raydell muttered. "Look at 'em all dressed down in their color. You know how they got the name, right? It's what they do. What they trade."

"Some kind of drug?" Joshua guessed.

"Yeah, man. Ice. You know ice? It's the white man's pleasure."

"Methamphetamine," Sam clarified for both Joshua and Pastor Stephen. "Crystal meth hypes a person up big-time. Listen, we need to get inside. I'll call for a patrol."

"Don't call the man, yo." Raydell had squared his shoulders and was eyeing the gangsters as they sauntered along. "They think Haven's a gang almost like them. Uncle Sam, you got to be the shotcaller here."

"We're not a gang, and I'll be the shotcaller from inside my building. And if you want any more door duty, Raydell, you'll come with me. Let's go, Duff. Pastor Stephen, gather everyone and head inside."

"They armed?" Joshua asked Raydell, for the moment ignoring his friend's orders.

Raydell's nod was all but imperceptible. "Oh yeah, they're packin'. No doubt."

"What've they got?"

"Anything. Gats, knives, you name it."

"Explosives? Grenades?"

"Naw. You ain't gonna find nothing like that in the city."

"Not yet." Joshua closed his eyes as the image of a marketplace ravaged by a suicide bomber surged into memory. Blood. Torn clothing. Body parts. People screaming.

He shook it off.

"Duff, Raydell," Sam barked from the doorway. "If I'm calling the shots, you'd better start listening. I want my people inside. Now!"

Keeping his eyes focused on the young men across the street, Joshua shouldered the shovel. Raydell muttered curses as he headed for the building.

"How do you plan to protect an outdoor basketball court and playground, Hawke?" Joshua asked. "You're going to have to stand up to them sometime."

"Not now. Not without backup."

"They don't look like much to me."

"Mo Ded is no idiot. He sent his gangbangers out to patrol this street because he knows exactly what we're planning for the empty lot. We're expanding our turf, and they don't like it. Believe me, they're well armed and looking for trouble."

"Trained?"

"Absolutely. Don't let the slacker attitude fool you. The baggy pants, the headgear—means nothing. You saw what happened last night."

"Do you have a plan?"

Sam put his hand on Joshua's back and nudged him inside to safety. "I told you last night about my plans for Haven. I want a place where kids can earn GEDs, learn job skills, find work, raise families, make better lives. I want kids to play outside without fear of a stray bullet. I've got plenty of plans, Duff. What I don't have is a *way*. A way to make my plans come true."

Joshua looked into his friend's blue eyes. They both knew the answer. The *way* had been built slowly, through years of training and experience in the sands and high deserts of a distant country. Joshua knew the *way*. He had seen the path out of such places, and he could find it again. Find it here.

But an oil field on the edge of the Texas plain beckoned Joshua. His father had called countless times since his return from Afghanistan. How long could he continue to shirk his family duty?

"Sir, please!" Pastor Stephen hurried toward him. "My wife! She did not enter the building with the others. Mary is missing!"

Police cars lined the street outside Haven as Liz pulled into a parking space opposite the building. A curl of warning slid into her stomach. All morning she had fretted about her agreement to let Shauntay braid her hair. It would be so easy to claim she was too busy to meet the Saturday commitment. Unlike Molly, she had brought home a tote bag full of files bearing forms that would take most of the weekend to complete and organize.

Besides, Liz had seen Shauntay run away the other night, and she knew it would be difficult for the girl to return to Haven. Shauntay had done more than lure the door guard away from his duties. Her behavior had opened the way for the Hypes to steal Duke, a misdeed that ended with conflict, knives, the police. And the possible death of the dog.

Shauntay would not be at Haven, and Liz certainly shouldn't be there.

Now that she'd seen the squad cars, Liz had every excuse to head home. But the scene troubled her. What if something serious had happened? An attack? An injury?

Liz couldn't hold back the memory of Joshua Duff's face as he had ushered her into her car. The clash with gang members had catapulted him into some sort of flashback, and his fear for her safety was visibly etched in his eyes.

Despite the warning flags in her heart, Liz knew she had to see him again.

After scanning the street, she pushed open her car door and stepped out. Hoping to appear detached, even unconcerned about the other night's incident, she had dressed as if she had other plans—running shoes, nylon shorts, a light T-shirt. She had just dropped by, she would say. This was true, of course. She was just checking in. On her way to the gym.

Her thoughts caught up in the plan, Liz was surprised to spot Mary Rudi hurrying down the sidewalk toward Haven. Head bent, the frail Pagandan woman focused on the ground as she beat a path toward the front door.

"Mrs. Rudi?" Liz reached out a hand to stop her.

"Eh?" Mary lifted her head, her spectacles catching the midday sun. "Excuse me, please. Please, please!"

Before Liz could stop her, Mary had brushed past and stepped through the door. Surprised at the woman's unwillingness to engage in a traditional African greeting ritual, Liz glanced down the street.

A group of young men clustered near a streetlamp. Liz recognized three of them. Chilled at the sight, she entered the building after Mary.

"Hold on! Hold on!" Raydell's long arm blocked her at the inner doorway. "Nobody else gets in now. Stand right there. Don't move."

Stepping out in front of her, he lifted his fingers to his lips and sounded a deafening whistle. "Uncle Sam, T-Rex! Yo, Sarge, she just walked in. The missing lady. Look—right there!"

Liz backed up against the cool wall and took in the scene. Two police officers sprinted across the basketball court after Mary Rudi. Stephen Rudi let out a whoop of joy, throwing up his hands and running to his wife. Sam Hawke and Terell Roberts headed for Mary, as well.

"You saw her come in?"

The voice at Liz's ear made her gasp. She turned to find Joshua standing at her elbow.

"You scared me to death." She gave him a gentle push. He didn't budge. "How did you get over here?"

"I've been waiting for you. As I recall, you've got an appointment for a goddess braid."

"Don't sneak up on me like that." She threaded her fingers back through her hair. "This place makes me nervous. I didn't want to come here to begin with. Then I saw the police cars. Now you."

"The best part of the package." A small grin softened his features. "You're trembling."

He took her hand. Tucking it into the crook of his elbow, he leaned against the wall beside her. "So you saw Mary Rudi come in?"

"I was right behind her."

"Where had she been?"

"Out on the sidewalk like me and everyone else. What's going on?"

"She went missing a few minutes ago. Pastor Stephen couldn't find her and started freaking out. Hawke called the cops. They were preparing for a sweep of the neighborhood when she showed up. Any idea where she might have gone?"

"Shopping?"

Liz knew she should move her hand from his arm. The warmth of Joshua's skin and the mound of solid muscle beneath her fingertips made her uncomfortable. Yet a sense of peace had paralyzed her. It was the same certainty of power and protection she had known the other night, and she liked it too much to step away.

"Mary was gone ten minutes—tops," Joshua said. "No time to shop. She doesn't have money, anyway. Pastor S. told me they made it to St. Louis with seventy-three dollars. Hawke put most of that in the office safe."

"Maybe she went for a walk—to get some air."

"She'd have told him. No, something happened. She was outside with us. We had just started work on the new rec project in the empty lot. The Hypes walked by on the other side of the street, and Hawke sent everyone back into the building. Somewhere in there Mary vanished. Pastor Stephen hit the panic button, and Hawke summoned the heat. And now here she comes."

"I saw those three men outside." Liz looked into his eyes. "The ones from the other night."

His body went rigid. "They're out there? How far?"

"Down the street."

"Was she with them? Had they gotten to her?"

"Mary? No, they were standing at a distance watching me. She was rushing back to Haven like she'd been out on a mission and wanted to get home."

"A mission?"

"An errand. Maybe one of the kids needed medicine? Or a toy or special snack? Maybe Mary had seen something in a store window and wanted a closer look. She's not a prisoner here, is she?"

He regarded her in silence.

"Maybe she is," Liz said. "At least she will be until you set the family free. How is that going, by the way?"

"I can't find the brother. The address in their letter is bogus. No such street. His name isn't turning up in any phone book or Web directory. Maybe they'll hear from him one of these days, but until then, they're all mine. I took Pastor S. and the missus out to apply for jobs yesterday. The best he's going to do is minimum wage—dishwashing or janitorial. Too bad, because he's educated and smart. His English isn't bad, either, once you get used to the accent."

"Is he willing to work an entry-level position?"

"He'll have to. And the guy keeps right on talking about starting a church here. Like that's going to pay anything. He won't give it up, especially after he learned about the family breakdown and the gang situation. Thinks he can save the world."

Liz bristled, recalling Molly's teasing.

"What's wrong with wanting to make a difference?" she asked. "I admire him. We need more people willing to get involved. And we certainly need someone who can minister to the people in this neighborhood. Cut him some slack."

"Keeping that dream alive, are you?" He turned

his back on the cluster of people gathered around Mary Rudi. Facing Liz, his navy eyes went deep. "Still headed to Africa?"

She looked away. "As fast as you're headed to Texas." Before he could speak again, she stepped aside. "Listen, I've got to get going. Mary's safe now, and it looks like you're taking good care of the family. I doubted Shauntay would show for the hair appointment. Better run."

He caught her arm and swung her close again. "When am I going to see you?"

Her heartbeat faltered. "Don't do this, Joshua. We both have plans. And nothing in common. Really, I need to go."

"Tonight? Let's do dinner and a movie. Or ice cream, if that's too much."

"Thanks, but it's not a good idea. You know that."

"I'm not asking for a lifetime commitment."

For a moment, she couldn't make herself speak. Everything written on his face belied those words. Joshua Duff *was* looking for a commitment. He wanted a connection . . . a permanent link to sanity, reality, hope, joy. These things eluded him, and he was seeking them as surely as she was looking for peace.

She stepped away a second time. "If you see Shauntay, please tell her I came on Saturday like I promised."

Hurrying toward the door, she spotted Sam Hawke waving at her. A tall, thin woman—almost too beautiful for such a gritty setting—stood at his side.

"Liz, come here a second." He beckoned, and she could do nothing but cross to the edge of the basketball court where they stood. He indicated the lovely, dark-eyed creature in her white blouse and khaki slacks. "I want you to meet Ana. Honey, this is Liz Wallace—the woman from Refugee Hope. Duff's girl. Liz, this is my fiancée, Anamaria Burns. Excuse me a second while I see Officer Ransom and the other guys out."

"So nice to meet you, Liz." Ana held out her hand. "Sam told me about your work with the refugees. I admire you. I'm a reporter for the *Post Dispatch*—which means I spend way too much time in front of a computer screen."

"I'm at a desk most of the time, too." Liz shook the woman's slender hand. Like a giraffe, Ana was elegant and ethereal. No wonder Sam had fallen in love with her.

"I just met Joshua this morning," Ana said. "Great guy. He and Sam served in the war together. So many stories! I've invited Joshua to join us at my apartment for dinner after church tomorrow. Would you like to come?"

"Oh, thank you, but I've got so much to do. The files are endless." Liz read the disappointment on Ana's face, but she couldn't back down. "Maybe some other time. I'm sure our paths will cross again."

"No doubt about that." Ana smiled. As Liz made for the door yet again, Ana fell in step. "Sam mentioned that refugees from war-torn nations are being resettled in St. Louis faster than people realize."

"Possibly. Surely the schools are aware. Businesses, too, I'd imagine."

"It has to be impacting the area. I'm going to talk to my managing editor about doing an article. Could I call you for an interview?"

Liz glanced at the wall where she and Joshua had spoken. He was gone. Letting out a breath, she dipped her hand into her bag and brought out a business card.

"Call me anytime. I'd love to talk about the needs at Refugee Hope. We're desperate for volunteers."

"Everyone is." Ana shrugged. "Haven sucked me right in. I put it off as long as I could. Didn't want to get involved. You know how it is. But Sam kept after me. Now I teach three writing classes on Saturday afternoons."

"Three?"

"Poetry, believe it or not. Song lyrics are the draw. Everyone wants to be the next king of hip-hop. We do a lot of rapping."

Liz laughed along with Ana. The idea of this elegant creature teaching kids how to write the kind of music that thumped from car stereos amused them both.

"You sure you won't join us tomorrow?" Ana asked as Liz stepped to the door. "Terell is bringing the new youth director from his church. Sam and I haven't met Joette, so it's going to be fun. She doesn't suspect she's soon to be the new Mrs. Terell Roberts. It would be great for everyone to get to know you better, too."

At that, Liz had to stop her. "Listen, Ana, I appreciate the invitation, I really do. But I have to tell you there's nothing between Joshua and me. I honestly have no idea why he would give Sam that impression. We've barely met. A couple of conversations. I dropped off some paperwork here, and suddenly I'm his girlfriend. He's nice enough, but like I said . . . Okay?"

Ana nodded. "Sure, Liz. I didn't mean to jump to conclusions. I'll talk to Sam about it."

"Thanks." Liz touched Ana's arm in gratitude, then she pushed the door open and walked out.

Two steps later, Joshua was at her side. "About what I said in there. The thing about a lifetime commitment—"

"I know—and would you stop jumping out at me?" She held up a hand and kept walking. "Don't worry about what you said. You were just asking me to dinner, and I'm being skittish. It's no big deal."

"But what I told you wasn't true. I've tried to convince myself I'm not looking for a lifetime commitment. Not with the military, not with my father's oil business, certainly not with a woman. But I'm lying to myself."

Liz paused at the curb. "Joshua, don't say anything else. Please, just stop talking, would you? Let me go. Let me run at the gym, and work on my files, and help the refugees, and eventually fly away to Africa. I need to do that. It's what God wants from me. What He called me to do."

"*Called* you?" His eyes narrowed. "Did you hear God's voice or something?"

"More like I saw it. I saw the United Nations refugee camps when I was in Africa. I saw the tents and the fences and the dust. I saw the medical clinic and the feeding station. I even saw where the aid workers live—my own future home. God didn't have to speak audibly. I knew I was meant to be there. Joshua, I'm going back to Africa."

"What will you find there?"

"Purpose." She couldn't help but falter. "I have a purpose here. I know that. Please don't argue with me."

"I wasn't."

"I'm arguing with myself. If you must know, it's a struggle for me right now. At one time, I knew I was supposed to go to Africa. But now . . . Why am I telling you this?" She threw up her hands and stepped down into the street. "You're the one who should be talking. You've got PTSD, not me. I'm fine, perfectly fine. I know who I am and what I'm going to do."

"You're not at peace about it."

"Don't talk to me about peace—you with your tattoos and your buzz cut and your hidden knife. You're a man of war. I don't want that. I don't want you. Leave me alone."

"Why did you come back to Haven today? I was sure you wouldn't, but you did. And don't tell me it was for Shauntay. You knew you'd see me, Liz. You're as curious as I am about what's happening here. There's a connection."

"No connections. No bonds, no links." She squeezed her eyes shut. "All right, maybe there is something. But I don't trust it. Something so spontaneous can't be right. Besides, it can't go anywhere, and you know that."

"Couldn't we just have fun? Friendship? Ice cream?" He looked away, rubbing the back of his neck. "Who am I kidding? That's not going to happen."

"Goodbye, Joshua." Liz held out her hand just as Ana Burns had done earlier. "You're doing a good deed for the Rudi family, and I admire your service to our country. Let's go our separate ways and do the things we're meant to do. You have my card, right? E-mail me from your office sometime. I'll write you back from my headquarters in Africa."

Joshua took her hand. He held it for a moment. Then he turned it over and kissed the sensitive skin on top.

"I won't forget you," he said. "I'm a Marine—always faithful. You know, Semper Fi and all that."

With a salute, he stepped back to watch as she walked to her car and drove away.

Chapter Seven

"I shall be very pleased to assist in the cooking of these foods." Pastor Stephen Rudi gave a slight bow of appreciation to the manager of the fast-food hamburger restaurant two blocks down the street from Haven. "Thank you for your kindness upon accepting my application, sir."

The manager smiled. "Uh, sure. See you tomorrow, then."

"Mission accomplished." Joshua set his arm around the smaller man's shoulders as they headed for the exit that Monday morning. "Slinging burgers isn't a bad job, and it will introduce you to the American way. You'll be earning minimum wage with no benefits, but it's only a matter of time before you work your way up the food chain."

"The food chain?"

Pastor Stephen held the door for Joshua. Then he led his little wife outside. In her crazy head scarf and enormous glasses, Mary Rudi had followed a good five paces behind the two men all morning. She wouldn't say a word and knew almost no English, so any hope of work among the public was impossible. In addition to the language barrier, the Rudis' immigrant status made them unwelcome. Joshua had displayed their legal documents, passports, visas and work permits to little avail.

As immigrants, they were *different,* he was told. Who knew where they had come from and what they might do? More than one potential employer made it clear he hired only English-speaking Americans. People who spoke a foreign tongue were unwanted and distrusted.

"Our country needs to take care of its own," one woman had informed Joshua as she cast a wary eye on Pastor Stephen. "We ought to seal our borders and keep these people out. It's the only way to make sure we're safe."

Joshua had refrained from pointing out that America's prisons were bursting at the seams with her own citizens. But no one wanted these strangers. None but the manager of the fast-food restaurant, himself a second-generation Irishman.

At least one thing about the Rudis could be remedied.

"Hold up a second, Pastor Stephen," Joshua said. "We have the custom of courtesy here. It may seem a little medieval, but it'll get you a long way in America."

"Have I committed an error?"

"No big deal. Just remember that in this country

the woman gets treated as an equal. Sometimes like royalty."

"Like a queen?" He stared at his wife, as if the idea wouldn't register.

"A man always holds a door for a woman. You open the door and stand aside, she walks through, and then you follow. On the sidewalk, you take the position nearest the street. Keeps your wife safe from muddy car tires and other indignities. And whenever possible, walk together."

Pastor Stephen shook his head. "My wife will not go along beside me. It is the woman's place to walk behind. The man must be the leader. In this way, he protects his family from dangers ahead."

"Yeah, well, not here. Not while you're walking with Mary, anyway. Now let's see how you do with this car door."

As the two Pagandans discussed the instructions in their rhythmic lingo, Joshua checked his messages. Three calls from his father that morning. Knowing the subject of those communiqués all too well, he deleted them without bothering to listen. He was expected at home.

Since Joshua's arrival in St. Louis, both his father and mother had phoned countless times to admonish their son for fleeing before they'd had the chance to give him a proper welcome. That meant parties and chitchat and hobnobbing—all among the things he detested most about civilian life.

Not only had Joshua failed to meet his social obligations, but he was needed at Duff-Flannigan Oil. A few weeks before his discharge from the military, his father had reassigned the man who had been running oil field operations. How much longer could the situation continue without Joshua's presence? The elder Duff had pressed the question again and again. It was time Joshua assumed his rightful position in the company. Family tradition demanded conformity. It was a Duff thing.

"Like this!" he said, with more force than he intended. Both Stephen and Mary had been grappling for the door handle, their conversation heating into an argument. Now Joshua brushed both sets of hands aside, pulled open the door and waved Mary in.

"Mrs. Rudi, you go first," he said too loudly, and the expression behind her spectacles startled him. Fury. Even hatred.

"Tell her it's the American way," he ordered Stephen. "It's polite. If you two can't bend your Pagandan traditions about something as small as this, you're sunk."

"Sir! You have frightened my wife," the smaller man said. "Please. She has endured much hardship."

Haven't we all? Joshua wanted to drawl. But he kept his mouth shut, indicated the passenger's seat for Stephen and walked to the driver's side.

The past weekend had not gone well, and Joshua had made up his mind to leave St. Louis before the next one rolled around.

As he drove toward a janitorial service where he hoped to place Mary Rudi in a cleaning job, he mulled the past couple of days. Saturday morning, the second incident with the Hypes had put a halt to Sam's outdoor construction project. A large purple gang sign spray-painted on Haven's wall sometime that night had sealed the deal. There would be no basketball court, playground or pavilion. Not until the street was secure.

Mary Rudi, still traumatized from whatever had happened to her in Paganda, was unable to explain what had separated her from the group that afternoon. Hunkered down on the bed in the little room she shared with her family, she had refused to speak a word. Not even her husband could make sense of the few syllables she muttered. He finally told Joshua that she must have run away in terror when the Hypes showed up. Once she lost sight of her family, she hurried back.

As if Saturday weren't bad enough, Sunday turned out worse. Watching Sam and Ana cook lunch together had been close to agony. So much in love they hardly noticed their guests, they had laughed and teased each other while tossing a salad and keeping an eye on the curried chicken casserole that had been heating through church. Joshua could think of nothing but Liz Wallace.

Terell, of course, was strutting his stuff for the beautiful Joette Plummer. To Joshua's amusement, the woman began to melt right before their eyes. Well educated and now in her second position as director of a church youth ministry, she might as well have been a teenager the way she giggled at everything Terell said. He told stories about his NBA glory days and his fall from grace. Then he and Sam regaled both women with tales of their efforts to raise Haven from the rubble and transform the shattered lives of the neighborhood children.

Impressive stuff. Joshua sat in a chair by the window and thought about the streets of Kabul and the oil fields of West Texas. What had he done with the life he'd been given? What did he have to offer for the future?

"Have we not passed the cleaning service? I saw the sign of the street just one minute ago." Stephen Rudi's voice brought Joshua back to reality. And yes, he had driven right by the office advertising part-time work.

A spin around the block took them back to the address. Inside, Joshua again presented Mary Rudi's legal documents and passport. To his surprise, the manager offered her a job on the spot. Housekeeping positions, it seemed, were difficult to fill in downtown St. Louis. Mary would work a night shift cleaning office buildings.

"She'll have to ride the bus to work," Joshua

explained to Stephen as they left the cleaning service. “Does Mary know how to do that?”

The two Pagandans conferred about this in low voices, then Stephen turned to Joshua. “My wife says she used to ride a bus from her village to a larger town once a month for shopping. I shall accompany her until she can succeed in St. Louis.”

“Good plan.” Joshua pulled the Cadillac out into the street again. “She’ll be working with a crew of five, so they can teach her the ropes.”

“The ropes?”

“The methods.”

Speak in concrete terms, Joshua reminded himself. Idioms were difficult to translate. It had taken several years for him to understand Afghan humor. He reflected on the beloved Mullah Nasrudin stories, confusing and illogical to Americans but side-splittingly funny to the locals. And Afghan proverbs were so enigmatic he never had learned to make sense of them. What good was all that now, anyway?

Once again feeling off-kilter in his own country, Joshua handed a sheaf of instructions to Pastor Stephen.

“Mary will be emptying trash, dusting shelves and vacuuming floors. Routine work. A landscaper takes care of the indoor plants, so she won’t have to do any watering or feeding. A window-washing company does all the glass in the buildings. Mary will get regular breaks, too.

She ought to take some spending money along if she wants to buy something to eat. Every building will have snack machines."

Again, the Pagandans discussed the situation. Each time they talked, it appeared to Joshua that Mary's unhappiness increased. Sprinkling her complaints with a liberal dose of grunts and mumbles, she didn't care for anything her husband had to say.

But when Stephen reported back, he made no mention of his wife's discontent. "We do not understand the meaning of *vacuuming,*" he said. "Is this a type of American floor washing?"

Joshua pictured the concrete or dirt floors on which the family must have lived in the villages and then in the refugee camp. "A vacuum is an electric machine for cleaning carpets. You plug it in, press a button and it sucks up dirt."

"Sucks dirt? Pardon me?"

"Yeah, it's hard to explain. Trust me, it gets the job done. Mary's supervisor will teach her."

As he drove back toward Haven, Joshua was pondering the wonder of the vacuum cleaner when a sign caught his eye. Veterinary Clinic. He made a hard right and pulled the car to a stop.

"I think this is the place Hawke mentioned the other night," he told Stephen. "They took Duke to the emergency vet here. I'm going to check it out. You and Mary want to come in with me?"

"We shall await your return." Pastor Stephen

cast a quick glance at the woman in the backseat. "I believe my wife is eager to return to our home."

"About that. Haven is not your home, Pastor Stephen. Sam and Terell have let you stay on there because I've assured them I'll move you out by the end of the week. Don't get too comfortable, okay?"

"Oh, we are not at all comfortable."

Joshua had his hand on the door, but now he leaned back. "You're not? Something wrong?"

The man bent his head. "Not wrong, but also not right. My wife's brother led us to believe he had a good home for us to share with him in St. Louis. He wrote that he would help me find a church to serve as pastor. Indeed, he promised us good work and much success here. Now we find that our circumstances are quite different from these expectations. Had we known this, we should have remained in Atlanta. There is a large Pagandan community in that city."

"I've done everything I can to find your brother-in-law. I'm sorry."

Stephen nodded. "I also am sorry."

"Listen, Liz Wallace mentioned the need for spiritual direction among the refugees here. Not to mention the whole gang thing going on. I'm not sure there are many Pagandans in St. Louis, but maybe Liz could introduce you to some of the other Africans she has helped resettle. There must be a lot who speak Swahili."

"I would appreciate this very much. You will place the call?"

Joshua hesitated. "You've got her card, right? Here's my phone—and by the way . . . don't call Paganda."

Stephen was smiling and pressing buttons as Joshua crossed the sidewalk to the clinic. He opened the door and a familiar antiseptic odor slammed him. Instantly, he was whisked to his base's medical facility. He reached for a chair near the door, leaning onto its back for support.

Post-traumatic stress disorder, a voice echoed through his head. Those words had been repeated again and again to the group of men and women with whom he had served on the most dangerous assignments. *PTSD. PTSD.*

Your Global Assessment of Functioning Responses meets the screening criteria for this mental disorder.

Mental disorder?

No way.

You qualify for mental health services now and after you're discharged. Please seek help.

The antiseptic smell—a trigger. A spurt. *Shake it off, Duff.* He could get through this transition on his own. The triggers would come. The nightmares, too. He knew the symptoms. Concentration problems. Fatigue. Sleep disturbance. Hyperarousal. Depression.

And everyone's favorite. Avoidance behavior.

Yes, he would avoid almost anything that forced him to deal with it. But now a chorus of yips and howls from the distance brought him back.

He was not in Afghanistan. Not on base. He was here in America. St. Louis.

“May I help you?” The voice of a young woman behind the front desk pulled him the rest of the way out.

“I’m here to check on the status of a dog. Duke.” Recalling now the cause of the injury, he found it hard to meet her gaze. “He’s a German shepherd.”

She pressed buttons on a keyboard and searched a monitor. “Oh yes, Duke came to us with a knife wound. Punctured lung. He’s had some fever, and the doctor put him on antibiotics. Come on back.”

Joshua hesitated. “I just wanted to know how he’s doing.”

“It’s okay, you can see him. Follow me.” She vanished behind a swinging door.

At the end of a long hall, they stepped into a large, open room two stories high with several skylights. It was filled with small trees, fountains and green plants. A long row of cages held dogs of every imaginable breed, and the entrance of the two humans incited a round of loud greetings and much tail-wagging.

“Here’s Duke. Come on, sweetie.” The assistant knelt, opened a cage door, slipped a lead around the dog’s neck and urged him out. “I’m pretty sure he’s not ready to go home yet, but I’ll check with the doctor. You can spend time with him in our visiting area."

She handed Joshua the short strip of nylon and pointed him in the direction of a small room. Aware that the Rudis were waiting in the car, he considered calling the woman back. But one look in the dog's large brown eyes, and Joshua knew he couldn't leave.

"So, Duke, nice digs you have here." He led the limping dog into the small room and shut the door behind them. As Duke dropped to the floor, Joshua noticed the patch of shaved skin over his ribs.

"Sorry about that, boy." He knelt and stroked the hair between and around the dog's ears. "You were just doing your thing the other night. Me, too. I guess we have some kind of crazy instinct. They trained us, and now look. We're both . . . both wounded . . . both messed up."

Unable to continue, he propped his arms on his bent knees and pressed his face into the crook of his elbow. A cold, moist nose nudged his side. Then the dog edged closer and laid his head on Joshua's lap. It was too much.

Tears came from nowhere. Joshua sank his fingers into the thick fur around Duke's neck. The pain wouldn't be held back.

"I didn't mean it. Didn't mean to hurt you," he choked out. "God forgive me. I don't know what happened out there . . . what's wrong with me. It's hard to feel okay. Hard to love myself after what I've done. Some of the stuff . . ."

He broke off, now burying his face in the dog's neck. "I can't sleep. Feels like my chest will explode. Cold sweats. Nightmares. I'd give everything I own to have one night of good sleep . . . a day without remembering pieces of something that happened. And it's all pieces. Bits and pieces jumbled together."

Again, he couldn't go on. He didn't want to talk, didn't want to say these things. But the dog was warm, his breathing a comfort. And it came again.

"Anyone who gets within ten feet of me, I size him up and analyze how to take him out." Joshua heard his own words with a sense of disbelief. But they were true. "I'm always trying to figure out a plan of escape so I won't get killed. That night in the street . . . I saw those guys. Something switched on inside me. I'm an IED. A bomb hidden inside a human body. A corpse waiting to explode."

He clung to the dog, his mind crouching in the dark corner of a hideout, his Barrett .50 caliber sniper rifle at his side. Or was it the M-40A3? He searched for the target, reached for the weapon.

Prepared to engage.

"Guess what! You can take him home!" The bright voice snapped through Joshua's brain like a Taser. The words continued. "The vet told me Duke's temp was normal at the last check, and she was just about to call you to come get him."

Blinking, he looked up. “What?”

“Aw, your puppy’s going to be okay.” The receptionist dropped to her knees. “I love it when I see how much a man cares about his dog. Don’t be sad, okay? I’m Allie, by the way. Nice to meet you.”

He shook the outstretched hand. “Duff.”

The young woman’s face was open, eager. Allie? She had pretty blue eyes and long blond hair. With a coy tilt of her head, she touched the deep V neckline of her knit top. It was a signal he recognized, but he didn’t have the energy to respond. She couldn’t be much older than eighteen.

“Well, then . . .” She shrugged and looked away. “If you’ll follow me, I’ll check Duke out. He needs to stay on his antibiotics, and the doctor wants to see him again in a week.”

Still dazed, Joshua followed her back down the hall. He hadn’t heard the door open. Hadn’t seen the receptionist walk into the little waiting room. Was he losing his mind?

“If you’ll sign right here, I’ll put the medicines in a bag.” She held out a clipboard and pen.

Joshua scanned the document. A record of the dog’s surgery and medications. A list of postop instructions. A bill.

He pulled out his wallet and thumbed off a few notes. Allie gave a little exclamation as he handed over the money.

"Cash?" she squeaked. "But we don't have change for that denomination in the drawer."

"It's okay. Whatever's left—use it to take care of the animals."

He took the bag of medicines and the receipt. Feeling frayed and disoriented, he headed for the door.

Should he visit the VA office? Were these incidents going to get worse? After past deployments, he had transitioned all right. It took a few weeks, maybe months.

Afghanistan . . . In the beginning, it had been easier than Iraq. But this past stint was rough. Not only the door-to-door hunts for insurgents in Kabul and Kandahar. He had spent months high in the Hindu Kush. Seen overturned cars and buses rusting at the bottom of the Khyber Pass. Searched caves along the border with Pakistan. Scrambled over rocky terrain at an altitude where he could hardly breathe.

"You have brought the dog?" Stephen Rudi flung himself out of the car. With an expression of alarm, he focused on Duke. "But where can it sit?"

Joshua rubbed his forehead. "The back."

"With my wife? Oh, sir, this will not be good. Please put the dog in the front. I shall stay with Mary."

"Whatever suits you." Joshua helped Duke into the passenger's side. But the moment the animal was seated on the floor, his ears perked up and a guttural growl rumbled from his throat.

"What's the matter, boy?" Joshua tugged the leash, trying to draw the animal's attention from the small woman in the rear. "Settle down. I'm taking you for a short ride. Back to Haven."

Now Duke was struggling to rise, eyes pinned to Mary Rudi. His neck ruff bristled as the low, chest-deep snarl began again. Joshua laid his hand on the animal's head, smoothing fur and stroking ears.

"Come on, Duke. Everything's fine. Down. Sit down." He started to shut the passenger door, but the dog barked.

That's all it took. Mary Rudi screamed and fled the car. Stephen ran after her. Down the sidewalk they dashed, and this time she was definitely in the lead. Joshua shook his head.

"Well, you did it now, buster. Scared the living daylights out of them." He closed the door on the animal, rounded the car and slid into the driver's seat. Duke had slumped, his head low and his breathing labored.

"I'm chauffeuring a dog while my refugees run for their lives through the streets of St. Louis." He switched on the ignition. Wonder what Liz would think of that?

Liz took out her scrapbook and laid it open on the spread. One-thirty in the morning. Memories and questions filled her head. Three hours of lying in bed unable to sleep had finally left her pacing the apartment floor and debating the merits of various over-the-counter sleep aids. None worked well.

Standing, she studied the first page of photographs in her well-thumbed album. The KLM jet through the terminal window. Faces of church team members who had gone with her on the journey to Congo. A brief stopover in Amsterdam with a visit to the Anne Frank house and museum. Genocide in another century.

She flipped through a few more pages. Now she saw the Congolese people—mothers with babies on their backs, a man proudly showing off his scrawny goat, a little boy with a bad burn on his stomach. Children playing soccer, their ball made of plastic bags they had salvaged from a dump and wound with twine. A girl staring at the camera, her eyes forlorn, her dusty cheeks streaked with tears.

Liz studied the face, saw the emptiness and need. What could she have done to address that child's hunger, illiteracy, hopelessness? Nothing while on the mission trip. Everyone in the group had understood there was no way to meet all the needs in the village. A few dollars, some bags of rice, penicillin capsules, even a newly built medical clinic. None of the donated aid made much of a difference.

Abandoning the scrapbook, Liz crossed to her small galley kitchen and filled a glass with water.

If she had been able to do so little before, could she expect to do anything *more* now? She still didn't speak Swahili well enough to be considered fluent. She had no health care training. No teaching certificate. Nothing but the desire to help.

She took a sip of water and let the cool liquid slide slowly down her throat. Then she returned like some windup toy to the photo album. She studied one page and then the next. On leaving the DRC, she had been so certain of her mission in life. She must return to Africa. God wanted her to go back and do something significant.

But what could she really accomplish? Process paperwork for refugees in a camp somewhere? Try to find a way to send them to America or some other haven? And then what?

A melody suddenly rang out in the empty apartment. Liz coughed and swallowed the last sip of water. She recognized the music as her phone's ringtone. Where had she left her purse? Who would be calling at this hour?

Spotting her purse on the sofa, she dug out the phone and studied the caller ID.

Joshua Duff.

That afternoon she had answered a call from the same number. Stephen Rudi had told her he was using Joshua's phone. He needed to discuss certain matters with her. Matters of great significance. They had been cut off midsentence.

Though Liz had tried Joshua's number several times, she got no reply. Unwilling to decipher her motive, she had entered the man's name and number into her own phone.

Holding it to her ear now, she steeled herself to what Joshua might want to say. "Hello?"

"I have your friend's phone."

The voice did not belong to Joshua Duff. Or to Stephen Rudi.

"Oh," she managed.

"My boys were following the car," he continued. A husky timbre, male, slightly slurred. "One of 'em picked it up. Your friend want it back?"

Her heart lurching, Liz sat down on the end of her bed and curled her knees up to her chin. Who was using Joshua's phone? Why would this man call her? What did he mean that his boys had been following the car? Was someone stalking her—or Joshua?

"You still there?" the man asked.

"Yes." She swallowed. "I'm sure my friend wants the phone."

"Good. Tell her to meet one of my people at Podunk's. You know Podunk's?"

Liz recalled the Cajun restaurant a block from Haven. "I know where it is."

"Tomorrow. Six o'clock straight up."

The connection clicked off. Liz stared at her phone. The number on the caller ID was definitely

Joshua's. But the man had told Liz to give the message about Podunk's to *her.*

Who was *her?*

No one could possibly mistake Joshua for a woman.

For a moment Liz considered calling back. But the voice on the other end had confused and frightened her. On the way to work in the morning, she would stop in at Haven.

Joshua Duff. An image of the man flooded her mind, pressing out thoughts of crying Congolese babies and frightened Pagandan refugees.

She would get little sleep on this night.

Chapter Eight

"Ninety-eight, ninety-nine, one hundred." Joshua set the barbell down and stared up at the ceiling of the weight room.

He would conquer this.

Sleepless nights. Terrifying dreams. Fight or flight. Adrenaline surging through him. Pumping iron helped a little.

Slices of sunrise slanted through the blinds as Joshua sat up from the weight bench. On the wall, a large mirror reflected his image. He didn't like what he saw. Bare-chested and glistening with sweat, he should be as fit, tough and healthy as he had been at the height of his military career. The body had changed little . . . but the face?

Joshua could see strain etched around his eyes. Weariness in the set of his jaw. Uncertainty in the line of his mouth.

With a grunt of frustration, he stood and stepped onto a treadmill. He switched on the motor and began a slow jog. Within moments, he had ratcheted it up to a near sprint.

The morning ahead would bring a trip to the neighborhood elementary school to enroll the two Rudi children. Neither spoke English well, and Joshua knew they would struggle. Pastor Stephen told him Charity had attended classes in the refugee camp. Her age made her a second grader. Virtue would start kindergarten.

After settling the kids, Joshua and Stephen would collect Mary from her job. The past two nights, she had joined a crew cleaning a large office complex not far from Haven. The three of them would drive to several apartment buildings that offered subsidized units for rent. Pastor Stephen did not want his family to live in such a dangerous part of the city, but for the time being, he had no other choice. They would select an affordable apartment and Joshua would provide money for essential furnishings.

That afternoon, while Stephen worked at the fast-food restaurant and Mary slept, Joshua would help with the after-school programs at Haven. A local gym, he learned, had equipped a weight room that summer. But with no one to monitor its use, Sam and Terell had been forced to keep the door locked. Joshua would settle the Rudis by week's end, but until then, he could make the weight room accessible to youngsters and teach them some lifting basics.

He would not think about Afghanistan and the men in his battalion who were continuing to serve without him. He would not think about his father or the office job waiting. He certainly would not think about Liz Wallace . . . the woman who . . . who even now was watching him in the mirror.

What?

Chills rushing over him, Joshua peered back at the apparition as he ran on the treadmill. An uncanny optical illusion of reality stood in the doorway of the weight room, her face beautiful and pale. Curls tumbled to her shoulders, gleaming in the light of dawn.

This was it, then. The psychosis he feared had finally settled in. He had tried so hard not to think about Liz Wallace that he was actually hallucinating her at this moment.

He notched down the machine, jogging, then walking, and finally standing. Gazing into the mirror, he stared at the figment of his imagination. His mind was gone. There she stood, looking as real as life. And he was totally insane.

"Excuse me, Joshua?"

He gripped the treadmill's handrails. Visual hallucinations. Auditory, too—he had actually heard her speak. He would have to tell Hawke. Get himself to the VA. They would check his records. Evaluate him again. Probably hospitalize him—rightly so.

"Sam opened the front door and let me in." The phantom image drifted into the weight room. "He needed to stay and unlock the office downstairs, so I came on up. I hope I'm not bothering you. I just have to talk to you for a minute."

Goose bumps sliding down his arms and legs, Joshua turned slowly toward the vision. She moved closer. She wore a pretty blue dress. Low black heels clicked on the tile floor. Her hair swayed as she neared.

"Are you all right?" she asked. "You look . . . odd."

He stepped off the treadmill.

"Do you want me to leave?"

"Liz?" He dared the word.

"Yes?"

"Can I touch you?"

Her eyelids fluttered as she looked away, cheeks flushing pink. "Well . . . what do you mean?"

Reaching out, he laid his hand on her arm. Warm silken skin met his fingertips. He traced the arm from shoulder to elbow. Cupped it. Brought her near. The scent of gardenias enveloped him.

"Liz," he breathed out. *"Thank God."*

She was real. The actual woman. Not a dream. He closed his eyes as he wove his fingers through hers and squeezed her hand.

"Joshua, you're scaring me."

"Don't be afraid. Not of me." Relief palpable, he slipped his arm around her shoulders and pulled her against his chest.

But her sudden gasp told him what he had done.

"Whoa, I'm sorry." He backed away, hands up. "Forgive me—I'm sweaty and you're . . . you're dressed for work. I apologize, Liz. I didn't mean to"

"It's okay." Her fingertips covered his mouth. "You didn't expect me here. I startled you."

"No, no." Shaking his head, he turned away. "It's me. My fault. I'm losing it."

"Why would you say that?" She followed him, circling until they were face-to-face again. "Joshua, please look at me. You're not losing it. You're fine."

"I didn't know you were real," he admitted. "The mirror. The light in this room. I thought I was seeing something."

"I'm real. And so are you."

"I frighten you."

"A little." She glanced at his chest. When she looked up, a smile tugged at her lips. "You're pretty fearsome with all those tattoos."

He tried to force a grin as he rubbed a hand over the blue markings inked into his flesh. "The things an eighteen-year-old will do to be cool."

"Aren't you going to ask why I came here this morning?"

"It doesn't matter *why.* I'm just glad you're an actual human being. I've been conjuring you up so often that . . ." He stopped himself. "Okay, why are you here?"

"Someone used your phone last night to call me. It wasn't you."

He thought for a moment. "I lost the phone. Rather, my Pagandan friend dropped it on a sidewalk somewhere."

"Stephen Rudi lost your phone?" She followed him to the rack where he had hung a white towel. "You shouldn't have let him use it. Never let the people borrow your phone, Joshua. It's in the Refugee Hope handbook I gave you the other day, remember? Didn't you read it? They all want to call home, and the costs are astronomical. You have to teach them how to purchase an international calling card."

He hooked the towel around his neck and studied her for a moment. "Are you always this beautiful in the morning?"

Her brows drew together. "Is that some kind of a line? I'm not here to flirt with you, Joshua. I came to tell you that some guy has your phone, and he called me in the middle of the night, and he wants you to meet him at Podunk's at six this evening. Only he thinks you're a woman."

"A woman?"

"Yes. He said, *'Tell her to meet one of my people at Podunk's'*—to return the phone, you know. Tell *her*. But the phone was yours. I know it was, because Stephen said you'd let him borrow it while you were in the vet's office. I was trying to tell him that he was not to use his volunteer's phone when we got cut off. I called back but I didn't get an answer."

"Because at that moment, my phone was lying on the sidewalk. See, I was putting Duke into the car when Mary Rudi got spooked and took off running with Stephen right behind her. He had my phone in his hand. When I caught up to them, they were all right but the phone was gone."

"The man I talked to last night told me one of his people had picked it up. He must have redialed the last call, and it was my number. Joshua, he told me they had been following you."

"Me?"

"Yes, and I'm worried they're stalking me, too."

"Stalking." At the word, his brain snapped to attention—instant analysis of the situation required.

Someone had been tracking him. Tracing the movements of his car, his person. They had watched him leave the vehicle and enter the veterinary clinic. Seen him return with the dog. Observed as Stephen and Mary Rudi fled. When Stephen dropped the phone, the tail had been right there. Snatched it up, took it to the man in charge.

Who would follow him? He scanned the mental list of possibilities. Insurgents. Members of an al-Qaeda cell. Sunnis. Shiites. Pashtuns.

He knew things, sure. Techniques, methods, skills, weaponry, even plans. Things the enemy might want.

The phone itself would do them no good. It would be a puzzle to anyone. He had coded his address list in such a way that no civilian could decipher the thing. For that matter, his closest buddies would have been at a loss to understand it. In fact, there was no identifying data on the phone. The only way to make contact would be to press the redial—and that had led them to Liz.

"No telling who's been trying to call you," she said. "That guy has probably freaked out all your friends. He sure gave me the creeps."

"My father," Joshua said. "My dad would have called several times since Stephen dropped the phone."

"God does work in mysterious ways, you know. Maybe the phone thief and your father had a nice conversation. Maybe he can go to Texas in your place, while you stay here to help refugees."

"Yeah, and watch you fly away to Africa?" He touched her cheek. "No thanks."

She looked down for a moment. "I'm late for work. I should go. So, you got the message—Podunk's at six this evening. But, Joshua, be careful. This business about the guy's people following you. I didn't like the way that sounded."

"I can take care of myself."

Her eyes crackled as she met his gaze. "Like the

other night? Do you want to end up in jail? Or dead?"

"Relax. I'm not going to—" He let out a breath. "You think I'm a loose cannon."

"Yes, I do. I hope this thing you're going through is temporary, but until it passes, please lie low."

She started for the door, and he kept pace. "I'm not ignoring it, Liz. The PTSD. They tell us to talk, and I am. I did."

"You did?" Halting, she turned. "Who did you talk to?"

He couldn't exactly admit his therapist had been a dog. A dog who didn't understand and couldn't respond. Still, it had helped him to speak aloud about the pain. Though he had rejected that method of healing, he knew the experts were right. Friends had been discharged from the Corps with PTSD or traumatic brain injury, and in letters or phone calls they had told Joshua the facts. Those who faced the problem, who talked to their loved ones and experts, who admitted the truth and worked on healing—they got better. Those who numbed it with alcohol or released it in fits of rage began to come apart.

"Never mind," she said. Holding out a hand to block him, she hurried down the steps. "Don't say another word. I came to tell you how to get your phone back. That's all. I'm going to work."

"Wait—when can I see you again? Liz?" He caught her wrist. "Look, I understand I'm different with the brain triggers and the trauma stuff. I can see how a woman might consider it a problem to spend much time around me. I know what you think of me, Liz."

"Please. You have no idea."

"Then what? What do you think of me?"

"Does it matter? No. It might matter if our paths were to keep crossing, but they won't. And now you have someone to talk to, so you definitely don't need me." She pulled her arm away and crossed the open gym area to the front door.

"But I do need you," he called.

His voice sounded weak. Childlike. He hated that, yet what he'd said was true. He needed Liz Wallace—in more ways than he could begin to count. Something about the woman drew him. He had tried not to think about her—working with the Rudi family, spending hours with Sam and Terell and their women, working out in the gym until his muscles ached. None of it had erased Liz from his thoughts.

Trying to think how to reach her, he lagged a couple of paces behind as she headed for the door. Volunteers who had come to work at Haven's newly opened day care center were beginning to filter into the building. Children, too. Teenage mothers knelt to kiss their toddlers goodbye. A girl who looked about fourteen handed her baby to a grandma-type with cottony hair and a delighted smile.

"Shauntay?" Liz paused near a young woman whose two little ones clung to her legs. "You're back. I'm glad to see you again."

The smoky gaze assessed Liz, then slid over her shoulder to the man behind. "You still with him?" Shauntay asked, her lip curling. "Me, I don't need no man. Raydell says I set him up. Told everybody I'm a Hypes queen. He don't know nothin'. I don't belong to no gang. I got me a job now."

"A job—that's wonderful."

A flicker of satisfaction crossed the young woman's face. "T-Rex said I could bring my babies here, even though I'm off Duke duty because of what happened. Him and Uncle Sam let Raydell stay on the door, but they took me off the dog. How is that fair, yo? They trust him more than they trust me."

"What happened the other night, Shauntay?" Joshua asked. "You were in charge of Duke, and Raydell was on the door. How come the two of you left your posts?"

"How come you followin' her around with your tongue hangin' out, dog?" Her voice dripped with sarcasm. "Look at you all buff with your big muscles—tryin' to be the man so you can impress your woman. Yeah, don't think I'm blind. You and her ain't no different from me and Raydell. What happened that night happened—but it wasn't all my fault. Raydell was givin' me the look, too.

Anyhow, I'm done with all that. I got me a job and I don't need no man."

Liz touched the girl's arm. "Where are you working, Shauntay? Do you need a ride?"

"D'Shondra's Braids. I can walk . . . but . . ."

"Come on, I'll drop you off."

As Shauntay handed her children to a volunteer and the two women pushed open the door, Liz glanced back at Joshua. "Don't forget Podunk's."

He called after her. "It was Duke. I talked to the dog, okay?"

The door swung shut. Someone pressed something into his hands. He looked down into a pair of bright brown eyes. A baby.

"Do *not* go!" Molly grabbed Liz's shoulders and stared her down. "Are you nuts? It could be a gang thing like the other night. But instead of the dog, *you* could be the one who gets stabbed. Or shot."

"It's not a gang thing. Someone wants to return the man's phone, that's all." Liz felt around the bottom of her purse for her car keys. "It's a public place. Podunk's—nothing will happen there."

"If nothing will happen, why do you need to go? The guy is a Marine, for goodness' sake. Let him take care of it himself."

"That's exactly why I need to go. He said it himself—he's a loose cannon."

"And you can fix that?" Molly maneuvered until she stood between Liz and the cubicle's exit. "You will not go, Elizabeth Wallace. You will drive home, make yourself eat dinner and sleep."

"Sleep is overrated."

"Look at you, Liz! You haven't slept in weeks. You're a wreck, and I'm scared something is going to happen to you. Even without that nutty man around, you'll probably drive into a wall. You can barely hold your eyes open. And now you're going to some restaurant to protect the guy from a stalker?"

"I can't protect Joshua Duff from anyone. But I can at least be there. From a safe distance, I can watch what happens. If there's a problem, I'll call the police. Now move, please. The guy on the phone said six straight up."

"I'm going with you."

"You hate Cajun food."

"This is not about food. It's about your life."

"Molly, please don't be melodramatic. I understand your concern. The times I've been around Joshua were . . . strange."

"This morning he thought you were a ghost."

"He has a touch of PTSD. They all do—the war vets—and he insists he knows how to get through it."

"He said he's talking to someone, right? So it's probably another woman, Liz. He's found a girlfriend, and he was letting you know."

That possibility had bothered Liz all day. The Somali refugees she'd visited in the morning were having trouble rationing their food stamps and other vouchers. Their phone bill was outrageous from calling Africa. They had fallen into debt after only two months in America. One of the older boys—frustrated and angry over struggles with English—had stopped going to school. The mother seemed depressed, and the father had made a serious mistake at his new job. The family meeting lasted several hours, and Liz's efforts to communicate in Swahili illustrated how far she still had to go before she would ever be ready to live and work overseas.

Through the entire time she spent explaining that junk mail coupons did not entitle people to free money, she kept thinking about Joshua. His face in the mirror. The touch of his hand on her arm.

I do need you, he had called after her as she tried to run away. But did he? What could she offer him? The pull between them could only be physical. Or perhaps it was a result of Liz's constant drive to save the world, as Molly had so often chastised her.

"I do not have romantic feelings for Joshua Duff," she told her friend. "I'm concerned about his state of mind, that's all. Now let me pass so I can get to the restaurant on time."

Molly stepped aside. "This is such an about-face from what you said before. Come on, Liz. You have a schoolgirl crush on the guy, even though you know it will come to nothing. He's leaving for Texas. You have plans of your own. Don't keep finding ways to see him."

"I need to do this one last thing." Liz moved down the hall, her heart rate increasing with every step. "You didn't see those three guys the other night. They came at us, Molly. If Joshua hadn't produced that knife out of thin air, I don't know what would have happened. Besides, the man who called me on the phone sounded threatening. He said his people had been following Joshua. How can I stand back and let him walk into something dangerous?"

"You said this wasn't a gang thing! You said you knew you couldn't protect him!" Molly's accusations flapped overhead like laundry on a line. "You said you weren't going to try to do anything! You told me you knew how to handle this!"

"I do." Liz pushed open the door of the Refugee Hope office building. "Bear with me, Molly."

"Liz, you're my friend!" Molly looked as if she might cry. "I know we're both a little crazy. This refugee work is . . . it's nuts. People who give their lives to do this kind of thing have to be a little wacky to begin with. But you haven't slept and you're stressed out about Africa and now the Marine Corps has come calling. I'm scared for you."

"Don't worry. I'll phone you from Podunk's." Liz waved over her shoulder as she trotted to her car.

It was a short drive to the restaurant, but she was late. Her watch read five minutes past the hour. Stomach churning, she parked and hurried to the door. Inside, the place was crowded and dimly lit. She searched for Joshua but didn't see him.

"Next! What you want, lady?" The man behind the counter was impatient, tapping the side of the cash register.

She elbowed between people waiting to pick up their orders. A quick glance at the menu revealed a list of things that would mess up her already fragile digestive system.

"We got a po'boy special. Shrimp. You want that?"

"I'll take red beans and rice," she told him. "And water to drink. Nothing else."

He shouted the order over his shoulder as she dug for cash. As she paid, she spotted a familiar figure in one corner of the restaurant. Senses prickling to life, she took her number and stepped away from the counter.

One hand propped on the wall, Joshua stood facing a smaller man. Their conversation was earnest, animated. She could see the exchange heating up. The man leaned closer, punctuating his words with a pointed finger.

Scrawny, he had pimpled caramel skin. He wore a purple do-rag. Hypes?

He would not be alone. She looked around, searching the gloom. There, near the front door.

Two young men waited, hanging back, watching. One sported a gold chain necklace with an emblem pendant she didn't recognize. The other was heavily pierced—both ears, eyebrows, lower lip. He had a skinny goatee that ended in loose wisps of hair.

Her heart stumbling over itself, Liz tried to edge casually in the direction of the two by the door. She reached into her purse and palmed her phone. The emergency number was a single button away.

"He gonna just give it to him?" the man in the necklace asked the other in a low voice. "Dog, he better not give that thing away without makin' the contact. It's all we got."

"Mo Ded's watchin'. He'll make sure it goes down right."

The name jangled Liz's nerves. Mo Ded. The leader of the Hypes. How could he be watching? Surely she would have noticed the man. She scanned the restaurant again. A couple of businessmen in suits, their ties loosened, sat in one booth. At a table, a family with four restless children dropped napkins, knocked over glasses, squabbled. A teenage couple laughed as they ate. She saw no one who could fit the description of a gang leader.

"I recognize him now, yo." The youth with the piercings elbowed the other and pointed at Joshua. "He's the guy from the other night. The one with the knife."

"You sure?"

"Yeah. How come he here and not her?"

"Maybe he her homeboy."

"Naw. He gotta be the shotcaller. Look at him, dog. We better step in."

"Number forty-seven! Lady, I called you three times already!"

Liz flinched as she realized the man behind the counter was shouting at her. Swallowing, she left the two by the door and took her tray. She tried not to tremble as she carried it in front of them and found an open table. Now her hand was off the phone, and she could see that Joshua and the other man were arguing.

As she set the tray on the table, Joshua grabbed the pimpled kid's T-shirt at the throat. He lifted him off his feet and gave him a rough shake. At that, the two by the door set off across the restaurant in the direction of their friend.

"Joshua!" Liz cried out.

She moved toward him, but another man stepped into her path. She saw little of him. A white T-shirt. A leather strap collar with a single purple bead. An angular face. Green eyes. The stench of dried sweat . . . and something else . . . flooded her nostrils.

His hand clamped her shoulder, shoved her down into the chair.

"Stay put."

She knew that voice. Grabbing her purse, she

searched for the phone. When she lifted her head, it was all over.

The men had vanished. A waitress sauntered past and straightened bottles of hot sauce on Liz's table. No one in the restaurant seemed aware a confrontation had occurred. From a booth against the far wall, one of Joshua's legs jutted out. At an odd angle, it didn't move.

With a gasp, Liz lurched up from the chair and ran to him.

Chapter Nine

As Liz reached the booth, Joshua stood. Circling, he wrapped his arms tightly around her and pushed her behind him. And then they were both seated, pressed together against the wall, hidden from view by the high bench on the other side of the table.

She covered her face with her hands and blew out a breath. "I don't believe this."

"Why did you come?" he demanded.

"You should have brought Sam and Terell!" She couldn't hold back the anguish. "What were you thinking? They could have killed you. It wasn't just that one guy, you know."

"It's never just one. Liz, this is what I do. My job for the last ten years—it's what I know. Why are you here?"

"Because I figured you'd do something stupid

like this. I knew you wouldn't ask for help, and then you'd get hurt."

"I'm not hurt." He set his cell phone on the table and gave it a spin. "See? Got 'er back."

"Oh!" She grabbed the thing and shook it. "For this you risked your life? For a dumb phone?"

"And you? Why did you risk your life?"

"My life wasn't at risk. I was standing way over there. That's my tray, see? That table by the door. And I saw two guys watching you, keeping track of the whole thing. There was someone else, too. When I tried to reach you, another man stopped me. He smelled . . . awful."

"So that's four. I'll bet there were more." He studied her face. With his thumb, he brushed her cheek. "Liz, this morning you said you'd given me the message and that was it. I thought you were gone. I thought you were finished with me. Now this."

"I *am* finished with you." She pushed at him with her shoulder. "Move over."

"Why? I like this." He leaned in. "As opposed to Mo Ded, you smell great."

"That was him? Did you know he was here? Had you seen him when you came in?"

"Didn't I just tell you this is what I do?"

"Why did the Hypes have your phone? Why had they been following you?"

"Not sure about that part. I tried to get it out of the little guy. He wouldn't talk."

"What did they want, Joshua?"

"Contact." He rubbed his brow. "I can't figure it out. It looks like a gang thing, so I don't understand the connection to me. What I did—Iraq, Afghanistan—it was tracking insurgents with a focus on counterterrorist stuff. Mainly al-Qaeda, mujahideen, the Taliban, you know, the groups go on and on. That was my work, and I'm good at it. But St. Louis? I never heard about cells or other activity like that before I came."

"They must have traced you here."

"And put *kids* onto me? They're punks. Trained, maybe. Smart, probably. I'll give them a little credit for savvy and tactics. But they're nothing like the men I knew over there. Those guys are warriors, fierce, eager to die for their cause. The boy who gave me the phone? He was a baby. The whole thing with the purple colors, the body piercing, the tattoos is a puzzle, too. Muslims don't do tats, Liz. Marking the body is forbidden in Islamic law. Even with my Muslim allies, these things caused me problems."

He gestured in disgust at the symbols on his upper arms. Then he shook his head. "Nah, I have to think it's something else. But the gang stuff is Sam's problem. A turf war. So why would they come after me? Why grab my phone?"

"The phone was just a way to meet you."

"They know how to do that. They met me the other night." He leaned back against the bench and shut his eyes. "Could the Hypes be connected to terrorism? Al-Qaeda isn't above using anyone—women, children, even the disabled and mentally handicapped. They'll do whatever it takes. But these scrawny St. Louis kids? I can't make it all add up."

Liz couldn't resist laying her hand on his arm. "Joshua, why don't you go on home to Texas now? You didn't ask for this gang problem, and you've done everything you need to do in St. Louis. I'll take care of the Rudi family. I remember what I said when you first came to my office, but I really don't mind helping them on the side. They're nice people, and I have the contacts and the skills."

"That girl just dumped your tray." He was looking across the room. "She works here. She thought you'd gone."

"I don't care about my dinner." She slid her hand down his arm and wrapped her fingers around his palm. "Joshua, I care about *you*."

His head swung, his eyes focusing on her. "There are still three of them in here, Liz. *Keep looking at me*." He reached up and touched her jaw, tipping her head in his direction.

"They work in threes," he murmured. "I need to get you out."

She tightened her grip on his hand. "Joshua, this is about you, not me. They're going to hurt you."

"These three are only on watch. Keeping tabs.

The conflict is over for now." He smiled at her. "Liz Wallace, you're following the wrong man around. I'm dangerous."

"Dangerous but not crazy."

"True. When the guy with the phone kept poking at me, I triggered. But I didn't go into a zone. I stayed with reality."

"So that's good."

"But the work I did, the people who gravitate to me because of my past—bad. The three kids over there—*don't look, Liz*—they're after something. I don't know what it is, but they need it. Their boss stationed them in here because he's desperate. There's an anxiety I recognize." He paused for a second. "And here comes the waitress."

"Did you want to see a menu?" The young woman slouched one hip out, pen poised over a pad of paper. "We've got a po'boy special tonight. Shrimp."

"Bring us two," Joshua said, holding up fingers. "You got hot tea?"

"I can make some, I guess. We have tea bags."

"Two cups." He glanced at Liz. "I hope that's okay. Gotta have my tea. Make it the green stuff with the cardamom in the bottom."

"We don't have anything like that at Podunk's." The waitress was frowning. "Ours is brown."

"Fine," he said. "We'll take brown tea. Milk and sugar, too."

As the waitress walked away, Liz made a subtle

effort to search the room for the three gang-bangers Joshua had mentioned. Or terrorists. Or whatever. She could see almost nothing as the light faded outside. The little restaurant relied mostly on candles in red jars centered on each table.

"I thought we were leaving," she said as he relaxed, leaning his shoulder against hers. "A few minutes ago, you wanted to get me out of here, remember?"

"Changed my mind. Might as well eat. Besides, I like this." He focused on their clasped hands. "I don't know what to do with you, Liz. I need to keep you as far away from me as possible. But I want you to stay close, too. Close enough to touch."

"Rumor has it you're dangerous and crazy. I ought to run."

"Maybe not." He toyed with her curls. "A woman who would go to Africa must like a little danger. Maybe she's a tad crazy, too."

"I'm not crazy like that. Everything I do is serious, focused. I take risks, but they're well-calculated ones. My family is conservative, religious, socially conscious. We're descended from William Wallace of Scotland, if that tells you anything."

"*Braveheart*. Dying for the cause."

"That's us."

"Wallace was pretty crazy, wasn't he? The blue face paint and the yelling?"

"Not my branch of Wallaces. Somber as the grave. My two sisters and I grew up doing activist things with our parents—protesting and marching. But all for severely rigorous concepts. No liberal agenda. We were about changing the world through Christianity. Protecting the unborn. Shutting down smut peddlers. Stuff like that."

"My upbringing was a bit different. We went to church, sure. But Dad was busy making money. I guess materialism and capitalism would be the little idols in the Duff family closet. As for socially conscious—oh, yeah, if you're talking about the social scene at the country club. We were very conscious of that."

She laughed. "I painted signs. Good handwriting, you know. Lettering slogans was always my job before we went out on protest marches. My older sister hammered the poster boards onto pickets for us to carry. My younger sister packed meals."

"Family fun."

"Quite adventuresome if you didn't mind the occasional rotten tomato. Effective, too. My family helped shut down smarmy businesses and open prison doors and get legislation passed. TV cameras couldn't resist three little curly-haired girls in matching polka-dot dresses toting placards around. The Wallace kids made the nightly news a lot—Lucy, Liz and Laura. We turned out all right, I guess. Lucy is a missionary doctor in India.

Laura has a law practice in California. Immigrant rights."

"And Liz is going to Africa under the blue banner of the United Nations."

"That's the plan."

"Any of you married?"

She shook her head. "I'm not sure how well political activism mixes with raising families, though our parents did a pretty good job."

"You don't want a husband? Kids?"

"I don't think about it much." Looking into his snow-flecked cobalt eyes, she could read nothing. "What about you?"

"Not till now."

Before she could respond, the waitress slid a couple of plates across their table. "Two shrimp po'boys. I couldn't find teacups. Sorry."

She set foam take-out cups filled with steaming water in front of Joshua and Liz. Each held a tea bag seeping brown color into the hot liquid. A handful of artificial creamers and sugar packets spilled out of her pocket onto the table.

"I asked for milk," Joshua called after the waitress as she sauntered away. He muttered, "Nondairy creamer. Among America's worst inventions. So, do social activists bless their meals in public places?"

"Always. I guess praying out loud is not such a great idea in Afghanistan."

"Not if you want to keep your head on."

He smiled, leaned closer and murmured a brief prayer. When Liz opened her eyes, he was already biting into the sandwich. She thought about asking him again to move over. He had wedged her against the wall, without elbow room or even much breathing space. But something about their closeness appealed to her. Her life was spent keeping a careful distance—from the refugee families, from coworkers, even from the men she dated.

Joshua was an invader. He had walked into her office cubicle and demanded attention. She wasn't able to dislodge him from her private space then . . . or now. And she had come to welcome his presence even as it disturbed her.

"This is the worst tea I've ever tasted," he announced, finishing it nonetheless. "Criminal. I'll make you a proper cup one of these days. Most guys leave with trinkets from the bazaar or souvenirs someone was hawking on the street. I came back with lots of tea."

Joshua had downed the po'boy faster than Liz had ever seen a sandwich disappear. He ate one-handed, his right hand holding the food while the left stayed in his lap. A Muslim custom, she recalled from her agency's literature. He had learned to blend well. She made barely a dent in her own meal. With her stomach in knots, she couldn't eat.

"So, it wasn't all bad over there?" she asked. "The tea sounds nice."

"Bad? Nah, lots of good stuff. The languages are beautiful—Dari and Pashto. The Hindu Kush—those mountains are spectacular. The Bamyam region where the two Buddhas used to stand before the Taliban destroyed them. Amazing. Kandahar and Kabul are fascinating cities. Afghan food tastes great. Naan is the bread, and shish kebab is a staple wherever you go. Pilau is a mix of rice, orange peel, almonds, raisins and chicken. Nothing better."

"You liked it out there in the big, wide world."

"I like it right here." He slipped his arm around her shoulders. "That's another line, in case you didn't catch on."

Her cheeks went hot. "I caught it."

"You smell good, Liz."

"You mentioned that. It's nothing, though. I don't wear perfume."

"It's you." He gently kissed her cheek. "This morning when I held you for a second . . . I couldn't stop thinking about it all day. I was worried because you were in your dress and I'd been sweating."

"I remember." She sighed. "I tried to recall being scared, but I couldn't. I'm not sure why, Joshua, but you don't frighten me. Some of the things you do, maybe. But not you. You're . . . comfortable."

"Me?" He chuckled. "Now that's a first."

She leaned her head back on his arm. "I feel safe."

"You're not safe, Liz. I'm plotting against you all the time."

"No, you're not. You're always protecting me. I like that."

"If only you knew. I'm scheming for your downfall. Thinking about holding you. Thinking about kissing you. Thinking all kinds of things."

She closed her eyes. "Good luck, soldier. I'm a labyrinth. You'll never find your way through me."

"And I'm a tracker. I can get to the center of any maze you design."

"Stop talking and drink my tea. I'm tired."

Despite the crowded restaurant, the clinking plates and the chatter of diners, Liz was suddenly so relaxed she could barely focus. The New Orleans jazz playing in the background and the scent of melted candle wax oozed through her, and she felt herself drifting. Something about the solid muscle of Joshua's arm behind her head . . . the warmth of his hand on her arm . . . the press of his lips against her temple . . . the touch of his fingertips in her hair . . .

"Liz! What are you doing?" A shrill voice streaked through the night. "You promised to call!"

Jerking awake, Liz focused on a wiry figure sliding onto the seat opposite her. "Molly?"

"I've been sitting at home dying of nerves waiting for you to let me know you're okay, and here you are snuggling with the Marine while I'm freaking out that you're lying dead in the street with a gang bullet in your head!" She dropped her purse on the table. "I have to call my boyfriend. Joel wouldn't drive down here with me, and I said, listen, if you can't support me enough to help me find my best friend, then we're through. Now I see you're perfectly fine, and I just dumped the one decent guy I've met in years."

"A decent guy would have come with you," Joshua observed.

"What do *you* know—you with your post-traumatic whatever-it-is? Look, there are two kinds of men, losers and keepers. You're neither one, right? Liz can't lose you, because you're always butting into her life and messing with her mind. But she's sure not going to keep you."

"Molly!" Liz cut in. "You don't know Joshua. Get off his case."

"I know you," Molly said. "This man won't tie you down. That's clear enough."

"It is?"

"What, you think you can talk her out of going to Africa? Good luck with that—I've been trying to convince her to stay in St. Louis for two years. And there's no way she'll ever be a Texas oil baron's wife. So why don't you leave her alone?" She blinked. "Liz, were you *asleep?* You were! You fell asleep!"

Sitting up, Liz pushed her hair back. "I guess so."

"Oh, this is great. The only time she sleeps in weeks is on your shoulder." Molly pressed buttons on her phone. "I'm coming home, Joel. Yes, I found her, and she's fine. She's sleeping with the Marine. Well, not with him, but on him. No, that's not right. Just don't leave, okay? I'll be back in half an hour."

She snapped her phone shut and took Liz's hand. "Come with me. Out of the way, soldier-boy. I'm making sure she gets home safely, and that means you stay here."

"Molly, I'm fine," Liz protested as her friend dragged her past Joshua and pulled her to her feet. She wanted to shut Molly up. Linger with Joshua. Try to understand what was happening between them. But she had slept for the first time in months, and now she felt off balance. Maybe she was even a little relieved that Molly had taken charge and was helping her get away from something that scared her more than she liked to admit. "We were just talking."

Now Molly was wagging her phone at Joshua. "You leave her alone. She's a good girl, and you're bad news. Just because you put her to sleep, don't think that gives you brownie points in my book."

Liz glanced back to see Joshua standing beside the booth, his arms crossed. "It's been nice knowing you," she called. "Bye."

Molly wrapped an arm around Liz and pushed

her out the door. "Gangbangers and Marines and who knows what else you're going to attract," she said. "Go home and get some sleep, honey. Life will be a whole lot clearer in the morning."

Liz slipped into her car, then waited until she and Molly pulled out at the same time. With some anxiety, she considered circling the block and returning to Podunk's and the man with warm lips. But she decided, after all, that would be dangerous.

"You are a man who knows the right thing to do." Stephen Rudi laid a ribbon marker in the open Bible and closed his book. He intended to begin reading, but Joshua had mentioned a gang task force meeting that evening at the police precinct.

Glasses perched on the end of his nose, the pastor now regarded his friend. "You should have gone with Sam Hawke to this assembly of leaders. You are a warrior. In my tribe—before the civil war and before the British—we were also warriors. My people were not farmers, digging with hoes and planting beans and maize. We kept cattle. Our flocks of sheep and goats were very large."

Inside the Rudis' small room at Haven, Joshua had turned a chair around, sat down and propped his arms on the back. "I hate to tell you this, Pastor, but a warrior and a cow herder are not the same thing."

"Young boys stood watch over the herds. At the

age of initiation, they became warriors. With spears, we protected our tribe and gained wealth for our families. Then, after many years, we became the elders who weighed judgment on all problems."

"I have trouble seeing you as a warrior, Pastor S.," Joshua told him. "You don't look like the spear-carrying kind."

"I never became a warrior because the British confused our system. We had been nomadic, but they forced us to settle on land that was very bad for keeping cattle. They made us live in a region of Paganda near Lake Victoria. They gave us boats and nets and tried to teach us how to become fishermen. Our old ways became difficult. Those British told us to choose a chief who would report to the district commissioner, and they encouraged us to put away our tribal life. Then one day the British granted independence to Paganda and went away, leaving the people untrained and lacking good leadership."

"I know enough about tribes to figure out what happened next."

"Yes, our country fell into chaos. And that is why *you* must stay here, in St. Louis."

"St. Louis is not Paganda or Afghanistan. You can't equate the local gangs with tribes."

"Certainly not. In a tribe, the fathers lead their families. Important decisions are made by a council of elders. Each person supports the others.

Enemies can come together to discuss disputes over territory. Everything is well organized. These gangs are not tribes—they are hooligans bent on thuggery. They are the cause of chaos in St. Louis, America."

"And I'm supposed to fix that?"

"Look at my children, sir." He indicated the two small, sleeping figures in the bed. "Shall they grow up in this wicked society?"

Joshua's heart softened as he studied the children. Curled together, Charity and Virtue clung to each other almost as if they were still inside that metal water drum . . . as if terror haunted them even in their dreams. He knew that midnight fear all too well.

After a full day at school, the two youngsters always returned exhausted. They did their homework and then ate a dinner prepared by Mary, who by then had already gone off to her cleaning job. Joshua took to joining the family meal, then helping out as their father bathed his children and read a few verses from the Bible—a quiet time that put both kids right to sleep.

"You're moving into the new apartment tomorrow," Joshua reminded Stephen. "It's a better environment."

The man turned his head away and grunted in disgust. "Would you permit your own family to live in such a place? Would you send your children to these schools? The teachers are sincere, but what sort of friends can my little ones find? If I am not very careful, Charity will suffer the same future as those young girls who bring their babies to Haven every morning. Virtue will stand on the corner with a gun in his pocket and drugs in his shoe. How can I bear this?"

"Not every kid in the area ends up that way."

"You would not bring your children here!" He thumped the Bible down on a bedside table. "If you were forced to live in such a city, you would use your training as a warrior to protect your family. I speak the truth. Do not abuse me by denying it!"

Joshua stood. "I can't stay and watch over your kids, Stephen. I have other responsibilities. You talk so much about family loyalties. Try telling my father what you want me to do. Tell him that the son who walked out on him to enlist in the Marine Corps is not coming back to Texas. Tell him that his son will never fill the job he's been holding open all this time. Tell him every expectation, every hope, every prayer has been in vain. You—of all people—should understand the obligation I feel to my father, to my family."

"Haya." Stephen muttered a Swahili expression of grudging acceptance that Joshua had heard a hundred times since he began to help the Rudi family. "Even so, you should attend the meeting tonight for speaking with the police and the government people. You can help them very much."

"Did you hear a word I just said?"

"Yes, I heard you speak of your father. But you have told me you are a Christian, as I am, and so you have another Father, my friend. A greater Father. He is not of this earth. He cares for His people here, yet they suffer. This Heavenly Father has trained you to be a courageous warrior, a man of battle who can protect the defenseless. Shall you make petrol instead?"

As Joshua opened his mouth to respond, the phone in his pocket vibrated. Certain it would be one of his parents, he checked it anyway. It was never Liz. He had not seen the woman for almost a week. Rather than helping him forget, her absence grew more painful each day.

"Dad, hey, how are you this evening?" he asked as his father's voice came through the receiver. He gave Pastor Stephen a nod and pointed to the phone.

"There you are! Your mother and I have been trying to reach you. We've left several messages. I'm sure you've been busy having fun with your friends, but you might at least return our calls, Joshua."

"I've talked to you every day, Dad. I explained about Haven, remember? The new basketball court. The fitness room."

"Your mother is wondering when to expect you home. She had a lot of hopes and plans built around that original homecoming date you gave us, and then, you know, you turned right around and walked out on her. Joshua, we've done our best to understand that you needed some time to unwind with your friends, but I have to say that this behavior of yours has been disappointing for everyone. Not just your mother and me, but your brothers, their wives, your friends. I understand about the camaraderie of the military, but you do have good friends here in Amarillo, too."

Standing in the doorway of the small room, Joshua watched Stephen Rudi tucking a blanket over his children. In silence, the man laid a hand on each child and bowed his head. His lips moved as he whispered a prayer. Then he settled into his chair again, put on his glasses, opened his Bible and began to read in silence.

"Dad, I know I've disappointed you and Mom," Joshua began. He stepped out of the room into the long, empty corridor. The sound of kids playing basketball downstairs echoed through the building. Rubber-soled shoes squeaking, whistles blowing, young voices shouting.

He leaned one shoulder against the wall. "I'll come home soon. I promise you that."

"Can you give me a date? The other day you said you were hoping to leave at the end of this week. But here it is Friday again, and we still don't have any idea of your arrival time. I'd be happy to send a car to pick you up at the airport if you'll just give me a flight number."

Joshua clenched his jaw. The battle inside him waged with as much intensity as any he had known in Iraq or Afghanistan. Stay and continue to help the Rudis . . . use his training to impact the city for good . . . see Liz Wallace again? Or go home . . . honor his father by assuming the mantle for which he had been intended his whole life . . . bring his mother the joy of watching her son settle near his brothers and work in the business that bore the family name . . . be obedient to those who had raised him with such love?

"Dad, give me one more week," he said, the words coming out in a rush of breath. "Tell Mom to plan a poolside shindig for next Saturday night. I'll be there with my boots on."

"Now, you're sure about this? Because you know how your mother is with her parties, Joshua. These social occasions are very important to her, and she'll be inviting all her friends, including some lovely young women."

"The bumblebees?" He rubbed the back of his neck, recalling the local girls who had swarmed him from childhood through college. "Listen, please ask Mom not to get all worked up about introducing me to any lovely young women."

"You have a girlfriend? You never mentioned this. We'd love to meet her, Joshua. Is it serious? Why don't you bring her with you?"

"No, Dad. It's not . . . not like that . . ."

The silence on both ends grew uncomfortable.

Joshua checked his watch. The meeting of the gang task force had begun. He had told Sam to go on without him.

But now he spoke quickly. "Hey, gotta head out, Dad. Give Mom my love. See you in a week."

Pushing the phone into his jeans pocket, he started down the hall. By the time he reached the stairs, he was running.

Chapter Ten

As Joshua slipped into the room, he spotted Sam near the head of a long conference table. A surprising number of people had gathered at the precinct station to discuss the gang situation, an indicator of how serious the crisis had become. Sam paused while describing the work of Haven and beckoned Joshua.

"Grab a chair, Duff." He leaned forward to address the others. "I'm counting on this guy to play a key role in our strategy—Sergeant Joshua Duff, USMC. He just got back from Afghanistan. Counterterrorism. He's an expert marksman. Tracks insurgents like a hound dog. Sniffs out trouble and handles it before anyone else even knows there's a problem."

"Hawke's a known liar," Joshua drawled. "Never trust a word out of the guy's mouth."

Low laughter accompanied a rumble of greeting as he set his chair beside Sam's. A quick scan of name tags revealed police officers, ministers, representatives of charitable foundations and others.

"I believe we've already met." A tall man at the head of the table nodded at Joshua. "I head the law enforcement division of this task force. Name's Ransom, St. Louis PD. So, how's the dog?"

Joshua recognized the cop who had taken his knife on the night of the conflict outside Haven. The two assessed each other, and Joshua sensed an equal in both intensity and skill.

"Recovering." He kept his focus leveled on the officer's eyes. "Neighborhood's not faring too well, though."

Ransom nodded, accepting the retort. He slid a sheaf of stapled papers across the table toward Joshua. "If you've got answers, we're listening. We have a lot of groups tackling the problem, and we welcome the Marine Corps' help."

"I'm off-duty, friend—discharged a month ago. But I'm listening."

"Good. Sam, you were describing the new day care at Haven. And we'd all like to hear why you had to stop the construction of your outdoor recreation area."

"Why don't we introduce everyone to Duff first. Go ahead, Ransom. You pulled this task force together."

The cop tipped his head in acknowledgment. He made the round of the table, putting faces to the names of organizations Sam had mentioned. The task force included law enforcement officials from St. Louis city and county, as well as the Missouri State Highway Patrol and the Bureau of Alcohol, Tobacco and Firearms.

Ransom's unit worked with a number of non-profit agencies—the Gang Resistance Education and Training program, CeaseFire, INTERACT, African-American Churches in Dialogue, the St. Louis Gang Outreach Program, Central Baptist Family Services, the Regional Violence Prevention Initiative and the North Patrol Initiative. Representatives from DEFY camp, the Weed & Seed Jobs Program, the SafeFutures program and the National Guard Show Me Challenge were also in the room.

"We're missing someone," Ransom said. As he scanned a printout, the door opened. "And just in the nick of time, our newest task force member. Everyone, this is Liz Wallace from Refugee Hope. I asked her to help us understand how we can work with the influx of immigrants being resettled in the city. Welcome, Liz Wallace."

Joshua tried not to gape as she took a chair across the table from him. After the evening at Podunk's, he had called Liz's office a couple of times and left messages on her phone. She didn't respond, and he knew why. Refugee camps in Africa were her future—not an ex-Marine oil company vice president with a touch of PTSD.

He'd told himself he would never see her again. It would be best for both of them. In time, his memories of her would fade. His desire for her would weaken. Other women would replace Liz in his thoughts. He'd meet some pretty girl in Texas—maybe one of the bumblebees from his childhood had matured enough to be interesting. If civilian life didn't work out, he would start looking in the ranks. Or he could go on as he had for so long . . . keeping women at arm's length, focusing on his work, preferring his own familiar and reliable company over the distraction of female companionship.

But as Liz propped an elbow on the table, something stirred to life deep inside him and he knew it wasn't over.

"Sorry I'm late, Daniel." She smiled at Sergeant Ransom. "A new family from Iraq arrived this week, and the kids had a bad experience at school today. I hope you haven't all been waiting for . . ."

Her brown eyes settled on Joshua. Her lips parted. "Oh, I didn't realize . . ."

"Miss Wallace, good to see you again." Joshua tore his focus from her face as he spoke. "So, Sam, the new day care at Haven? Looks like it's going well."

His friend took over. "Yeah, sure is. More kids than we know what to do with—and I'm talking about the moms as well as their babies. We only take teenage mothers, and our goal is to return them to high school, help them earn their GED or find them a decent job."

Joshua saw that Sam had read the uncomfortable situation and stepped in as he always had. Nothing like the brotherhood of the military to attune men to each other. After telling task force members about the child-care program, Sam went on to outline Haven's effort to build an outdoor recreation area. While he spoke, Joshua hunted for a pen, found one and took notes on the agenda he'd been given. Anything to avoid those big brown eyes across the table.

"Sam, are you sure the sign sprayed on your wall was done by Hypes?" Ransom was asking. "Some of these gangs are using a graffiti code we haven't deciphered."

"It was purple paint."

Ransom's brows rose. "Did you understand the symbols?"

"Pretty obvious—my name with a big X over it. For some reason they've singled me out as the target. My partner, Terell Roberts, keeps a low profile, but they know him. The Hypes want Haven. Our street cuts through their turf, and they don't like it."

"Haven stands in opposition to everything the Hypes promote," Joshua spoke up. "I've had a couple of encounters with them now. They create chaos and violence in an effort to build gang loyalty. Haven is about education, job training, employment, meaningful recreation—everything designed to keep kids out of gangs. The message to gang members from your task force should be clear. If you engage in criminal activity, we will bring you to justice. If you want to turn your life around, we'll be there to help."

"Your task force?" Ransom glanced at Sam. "I thought your friend was part of Haven's team."

"We're working on that," Sam said. "Duff has . . . commitments."

With a shrug, Ransom turned to Liz. "Haven has brought a lot of good changes to the neighborhood, but we've got big problems growing, too. This refugee resettlement thing is another new wrinkle. What can you tell us about that, Liz?"

She stood and Joshua's mouth went dry. As if he were on sniper patrol and had just spotted his target, every sense beamed in her direction. Smell, taste, sound, touch . . . and sight, of course. Liz wore a modest pink blouse, but the short sleeves revealed her slender arms. Her narrow waist. Her perfect curves. That voice dripped into him and lit up every nerve. He was a dying man, stretched out on a gurney, and she was the lifeblood flowing into his veins. He could hear his heartbeat in his ears, feel the pressure in his chest.

"Refugee Hope," she was explaining, "views any immigrants' potentially greatest problem as a failure to assimilate to American culture. Now we understand there's something worse. That is the integration into the wrong American culture."

"By that, you mean gangs?" Ransom asked.

"Any unhealthy lifestyle." She smiled at him again. Joshua's eyes darted to the man, recognized the cop's admiration and swept back to Liz. Was she aware? Was she flirting with this guy? They were on a first-name basis. So what was going on between them?

"Our African refugees are particularly susceptible to the hip-hop culture in St. Louis," she told the group. "Kids mingle at school. Adults meet on the streets, in the grocery stores, at work. In people's eyes, their skin color automatically classifies them, even though the original ethnicity—their tribe, their language, even their experiences in the refugee camps—could not be more different. We're seeing the African-born immigrant children try to adapt by mimicking customs they see in their new neighborhood. This is fine if the role model is healthy. But too often, our refugee youth are falling in with the gang subculture."

"Aren't a lot of these immigrants Muslims?" someone asked. "I heard they were, and I didn't like the sound of it one bit."

"Refugee Hope is a Christian organization, but we resettle people from many religious backgrounds."

"So you're saying these refugees might be

bringing a Muslim ideology into the Molotov cocktail these gangs already represent?"

"Possibly. Does religion play a part in gang culture, Daniel?" She looked again to Ransom. "I wasn't aware of that."

"These kids aren't religious," he said. "They may have been raised around some form of faith—grandmothers reading Bibles and saying bedtime prayers. But the only time they crack the door of a church is to attend the funeral of one of their homeys."

"What about the Hypes?" Joshua spoke up. "Something is holding them together, and it's not race. Not turf. Not even bloodshed. They don't have anything going for them that I can see."

"Their leader is the catalyst." Ransom picked up another stack of papers and began handing them out to the people gathered at the table. "You're correct, Sergeant Duff. The Hypes are an unusual gang. Once we recognized their shotcaller as Mo Ded, we started watching him. He's definitely a different ball of wax. This document is a summary of data we've gathered about the Hypes. The broad dimension of their activity goes beyond drugs and weapons to include politics and interracial issues. We do see some religious undercurrents. There may even be possible terrorist connections."

"Terrorist?" The word rippled around the room.

"Hear that, Duff?" Sam stuck a thumb in Joshua's direction. "Right up your alley."

"Hey," Joshua protested. "I'm just here to listen."

Ransom grunted. "Well, if anyone on this task force learns something other than what's printed on this fact sheet, please let me know immediately. We have some concern that Mo Ded's group may be working to purchase arms, perhaps even mines and other explosives."

Joshua held up his hand and rubbed his fingertips together. "Gotta have the dough for that. How are they paying?"

"We're seeing a lot of ice moving on the streets these days. Methamphetamine is Missouri's hallmark drug. It's been the white man's domain for a long time, but these days it's moving across racial lines. Latinos, even blacks. We think Mo Ded is behind the St. Louis trade."

"Have you traced his roots?"

"As far back as we can get—which is nowhere. He came here from some big city is all we know. Detroit. Chicago. Could be one of the coasts."

"You need to map out his pedigree," Joshua said, vaguely aware he was leaning forward on the table. Without realizing it, he had been swept into the discussion. "Track the guy back to where he came from. That'll tell you a lot. Who shaped him, who influenced him, what incidents triggered his patterns. Parents, education, religion. Check his documents."

"Documents? We don't even have the guy's real

name. We can't find a rap sheet on him. He's not turning up in records anywhere. It's like one day he just appeared out of thin air. The next day he had built a gang out of a bunch of scrawny rejects. Then he started moving ice. Now we're hearing about weapons, including some big stuff."

"Why would Mo Ded want mines or grenades? That's heavy artillery for a street fighter. Too heavy, if you ask me. With your men looking over his shoulder he'd need to have strong motivation and a major plan. Purchasing that stuff would require a lot of cash. He wouldn't even think about it unless he had a big target in mind. What does this Mo Ded want? And who does he have to take out to get it?"

The silence in the room told Joshua what he needed to know.

"He wants it all," Joshua declared as he looked around the table. "He wants to control the police force, the schools, the businesses, the streets. He wants to own this city."

Joshua made a point of talking to Sam as the meeting ended. He knew Liz wouldn't want an uncomfortable encounter. Neither did he. All the same, it was hard to keep his focus on his friend as Liz spoke briefly with Sergeant Ransom and then hurried away.

"I've asked my dad for another week," Joshua said. The two men stood to one side. "I haven't been fair to him, or to my mother. They were hoping I'd come home and blend right in."

"You? Blend in?" Sam chuckled. "You blend like a chameleon into the Afghan high desert or the streets of Baghdad, but you'll never belong in a Texas office building, Duff. Accept it."

"Maybe not, but it's my destiny. Duff tradition. I've thought, I've prayed and I don't see any other way. But I'll give you this week. It's the best I can do, Hawke. Everything I've got, I'll put to work unlocking your enemy's background, MO. Plans. After that, it's pool parties and that executive office for me."

Sam shook his head. "I've been there, you know? Got back from a deployment, was discharged, headed to New Mexico, tried to fit in with my family again. My dad, my brother. I couldn't find anything to keep my attention or satisfy me. I was about ready to re-up when I got back in touch with Terell. We bought the old building and started Haven. It's been touch and go, but I never looked back."

"The things we did over there . . . the missions . . . they gave my life meaning. I promised I'd go home, and I never break a vow. But if I can make my dad understand, I may go back in."

"The Corps? Leave it to the younger men. Put your skills and training to use building up this country. We need you here, Duff."

"One week." He held up a finger. "I'm moving

the Rudi family into their new place tomorrow. Monday I'll check with the school, the restaurant, the cleaning business. Make sure things are working out. Meanwhile, I'll do what I can to track down Mo Ded. Saturday afternoon, this old man will be lounging by a pool with a couple of Texas bikini babes for company."

"Sounds good to me." Sam laughed. "I notice you and Liz didn't have much to say to each other. I thought that might go somewhere."

"Nah. Not really my type."

"Exactly your type—which is why you're running in the opposite direction. I know, I know. Did the same thing myself. A wife, kids, a house? Not for me. That's what I thought until Ana. Terell was a real ladies' man. Now Joette has him wrapped around her little finger. Did you know a junior college has been talking to him about a coaching job? If he takes that job and both of us marry, the bottom could fall right out of Haven. We need someone living in the building. We need you."

Joshua shook his head. "Lay off the guilt speech, Hawke. I'm giving you a week, and that's all I've got. You know what Pastor Stephen says about everything. God has a good plan for this. Haven is under His wing. It's going to work out."

"I'll take your week, but I'm praying you give your life." He nodded in the direction of the police officer. "I've got to talk to Ransom. We need more cars cruising our street. See you back at Haven."

"Later, Hawke." Joshua grabbed his jacket and pulled it on. Autumn was on its way. He had felt the crisp tang in the air that morning, and it reminded him of sunrise in the Hindu Kush.

Crossing the room, he recalled traversing the Shomali Plain north of Kabul. Despite evidence of decades of war and the presence of antiper-sonnel and antitank mines along the route, the countryside fascinated him. The people, too. He had loved the Istalif bazaar with its wooden shop doors and colorful displays of vegetables and fruits and open sacks of grain. Images of boys helping their fathers in the market and widows in blue burkhas begging on the roadside would never leave him.

Joshua pushed open the conference room door and started down the hall. Those early mornings had been so cold he had checked his fingers and toes for signs of frostbite. Though his memories were strong, he sensed he would never share them. His parents wanted little part of his past life. His military service alarmed and probably even disgusted them.

In his mind he would always carry images of those barren slopes—mountains still being born, thrusting upward more than two inches every year. Born yet dying. Younger ranges to the southeast blocked their rainfall and were slowly trans-forming them into desert. Bleak, remote, desolate, mysterious, the Hindu Kush haunted him.

"Joshua, I was wondering if I could talk to you for a moment."

The voice in the darkness pulsed out at him. He pivoted, tense and alert. His ears tuned to the click of an automatic rifle. His nostrils flared as he sniffed for gunpowder. Instead he smelled lavender.

She stepped out of the shadow, her eyes lowered. "I waited," she said. "You don't mind, do you?"

"Liz." He fought to control his breathing.

"Oh, did I startle you?" Now she looked up. "Joshua, I'm so sorry. I didn't think about—"

"It's okay. Walk with me, Liz." He had it under control. The spurt had triggered him, but he quashed any outward response. Relieved, he opened the door to the police building and escorted her outside.

"I hadn't expected to see you here tonight," she was saying. She moved beside him, closer than necessary. Perhaps it was the chilly air. "When Daniel invited me—Sergeant Ransom—he mentioned some of the groups represented, but he didn't say anything about Haven. I hope you don't think I was avoiding you in there."

"You *were* avoiding me."

"Okay, but it wasn't obvious, was it?"

"Yes."

"I apologize. I felt uncomfortable. These past few days, I've thought about you a lot. All the time, really. But after that evening at Podunk's—"

"Liz, it's all right." He turned, stopping her progress along the sidewalk. "It's fine. I know how your friend feels about me. I know you're busy. You have other plans."

"You're the one with other plans, Joshua. I didn't want to see you again and feel all these things and then have it just end when you went off to Texas. I thought it would be better to let it go."

"What were you feeling . . . *all these things?*"

"Nothing really. Just weirdness." She looked away and brushed at a curl that had settled on her cheek. "I was comfortable with you the other night. For me, that's unusual."

"You fell asleep."

"Don't be offended. Please, I—"

"I loved it." He began walking again. "We're a couple of high-strung people, but somehow we relaxed each other. I don't know how that happened, but it was good."

"I was embarrassed."

"Embarrassed, why? You were beautiful."

"No, don't say that kind of thing! How am I supposed to focus on my work when you keep butting in?"

"I'm butting in? You're the one who came to Haven and brought the paperwork. You showed up at Podunk's. I've been trying to hold back, but you're always around. And I like that. I want it." He focused on the sidewalk. "I don't know what's going on, Liz. But I want to be with you. That's all

I can see right now. It's the only thing that makes sense in my life."

"It doesn't make sense, though. I'm sure we stumbled into each other by accident. I believe God knows everything, of course, but He has such different plans for us."

"I don't like His plan for you. You shouldn't be attending a gang task force meeting. You can't get involved with thugs like Mo Ded. It's too dangerous. I'm trained. I know how to handle myself. You should stay in the office and do your filing."

"Filing!"

"Okay, go out and help people. But stay away from violence, Liz. And as for Africa . . . why do you have to do that? Can't you think of something more reasonable?"

"I suppose you call tracking al-Qaeda terrorists reasonable?"

"It made sense for me, and I did it well."

"Someone needs to work in those refugee camps, Joshua. The people will languish unless they're cared for. Schools, water supplies, food distribution, orientation classes, assistance with paperwork. There's so much to be done. I believe I could do that work. And why shouldn't I?"

"Because." He stuffed his hands into the pockets of his jacket. They had arrived at her car. "Because . . . okay, I have no right to tell you what to do. I never listened to anyone. Not even the people who loved me the most. I did exactly what

I wanted to do, and I don't have a leg to stand on with you."

She reached for her car door. "How about sitting, then . . . with me . . ." Her brown eyes met his. "There's something I'd like to show you, Joshua. It's in my apartment. And that's not a line."

He smiled. "Didn't think so. I'll follow you."

Before she could change her mind, he returned to his own car. In moments, they had both pulled out into the street. As he cruised along behind, Joshua searched his motives. He couldn't deny the anticipation. Being alone with Liz would leave time to talk . . . and more . . .

But he couldn't let it go too far. She would never allow that, and he didn't want to make mistakes. All the same, the temptation would be great. He dug out his phone and dialed Sam.

"Hawke, it's me. I wanted to let you know I'm headed over to Liz's place."

His friend's silence said more than enough.

"Listen, I know what you're thinking. I know what *I'm* thinking—and that's not going to happen. I need you to keep me on track, man."

"How can I help?"

"You already have. I'm telling you, so I'll be accountable."

"Do you love that woman, Duff? Because you're acting like a man in love."

"I haven't known her long enough. Have I? It doesn't happen this fast. It doesn't happen to people who can't take it anywhere. And we can't. We won't. We're both too smart, too dedicated to the right things. Hawke, I've been through deployments and transitions. But I'm scrambled right now."

"I'll pray for you—and that's not some lame cop-out. Joshua, hold firm."

As the men signed off, Liz turned her car into an underground parking lot not far from the apartment complex where the Rudis would be moving. Joshua frowned. The few cars in the lot were battered. Trash littered the concrete floor pad. This couldn't be right. She wouldn't live in such a place.

"What are you doing?" he asked as they both stepped out of their cars. "You don't live here, do you?"

"Fourth floor. What's the matter—scared?"

She crossed to him and slipped her arm through his. "Don't worry, Sergeant Duff. I'll protect you."

Chapter Eleven

As Liz fitted her key into the lock, she waved at an elderly woman who was carrying an empty glass casserole dish down the hall. "Good evening, Mrs. Gonzales. Thanks for the tamales you gave me yesterday. They were *muy deliciosos.*"

Turning to Joshua, Liz spoke in a low voice. "Her name is Socorro Gonzales. She brings food to everyone on our floor. She's been like a mother from the first day I moved into the building."

Now the woman trundled forward, speaking Spanish and gesturing with great animation at Joshua.

"Mi amigo," Liz explained. "This is my friend. I'm going to show him the pictures of Africa. *Mis fotos.*"

The door swung open, and all three entered the studio apartment. There would be no keeping Mrs. Gonzales at bay, Joshua realized. So much for private conversation with Liz. The woman was already rummaging around in the cupboard as though she owned the place.

"Galletas?" she asked.

"No, I don't have any cookies," Liz said. "It's all right. He's only staying a few minutes. *Unos cuantos momentos, no más.*"

"Ah!" Mrs. Gonzales nodded, firing off another salvo of Spanish words as she hurried out of the apartment. "I come back!"

"She'll be bringing cookies," Liz told Joshua. "Have a seat. Sorry it's not much of a couch. Refugee Hope isn't exactly a Fortune 500 company. This place is what I can afford. I like the location, too. It's close to work. Puts me right in with the people."

"Is that a good thing?" He took one end of the

bedraggled plaid love seat. "Liz, this can't be safe for you."

"Safety isn't a priority for either of us, is it?" She picked up the scrapbook and sat down beside him. "This is what I wanted you to see—my trip to Africa. Congo. I put the album together not long after I got back, but lately it's been haunting me. At night, I go through it, poring over the pictures and trying to remember everything. It's like I keep thinking that God will show me some new message. Some face I didn't notice. Some scene I'd forgotten. Anything to make sense of it."

"What message are you waiting for?" He searched her eyes as she opened the book, spreading it between them. "What questions need answers, Liz?"

"Don't ask me that. Just look at this. Tell me what *you* see. You and I are alike in how we process things, and I need to hear your thoughts."

He turned the pages, running his fingertips over the photographs as he absorbed the story of her journey. As Joshua pondered each image, Mrs. Gonzales returned with a tray of chocolate-chip cookies and two cups of piping-hot coffee. She stood, hands clasped, smiling at the pair on the sofa. Clearly she wanted to join them. But with a few words of gratitude and farewell, Liz escorted her neighbor from the apartment.

"Mrs. Gonzales is why I live here," she told Joshua as she shut the door. "When I moved to St.

Louis, I wanted to immerse myself in many cultures and languages. Socorro fled from Nicaragua years ago. She has no legal documents, though she paid taxes, social security and rent and even had a driver's license for a while. Her husband was an alcoholic who came in and out of her life at random. She raised five children—mostly alone. Her kids live nearby and support her now."

"She worked somewhere before?"

"Cleaning houses for wealthy gringos. She rode the bus to Clayton and Ladue. I've been trying to help her get her papers in order, so she can become a citizen. She's scared to death that the immigration authorities will knock on her door one day, cart her off to a detention center and ship her back to Nicaragua. She has no family there. Her parents and siblings were all murdered during the war years. Along with her grown kids, the people in this building are her support system."

"Do you work this hard on behalf of everyone you meet, Liz?"

"Molly says I have a messiah complex. But it's not that. I have no power on my own. No illusions there. I believe I can help, though, and the desire to make a difference gives my life meaning. You're the same, right?"

"I'm not sure you could put fighting terrorists for the U.S. government in the same category as ministering to refugees and immigrants."

"We're both working for a greater cause,

Joshua. We believe we can change the world in some small way."

Nodding in agreement, he studied the photographs in the scrapbook, but what interested him more were the notations and comments Liz had written in black ink below each picture. This journey to Congo had gone beyond a mission trip. The people, the land, the experiences had slipped into her heart.

She was sipping coffee as he leaned back, his arm along the sofa behind her. "I see why you want to go to Africa. I understand that—even without this album, I know."

"Then maybe you can explain it to me. What calls me? Why did I feel such an urging while I was over there, and how can I make sense of it now?"

"I never have understood what reaches inside some people and grabs them by the heart—yet leaves others cold, disinterested, totally indifferent. Is it their personality or education or upbringing or family? Maybe it's God. I don't know. I've met a lot of guys who set one foot outside their original safety zone, and they can't ever go back. The experience changes them too much. They have to find a way to keep their finger on the pulse of the world or they're always uncomfortable."

"What about you, Joshua? You were changed. You're one of those who can't go back, aren't you? Afghanistan. Iraq. You saw what's out there. How are you going to live happily in Texas?"

"Happily?" He picked up his cup and took a swallow of the strong black coffee. "I'm not sure happiness is part of the equation. All I know is that to find contentment, I have to do my assignment."

"What assignment? Drilling for oil and building your family's bank accounts?"

"You make money sound like a bad thing. My family's wealth has done a lot of good. We have a foundation, we contribute to a lot of nonprofit organizations, my dad and brother sit on several boards."

"But do you really want to sit behind a desk, Joshua? I can't believe that would be fulfilling for you. What kind of a life will you have in Texas?"

"An easy one. And maybe that's as it should be. My father and grandfather built up Duff-Flannigan Oil to provide a life of wealth, comfort and privilege to their heirs. Am I supposed to turn that down? Am I supposed to shirk my own responsibility to the next generation? For ten years, my family accepted that I'd been assigned elsewhere. I did my job for the military, and now I need to fulfill obligations to my father."

As the coffee warmed him, Joshua drew Liz closer. His hand cupped her shoulder, soft and round. "Odd thing," he murmured. "Pastor Stephen says duty to my Heavenly Father supersedes the other. I wonder about that. If it's true . . .

if I can find a way to look my dad in the eyes and tell him I'm never going to run his oil field operation . . . I'd sure better have a good idea as to what God wants from me instead."

"You're a praying man. Do you have the answer?"

He suppressed an urge to tell her he was holding the answer in his arms. Beyond rational sense, Joshua knew only one certainty. He was intended for this woman. Liz Wallace had been sent to him. Placed in his path. Set so obviously in front of him that he couldn't pretend to have missed her.

But could he say that? Dare he admit something so preposterous? It was too soon. They had met only a couple of weeks before. And he had just returned from an intense assignment. He knew he was still suffering from PTSD, jet lag, exhaustion, sleep deprivation. Any rational assessment would declare his emotion a product of a currently unstable mental status.

"What happens when you pray, Liz?" he asked. "Do you hear God's voice telling you what to do?"

"Not these days," she acknowledged softly. "There was a time I had no doubt at all. But now . . . things feel different . . . unsettled. I can't sleep. I'm having a crisis of faith. Not in God—but in myself, in my ability to understand Him. Questions jumble my brain, as though a voice is demanding answers. I shut my eyes, and the barrage begins. Why are you studying Swahili? Why are you living in a big city in a run-down apartment building? Why do you work for a salary that can barely feed you? Why do you think you have to go to Africa? What's waiting there for you?"

He flipped a page in the scrapbook. Touching the face of a child with large, hungry eyes, he knew the response to her questions. "This is your answer, Liz. This is the voice you hear, and he has the answer to all those questions in your mind. This kid—and the hundreds more like him. They're calling you."

"And I know I should go. I wanted to go." Her voice grew small as she nestled against him. "But now . . . all of a sudden . . . things are so confusing."

For a moment, neither spoke. Though he could see the book, her written words, the little boy's eyes beckoning Liz, Joshua wanted to deny his own statement.

Liz should *not* go. Africa was dangerous, filled with war and disease and poverty and corruption. She might die there. She should stay right here on this sofa, tucked under his arm, pressed against him, safe and warm.

But what right did he have to hold her? What claim could he make on this woman? None.

Even as he acknowledged the truth, he bent and kissed her cheek. Her hair was soft against his hand as he touched it, curls threading around his fingertips like mist. Then she turned into him, lifted her face, pressed her lips to his. And it was too late. He could do nothing but pull her against his chest and lose himself in her. Her mouth, pillow-soft, worked a magic that spread through him like a flame. The scrapbook slid to the floor. His hands tested, measured, memorized her neck, shoulders, back.

"Liz," he murmured. "Liz, I can't keep you, but I want you. I want everything about you. Everything about you in my life."

"How can this be happening?" Her breath heated his ear, teasing sensitive skin. "Joshua, please make this feel wrong. Help me see how crazy it is."

"I can't do that. I may be crazy, but this isn't. It's too right to be wrong." As he kissed her again, Joshua heard a knocking on her door. It would be the Nicaraguan neighbor, worried—and rightly so.

He drew back. "Liz, let me see you again. Let me spend time with you until we're both sure. Either we'll know what's going on between us is good, or it will stop feeling right."

Leaning into him, she buried her face against his neck. "I can't keep seeing you. It's a mistake. Joshua, this is just physical, right? There can't be more to it."

"How will we know unless we're together? You have to give it a chance. It might be just physical or maybe just some temporary insanity. But it might be God."

The knocking increased, and she let out a little cry of frustration. "I have to get the door. It's Socorro." As she pulled away from him and stood, she laughed. "*Help*—that's what Mrs. Gonzales's name means in Spanish. And thank heaven for Socorro at a time like this."

Before he could rise, she was opening the door and welcoming the little woman inside. "Thank you for the coffee. *Gracias*." With a glance at Joshua, she shook her head. "Of course, with black coffee in my blood I'll never get to sleep . . . as if there were any hope of that after you . . . after this . . ."

He stood. "I won't sleep, either. I'll be thinking about you."

"Joshua—oh, please go now. I appreciate what you said about my scrapbook. You're right. That's the call. I have to remember the children, their faces. They need me."

"They're not the only ones." Picking up the coffee cups, he nodded at Mrs. Gonzales. "Did you know she's going to Africa? Liz is going away. Africa."

"Excuse me, please, I am not speak English good." The woman was smiling as she lifted both hands in an expression of helplessness. "I try, but I have no words."

"I don't have words, either. Not for this." He

focused on Liz. "Your neighbor needs you right here in America. Don't forget Mrs. Gonzales. All the refugees you bring in—they need you, too. And a war-weary Marine needs you, Liz."

He stepped to the door and handed the cups to Mrs. Gonzales. *"Gracias. Me gusta mucho su café."*

"Ah! You speak Spanish. Very nice!" She beamed at him and then at Liz. "This boyfriend, I like him much better to the other one. He is beautiful, no? The face? I like it."

Liz laughed. "Beautiful? Yes, I suppose he is."

Joshua bent and brushed a kiss on her cheek. Then he did the same for Mrs. Gonzales. Both women were giggling as he headed down the hall.

Just as Liz shut the door, her phone warbled. So soon? Joshua couldn't even have made it down to the parking garage, yet he was calling already. Her heart hammering, she answered.

"All right, it's me," she said. "What do you want—and be serious."

"You're the lady I was talking to before, right?"

The unexpected voice sent a cascade of chilled marbles spilling down her spine. She hadn't bothered to check the ID on her phone. Now a pair of green eyes flashed into her thoughts. That night at Podunk's came back in a rush. The vivid memory of a rank smell flooded through her body and made her stomach turn in revulsion.

Mo Ded.

Liz held her breath. He had called her before from Joshua's phone, and she believed that was the last time they would speak. But now his words came again.

"Look, I saw you in Podunk's, so I know it's you. I know you're with him. I got some things to say to that dude, yo."

"Call him, then. You have his number."

"He rigged his phone. I can't get through. But you and him are together, right? So you give him a message from me."

"What's your name? Where are you?"

"You know me. You know who I am. What I do. You know I own the streets, and I got my people everywhere. We watchin' you. We watchin' him. He just left your place. Goin' down the elevator to his fancy car right now. You want to keep him safe? You want me not to touch him? You want my boys to leave you alone, huh? Then you better listen up."

Liz glanced at her door, as if the green-eyed man might be standing just outside it. He or some of his Hypes were inside her building. They had followed Joshua as he left the apartment. They knew where she lived, what she was doing, who she spent time with.

Fear coursing through her, Liz gripped the phone. "You get out of here. Leave me alone. And don't you dare touch my friend."

"Him? I won't be touchin' him. It's you who should worry about gettin' touched, lady. You and maybe your Mexican friend down the hall."

The image of Mrs. Gonzales flashed through Liz's brain. The elderly woman would be tottering back to her apartment, coffee mugs in hand and a smile on her face. She would never suspect that Mo Ded's gangbangers might be spying on her from the shadows.

"What do you want?" Liz demanded. "Tell me. Tell me right now, and then you and your people get out of my life."

"I want you to give your man a message from me. You tell him to stay offa my turf. I can take out his friends—not a problem. I know how to immobilize them. And him . . . he better not mess with me, yo. You tell him that."

"Tell him what Mo Ded says, right?" she challenged.

"Oh, you know my name? Good. Then you got an idea what kind of organization you're up against. You better take what I say serious, yo."

"What do you want with Haven? Just leave it alone. It's a good place, a nice community center for kids. You don't need that block. Let it go."

"You tellin' me to back off?" He made a guttural grunt. "Tell that to *him.* Yo man be up there in a second. Yeah, here he come now. You tell him to back off."

As the connection went dead, someone hammered on Liz's door. Stiffening in fear, she called out. "Who is it?"

"Liz, let me in!" Joshua's voice sounded urgent.

She ran to the door and turned the dead bolt. He stepped inside. As she slammed the door behind him, he reached for her, pulled her against him, backed them into a corner.

"Did they touch you?" he rasped, breathing hard. "Did anyone get in here?"

"No, it was a phone call. Oh, Joshua, they were watching us the whole time. They saw Mrs. Gonzales! It was Mo Ded—I recognized his voice from the time before. He knows where I live. He threatened me! What made you come back?"

"A couple of his guys met me when the elevator doors opened. I got past them and ran up the stairwell to your place."

"Did they hurt you?"

"Not me. It's you they keep tracking. What do they want from you, Liz?"

"They don't want *me.* Mo Ded called here so that I would give you a message. He said he wants you off his turf. Haven. He told me he knows how to handle Sam and Terell—take them out, immobilize them. Those were his words. He's not worried about them. But he said you were not to mess with him."

Shivering, she wrapped her arms around Joshua and held him tight. "He knew you were coming up here to my apartment again. The moment before you knocked, he told me you'd be back and I was to give you his message. I'm worried about Mrs. Gonzales. He must be right outside this door—in the hallway somewhere. What if he hurts her? I'll never forgive myself if something happens to her."

"He's not out there now. I checked on my way through. The hall is clear."

"How can you be so sure about these things? You're not invincible, you know." She pushed away from him and took him by the shoulders. "Joshua, you have to get out of St. Louis. Leave and don't come back to this apartment. Don't even stop at Haven to pick up your things. Just get in your car and drive away. Let Mo Ded have his turf. Let him—"

"Liz, stop talking." He took her again, encircling her in his embrace. "Be quiet and breathe. This is about territory, not people. Especially not Mrs. Gonzales. Mo Ded is a bully—posturing and threatening and trying to make a statement. I'm not afraid of him."

"I am. I'm terrified. If he found my building, my floor, my apartment, who knows what else he could do?"

"Your building was never safe to begin with. You shouldn't live here. There's no door security, no alarm system, nothing. Anyone could get through that window. I could take your door down with my elbow. Tracking you would be a piece of cake. You need to get out. I'm going to transfer you to a better place. I'll put you in a hotel tonight, and then I'll move you into a secure apartment in a safe part of the city."

"You can't do that. This apartment is my home." She stepped away from him. "Everything was working fine, and then you came along and messed me all up. Why? Why do you have to be in my life?"

"Those questions are irrelevant now. I'm here and I'm not leaving. Not for a week. I told Hawke I'd give him that."

"Why? He doesn't need your help building his outdoor recreation area."

His eyes went deep. "Liz, I'm going to take care of Mo Ded for him."

"No!" She caught his hands. "No, Joshua. Please don't tell me that. I can't accept it. You're one man. Mo Ded has a whole gang. They're trained and armed. How could Sam ask that of you? What kind of a friend would place you in so much danger? You could get killed."

"It's you I'm worried about. Mo Ded knows I'm a threat to his operation. He said he can take care of Hawke and Terell, but he wants me out of the picture. That means he's got me figured out—at least to some degree. He recognizes I'm the real danger to his little terrorist cell, and he hopes by scaring and threatening you, he can get me to leave. But he could do worse than frighten you, Liz. He could hurt you."

He began to pace, head down, fingers toying with his lower lip. "Civilians are always a factor, but not like this. No enemy has ever been able to get at someone who matters to me. I've protected women and children, sure. People in their homes and on the streets. This is a whole new level. Mo Ded has the upper hand right now because he's got you in his sights. He knows I won't risk you."

"He doesn't know the truth about us," Liz protested. "You and I are friends, that's all. Mo Ded has put us together in his mind, but we're not together. Not really. I can stay here in my apartment, go to my job, do my work and keep my relationships with Molly and Mrs. Gonzales and everyone else. If you and I don't see each other again, he'll figure it out. He won't touch me."

Joshua had halted in the middle of the room. "Liz, I won't stay in St. Louis without seeing you."

"You have to. Just leave my apartment and my life. And if you're as smart as I think, you'll go to Texas where everything is safe."

She looked away, fighting unexpected tears. "We can't see each other anymore, Joshua. From the start, we both knew it wasn't best. And now that's even more true. I want to live in my own home. I refuse to become the kind of woman who buckles to fear. When I move to Africa, I can't walk around with constant terror that something bad might happen to me, or I'll never make it. And as for you, there's only a week left in this city anyway, right? You've given Sam your time to set up some kind of protection from the gangs. From Mo Ded. So you'll be leaving soon. And that's good."

"Then why are you crying?"

Brushing at the tears that kept tumbling down her cheeks, Liz shook her head. "I'm not crying. Not really. It's the shock of the phone call. Mo Ded's voice. The worry about Mrs. Gonzales. I don't know, but the tears aren't what you think. They have nothing to do with . . ."

At the thought that this might be the last moment she would ever see Joshua Duff, sobs welled up from deep inside her. She turned away, hurrying into the kitchen, opening cupboard doors, searching the shelves for some nameless object.

And then he was behind her, his arms circling her waist, drawing her close.

"Liz, let me hold you." His breath warmed her cheek. He didn't speak for a moment, and when he did his voice was husky. "I've never felt this way about a woman. Never intended to get so caught up in another person. Please let me take care of you. Let me put you somewhere safe. Let me fulfill my promise to Sam and come to you again. We'll talk and we'll take the time to figure out what's going on, what we're supposed to do. Please. Please do that for me."

The images he laid out glittered in Liz's mind

like bright jewels on a necklace of hope. A hotel. Safety. Good food. Maid service. Time with a man she had thought about constantly since the moment they met.

And then what? More precious diamonds. Love, perhaps? Maybe even marriage? A life in Texas. The wife of an oil tycoon. A large home. A swimming pool. Happy, healthy, well-educated children. Everything a normal, intelligent woman would want. And more.

How could she resist this man?

Turning in his embrace, she slipped her arms around his neck. For a moment, she could only drift in their kiss. It took away the fear, doubt and confusion. Joshua's strength and shield filled her with such joy. Such bliss.

And yet the call was always in her heart, whispering or lecturing or even shouting at her. The little boy with beckoning eyes. The hunger and filth and poverty and ignorance. How could she dance away with her glimmering necklace of jewels? How could she waltz away and never think again of the promises she had made? How could she stop listening to the words that called to her with such urgency?

"Joshua, I can't leave this place." She bit her lip, battling emotion. "I believe God wants me to stay here and eat Mrs. Gonzales's tamales and keep searching my scrapbook while I work for Refugee Hope. And I think . . . I really do believe . . . I'm almost sure I'm supposed to go to Africa and minister in camps on the Kenyan border. So please go. Go and take away the war and violence and gangs and terrorist cells and everything that came into my life when you walked in. Let me stay here in my little home and heal from you. Because I will heal. So will you. Just let that happen, all right?"

She stepped away from him. Grabbed tissues from a box on her kitchen counter. Fought the sobs. She would not say more for fear of confessing too much. For fear of revealing her heart.

He walked to the door. He stood in silence, and she could feel his eyes on her, searching. Clutching the back of a chair, she willed herself not to look at him again. Not to go to him.

And then he opened the door, stepped outside, shut it behind him. Before he could come back into her apartment—her life, her heart—she ran and turned the dead bolt.

Chapter Twelve

"Eat the fish head."

The gentle request came after Liz and that particular item in the soup pot had been staring at each other for about five minutes.

"Me?" Flustered, she glanced at Boazi, a Burundian refugee whose right hand had been cut off during the civil war. "You want me to eat the fish head?"

"No, no. *Him.*" Boazi gestured at Liz's coworker.

"I'm supposed to eat it?" Matthew Strong, a college freshman who volunteered at Refugee Hope, had accompanied Liz to the small apartment not far from the office. The young man had been assigned to help the newly arrived family with assimilation.

He blanched at the prospect of dining on the fish head. "I'm not really that much of a fish person, to tell you the truth."

"A fish *person?*" Boazi frowned. "A fish is not a person. A fish is a fish. In Burundi, the guest always eats the head."

"Maybe Liz would like it," Matt suggested.

"No, the man must eat the fish head, because the man is the head of the woman."

Seated on a blanket on the floor with his guests, Boazi smiled at his wife. Six months pregnant, Rahaba had been trying without success to corral her three excited children—all under the age of five. From the moment Liz and Matt stepped into the apartment, the kids had been jumping on the sofa, running around the living room, climbing on furniture, pushing each other, inspecting wall outlets and reaching for a large butcher knife that lay on the blanket between the soup pot and a large bowl of stiff cornmeal called *ugali.*

Now Rahaba dutifully dipped up a ladleful of soup—including the fish head—and poured it into Matt's bowl. She filled Liz's bowl with a second portion. The unidentifiable bits floating in a strong-smelling broth caught at Liz's nostrils and tipped her stomach on its side. But she recalled eating bush rat and monkey meat in Congo, and she could survive this, too.

An opportunity to spend time with one of her families was a rarity, after all. On taking a position as a caseworker with Refugee Hope, Liz had envisioned herself deeply immersed in the lives of people who had come to America from war-torn countries. She would bring them language, health, nutrition, education and, most of all, hope. The hope of a new beginning and, especially, the hope of a new life in Jesus Christ.

Instead, she spent most of her workday drowning in rules and regulations. Government forms flooded every file. Each time she began the process of helping a refugee family, the tap turned on and a gush of red tape came spewing out. School, food stamps, English language classes, job training. Any direction she turned to lend a helping hand, another faucet opened.

"Boazi, thank you for inviting Matt and me to join you for lunch," Liz said, casting her eye at the young man, who was prodding the fish head with the tip of his spoon. "We are pleased to share this meal with your family and learn Burundian traditions. But in America, we do have some customs that are different from yours. Would you be offended if Matt did not eat the fish head?"

Boazi sat in silence for a moment, staring at the delicacy in the young man's bowl. Then the corners of his mouth turned up. Covering his grin with his left hand, he began to laugh. His wife spoke to him in Kirundi, and with a chuckle, he explained the situation. Rahaba, too, began to giggle as if this were the funniest thing she had heard in a long time.

Liz tried to join the merriment, but she wasn't sure why the couple was laughing at their rejection of the gift. Another cultural mystery, she thought.

There were so many. Just as odd as the fish head was to her, American customs mystified the refugees obliged to learn the ways of their new homeland. Why was fried chicken eaten with fingers, while baked chicken must be cut with a knife and eaten with a fork? A napkin was used for what? A pepper mill? A microwave?

Why did American women wear trousers, panty hose, eye shadow? Why did they go without head coverings? For what purpose was a tie worn around a man's neck?

What was a table lamp? A vacuum cleaner? A rake? A lawn mower? Not only was the secret of opening a childproof medicine bottle unknown, but what exactly was a *dose?* Or a *tablespoon?* And how often should one take it?

The challenges were so great that Liz wondered how any of the refugees adjusted. Somehow most did. But the success rate varied, and she felt so responsible for the ones who drifted into squalor and disappointment. They had come from such anguish, war and deprivation. Yet America, with its brightly waving flag and glorious dreams, often failed to answer their prayers.

"It is no problem. Do not eat the fish head," Boazi told Matt. Then he looked at Liz. "But, for you, please take more soup."

Before she could declare that she already had more than enough, Rahaba poured another ladleful of the pungent broth into her bowl. Liz stirred it with caution. "So, Boazi, can you tell me how you like your job?"

"Very good. Yes, the job is good." With his better-than-usual command of English, Boazi had quickly found work at a landscaping company. "I put water on the plants. There is a pipe . . . many pipes . . . with water for seeds. I put water on the seeds and make the plants to grow."

"Wonderful." Trying to avoid the gaze of Matt's fish head, Liz dipped up a spoonful of her own soup. "I'm glad you like this work."

"Yes," Boazi said. "Thank you. But I have a question about papers."

"Papers." Liz muttered the word to Matt. "The bane of my existence. No doubt these are some more forms he has to fill out."

"I'll help him," Matt offered.

Boazi and Rahaba were speaking heatedly while

Liz sipped another spoonful of soup and watched the youngest of their children run shrieking from the other two. But when the boy slipped behind a television that had been balanced on a chair, she gasped. "Oh, Boazi, look at your son! That's dangerous. The TV could fall on him."

"I got it, Liz." Matt leaped to his feet and hurried across the room to steady the chair and rescue the baby. "Wow, look how many wires they've plugged into the outlet. That can't be safe."

"Please, how am I to get this money?" Boazi had dug several sheets of folded papers from his shirt pocket.

Rahaba beckoned her children as Liz spoke to her. "You must move the TV to a better place. Matt, why don't you put it on the table over there. That's their dining room table, but they prefer to eat on the floor. It looks pretty strong. Could you—"

"Madam, see this free money," Boazi cut in. Using his one hand, he spread the papers across his thigh. "Where I can go to get this money?"

Liz leaned over and scanned the pages. Coupons. Rebates. Credit card applications. Bogus offers of cash in exchange for opening bank accounts, testing products or performing in-home mailing services. Clearly Boazi and Rahaba had been saving the worthless flyers as if they were gold. Oh, dear.

"This is not *free* money," Liz said, lifting an

application with its shiny fake credit card attached. She searched her mind for the right Swahili words. "*Weka karatasi ndani ya basura.* Put the paper in the trash. It is bad—*mbaya.*"

Boazi scowled. "Bad? No, please. See here. It says one thousand dollars. Free." He pointed with his index finger at the figure and pronounced the English word with emphasis. "*Thousand.* One *thousand* dollars. I want this money."

"I understand, but this is a bad plan. This is not a smart way to—"

Liz's phone warbled, cutting off her effort to explain. As she crumpled the application, Boazi appeared distraught. She slipped her phone from her pocket. "Hello? This is Liz Wallace."

"Yeah, Ms. Wallace, my name is Jim Boggs from Apex Cleaning Company. The refugee place in the phone book gave me your number—said you could help me out. Listen, I've got an employee who hasn't been showing up for work. Last night was the third shift in a row, okay? No notice, no phone call, no nothing. I understand about the language problem, but I got people who could use that job. More important, I got buildings to clean."

"I'm so sorry, Mr. Boggs. We value your company's support of our work programs, sir. What's the employee's name?"

"Mary Rudi, and I have to tell you she never was much good to begin with. I kept losing her from the crew. She'd start out with us when the shift began, and then she'd vanish. I was about to have to fire her anyway."

"Mr. Boggs, Refugee Hope didn't bring Mary Rudi to St. Louis. We're not responsible for her." Liz let out a breath. "I do know Mary, though, and I'm aware of her situation. If you'll give her another chance, I'll talk to her and see if I can help. Maybe she doesn't understand what she's supposed to do. She recently came from a refugee camp in Kenya, and before that she was in Paganda."

"Yeah, we've had one or two of them before, from Paganda or thereabouts, but I gotta tell you it doesn't really matter to me where an employee comes from. What matters is that she shows up to work on time and does her job."

"I understand. It's just that Paganda is . . . There was a lot of violence. It's possible that Mary Rudi suffered terrible things. Unspeakable things. So, if you could give me time to talk to her, I'd appreciate it."

"I'll give her another chance. But if she doesn't show up tonight, I'll have to let her go. That's how the business world works, ma'am. We've all had one kind of trouble or another, whether we're from Africa or someplace else. I'll look for Mary this evening. And tell her to plan on working a full shift."

Liz thanked the man and put her phone away.

Boazi was again spreading the crumpled credit card application on his thigh. As he attempted to iron out the wrinkles with his palm, he shook his head.

"This is America, and here is money for my family. Please do not take this money from me." He looked at her with an expression of reproach. "You talk about Paganda on your phone. Paganda is violence, yes. But Burundi also. Much violence. You see my arm? Is bad people chop off my hand."

"I'm so sorry, Boazi. What happened to you was terrible."

"Many bad people in Burundi. I know Paganda is bad people, too. In my camp in Kenya are many refugees from Paganda. All have suffering. Burundi, Congo, Rwanda, Paganda— all come to the camp in Kenya."

He picked up the sheaf of flyers—these bits of magic that had somehow appeared in his mailbox in America—and shook them at Liz. "This is much money. For my family."

She set down her spoon and rubbed her eyes. As she searched her mind for the right words to explain that not everything in America was good, Liz saw one of the children dart in front of Matt, who was carrying the television toward the dining room table. He stumbled. The TV begin to topple. Though Matt quickly regained his balance, Rahaba yelped and scrambled on her hands and knees across the floor. All three children wailed. One little boy, reaching for his mother, toddled across the blanket on the floor, upsetting Matt's soup and sending the fish head rolling across the blanket.

As Liz reached for the bowl, Boazi laid his hand on her arm.

"Please, please." His dark eyes searched hers. "I have two brothers in the camp. My wife's mother and two sisters and their six children. All are in the camp in Kenya. Please, we need this free money. We must send money to our family. You understand? You understand, please?"

Liz nodded. Yes, she understood. Even more than she comprehended that this man had left his dearly loved family members to languish in a barren camp on the Kenyan border, Liz understood her own helplessness. What could she do? What could anyone do?

"You must watch this street like the cherubim of the prophet Ezekiel." Pastor Stephen Rudi gripped his shovel as he stood beside Joshua. "Those four angels appeared to Ezekiel in the first of his visions."

"Really? Well, you might want to remind me about that deal. I'm not exactly up to snuff on Ezekiel's visions."

A large group of neighborhood men and teens had gathered for the afternoon ground breaking outside Haven. Despite Mo Ded's threats, Sam and Terell had decided to go ahead and start work on the outdoor recreation area. With Joshua keeping watch, police vehicles cruising by regularly and the large number of people working in the empty lot, they trusted that the Hypes would not dare act out against them.

The day before, Joshua had briefly trained Raydell and two other promising young men in basic guard strategies and techniques. Duke was back in action, too. Though still a bit stiff and sore from his injury, the dog stood at Joshua's side, alert and vigilant.

"You do not remember the cherubim of Ezekiel?" Pastor Stephen shook his head. "You Americans have so many Bibles in this country! You should *certainly* know these Scriptures. I am shocked. Yesterday, Terell told me he did not remember the brave woman who drove a tent stake through the head of her sleeping enemy."

"A what?" Joshua glanced over in surprise. "A tent stake?"

Pastor Stephen gave a grunt of disgust. When he spoke again, his voice was filled with emotion. "It is important for all women and men of God to know Jael! She killed Sisera, a cruel enemy commander of nine hundred chariots. That man came into Jael's tent, and while he slept, she took her hammer and struck the tent stake so that it went through his head. That stake went through his brain into the ground. This account is in the book of Judges in the fourth chapter. Do you not know it?"

Joshua let out a breath. He was trying to make sure that Raydell and the other two teens stayed focused at the far end of the empty lot. With children milling around, the sounds of talking, shovels and jackhammers filling the air and curious onlookers gathering, conditions were ripe for trouble.

"Look, Pastor S., I appreciate your knowledge of the Bible," he said, wrapping the end of Duke's leash around his palm. "I'm glad you want to share it here in America. But I—"

"Ezekiel saw four cherubim," Stephen cut in. Raising his hands, he spoke as if he were the prophet himself. " *'And I looked, and, behold, a whirlwind came out of the north, a great cloud, and a fire infolding itself, and a brightness was about it, and out of the midst thereof as the color of amber, out of the midst of the fire. Also out of the midst thereof came the likeness of four living creatures. And this was their appearance; they had the likeness of a man. And every one had four faces, and every one had four wings.'* "

"Pastor Stephen." Joshua reached out and set his hand on the man's shoulder. "Calm down now, all right? We're not seeing visions here in St. Louis. We're watching for Hypes. I've trained Raydell and the other two men, and we've got it covered."

" '*As for the likeness of their faces,*' " Stephen continued, " '*they four had the face of a man, and the face of a lion, on the right side: and they four had the face of an ox on the left side; they four also had the face of an eagle.*' "

"I don't have four faces, Pastor, but I am on the lookout for trouble. And I'd do a better job if you and Ezekiel would march over there to where Sam is trying to mark out the basketball court. If you want stakes, that's where you'll find them. He's got a whole bucketful. And by the way, your son has his hands down in that bucket."

"Virtue?" The pastor swung around, spotted his five-year-old and hurried away. "Virtue, leave the bucket! Put down those stakes!"

Joshua couldn't help but grin. The fact was, he liked Stephen Rudi and his little Pagandan family—especially the children. Virtue loved to imitate his father, waving his hands and wagging his finger at people. More than once, Joshua had seen the little boy hauling around the big black Bible his father read so diligently every night.

Charity was blossoming at school, and Virtue ate up every minute of kindergarten. It was hard to believe how fast both kids were picking up the English language. Their father helped, of course, poring over their homework each night and correcting spoken language mistakes. Joshua had become fairly proficient in the tongues of Iraq and Afghanistan, but it had taken great effort. The

Rudi children were absorbing English faster than he ever could have hoped.

Joshua even admired silent little Mary Rudi. Focusing on the doorway of Haven, he spotted Stephen's wife standing in the shadow of the awning and watching the scene from behind her large spectacles. She wore her usual colorful head scarf and one of her three plain dresses, as she had every day since the Pagandan family appeared outside the youth center.

Arms crossed, Mary wore a pinched frown on her lips, as if everything she saw displeased her. The woman did not have the most welcoming personality, but Joshua believed she took good care of her two stepchildren and her husband—making beds, toting laundry down long flights of stairs to Haven's basement washers and dryers, cooking traditional meals on the hot plate Joshua had purchased, working long hours at her cleaning job.

The women in any war-torn country suffered the most, he knew. They were the spoils of battle. Sexual terrorism was not a term in his training manuals, but he had seen its effects in the faces of victims—women huddled by the side of the road begging for food, creatures cast off from society even though they were the ones who had suffered violations almost too atrocious to believe.

Inside the heart of Mary Rudi, there would be such a story, Joshua surmised. He doubted even her husband knew what she had suffered before their marriage in the refugee camp in Kenya. Her sour expression, terse comments and joyless performance of the acts in her daily living could be forgiven. She deserved some hope in her life.

To that end, Joshua had canceled their apartment lease. After leaving Liz, he realized he could never put the Rudi family in such a place. He hated the thought that Liz still lived down that musty hall in a tiny apartment behind a flimsy door. He chastised himself for abandoning her there. If he'd been thinking more clearly, he would have picked the woman up, tossed her over his shoulder and hauled her off to a hotel whether she liked it or not.

But her kisses had overwhelmed his senses. Her tears had caught him off guard. The strength of his own feelings for her had startled him. And when she sent him away, he went.

"Yo, Sarge!" Raydell's call from the far end of the lot alerted Joshua to a group of young men gathering across the street. At his side, Duke's ears pricked up and the hair on the dog's back bristled.

Hypes. Their purple do-rags and scrawny physiques gave them away. Baggy jeans hung low on their hips. White T-shirts set off colorful tattoos. Dark sunglasses. Chains with gem-studded pendants. They slouched, eyed each other, smoked cigarettes. Sullen. Brooding. Their facial expressions revealed pride and mockery. They thought Haven was a joke.

Joshua checked his young guards. They stood stiff and expressionless. Frightened. Their posture revealed too much. He would have preferred Raydell and the others to relax and monitor the street in a way that didn't shout alarm, trepidation, fear.

But the Haven youths *were* afraid. The Hypes were armed, and they meant business.

Pondering the best strategy for such a situation, Joshua started toward Raydell. The Hypes might be bluffing. Or they might have a plan to disrupt the work going on outside Haven. Joshua could hand Duke off to Raydell, cross the street and confront the gangbangers. Tell them he was tracking Mo Ded, that he would find him and put a stop to their nonsense.

Joshua had left Liz in her apartment four days before, and since that time he had concentrated his efforts on pinning down Haven's green-eyed adversary. He had no doubt he could find a way to snuff Mo Ded's reign of terror. But so far the method eluded him.

"How many you count, Raydell?" he asked.

"Nine. Look at 'em flying their colors. They're probably strapped, too. They go everywhere in threes, yo. Just like you said. Three of 'em came around that corner. Three were in the restaurant down the street. The other three, I didn't see where they were hanging before they joined up. They all got them phones stuck on their ears, and they never stop talking."

"Those phones are the way Mo Ded controls his turf. He's watching the set right now, but we won't see him out in the open. He'll be talking his people through every move they make. Man, I'd love to get my hands on one of those phones."

"You ain't never gonna do that, dog."

"U.S. Marine Corps, Raydell—*never* is not in our vocabulary. We do what has to be done or die trying."

"Die trying? Now you sounding like a gang-banger yourself. Maybe that Marine Corps of yours is a gang, huh?"

Joshua bent and stroked the fur between Duke's ears. "Troops, training, protecting turf. Could be a little bit like a gang. But we're not in the business of running guns or selling drugs. We defend our country. Do battle against America's enemies. The Marines don't make people jump off the porch to get in. No one has to get beaten in or go on a mission if they want to join. You just sign up and hope you've got what it takes. If you want out, you get discharged. Nobody kills you for leaving the Corps."

"Yo, we got more trouble now. There's D. Loc and Big Man down the way. They're Crips." Raydell began to breathe hard. "This ain't good, dog. You can't have Crips and Hypes on the same set. Not when one of 'em is staking out turf. We're about to have a problem, Sarge."

Joshua instinctively felt for his weapon—and

once again realized it was missing. He handed Duke's leash to Raydell. "Stay calm. I'll talk to the other guys on guard. Don't do anything, man. Don't make a move. We have to let this play out."

"Listen, D. Loc is a pipe head." Raydell caught Joshua. "Crack has him all messed up. But Big Man, he's a real hoodsta. You don't want to mess with him."

"Neither do you. If we handle this right, Mo Ded's people can mess with Big Man, and we'll be watching from the sidelines."

Joshua saw that his other two rookie guards were already aware of the trouble brewing across the street. Against his instructions, they had left their posts. Heads together, they gave off every possible indication of insecurity, fear and lack of preparation.

Though the four on duty were alert to the current gang problem, Joshua realized that no one else in the area was paying attention. Sam was directing kids as they staked out the basketball court. Terell was helping two teens examine a jackhammer someone had donated to the cause. So far they hadn't figured out how to start the thing. Children raced around the empty lot. A group of girls played jump rope on the sidewalk. Balls bounced. People shouted instructions, measurements, requests back and forth to each other.

And then Liz Wallace drove up. Her car pulled into a space across the street, directly in front of the growing collection of Hypes—now there were a dozen. Joshua couldn't believe his eyes.

But he was seeing reality. Liz left the driver's side of her car, straightened and hooked her purse over her shoulder. A young man with dark curly hair and a laptop under his arm climbed out through the passenger door. Oblivious to the stage they had just entered, they spoke to each other for a moment across the car's roof.

"Yo, that's Matt Strong." Raydell grabbed Joshua's arm as Liz moved onto the sidewalk to join the younger man. "He's got your woman with him. They walkin' right into the middle of the Hypes. Dog, we better do somethin'!"

As Liz waded through the cluster of purple do-rags and sagging jeans, a burst of adrenaline shot through Joshua's veins.

"Don't move," he barked at Raydell.

Eyes trained on the pretty woman in the green dress, he strode into the street.

Chapter Thirteen

Liz saw Joshua coming and leaned toward Matt. "Oh, dear. I didn't expect him to be outside. Not right here first thing."

"Who—the soldier-looking guy? You know him?" Matt shot Liz a smirk. "Is he your boyfriend?"

"Why do people always assume that? No. Of course not."

"Hey, there's Raydell with Duke." Matt lifted a hand to wave. "And Sam's over by the door. What are they all doing outside? I don't see T-Rex—oh, yeah, there he is. I haven't seen any of these guys since I was here last summer. Did I tell you I came to Missouri on a mission trip and helped set up Haven's computer system?"

Before Liz could reply, Matt was stepping out into the street. He greeted Joshua in passing but got no response. The teen hurried ahead, joined Raydell and vanished into the cluster of Haven volunteers.

"Liz, walk toward me." Joshua's voice was deep. He reached for her, caught her around the shoulders, pulled her close. "Stay right with me. Don't say a word until I get you across the street."

Sucking in a breath, Liz all at once understood. The people on the sidewalk around her. The vague tinge of purple. The dancelike movements as figures paired off, reformed, parted again. She looked for green eyes but didn't see them.

Joshua moved her out into the roadway, paused to let a car pass, pressed her in a fast walk toward the bustle of the lot beside Haven.

"I'm sorry. I didn't see them when I pulled up." She felt his chest against her shoulder. He was protecting her, shielding her from behind with his body. "I should have called ahead, but I was hoping . . ."

"Hoping to avoid me?"

"No, Joshua. Hoping it would be less intense between us if I just showed up."

"Don't worry. I'm on duty, anyway." He ushered her into the relative safety of the group outside Haven. "Hawke and Terell decided to go ahead with the rec area. I agreed to patrol. But the thing is out of control. The enemy is gathering force."

"I walked right into the Hypes."

"And a few Crips." He turned to scan the street again. "Can't tell if they're just watching, or if they've got something planned. Why did you come?"

"Mary Rudi." Liz spotted the small woman in the shadow of Haven's front awning. "I got a call today from Apex Cleaning. Her boss contacted me because he thought Mary came to St. Louis through Refugee Hope. She hasn't been showing up for work."

Joshua looked at Liz, his blue eyes truly focusing on her face for the first time since she arrived. His dark brows narrowed in confusion.

"I drive Mary to work every evening," he said. "I drop her off at Apex. Front door. Jim Boggs—the night shift boss. He's always waiting there with the others on her crew. She goes right inside."

"Evidently she accompanies the crew to the work site, but then she vanishes. Jim is planning to fire her unless she complies with his rules."

"She can't lose that job. They need the money. I've decided to put them in a better apartment, but it's going to cost an arm and a leg."

"I'll talk to her." She started toward the woman, then paused. "Joshua, you're doing good work with the Rudis, you know. I'm afraid this is how it often goes. Things are never easy for our refugees. Mary is probably overwhelmed by the job but hasn't figured out how to tell you. Maybe Matt or one of our other volunteers can stay with her for a few days until she learns the ropes and feels comfortable. We call it job shadowing. It helps them over the rough spots."

She stepped away, but he took her arm. "Liz, I wish you hadn't come down here. It's not safe."

"Joshua, look at all the people around you. Others are here—children, teenagers, grandmas. Why should I stay away?"

"Because three more Hypes just walked out of that alley. We've got more than a dozen of them milling around now. I'd almost swear they're taking up offensive positions. Crips are gathering, too, and I don't know how that figures into the equation. Hawke asked the police to step up their patrols of the street today. Right now would be a good time for a squad car to swing by."

"Joshua, the gangs are not after me. I have work to do here."

"Liz, you must not get hurt." He snapped out the words. "This place is . . . wrong for you. You should come to Texas with me. Take a break from the gangs and the refugees. Sit by the pool."

For a moment Liz couldn't move.

Joshua wanted her to go to his home. Sit by his swimming pool.

But he had said those things almost in anger. And what did they even mean?

She shook her head. "I'd better go talk to Mary."

"I leave in three days."

Liz studied the man. Eyes trained on the street and sidewalk opposite Haven, he hardly seemed aware of her. Yet she sensed that from the moment she drove up, she had been his central focus.

"Three days," she echoed. "That's not long. How will they make it without you?"

"They?"

"Haven. Your friends need your help." She gripped her purse strap. "And I've missed you."

Blue eyes darted to her and then away again. "I keep thinking I've got it licked. Wanting you." He gave a wry smile. "I'm doing a better job managing the PTSD."

"I don't know how to fix this, Joshua," she said softly. "I don't know how to make this thing with us work. But I can't go sit by a swimming pool in Texas."

He nodded. "I understand."

"I'll talk to Mary." For fear she might say too much, Liz hurried through the crowd.

As she approached, Mary Rudi noticed her and made a move to push open the door and step back inside the building. Liz called out.

"Mary, please wait. *Ngoja!*"

The small woman halted, hung her head, knotted her fingers together. She said nothing.

"Mary, I had a phone call today." Liz took out her phone to demonstrate. "Jim Boggs called me. From the cleaning company. He wanted to talk about you."

Head bent, Mary didn't move. Liz had no idea if the woman was understanding a word she said. Spotting Charity in the jump rope line, she beckoned the little girl.

"Do you remember me, Charity?" Liz crouched to the youngster's level.

Bright eyes flashing, Charity took her hand. "I am seven years old! I jump!"

"You're a good jumper. Can you please talk to your mother for me, Charity? Will you tell her not to leave her work at night? She must go to her job and stay with the group until all the work is finished."

"I am from Paganda," Charity said.

"Yes, I remember that. And now you live here." This wasn't going as well as Liz had hoped. "Does your mother understand English?"

Charity shook her head. Her whole body turned back and forth with the denial. "She can't talk English. Mary never do talk to me. She don't talk to Virtue, also. My father can talk English gooder than Mary."

Liz looked up to find that the woman had shifted

away from Charity. She was hunting for something in her purse. The little girl must find it hard to accept such a distant, unemotional woman into the family. Especially after her birth mother had been so brutally murdered.

"I will find my father," Charity said. "Wait!"

In moments, she had located Pastor Stephen. Holding his hand, she tugged him toward the two women. Liz called out a greeting.

"Thank you for helping out here, Pastor," she said. "Will you please explain to Mary that her employer called me this morning? He's very concerned about Mary's work. He wants her to stay with the cleaning crew for the whole shift. She can't leave. She has to remain with the others until the job is done. If she leaves again, he will have to let her go."

"Do you mean he will sack her?" Stephen's eyes went wide. "But why does this man say my wife is not doing her work? She tells me she is cleaning every night."

"There must be some confusion. Her boss says that after a short time, she stops working and leaves the rest of the crew to finish the job. Please tell Mary that if she needs someone to help her learn how to do the work, I will find a volunteer. She can succeed at this, and we want to help her."

Stephen spoke to his wife in the Pagandan language. The entire time, Mary kept her shoulder to him, as if she didn't want to hear the message.

After a long silence, she muttered a few words.

"Mary says she will stay with the crew," Stephen translated. "She does not need your help, because she knows how to do this work."

Noting that Charity had raced back to the jump-rope girls, Liz spoke quietly to Stephen. "Your wife seems very sad, Pastor. Is there anything I can do to assist with her adjustment to America? Refugee Hope has contracts with several counselors in the city. Maybe Mary should talk to someone about her past. I'm afraid she's not doing well here."

"This is always her way," Stephen confided. "Mary is a quiet woman who only wants to live a peaceful life. When I met her in the refugee camp, she was in a very bad situation. The rebels . . . they had harmed her. You understand my meaning? The soldiers did that kind of thing which is called rape. This was done to Mary. She was injured very much in this event—inside her body—but she refused to allow a doctor to examine her because of fear. She saw with her own eyes the killing of her husband and all her children. She had five children, all killed with machetes. She was just this same way in the camp. Very quiet. My situation there was also bad. So I suggested that we make a marriage to help each other."

"You do help each other a lot," Liz said.

He sighed. "Yes, and I hoped my wife would become happy. I thought that my children might make her cheerful. I pray for her every day that she may find the great joy of knowing God even in suffering. But now I fear this is not to be."

"Maybe one day she'll feel better. How long have you been married?"

"A short time. My name was on the list to go to America when I met her. Actually, she found me. Mary heard me preaching in the church at our camp. Afterward, she wanted to talk to me in private, to get some help. She told me some things that had happened in her life. I felt it would be good to marry her. I wished to assist her and also to give my children another woman who could be like a mother for them. I had to work hard to get Mary's name entered onto the list, but with God's mercy, I was successful."

Liz studied the small woman. Mary seemed to be drawing into herself even as they spoke. It was as if she wanted to shrink away into nonexistence.

"Would you object to the possibility of counseling for your wife?" Liz asked Stephen. "Or a physician? Maybe if Mary were able to talk to a female doctor about what happened, about her losses and her pain, she might let go of the past a little bit. Maybe if she could learn to accept the truth, she would find hope."

He shrugged. "I will speak to my wife about this. But she cannot talk English, and she will not be willing to tell another Pagandan what happened to her back there."

“Maybe *you* could translate for the doctor.”

“This would be impossible. I am her husband, and she does not wish me to know all of the things which she suffered. She believes I will reject her if I learn more about these bad events.”

“But you wouldn’t reject her. You love her.”

“Of course I do, but—”

The screech of car tires drowned his words. Deafening bangs split the air. Firecrackers? What? Why now?

Someone screamed.

Confused, Liz searched the crowd. Shrieking people ran for Haven’s front door. One crashed into Liz, nearly knocking her down. She smelled gunpowder.

Too late, realization hit. A drive-by shooting. Police vehicles rounded the corner, sirens wailing. Liz backed up against the red-brick wall as people surged into the building.

Scanning the chaos, she spotted him. Joshua was down. Hunched over, he huddled on the ground. Blood spattered across the dry dirt of the bare lot.

“Joshua!” Shouting his name, she ran to him. “Joshua! Joshua! God, please help us!”

As she fell to her knees, Joshua lifted his head. His blue eyes met hers. Then she saw another figure lying beneath the man. A boy.

“It’s Virtue.” Joshua grabbed her arm. “Get the medics, Liz. Get them now!”

She scrambled to her feet, but the police were

there already. They crowded around Joshua and the child. There was another victim, too. Near the edge of the empty lot, a group of people gathered, shouting at each other, pushing, yelling instructions. Before Liz could drink down a breath, the medical technicians arrived. And then Stephen Rudi began to howl.

Liz turned to the man who stood gazing down in horror at his fallen child. "Stephen? Pastor, I'm here with you."

She wrapped an arm around his shoulders as he covered his face with his hands and cried out. "My boy! My son!"

Her own tears spilling, Liz embraced the man. "Dear Lord," she prayed. "Please help us now. Save Virtue. Preserve this child's life."

"Where are you, my God!" Stephen raised his face and hands, shouting to the sky. "My God, my God—why have You forsaken me?"

"Baba?" It was Charity. Trembling, she clutched at her father's fingers.

Liz bent and scooped the weeping child into her arms. "Hold on to me, Charity. I'll keep you safe."

Reaching for her father, the girl babbled in her native tongue for a moment. Then she seemed to remember where she was. She put both hands on Liz's face to draw her attention.

"What happened to Virtue?" she demanded. Sobs tangled her words. "Why is my brother on the ground?"

“The doctors are helping him. They’re taking good care of him.”

“Did he get hurt?”

“Yes, but maybe not too much. I hope not.”

“Why is my father shouting? Why are you crying? I’m afraid!”

“Put your arms around my neck, sweetheart. Can you feel how tightly I’m holding you? Don’t be scared, Charity.”

“I want my mama!” She began to wail. “I want my mama! Mamaaaa!”

Liz swung around, searching for Mary. The woman was no longer by the door. The police moved about in the street, cordoning off the area in front of Haven. Several were talking to witnesses. But Mary? Had she bolted inside right after the shooting? Did she even know what had happened to her stepson?

“Let’s go find Mary,” Liz whispered to Charity. “She can make some tea for you and your father.”

“No! No, I want my mamaaaa!”

A stretcher lay near the spot where Virtue had fallen. Now the EMTs lifted the little boy onto it. Someone carried an IV drip overhead. In a quick, synchronized motion, they headed toward the open ambulance door.

Stephen danced alongside the stretcher, calling out, trying to reach between the medics to touch his son. Someone moved to him and caught his shoulders. Terell Roberts. The taller man drew Stephen aside.

Joshua remained on the ground where Virtue had fallen. Now Liz realized that a couple of medics were working on him. Heart in her throat, she set Charity down, took the girl's hand and hurried toward the cluster of men.

"Joshua?" She saw they were dabbing at blood on his arm. "Joshua, are you hurt?"

He looked up, his face ashen. "Go with the ambulance, Liz. Take Stephen. Make sure that boy lives!"

"What about you?"

"Those bullets were meant for me. One grazed my arm, but it's nothing." He swallowed as a medic began to blot his forearm. "It's the kid who was shot. Virtue. Someone else, too. Maybe one of my boys. From here it looks like Raydell. Duke's running around loose. I've got to get to that kid before they take him away. Liz, call me from the hospital."

"I'm not leaving you, Joshua. Don't ask me to leave your side."

"Do this for me. Please, Liz, go with the boy."

On an impulse, she knelt and kissed him. Then, taking Charity's hand again, Liz hurried away to follow a little Pagandan boy whose five years of life had known far too much tragedy.

Chapter Fourteen

"Are you following the violence?" Daniel Ransom asked Joshua. "Or is it following you?"

"What are you implying, Sergeant?" Joshua fixed his focus on Ransom. The two men stood just inside the hospital's emergency room door. Far enough from the other visitors for a private conversation. Or a confrontation.

"Since you arrived in St. Louis, I've responded to two emergency calls at Haven," Ransom said. "At both, you were the man closest to a bleeding victim."

Joshua bristled. "I resent the implication in that statement, Sergeant. In my military service I was often obliged to step into a conflict. But I don't cause problems. I solve them."

"Truce, Duff. I'm ex-army myself." Ransom's squared shoulders sagged as he let out a breath. "This gang situation is getting out of hand, and my men are outnumbered. The Hypes have introduced a new set of variables into the equation, and frankly the department is on the defensive."

"And I'm trying to help my friends defend Haven against Mo Ded. We're on the same side."

"I know that. You've given me the car's make and model. We got a good description of the driver and the backseat shooter. The gun wasn't much—a small-caliber weapon. Ballistics is studying the casings we took off the street. Did you notice anything else? Anyone on the scene? A clue as to why this action on this day?"

Joshua held his tongue for a moment as he assessed the situation. In the waiting room, Liz Wallace was seated with Stephen and Mary Rudi. Thumb in her mouth, little Charity had curled onto Liz's lap. Sam was pacing, waiting for his fiancée to arrive. Terell had stayed at Haven to clear the construction site and shut the place down for the rest of the day.

Virtue had not yet come out of surgery. A doctor had stepped out to report that a single bullet had entered and exited the boy's abdomen. Bleeding was controlled and vital signs were stable. No broken bones. But only the exploratory surgery would reveal the extent of Virtue's injuries.

Like Joshua, whose disinfected and sutured forearm throbbed, Raydell Watson now bore a mark of combat. A single round had slammed through his left hand, shattering a bone. Joshua knew the injury would garner the youth a generous dose of the admiration and respect he craved. Sporting a bright white cast, he had gone home.

"I can give you information," Joshua told the police sergeant. "You want the obvious? Or the theory?"

Ransom's eyebrows rose. "Let's start with the obvious. This was a Hype move. A reaction to Haven's expansion plans. What else?"

"When the spare lot began to fill with Haven's workers, Mo Ded stationed twelve men across the street. They came out three at a time, talking on their phones, taking orders from their shotcaller. Moments before the drive-by, two Crips entered the set. Not sure how they fit. Four of my people stood guard. Not enough. My fault. I hadn't anticipated that level of force."

"You think Mo Ded was onto you?"

"He knew everything. Mo Ded had the time of the work party, the number of guards we put out, the extent of our preparation. Within minutes, his men were taking up their positions. When the two Crips walked into the picture, it threw my boys off their game. They're barely trained, and the sight of both gangs moving into Haven territory spooked them. The minute we lost our concentration, Mo Ded initiated the attack."

"The drive-by car. You're saying he's that savvy?"

"Mo Ded is a smart guy. But someone at Haven is tipping him off. I don't know if we've got a snitch or if it's innocent stuff the kids have let drift out onto the streets. There was no way to keep my work a secret."

"You actually trained some of Haven's boys?"

Joshua had to chuckle. "Not sure I'd call it training. We talked about strategy, how to stay alert, what to watch for, methods of defense. A few hours of my time, that's all."

"Mo Ded's people aren't a whole lot better off, or they'd have hit their target."

"Me."

At this acknowledgment, Joshua glanced at Liz. Her brown eyes were locked on him. He had no doubt this event had affected her deeply. Her feelings for him would be impacted. But in what way? He couldn't guess.

"Mo Ded knows I've been sniffing his trail," Joshua admitted. "He may even know a little of my background, my expertise. But he can't have a lot of information."

"I heard he got his hands on your phone."

This news surprised Joshua. "Who told you that?"

"Liz."

The two men assessed each other. Joshua realized Ransom was baiting him. The police officer clearly understood there was some kind of relationship between the refugee worker and the ex-Marine. And he was no more immune to Liz than Joshua.

Ransom wanted it known that he and Liz had talked to each other apart from official settings such as the task force meeting. That Liz had shared private information with him. That if Joshua wasn't very careful with her heart, another man was ready to step in.

"So, you're tracking Mo Ded," Ransom said, returning the conversation to its original focus.

"I'm not surprised Sam and Terell asked you to help. Put your skills to use."

"I've done a little digging. Canvassed the area. Talked to anyone who would open up. The Hypes are not welcome in the hood, so the older folks will tell what they know. It's not much."

"What can you give me?"

"He showed up in St. Louis this past spring. Some say he's from Detroit, others Chicago. Cocky. Mouthy. Disrespectful. But he's smart—they all acknowledge that. Right away, he began drawing in the misfits. Anyone who couldn't make it in other gangs heard about the Hypes and found Mo Ded. He welcomes the disabled, the scrawny, the multiracial, the eccentrics, even the nerds. You saw him at Podunk's, right? He's a mixed bag himself. Some Asian, maybe a little black and Hispanic. Definitely a big shot of Caucasian. Green eyes, light brown skin, pock-marks. Weird hair and bad teeth."

"Don't forget the smell." Liz stepped up to the entry area where the two men had been talking. Joshua looked over her shoulder to see that Charity had fallen asleep on Stephen Rudi's lap.

Liz shuddered. "I will always remember how bad that guy smelled. Body odor, but something else, too."

"Meth," Ransom said. He glanced at Joshua. "But I guess you know."

Joshua didn't know. "Meth smells like cat urine?"

"Or worse. Mo Ded isn't just dealing the stuff. He's cooking it. But we don't know where he set up his kitchen. Could be a traveling lab—all the equipment will fit in the trunk of a car."

"If he's cooking, is he using?"

"His bad teeth would suggest that. But if he is, he's dumber than we give him credit for. Ice cooks who use don't last very long."

"That guy gave me the creeps." Liz edged closer to Joshua as she spoke.

At the gesture, gratitude and relief flooded his chest. He slipped his arm around her shoulders.

"So, Mo Ded is cooking and selling methamphetamine," Joshua recapped as he drew Liz against him. "He has assembled a motley crew. Done a little training. Armed his boys with peashooters. And now he's determined to rule St. Louis? Seems far-fetched."

"We thought so, too." Ransom paused, studying the surroundings for a moment before he spoke again. He lowered his voice. "Over the weekend, my men brought in some disturbing information. We'd been hearing rumors that the Hypes may be facilitating the movement of heavier arms. Serious firepower. Now there's talk that Mo Ded has his hands on a Claymore."

"In St. Louis?" Joshua could hardly credit this possibility.

"What's a Claymore?" Liz asked.

"A directional antipersonnel mine," Joshua

explained. "It was originally a U.S. military weapon, but other countries have them now. In Afghanistan, we saw Soviet versions. A Claymore is a rectangular device in an olive-green plastic case. Looks like an oversize camera—even has a sight window. Comes with short scissor legs, kind of like a tripod. It can be detonated by a signal from a distance or by trip wire. There's also a time-delayed mode. Fires shrapnel—seven hundred steel balls—across a sixty-degree horizontal arc. Up to a hundred feet for maximum casualties."

Her brow furrowed at the image. "Why would anyone want to do that?"

"In wartime," Joshua said, "a Claymore is an anti-infiltration device against enemy infantry. It can be pretty successful against soft-skinned vehicles, too."

He studied the police officer. Ransom's expression told him the seriousness of this situation.

"But the truth is," Joshua told Liz, "the Claymore mine is used primarily for ambush."

"Ambush? Who would the Hypes want to . . ." Her words drifted off as she, too, focused on the policeman.

"A Claymore is especially effective," Joshua added, "because it can be directionally sighted to provide fragmentation over a specific area."

Ransom made a sound of disgust deep in his throat. "In layman's terms, there's a peephole in the thing. You can set it up, angle it just the way you want and detonate it from a distance. You don't have to rely on your enemy to stumble across it by chance."

"If the opposition comes within range of the Claymore," Joshua continued, "all you do is trigger it. I'm not crazy about that mine, though. The thing is unstable. The electrical firing device isn't safe. Premature detonation has been a big problem. We didn't like to use them."

"Evidently Mo Ded disagrees." Ransom hooked his hands in his pockets and gazed through the emergency room doors into the night. "If it's true . . . if he's got a Claymore mine . . . if he intends to use it for himself rather than selling it . . . then we've got serious trouble."

Joshua knew the officer was right. Without much difficulty, Mo Ded could set up a disturbance to draw police into an ambush, and then inflict major casualties. "Do you think your source is reliable?" he asked.

"Hard to say. Either way, it's bad. Trouble is, we don't have the manpower to focus all our attention on the Hypes. You were both at the task force meeting. My people are doing all we can to combat gang activity. Not just us—the city, schools, parents, churches. But how do you go up against a Claymore?"

Joshua bent his head, thinking. "I'm not confident you've got your information right, Sergeant.

A Claymore won't be floating around for sale just anywhere. You can't pick one up at an army surplus store. Mo Ded would need major connections to get his hands on that kind of firepower. Not to mention a boatload of cash."

"He's got cash."

"You told me meth was a white man's drug. How can Mo Ded be moving that much of the stuff in downtown St. Louis? I've had my eyes open since I got here. I don't see a lot of Caucasians hanging around on street corners doing drug deals with guys in purple do-rags."

"He's taking it out of the area into places where he can maximize sales. But the city is a great location for him. Mo Ded uses his gangbangers to buy one of the main ingredients—the decongestant chemical in cold medications. Missouri has strict controls on the sale of that stuff now. Most of it stays behind the counter at pharmacies. But Mo Ded has a whole army of innocent-looking, bony misfits—some of them girls—that he can send around the city to do his buying. No pharmacist would suspect a kid like that to be packing a gun or communicating with his shotcaller by Bluetooth. But it's becoming a major operation."

Joshua studied the police sergeant. The man's uncomfortable focus on the darkness outside the emergency room door told him there was more to this story. Something Ransom had not yet disclosed.

If the cops needed to keep certain aspects of their investigation a secret, he could understand. But if they wanted his help, they would have to trust him.

"This cash Mo Ded's got his hands on—it's not just coming from the sale of meth. He has another source, right? There's something else going down here." He saw Ransom's eyes widen slightly. "You planning to let me in on that?"

Ransom glanced at Liz, then looked at Joshua again. "I hear you're leaving town in a couple of days."

"I'll be here till Saturday."

"So, you're not much good to me, are you, Duff? I've told you my men are up to our ears in this gang business. Even with all the civic groups pulling together on the task force, we need help. Expertise. With your training and experience, you might turn the corner for us. I believe we could even bring Mo Ded down."

"But not if I'm in West Texas. I hear you, Ransom."

The officer blew out a breath as he shook his head. "Look at you, man. Standing there. You know exactly how to crack a terrorist cell, don't you? You know how to ask the right questions, be in the right places, hunt down the right people. You've got everything we need locked up inside your brain. You've got the physical fitness to do the job. And you've got the best woman around standing by your side. But you're planning to fly off to Texas—and let my men walk right into the fragmentation zone of a Claymore mine."

With a contemptuous grunt, Ransom nodded to Liz and walked through the sliding-glass doors of the emergency room. Joshua started after him, but a commotion in the visitors' area drew his attention.

A doctor had stepped into the room. Stephen Rudi leaped to his feet. Charity woke with a cry as her father hefted her against his chest. Liz pulled away from Joshua's side. He followed.

"The surgery went well, Mr. Rudi," the physician was saying. "Your son is still in critical condition, but he's stable. We have him in recovery right now. When he can be moved, we'll transfer him to the ICU. Then you'll be able to see him."

"What is this man telling me?" Stephen asked, grabbing Liz's arm. "Is my son going to live? Will he recover? What is he telling me?"

"Virtue will be all right," she assured him. "Your son will live."

"Praise be to God! My family is—" Stephen swung around. "Where is Mary? Where has my wife gone?"

"Maybe she's in the bathroom. I'll check." Liz took his hand. "Pastor Stephen, you must wait a little while before you can see Virtue. He's resting now after the surgery."

"But what of his health?" He turned to the

doctor. "Will my son walk again? Can he eat and play and go to school just as before?"

"It's going to take a few weeks. But yes, your son should make a complete recovery. Mr. Rudi, if you don't mind—may I ask where you're from?"

"My home was in Paganda."

"I visited Paganda last year." The doctor's face broke into a smile. "Some fellow physicians and I went on a mission trip to a town near Lake Victoria. We worked in a clinic for three weeks."

Joshua watched as Stephen's face softened. The panic in his eyes vanished, and he took the doctor's hand. "Then you know my people," he said. "You understand my country. Come, sir, can you sit here with me and tell me what you saw in Paganda? I lived in a refugee camp in Kenya before I came to St. Louis, and I have not been to Paganda for many years. What news do you have of my homeland?"

The doctor looked at the others in the room for a moment. Then he smiled. "Sure, I'd love to talk to you for a few minutes. Going to Africa was the best experience of my medical career."

Joshua looked at Liz and knew she would be eager to join in the conversation. Her short trip to Congo had altered the course of her life. Now she had found a kindred spirit.

Pastor Rudi sat down and nestled Charity's head in the crook of his neck. The doctor settled into one of the soft chairs, leaned forward and began to talk to the African. As he did, Liz took Joshua's hand and drew him away.

"Mary left," she murmured. They found a shadowed corner of the waiting room. Obviously exhausted, Liz leaned against the wall. "She told Stephen she was going to the bathroom, and maybe she's still in there. But I have a bad feeling she fled the hospital. Why wouldn't she stay with her husband, Joshua? Why didn't she want to look after Charity? This is a terrible time for them, and she just vanished."

"The woman is traumatized. You can see it in her eyes. She lives in some kind of a zone. As much as I hate to admit it, I understand where Mary is coming from. The things you feel when you witness violence firsthand . . . when you're part of it . . . you don't recover easily. Some of us learn to cope. I'm getting better every day. I can feel the changes in myself, and I have a lot of hope. But Mary Rudi? Liz, she may never get past the things that happened to her over there."

"But she needs to at least *try* to get help. We have resources. I've offered to make her an appointment with one of the counselors who volunteers at Refugee Hope. If Mary doesn't make some effort to heal, her life here in America isn't going to be successful. I'm very concerned about the family. Especially her relationship with the children."

"I'm concerned about that and a lot more." He

shoved his hands into his back pockets and studied his feet. "There's something I need to do, Liz, and I don't know how to go about it."

"You have to talk to him in person," she said.

He lifted his head in surprise. "Who?"

"Your dad. Go home to Texas. Tell your parents about the situation here. And then come back, Joshua. Please come back."

Though it was a public place, the corner was dark and he took her into his arms. "I don't know how this happened, Liz. Everything is out of my control right now. I dropped in on St. Louis to touch base with an old buddy and then head back home to my new life. Instead I'm training a ragtag little army to protect Haven. I've been involved in two street conflicts. I even got shot—my first bullet wound after a military career spent in two war zones—and it happened in a gang drive-by. The police say they need me. Haven needs me. And worst of all . . . I need you."

"Those all sound like bad things," she said, looking up at him. "Even me."

"Not bad, just unexpected." He laid his cheek against her head, enjoying the soft brush of her curls on his skin. "You, Liz. You're the biggest surprise. And the best."

Her arms tightened around his back. "Oh, Joshua, when I saw you this afternoon . . ." Her voice caught. "You were down on the ground, and there was blood, and I thought . . ."

"Maybe now you understand how I feel about your plan to spend the rest of your life in a refugee camp in Africa. When you care about someone—" he kissed her cheek "—when you feel about someone the way I feel about you, Liz Wallace, you can't stand the thought that anyone might hurt them."

"That sentiment ought to make me want to pack you off to your family's office building in Amarillo."

"But it doesn't?" He stepped back and studied her eyes.

"I want you here, Joshua. In St. Louis. With Haven and the kids and the police. And with me."

Captured by her words, he pulled her against him and kissed her hard, unable to hold back the tide. He had never wanted a woman this way. Never desired anyone to such great depth.

Her hands slid up his back, molding to the muscle and keeping him close. Her lips met his again . . . and then again. She kissed his cheek, his ear, his mouth.

"Joshua, I know what I ask is wrong," she breathed. "Your parents love you so much. Their dreams for your life, their hopes and plans, those all supersede any request I could ever make. If I really cared about you in the right way, I would encourage you to go home and follow the path they've laid out. That would be the noble thing for me to do. You'd be happier. You'd certainly be safer. But I can't. I'm too selfish."

"What about me? You think I can stand here and encourage you to fly off to Africa?" He dipped his fingers into her curls and lifted them from her shoulder. "I see your heart, Liz. I read your face. You'd like to be sitting over there right now with Stephen Rudi and the doctor, talking about Paganda. Just the mention of Africa lights up your eyes. You told me God called you there. *God!* And I have the audacity to ask you not to go? But I am asking. I'm begging. As much as you want me to disobey my parents, I want you to disobey God. It's wrong—dead wrong. But I'm selfish, too."

At that, they came together again, holding each other, unable to speak.

So aware of the sweet curves of her body, so conscious of the stunning beauty in his arms, Joshua ached to do everything in his power to make this woman his own. But years of military training had taught him how to control his passions, to subject his own will to the greater good.

He drew back from her. Dropped his hands. Stepped aside.

"I need to go find Ransom," he told her. "There's more to his story. And Mo Ded. I'm going to hunt that guy down. I've only got three days before my flight, but I'll do everything in my power to break his hold on the streets of this city. I will go back to Texas, Liz. I made a promise, and I never break a vow. You're right in what you said. I need to talk to my father. My parents have waited a long time for me. They want my presence, my skills, my education and training . . . they want—and deserve—a say in my future."

"So, I'll just be here," she said with a shrug. "Studying Swahili and searching for messages in my scrapbook in the middle of the night."

Fighting the urge to take her in his arms again, Joshua turned away. The path across the waiting room, past Stephen Rudi and his sleeping daughter, out into the hospital parking lot and all the way to his car, was the longest journey of his entire life.

Chapter Fifteen

"Mary?" The name echoed through the ceramic-tiled hospital restroom. "Mary Rudi? Are you in here?"

Liz bent over and looked under the stalls. All empty. As she straightened, she caught her reflection in the mirror over the row of sinks. Pink-stained, her cheeks gave evidence of the flush of emotion coursing through her. Desire, joy, exuberant passion in Joshua's arms. Terror and shock at the shooting outside Haven. Deep sorrow over the prospect of losing so much she had come to love.

Stepping to the mirror, Liz wiped a smudge of mascara from under her eye. Her curls were a little mussed where Joshua had crushed them as he held her so tightly. Her lips were swollen from his kisses.

Did she love Joshua? Was it possible to love a man so fervently in such a short time? Reason cautioned her. This couldn't be much more than a physical attraction. A crazy magnetism born during the moments of excitement and danger they had experienced together.

Did she really know Joshua Duff? Did he know her?

She tugged a length of paper towel from the dispenser, wetted it and pressed it against her cheeks. Joshua claimed to want her, even need her. She could hardly imagine her life without him. But when the time came to make a decision about loyalties, neither was willing to commit.

Joshua would go home to Texas. And she would go to Africa—just as they had planned long ago.

She had to accept that he was concerned about Haven and his friends. That he cared deeply about her. But that he would never return to live in St. Louis.

Why would he? His family needed him and expected his loyalty. He had promised to do his duty by them, and his feelings for Liz wouldn't keep him from that. Of course it wouldn't, because she had not given Joshua a single shred of commitment. When he mentioned her plan to go to Africa, she said nothing. For all he knew, she really would spend the rest of her life on that continent.

Her call, Liz admitted as she studied her reflection in the mirror, had not died away the moment she laid eyes on Joshua Duff. Or felt his arms around her. Or heard his words of desire. Nothing, in fact, had silenced the constant whisper in her heart.

It was this call that took her back out of the restroom and into the visitors' area to the row of chairs where Stephen Rudi sat. Charity lay on a sofa now, her eyes shut as she found escape through sleep. The doctor had gone away, no doubt to tend to yet another of the emergencies sent by the streets of St. Louis through those doors each night.

"I can't find Mary," Liz gently told the pastor as she took a seat near him. "She wasn't in the restroom."

He nodded. His dark eyes were tired, bloodshot, lifeless. "I can only pray for my wife now," he said in a low voice. "She will not be helped except by God."

"I'm sorry, Stephen."

"You are sorry?" He looked across at her.

"For your suffering. I'm sorry that this terrible thing happened to your son. That your wife is struggling to adjust. That you came all the way to America only to find that life here can also be very difficult."

The corners of his mouth drew downward as he nodded again. "I did not expect this. None of these bad things were revealed to us in that film we saw in our orientation class in the camp. We saw American people eating from a table covered with food—large chickens and potatoes and bread and yellow maize. We saw shops full of things to buy on shelves that stood from the floor to the ceiling. We saw yellow school buses and children sitting at desks in rooms with big windows. Each child had a book and a pencil and clean paper. We saw houses and gardens and nice cars and American flags waving everywhere. But this country is very different from that film."

"There are places like you describe, Stephen. America is a land of plenty. But this nation also has problems. There are poor people here. Some lack education and good jobs, and they live in slums or other areas where there's violence. I'm sorry that refugees arrive in America at the lowest level, not at the top where life is easier. Without knowing our language and culture, without work and transportation, people have a hard time rising above that low level. It's hard even for many of those who were born into it right here in America."

"Yes, this is what I understand now." He rubbed his eyes. "I understand much more than I did. You know I am a pastor, and I have been educated about the Bible. I read it every day. I also pray very much. In Paganda and in the refugee camp in Kenya, I preached the word of the Lord—words of hope and salvation and new life. Now, I sit in this hospital, and I cannot pray."

"Why not?"

He gave a low laugh. "If I pray, how will my words reach God? Where is He? What is He doing? At this moment, I wonder who is more powerful—God or His enemy?"

Bending over, he rested his elbows on his knees and rubbed his hands across his eyes. His voice was filled with anguish. "My beautiful wife and my sweet children were chopped to pieces in Paganda! They died a terrible death. My two remaining children and I struggled to survive in that refugee camp, eating rations from the relief agency and drinking water from a dirty river. Now, here in America, my only son has been shot with a gun, and my second wife is so frightened that she runs away from even me, from her own husband. I look at that child lying there—my little daughter—and I wonder what kind of a future I can give her. It is difficult . . . very difficult . . . for me to see God now."

Liz laid her hand on the pastor's shoulder. "I don't have easy answers for your questions, Stephen. I wish I did."

He sat in silence, staring blankly at the floor. "In the end, there is only faith. That is all I have. That is the only answer for my questions."

"Faith?"

" '*The assurance of things hoped for.*' " He sat

up, his dark eyes focusing on her. "If I have faith I can be certain that God loves me, that He is powerful, that He has a very good plan for me, Stephen Rudi . . . oh, those are hard things to accept at such a time. But do you know? Do you know what I have discovered whilst sitting here at this hospital tonight? I can do it. I can believe in God. I do believe in Him."

Liz swallowed. "How, Pastor Stephen? How do you have such faith?"

"Because I choose to have it." He said the words simply. Then he shook his head. "When I was a young boy, I did not have any understanding of God. I was not good in those days. I did many bad things. But then someone told me about Jesus and His love. It was my employer at a job I hated. He said that Jesus had carried my sins on His own back all the way to death. And that is when I began to choose faith. If God would do this great and terrible thing for me—letting Himself be killed because of my sins—then I should take any risk for Him."

"So now you're continuing to have faith. And you call it a risk because you choose it, not because you have proof that God loves you?"

"Yes." His dark eyes met hers. "I could stop believing. That would be the easy way. The educated way. Look at my life . . . all these evil things that happen to me and my family year by year . . . Do they prove that God is good? That He loves me?"

Leaning forward, he held up one finger. “Yes, they do! For now—here in this chair in the hospital—I have remembered that God did not promise me a happy life on this earth. He did not say He would show His love by giving me a nice table with a big chicken and yellow maize, or by putting me into a fine house with a garden. Or even by making my family safe.”

Liz studied her hands. With every fiber of her being, she longed to contradict the pastor. She wanted to talk about God’s constant protection from harm and the earthly abundance that rewarded true faith—all those lofty promises.

But she had walked in Africa. She had seen great pain, hunger, disease, poverty, need. She knew that the finest and most faithful of Christians often suffered more than anyone.

“The bad things that have happened to me,” Stephen went on, “are teaching me that I must trust God more. I must be willing to give everything to Him. Even . . . even my wife and my children . . . even my only son. My Virtue.”

As he said the name, Stephen bent over again and covered his face with his hands. Liz saw his shoulders shaking as he wept, but she knew that nothing she could say or do would change the realities in this man’s life. She couldn’t bring back the village on the shores of Lake Victoria and the family he had loved there. She couldn’t heal Mary’s scars, or erase Charity’s memories of the steel water drum, or save Virtue from violence.

This was the same reality she faced every sleepless night as she stared at her photographs. If she went to Africa and worked her whole life in a refugee camp, what difference could she truly make?

"God has a strong plan for me now." Pastor Stephen sat up and rubbed his eyes. "This is what I have seen, this task. Do you know—one night when I first came to St. Louis, I was talking to Joshua Duff about Paganda. I told him about the old days when the men of my tribe were warriors. I said I did not become a warrior, because the British changed our tribal system when they ruled Paganda. But I made a challenge to Joshua. I told him that he is a warrior, and he must use his courage and skill to protect the innocent people in this city. Now I understand that I, too, must become a warrior."

Dread prickled the back of Liz's neck. "What do you mean, Stephen? You can't seek revenge on the men who shot your son."

"Revenge?" He scowled at her. "Revenge is for cowards. No, God has chosen to shape me into a man like those brave warriors of the Bible. You remember the ones I am telling you about? Daniel was put into a pit of lions. Jeremiah was put into a pit of mud. Deep pits! Paul was whipped and locked in prison. And Stephen? The man whose great name I took when I became a Christian and received my baptism? Do you remember what happened to him?"

"Stephen was stoned to death," Liz said softly. "But what are you saying? God doesn't expect every Christian to die for the faith."

"To be *willing* to die!" Now his eyes flamed. "I have been brought to this city to preach the Gospel of Jesus Christ! I shall do that! I can now see how it must be for me . . ."

As he continued to speak, Liz heard her phone ring. Holding up a hand to silence the man, she dug in her purse until she found it. The ID showed the caller—Joshua Duff.

"Joshua," she murmured. She stood and stepped away from Stephen. "Are you all right?"

"Yeah, how are you?"

She let out a breath. "I'm fine—at least I think I am. Pastor Stephen is . . . I don't know whether he's losing his mind or making perfect sense. He's agitated. He's pacing the room right now—telling a nurse about his plan to preach the Gospel to St. Louis. The man has had so much trauma. I'm afraid he's coming unglued."

"You can tell him I found his wife. She's okay."

Liz turned away so Pastor Stephen couldn't hear as she spoke to Joshua. "Where is Mary?"

"Here at Haven. I found her in the room. She was pretty nervous when I went in, but I got her calmed down enough to talk. She speaks English better than we knew. I realized she was understanding me, so I used a few subtle techniques to get her talking."

"How did it go?"

"Not good. She's unhappy about everything."

"Because you still haven't been able to find her brother?"

"She didn't even mention the brother. It's like she forgot all about him in her frustration with this situation she's in. As near as I can tell, she hates her job, America, the city, even the new apartment I found for the family. Liz, I need your help. You've got to try to talk to Mary. Can you swing by here on your way home tonight? This is really important."

"What's going on?"

"It's Stephen," he said. "Mary is planning to leave him."

Joshua opened Haven's door to let Liz inside. She brushed past him, trying not to make contact.

It was a wasted effort. He took her in his arms, kissed her gently, held her close. The cavernous room around them was dark and silent.

"Thank you for coming," he murmured. "How's Virtue?"

"They moved him into the ICU. Stephen and Charity were with him when I left. The doctor gave us a little more information. There was a lot of bleeding. Virtue is weak. The doctor told us it was touch and go for a while in the OR. But he said they expect Virtue to make a complete recovery."

Joshua tilted her chin. "What about you? Are you all right?"

"Tired. It's been a long day. My nerves are jangling. Where is Mary?"

"Upstairs. Their room. Terell and Sam have both tried talking to her. Sam's fiancée was here for a while. Ana made a stab at it, too—but nothing. Mary won't look at anyone, won't do more than mumble a few words. It's PTSD. I can see it in her demeanor, Liz. Somehow I need to convince her that she can't just surrender. She has to keep living, keep moving and breathing and trying one day at a time."

Liz couldn't resist running her fingertips across the stubble on his jaw. "Are you talking about Mary—or yourself?"

"It's a journey we're both making. I want to get well, Liz. I have a lot of good reasons to heal. But Mary seems to have given up."

Hands entwined, they crossed the room and started up the stairs.

"You can't force this woman to embrace life, Joshua," she told him. "Do you know the terrible things . . . the atrocities that happened in Paganda during the last conflict? Hundreds of thousands of women and children were raped. Babies as young as ten months were ravaged by warring soldiers. I read the accounts. Physicians reported having to do surgical repairs because of rape that involved sticks, guns, even molten plastic. The doctor tonight at the hospital—he mentioned it, too. He started to tell about some of the things he had seen, and then he noticed Stephen's face."

Joshua groaned. "Oh, Liz. Stephen did open up a bit about what Mary endured."

She nodded. "None of us—even Stephen—knows exactly what Mary went through before she made it to that camp in Kenya. When I got the job at Refugee Hope, the head of my department asked me to read documents about the atrocities so I would have some idea of what goes on. So many of the refugees we bring in from all around the world have suffered these horrors—yet we fly them here and expect them to waltz right in and become perfectly happy, law-abiding American citizens."

Wrapping one arm around her shoulders, Joshua paused in the stairwell. "I wish I could erase those images from your mind, Liz. You're too good, too innocent to even know about stuff like that."

"The women and children in these countries are no different from me, Joshua." She began climbing again. "They were just as innocent before whatever conflict tore their nation apart. In Paganda, little boys like Virtue were captured by warlords or rebel leaders. Forced to walk for weeks on end. Beaten and tortured and then handed guns and trained to become soldiers."

"Stop, Liz." He pulled her against him again. "Stop talking about it. You'll make it seem real."

"It *is* real. It's the kind of terror that Stephen and his children saw and heard about every day. Yet somehow . . . somehow Stephen still believes in God. He still sees God's hand in his life."

She gave a dry laugh. "I can't believe how determined he is to preach here in St. Louis. Tonight, he told me of his plans to start a church. His son is lying there with a bullet wound, and Stephen is talking about hopes to teach the Bible in the homes of the children who come to Haven. He's on a mission—on behalf of a God who let his wife get hacked to death . . . *chopped* is what Stephen said . . . *my wife was chopped to pieces.*"

Crying now, she sagged against Joshua. He held her, and as her tears slowed, she heard his heart beating and felt the rise and fall of his chest as he breathed. This man was a soldier, too. Had he done things like that? Terrible, wrong, sinful things? Members of the American military had been implicated in torture, rape and even the murder of innocents.

With a shudder, she pulled away and climbed the last few steps to the second floor. As she walked down the darkened hall, she could feel Joshua's presence beside her, huge and looming. He might have done anything in the past ten years of his life in Iraq and Afghanistan, she realized.

He admitted that certain events had traumatized

him. Maybe some of those events involved acts that he himself had committed. Liz had witnessed his anger, his swift and combustive reactions, the confusion and pain that had scarred his mind.

As she stood before the room where the Rudi family had been staying, Joshua's arm came around her, his hand knotted into a fist as he knocked on the door. When no one answered, he turned the knob and pushed open the door. The room was empty.

He stifled a guttural curse. "She was just here." He stepped inside, switched on a lamp, looked around. "I don't believe this woman."

Liz moved past him toward the beds. "Her things are still here. She'll be back. Maybe you scared her."

"Me? I didn't do anything to her." He leaned out the open window and studied the steel fire escape. "I play no part in this."

"You said you manipulated Mary into talking."

"It's a technique." He turned on her. "Wait—are you accusing me of something? Because I don't like what I'm hearing in your voice."

Liz pushed her fingers back through her hair. It was after midnight, she was exhausted and she hardly knew how to explain the tumult of emotions roiling inside her.

"It's just that you put a lot of pressure on people sometimes, Joshua. You're intense, and everything you do is *strong*. You storm through life in a forceful way, like you're on a mission. That's not always good. Sometimes it can be overwhelming."

"Look, I didn't touch Mary Rudi, if that's what you're getting at. I did nothing but talk to the woman." He was at the closet now, picking through her few shabby dresses. "I'm trained to watch people, to study their body language. When I talked to Mary earlier this evening, I could see she was understanding me. She was responding. So I knew she had a little English, and I moved in on that."

"Moved in on it?"

He swung around. "It's an expression. What are you implying with these questions, Liz? I didn't do anything wrong. I need to find out why she keeps running away. She bails out on her job, her family, even an injured stepson. I'm leaving this town in three days, and I have to make sure the woman is functioning. She has to move into the apartment I've rented, she has to keep going to her job and she has to at least try to act like a wife and parent."

"Joshua, maybe she can't do all those things right now."

"Yes, she can. She will." He took a faded cotton dress off its hanger and stuck his hands down in the pockets. "Mary made some deals in this life, just like everyone else. It's her responsibility to follow through on those promises. When she married Stephen Rudi, she accepted a role. She agreed to play a part. That agreement is important to him and those kids. People make bargains, Liz. We all do. Life is all about give and take, and Mary Rudi is not playing by the rules."

Liz crossed to the closet and stepped in front of Joshua. "Stop messing with Mary's clothes. You're digging around in her private possessions. You can't do that."

"I can do whatever I want. I'm in charge here, and she's a deserter."

"Joshua, this is not the Marine Corps." She was surprised at the heat in her voice. The weight of the day had crashed in on her, and she was angry. "Mary hasn't gone AWOL, and you don't have the right to treat her like a disobedient recruit. You're not *in charge*. No one is—not even a refugee agency. You agreed to help the Rudis, but that doesn't mean you can pry."

"Pry?" He threw up his hands. "I'm looking for clues here. The woman has had a rough life, granted. But she struck a deal with Stephen, and she owes him the courtesy of sticking around and trying to cope."

He reached over Liz's shoulder and lifted another hanger from the rod. As he spoke, he held the dress to the light, studying it. "Mary's got more going for her than she lets on. The woman isn't stupid. She can understand English. Even with PTSD, she got herself to that refugee camp and found a man to marry her and take her to America. She's a survivor. She's a manipulator, too. I don't like being manipulated."

"Stop this, Joshua." Liz snatched the dress from his hands. "What are you looking for? What do you think you're going to find in Mary's pathetic little dresses? You're acting like she's some kind of criminal for bolting. Put yourself in her shoes."

"I'm not in her shoes, Liz. I'm in mine. I have a job to do, and she's messing it up. I don't like that. She bothers me."

"Bothers you? Oh, get real. The woman is barely visible. She hides in the shadows. She never opens her mouth. She might as well not exist."

"Except that she does exist. By hiding or running away all the time, she's making her presence felt in a big way. She might as well be screaming at me."

"What is she screaming, Joshua? What is that terrified little woman saying to upset you so much?"

He took the dress from her and hung it back on the rod. "She's shouting at me. That's all I know how to tell you. Her actions are shouting messages that I can't decode right now. But I'm going to understand Mary Rudi. I'm going to find out what she's saying, and I'm going to talk back to her in her own language until we have an agreement between the two of us."

"Is this some kind of PTSD language? Because you're making no sense to me." She wrapped her arms around herself. "You're scaring me."

He focused on her, his blue eyes blazing. And then the air went out of him. His shoulders sagged. He turned away.

"Never mind," he muttered.

"Joshua, what's going on?" Liz touched his arm. "Why are we yelling at each other?"

"I don't know." He rubbed the back of his neck. "I feel a little bit off right now, Liz. A long day. Working with Raydell and the other guys. Hypes and Crips across the street. Gunfire. Virtue bleeding on the pavement beside me. The smell of the hospital. Mary vanishing twice. A lot of triggers, I guess."

"We're both tired."

"Yeah, but I scare you. I'm too intense." He absently pulled open a drawer in the table beside the Rudis' bed. "What was it you said about me? I put pressure on people. I storm through life. I overwhelm you."

"Don't be so hard on yourself, Joshua. Maybe your own PTSD is making you act this way toward Mary. And toward me."

He straightened. "I'm no good for you, Liz. You're right—I'm intense. I always was, and I always will be. This is who I am, a guy who studies people and hunts them down and looks for clues to break everything apart and try to understand. I'm relentless, okay? I want the things I want. I can't help that."

"What are these things you really want, Joshua?"

"Right now I want to break up the Hypes and put Mo Ded someplace where the sun never shines. I want Mary Rudi to shape up and quit pulling these vanishing acts on her family. I want Virtue to get better and Charity to sleep well at night. I want both of them to live a good long life without any more problems. And I want *you*. I want you, Liz. I want you in a way that's intense and overwhelming and all the things that scare you. That's just how it is."

With that, he looked down at an envelope he had taken from the drawer.

"This is the letter the Rudis had with them the night they arrived at Haven—the letter from Mary Rudi's brother." He looked up at Liz. "This post-mark . . . The letter was mailed from Atlanta."

A ripple of chills slid down her arms. "Atlanta? But I thought the brother lived in St. Louis."

"Someone in Atlanta mailed this letter to the Rudis not long after they arrived in Atlanta. Someone wanted them to believe that Mary's brother was here in St. Louis. Someone wanted them to leave Atlanta and take that bus ride all the way to St. Louis in search of a man who doesn't live here and an address that never existed."

He jammed the envelope into the back pocket of

his jeans. "Sorry, Liz, but I need to cut out on you right now. I have to go find Mary Rudi. I've got to get to the bottom of this."

She was still standing in the room when she heard his footsteps in the stairwell.

Chapter Sixteen

When Liz looked up from the file on a family soon to arrive from Bhutan, she saw Daniel Ransom standing just outside her cubicle. He was talking to Molly.

Sergeant Ransom was a good man. An honorable man. Exactly the kind of man Molly kept at arm's length in favor of grunge band drummers, street poets, painters, unpublished playwrights and other romantic dreamers who could provide her with neither the strength nor the stability she needed.

Seeing an appreciation for Molly's perky humor and pretty face in Daniel's eyes, Liz felt her heart soften. This was the right kind of man to fall for. Not this police officer in particular, but someone like him. Someone calm, competent and at ease with himself. Certainly not a wigged-out ex-Marine who kept storming in and out of a woman's life and messing up what little serenity she had been able to find.

Since meeting Joshua Duff, Liz felt that everything in her life had gone haywire. She no longer felt secure in her little apartment. The day after the phone call from Mo Ded, she and Mrs. Gonzales had rigged makeshift alarms at their windows—strings of jingle bells that would wake them should anyone try to break in at night. They had the building manager install new locks on their doors. And they programmed their phones to dial each other as well as the police with the press of a couple of keys.

Liz's current life was a wreck, and Joshua had done nothing to help her feel better about the future, either. She was more confused than ever—still spending half the night thumbing through her scrapbook and reading her Bible in search of answers.

As for her heart . . .

"Hope you don't mind a drop-in visitor." Daniel stepped into her cubicle. "Your friend said you were doing some filing. She thought it would be okay for me to talk to you for a minute."

"That's Molly Sims," Liz said, standing. "I'm glad you met her. She's great."

"Nice lady." His eyes softened as they focused on Liz. "So, uh . . . Liz. I was wondering if I could steal you away from this place for an hour or so."

"Me?" She touched her throat in confusion. As his request sank in, her cheeks went hot—and all at once she understood the power of her attachment to Joshua. Daniel Ransom was a good man, certainly handsome, concerned about the community, responsible, stable and every other dependable thing a woman could ask for.

But Liz didn't want him. She wanted Joshua.

"I'd love to get away, but I'm totally swamped," she told the police officer. "I'm preparing for the arrival of a family from—"

"It's the gang task force," he cut in. "After the shooting at Haven yesterday, I decided to call an emergency meeting. This is last-minute, so I can't get everyone together. But I'd really like to have your input, Liz. We need to stay on top of the situation. Especially with some of the reports coming in."

"Reports?"

"A couple of officers from my precinct contacted me this morning. They patrol the area where your agency has relocated refugees. News of the shooting has everyone upset. They believe the little boy was shot on purpose because of his ethnic background. Our country's general hostility toward immigrants is clear to these people—even if they don't speak English that great. They say the police aren't protecting them well enough, and they're being targeted by gangs. Molly confirmed that Refugee Hope had a slew of phone calls this morning—similar complaints."

"She didn't tell me that. I guess she's been as busy as I have." Liz glanced at her file as she stepped around her desk. "When is the meeting, Sergeant?"

“I’m on my way there. Could you follow me?”

Liz hesitated only a moment before picking up her purse. She would need her jacket, too. The morning had brought the first frost of autumn to the city. Her windshield had been covered with a glaze of white lace. Scraping it off had made her late to work.

Liz lifted the receiver on the office phone and pressed Molly’s number. “I’ll be out for an hour or two, Mol. Emergency gang task force meeting.”

“That guy is after you, girlfriend.” Molly’s voice was breathless. “What a hunk! Two men in one month. You have all the luck.”

Turning away, Liz spoke in a low voice. “Why didn’t you mention that we got calls about the shooting?”

“I’ve been buried all morning—schedule problems at the chicken factory where my Burundian women work. Have you ever seen such big brown eyes on a man? You could swim in those chocolate puddles! And that chin—”

“Tell the boss where I’ve gone, Moll. Don’t forget.”

Liz glanced at Daniel and hoped he hadn’t overheard her friend’s exclamations. He was gazing at her from the doorway, his face inscrutable.

“All right,” she told him. “I’ll be right behind you.”

The short drive unraveled the last threads of Liz’s frazzled nerves. All morning she had managed to elude the memories of the previous day.

Now, stalled in noon traffic and staring at the back bumper of a police cruiser, she recalled walking out of the Rudi family's little room alone. She hadn't spoken to Joshua since.

Before she left Haven, Sam and Terell talked to her for a few minutes—confirming what she already knew. They had asked Joshua to stay on in St. Louis as a permanent member of Haven's staff. He had been evasive, they told Liz. His father's expectations, his sense of duty, his obligation to family and heritage—all were pulling him toward Texas.

But there was more. Joshua's friends told Liz they had no doubt he was deeply in love with her. Sam insisted Joshua was a man of total commitment. If he made a statement, it was true. If he gave his word, he kept it. If he set out to do something, he did it.

"He loves you," Sam told her. "Nothing's going to change that. I know him too well."

What about his behavior? she had asked. What about the PTSD? Wasn't that having a major impact on Joshua's outlook—including his feelings for her?

Sam insisted his friend had always been edgy and high-strung. Joshua's experiences in the war had heightened that, had given him moments of confusion and made him a little disoriented. His behavior was not unusual for a soldier recently returned from Iraq or Afghanistan.

And Joshua was adjusting. For the most part, he had control of the reaction triggers. He was focusing now on doing what he could to make a difference at Haven in the short time he had left. Sam told Liz the only wavering he saw in his friend occurred as Joshua tried to decide how to handle the conflict between his commitment to his family and his feelings for her.

Blinking back unexpected tears at the memory, Liz executed a near-disastrous parallel parking maneuver for the benefit of Sergeant Ransom of the St. Louis Police Department. Her car's front right tire rolled up over the curb, then dropped down again before she finally gave up and switched off the engine. The officer was stifling a grin as she stepped onto the sidewalk.

"I should sign you up for driver's training demonstrations," he said. "How *not* to park a car on a city street."

"Okay, write me a ticket. It won't be my first." She brushed past him. "I barely passed that part of the exam ten years ago. I have no doubt I'd fail it now."

"You just need to practice." He chuckled as they walked into the police precinct building. "Looks like we have a bigger crowd than I expected. You might need to grab a chair if you want to sit by your boyfriend."

Liz pulled up sharply at the comment. She didn't like Sergeant Ransom's tone. And for some inexplicable reason, she had not expected to see Joshua at the meeting. He had been at the last one, of course, but she knew he was busy now, hunting Mo Ded and trying to put a stop to the Hypes.

Then she saw Joshua's blue eyes lock on her as she took a seat at the end of the table opposite him. Ransom began the meeting with the police report of the shooting incident. Liz did her best to focus on anything but Joshua Duff. As people spoke up, asking questions and offering comments, she stared at her fingers interlaced on the tabletop.

"The police believe that refugees play only a minor part in this," Ransom said, drawing Liz's attention. "We know they're in the area and they affect the workforce, the schools and, to some degree, the streets. But the police have found no direct link between gang activity and refugees. Would you address that issue, Ms. Wallace?"

Liz realized everyone was waiting for her to respond.

"Refugees can become disenfranchised and vulnerable to problems," she told the group. "If no one helps them adapt to American culture when they arrive—if they have trouble with the language or they can't find housing and jobs—they can become very unhappy. Even angry. Refugees with a Muslim background could drift toward extremist cells. Refugee youth who struggle in school might be attracted to gangs. Local residents may resent the influx of immigrants and treat them badly, which increases the refugees' sense of alienation. My agency, Refugee Hope, works hard to prevent these things from happening."

"Have you seen anything that would lead you to believe the shooting of the Rudi boy was tied to problems like the ones you've mentioned?"

"Absolutely not. I'm convinced Virtue Rudi was shot by accident. It was random gunfire—"

"Not random, Liz." Joshua's voice silenced her. "The Hypes had a definite target yesterday. My name—with an X across it—had been sprayed in purple paint on the wall of Haven. Mo Ded staged the shooting down to the last detail. Virtue was in the line of fire, but that bullet was meant for me."

"I have to agree with you," Ransom said. "That's the talk we're hearing on the street. You've earned quite a reputation in the short time you've been in our city, Sergeant Duff."

"Excuse me, Officer Ransom, but I have a question for this man." A woman Liz recognized as a representative of one of the school groups affiliated with the task force spoke up. "Sergeant Duff, it has come to my attention that in the Marine Corps you were a sniper. Is it true that your job was to stalk the enemy in advance of the front lines—and then kill them?"

Her heart hammering, Liz studied Joshua. How would he respond to this direct query? She saw his Adam's apple rise and fall before he answered.

"Your information is correct, ma'am," he said. "Anticoalition militants in Iraq and Afghanistan are well versed in evasion tactics. The battalion I led was assigned to disrupt terrorist activity. It was my duty to identify and eliminate key enemy personnel."

"Then it's true what they're saying about you," she responded. "You're an assassin."

A buzz of discomfort rose in the room.

"Mrs. Hardy, a Marine sniper is not an assassin." Ransom's deep voice silenced the onlookers. "This country is grateful for the service of men like Joshua Duff. And Haven is fortunate that he's willing to lend a hand there. Sergeant Duff, can you explain to the task force what you've been doing on the streets?"

"Simple stuff, mostly," he responded. "Getting my message to the Hypes."

Though Joshua's voice was steady, Liz could see the gratitude written in his blue eyes. It was good to know these two men would defend each other—not only in person, but in reputation, as well.

"I want the gang to know I'm keeping an eye on their leader," Joshua continued. "Yesterday's incident confirmed that Mo Ded considers me an obstacle in his effort to shut down Haven. Failure to anticipate the level of his response was my error. I should have been more careful. I take full responsibility for the little boy's injury."

“I wouldn’t go that far,” Ransom said. “Our officers patrol these streets, and we’ve learned how hard it is to predict violence. My men risk their lives every day, and the current situation is the most volatile it’s been in years.”

As he continued to speak, Liz saw Joshua’s focus flick toward her. She knew he was recalling the information Ransom had given them the night before in the emergency room.

What greater violence could be lurking for the St. Louis Police Department than a Claymore mine? An ambush could kill a significant number of law enforcement officers. Many would be left injured, perhaps permanently. Such an attack would leave the streets unprotected and vulnerable.

Exactly what Mo Ded wanted.

Mrs. Hardy spoke up again. “And it’s the police who should be dealing with these matters. I, for one, am uncomfortable with sending a sniper out to hunt gang members. This task force should not condone subjecting our citizens to some outsider’s target practice.”

“I know the law, ma’am,” Joshua told her, his blue eyes crackling. “Anything I do is well inside that boundary. As a civilian, I don’t carry a weapon. And as for *target practice*—”

“Actually, Sergeant Duff is exactly the kind of man we do need in St. Louis.” Liz spoke over Joshua. “On his own initiative, he took personal responsibility to resettle a refugee family here. He found jobs for both parents, settled the children into school and located an apartment where they can live. He has also been working closely with the staff at Haven, even training some of the young men who protect the building and the kids who spend time there. Personally, I think this city has benefitted from Sergeant Duff's efforts, and as a task force, we owe him our gratitude."

Amid a smattering of applause, Ransom thanked everyone for attending the impromptu meeting. "Before we close," he said, "I'd like to let everyone know about a report I was handed a few days ago. It has to do with the movement of cash and weapons in the area."

Liz glanced at Joshua. This time, she clearly read the message in his eyes. He was grateful she had joined Daniel Ransom in rising to his defense.

But those deep blue eyes told her much more than that. What she saw was love. Genuine admiration, passion, desire, devotion, commitment were written in the gaze across the expanse of oak table. All those things Sam and Terell had insisted were true the night before shone with such clarity Liz could never mistake them.

Yet Joshua planned to leave on Saturday. And why not? Neither of them had been willing to admit their true feelings. And neither would agree to change the course of their life.

Liz sensed the depth of Joshua's passion for her,

and it frightened her. The thought of trying to recover after he left was enough to cause her to pick up her purse. But as she reached for her jacket, Sergeant Ransom's words caught her attention.

"Platinum," he said. "It's a precious metal—looks like silver to me, but it's more valuable than gold. In my years on the force, I've seen all kinds of currency on the street. Counterfeit bills, diamonds, drugs, prostitutes—you name it, if something has value, people will use it in trade. But this report about platinum changing hands has our people baffled."

"Where's it coming from?" someone asked. "Missouri doesn't mine platinum, do we?"

"Definitely from out of state—probably out of the country. South Africa and Russia are the world's largest producers. We can't figure out who's bringing it in. The stuff is rare and very expensive. What we do know is that it's on the move. Someone has imported a large supply of platinum, and it's gotten wrapped up in gang activity here in St. Louis. The Hypes seem to be playing a role in the movement of the metal, but we can't pinpoint how they're getting their hands on it. We would ask that you keep your ears tuned to any mention of platinum, especially if you can get a sense of who's actually bringing it in."

As he spoke, Liz looked down at her hands. On special occasions, she wore the wedding ring that once belonged to her great-grandmother. At her sixteenth birthday party, her father had slipped the ornate platinum circlet set with three diamonds onto her finger. It had cost a fortune, he told her, but the Wallace family was wealthy in the early days. Through passing generations the affluence had eroded—bad investments, the Depression, a costly divorce. Now all that remained was the ring.

Deciding to study it more closely that evening, Liz stood as Daniel Ransom concluded the meeting. And then Joshua was at her side.

"The Claymore shipment," he said, speaking in a low voice as he took her elbow. "Intercepted it. That's why Ransom didn't mention it just now. We got the thing off the street."

She caught her breath. "Last night?"

"After I left you, I went looking for Mary Rudi. I found something a lot more interesting to the police."

"Listen, Duff, I contacted the Feds." Daniel Ransom joined them as they left the conference room. "Sorry to interrupt, Liz, but I need to talk to Duff before you two get away. You can hear this, too, but don't forget the task force is sworn to secrecy."

"Of course," she said.

"The ATF suggested we notify the FBI," Ransom told Joshua. "Two agents from the Joint Terrorism Task Force are on their way here. They arrive this evening."

"You planning to do what I suggested?"

"It's risky, but we think it's the right thing."

"Wait." Liz held up a hand. "What's going on here?"

Joshua spoke. "Last night while I was hunting my missing refugee, I learned the police had good information about arms movement in the city. My contact told me that a local dealer tied to the Hypes was offering military hardware for sale—hand grenades, a fully automatic M-16 rifle. And a Claymore mine."

"For several months, we've been working to link the Hypes to the weapons trade," Ransom told Liz. "But we began to figure out that most of the kids aren't real criminals. They're just pimple-faced misfits and social outcasts."

"They were until Mo Ded pulled them together," Joshua clarified. "Now they're killers."

"Killer wannabes. All the same, few of them have felony convictions. That meant our usual charge—felon in possession of a firearm—wouldn't work. But selling a firearm to a convicted felon carries the same maximum penalty as being a felon in possession."

"What's the sentence?" Liz asked as the three walked down the hall toward the side door of the precinct building.

Joshua answered. "In this state, selling a firearm to a felon will get you ten years in prison. Ransom figured if he could put Mo Ded away on that, the gang would fall apart. So he enlisted an informant with a felony record to start buying guns."

"Hold on—did you say *ten years* is the max for firearms charges?" Liz asked. "That doesn't sound like much."

"You take a gangbanger like Mo Ded off the streets for ten years, that's something," Daniel told her. "We've been using our snitch to buy assault rifles, sniper rifles, combat shotguns, pistols, even hunting rifles. Almost all the weapons had been involved in crimes. Two were linked to murders. One to armed robbery. Another played a part in the killing of a police officer. Several of them were used in drive-by shootings."

"So, you're clearing the streets and linking the weapons to Hypes," Liz said as they emerged and started down the steps to the sidewalk. "This guy who's been selling weapons—is it Mo Ded?"

"No. He's working with Mo Ded, though. Taking orders, bringing in what the Hypes want. We still have some dots to connect before we can tie Mo Ded to direct criminal activity."

"But your seller did have the Claymore?"

Daniel nodded. "After Duff contacted us last night, our informant talked to him. The guy didn't want to let go of it. Said he'd promised the mine to someone else—brought it in on special order. But eventually our man was able to buy it."

He fell silent. Liz pondered the information. Someone—probably Mo Ded—had wanted a mine. The rumor that gang members intended to lure the police into an ambush must be true.

No doubt the Hypes were keeping a close watch on the cops. Certainly they knew as much about the movements of the force as the police knew about gang activity.

Kill or be killed.

Liz recalled the gruesome tales of genocide she had heard from refugees. Then she flashed on the memory of Stephen Rudi, head bowed, shoulders heaving in anguish over the wounding of his son.

What answer was there for such evil in this world? he had asked. Then he answered his own question. God.

As Liz studied the busy street, she struggled to feel His presence. The two men continued their discussion.

“The FBI will disarm the mine for you,” Joshua predicted to Daniel. “Did you ask them about installing a tracking device?”

“Yes,” the officer replied. “They told us they will render the Claymore inert. Then they’ll wire it so we can follow its movements.”

Liz shivered as a chill wind bit through her jacket. “If the Hypes can afford to buy a Claymore, can’t they buy almost any explosive?” she asked. “And what about the platinum suddenly showing up? This sounds much bigger than gang activity. It makes me wonder if Mo Ded really is who we think he is. I almost hate to ask—but is all this somehow tied to global terrorism?”

Joshua shot a look at her. "I'm checking into that. It's possible."

Memories of the green-eyed stalker making her shudder, Liz turned to the police officer. "Daniel, why don't you arrest Mo Ded? Surely you can get him on some kind of charge and take him off the street."

"We don't want to do that until we can lock him away for a long time," Ransom said. "He's too dangerous. We're putting the Claymore back out there. We'll track its movement, see what Mo Ded is up to. Duff, I want you to keep a close eye on Haven. If the violence on that street keeps heating up, we'll have to shutter the place."

"You can't do that, man. It's all the kids have. GED classes, the single moms' nursery, job skills training, sports. Now the new outdoor rec area. Haven is doing too much good in the community. You close it down and you'll be playing right into Mo Ded's hands."

"We'll do what we have to do to keep the city quiet. Thanks for coming to the meeting, Duff. I really didn't expect to see you again."

The men shook hands, and then the police officer excused himself. As Joshua turned to Liz, she saw the desire in his eyes and knew what would come next. He would take her in his arms, hold her, kiss her. She would melt, and all her distress and confusion would dissolve. For a moment.

As he reached for her, she put her hand on his

chest. "I didn't expect to see you again, either, Joshua. You walked out on me last night."

"I had to look for Mary Rudi."

"You went hunting that Claymore, Joshua." Hands in her pockets, she took a step toward her car. "Listen, I talked to Sam and Terell for a few minutes after you left. They said you're doing well—adjusting and focusing. Most important, they confirmed that you're leaving for Texas on Saturday. So, let's acknowledge the facts and make everything easier on ourselves, okay?"

He looked away from her, his eyes a deep gray-blue. "What facts are you talking about?"

"The ones we keep admitting and then denying. For one reason or another, we've been attracted to each other. Things have been good—intense but meaningful for both of us. Now we have to get on with life. I didn't intend to see you today, Joshua. The truth is, I don't want to see you again. I think you understand why."

Nodding, he focused on her again. "I do understand. Out on the streets last night, I was working, but I was thinking, too. Thinking about you, about us. There's no way around it. I love you, Liz."

She caught her breath. "Don't say that. Just don't say it." She reached for her car door. "I have to go."

He grabbed her hand. "Don't touch the car."

"What?"

"Your tire."

Liz looked down to find a streak of purple paint on the black rubber. "Oh, no."

As she spoke the words, Joshua turned her into his arms, moving her under the protection of his body and rotating her away from the car.

"Across the street," he breathed into her ear. "He's watching us."

Chapter Seventeen

As Joshua pulled the Cadillac away from the curb, his phone rang. When he reached for it, he saw that Liz was crying. In the passenger's seat, head bent, she searched her purse for tissues.

"Duff here. What's up, Pastor Stephen?"

"We need your help now." The man's voice was tight. "Those bad young men were outside. They broke windows."

"Haven's windows?"

"Yes, and they sprayed paint. We chased them away. So you must come. We have decided we shall go after them."

"Hold on, now. You can't do that. The Hypes are armed and dangerous. Does Sam Hawke know about this attack? Has anyone called the police?"

"We are all together in our decision—Sam, Terell, Raydell, everyone. We shall not call the police. Instead we shall go walking out there in the streets where our enemy is hiding, and we shall pray for them. You must come with us."

“Whoa, now.” Joshua had been driving toward Refugee Hope, but he swung the car down a side street, made a U-turn and headed for Haven. “This is not sounding good to me, Pastor. Can you put Hawke on?”

“I cannot. He has given me his phone for the purpose of calling you. He is very busy at this moment. We are making a small group here, a Christian army. And we shall go out in the name of God to pray for those who spitefully use us.”

“Pray?”

“Prayer-walking! Do you not know this?”

“Uh, no.” The last thing Joshua needed was a bunch of zealous civilians making some crazy march into enemy territory. He could see Liz was having no luck drying her tears. Reaching across her, he pressed the button on his glove compartment. Nothing inside but the owner’s manual and a map of St. Louis.

“Try this, honey.” He handed her the map. “It’s all I’ve got.”

He turned his attention to the street again—and the phone. “Do not leave Haven without me,” he ordered. “I know you have good intentions, Pastor Stephen, but this is not a smart way to handle the situation. Trust me. You need the police.”

“We have someone much better. We have God.”

“Yes, and God works through the police force. So that’s who we need to depend on to help Haven get through this crisis.”

"We shall prayer-walk until the enemy is defeated!"

"No. No, we will not do that. No walking in the streets." All Joshua could see at the moment was a Claymore mine, small and green and rigged to spray shrapnel through the bodies of people he had come to love. The one he found the night before was being disabled, but there could be others.

"Do not leave that building, Stephen Rudi," he warned. "You might be ambushed. There will be no prayer-walking."

"Sir, which Bible name did you take when you became a Christian?"

"I didn't take anyone's name. I already had a name. Joshua."

"Joshua—yes! Do you know what Joshua did—that great man in the Bible? He *walked* around the city of Jericho. And on the seventh day, what happened? The walls fell down. The enemy was defeated. Who was the leader of this great prayer-walk? Joshua!"

A low growl rising from deep in his chest, Joshua turned onto Haven's street. He saw police cruisers out front, lights flashing. Someone had called them after all. Probably Hawke. Good. Maybe this prayer-walking business was just Stephen's way of dealing with all the tension.

"How is Virtue this afternoon, Pastor?" Joshua asked, hoping to deflect the man's focus until they were face-to-face. "Have you talked to the doctor?"

"My son is much better today. I was with him this morning, and he knows me. He smiles. He holds my hand."

"Great. That's good. Listen, I'm at Haven now. I'll see you in a minute." As he steered toward a parking space, Joshua glanced at Liz. She was sniffling, but not crying.

"Oh, baby." He switched off the car and pulled her into his arms. "You scared me, girl."

"What scared you? Me—crying? Joshua, you saw that paint on my tire. You saw Mo Ded looking at us from that storefront across the street. You found the Claymore last night. You know the kind of violence that's going on in this city. And a crying woman scared you?"

"Liz, that other stuff is normal to me. *You're* outside the range of anything familiar in my life. Why do you think I left you last night? I ran toward my comfort zone. The streets, the hunt, the danger. That's where I feel safe. We had been arguing, remember? Arguing and fighting and wanting each other and all kinds of things I don't know how to handle. I couldn't take it. And now, more problems at Haven."

Liz looked at the police cars. "So it appears."

"Stephen Rudi is planning some kind of 'Onward, Christian Soldiers' march into Hypes territory. He wants to pray for the enemy."

"Prayer-walking. It's a good idea."

"It's insane. Did you hear what Ransom and I were talking about, Liz? Mo Ded is trying to buy a Claymore mine. He may already have a stockpile—mines, grenades, no telling what else. He wants to ambush the police—or some other enemy. I can't let Stephen just walk into his hands."

"Looks like it will be more than just Stephen." She pushed open her door. "You're in the crowd-management business now."

Joshua focused on the large group of people gathered around the steps at the entrance to Haven, and his heart sank. This was not a good sign. He spotted Stephen Rudi under the awning. Arms waving, voice raised, he exhorted the crowd.

Before Joshua had time to unbuckle his seat belt, Liz was halfway down the sidewalk.

Throwing open his door, he strode toward the crowd. This was not going to happen. Stephen Rudi was Joshua's refugee, his Pagandan, his charge. The man would do what he was told.

As he neared, Joshua took in the destruction the Hypes had wreaked. Broken bottles and beer cans littered the new rec area. Glass from shattered windows lay on the sidewalk. A purple gang sign had been sprayed on Haven's outside wall. Again.

"Jesus is the only answer," Pastor Stephen was shouting. His thick accent tinged with a British lilt held his audience spellbound. "We must love our enemies! We must pray for them! In my country—in Paganda—we experienced much violence. When one group attacked, the other went out seeking revenge. This is a cycle that never ends. But we are the ones who can stop it!"

Joshua worked his way through the throng and up the steps. "Pastor Stephen. Hey there, my friend."

"Christ is the only way to change lives! We must reach out in love. We shall join together and pray for this city. For this nation!"

"No, we won't," Joshua muttered, linking his arm through the African's. "Not today. Not here. Come on, Pastor. Let's head inside where it's warm."

Stephen Rudi refused to budge. "We shall follow the example of Jesus!" he shouted, pumping a raised fist. "Like a lamb to the slaughter, He opened not His mouth! Like a sheep before the shearer, He was dumb!"

"And in we go." Half lifting the smaller man off his feet, Joshua forced him toward the door. The pastor's determination was no match for the ex-Marine's strength.

Joshua called over his shoulder. "Excitement's over, everyone. Head on back to what you were doing."

But this crowd was not so easily dispersed. As Joshua propelled Stephen inside, the people followed. Pushing, edging their way into the building, they overwhelmed Raydell's efforts to herd them through the metal detector. Duke, pacing restlessly, began to bark.

"Into the streets!" Stephen shouted. "Into the streets with prayer and love!"

"What's going on here?" Sam Hawke left a pair of police officers and hurried toward the mob. "Duff, what are you doing?"

"Pastor Stephen, send the people outside," Joshua ordered. Taking the man's shoulders, he turned him toward the agitated group. "Do it now."

Stephen didn't miss a beat. "Go out and pray! Pray in the streets and in the shops and in your houses. Pray for God's peace. Love your enemies!"

Joshua wiped a hand across his forehead as he watched Sam, Terell, Raydell and the police officers steer everyone back outside without incident.

Too close. Way too close.

"Any one of those people could have had a gun, Pastor Stephen," he barked at the small African. "Any of them could have been with the enemy. Do not do that again. We've got enough trouble on our hands—"

"Are you gonna preach tonight, Pastor?" A young woman caught the African man's arm. Her brown eyes glowed. "People are asking. We think you should preach out on the street. Help us pray for peace."

"Yes. Of course I shall preach." Stephen beamed as he waved at the stragglers. "We shall pray together!"

"Good! I'll spread it around." She slipped away.

"You will not preach out there." Joshua urged the pastor toward the office near Haven's front door. "Do you know who that female was? That was Shauntay. She's the one who lured Raydell away from his duties the night I scuffled with the Hypes. The night Duke got stabbed. Pastor, that young lady is a gang queen."

"She is not." Liz stared him down. She had emerged from the crowd, and now she stood at the pastor's side. "Shauntay told me she was framed by Mo Ded that night, and I believe her. Joshua, the people are hungry to hear Stephen. His message is good. Stop trying to silence him."

"Every minute he stands out on that street, he puts his life in danger." Joshua strained to keep the fury from his voice. "Pastor, your son is in the hospital right now with a bullet wound. You know the danger here. Why are you stirring up trouble?"

"I am stirring up peace!" The African squared his shoulders. "Sir, I am not one of your soldiers. I am in the army of God."

"So am I. I'm a Christian, too, and you need to let me do what I do best. I promised to hunt down the punks who trashed the building today, and I will. I'll bring them in."

"And you must let me do what I do best,

Joshua," he countered. "You may hunt, but I must preach. Each must serve his place in the Kingdom. Now let us prepare for our prayer-walk."

"Aw, man, this is a bad scene." Terell Roberts joined them. "The police are saying they have to shut Haven down. They were just telling Sam and me that we don't have enough control over the building—and now look what you did, Pastor. Bringing in a whole mob? That was a bad move."

"I was preaching *outside*." He pointed at Joshua. "This man opened the door."

Joshua shook his head in dismay. "Listen, the crowd is gone and I'll talk to the cops. We're almost to the bottom of this gang thing. I'm closing in on Mo Ded, and I plan to do all I can to take him down before I leave St. Louis. I'll give Sergeant Ransom a call. He'll keep the building open for you."

"What about the prayer-walk?" Terell asked as he approached with Sam a step behind him.

The edges of a trigger tickling at his nerve endings, Joshua scowled at the tall man. "A prayer-walk? Are you telling me you all agree with Pastor Stephen? You people want to leave this building and march straight into Hypes territory—with nothing but prayer to protect you?"

"What armor can be stronger than prayer?" Stephen asked. "We must go about doing good. We must take back this city for God."

Joshua studied his fellow Marine. Head down,

Sam Hawke clearly was weighing the situation. He would make the right decision. The man had served in Iraq during the worst days. He'd been through a lot and come out the other side. He understood the need for timing, for protection, for technique and patience.

"Would you lead us, Duff?" Sam lifted his head, eyes pinned on his friend. "If we walk through this neighborhood, praying the whole way, will you go ahead of us? We need you."

The question sucked the air out of Joshua's chest. "Are you serious about this, Hawke? You realize the kinds of arms those thugs have? We could step into an ambush and never come out. Mo Ded would like nothing better than to take you out. You, too, Terell. The Hypes want Haven. They've declared war on you. And you want to walk right into their hands?"

"In prayer." Sam nodded. "Yeah, I think we can do that."

Liz had never been so afraid in her life. Not during her visit to Congo. Not while touring a refugee camp at the edge of a battle-scarred no-man's-land. Not in her apartment listening to gunfire in the alley below. Not even when Mo Ded had called, his voice recording the soundtrack of her future nightmares.

But that evening she was back at Haven anyway. After Liz returned to work and finished the day's business, Molly had taken her to the police station where her car had been checked out and declared clean. Then Liz had hurried to her apartment, eaten a quick bite, dressed in jeans and driven to the youth center where a small band of prayer warriors—Haven staff, Stephen Rudi and a collection of passionate neighbors—had gathered. Mary Rudi had shown up at Haven sometime that morning with an explanation of her disappearance that no one really understood. Later, she went to the hospital to sit with Virtue. Several of the recreation center's older volunteers agreed to watch Charity and other children while the adults went out. After instructions and warnings from Joshua and Sam, the group set off into the streets of St. Louis.

To her left, Liz held the hand of Ana Burns. The tall, beautiful, model-perfect fiancée of Sam Hawke had arrived not long after Liz. To the consternation of everyone, including Sam, she had brought a newspaper photographer.

Shauntay held Liz's right hand. The young woman with two children and a history of violence, instability and probably prostitution had blossomed in recent days. She whispered her story as they walked.

"I like Pastor Stephen," she said. Though others around them were praying—some aloud and some in silence—Shauntay had too much to tell. "He different from most of the men in this hood, yo. He sticks with his wife and kids, and he works hard. I see him over at that restaurant where I eat when I'm takin' a break at the hair shop. He says hi to me every time, and he knows my name, too. He always talks to me about God."

Liz tried to smile. She, too, admired Stephen Rudi. The pastor was walking with Joshua at the head of the growing crowd, but the two men could not have looked more different. While Stephen prayed loudly, calling down God's blessings and protection on the people of St. Louis, Joshua moved in silence. His eyes searched the buildings—high, low, scanning alleyways, taking note of every storefront, studying each open window. His broad shoulders were squared, and his hands hung loosely at his sides. Liz wondered if somewhere on the man's body he had concealed a knife. Or a gun.

"Pastor Stephen makes God sound real," Shauntay confided, leaning close. "Like you can talk to Him and He listens. When his baby got shot yesterday, I figured that would be it between Pastor Stephen and God."

It almost was, Liz reflected in silence. She recalled the man's despair in the waiting area of the emergency room. His words had filled her own heart with anger toward God. Why wouldn't a loving Heavenly Father protect this faithful preacher who had come so far with his traumatized wife and children? Did God have to allow even more agony? More sorrow?

"But look at him now," Shauntay said. "This morning, Pastor S. told me God don't make things right. God makes *people* right. Sometimes that means they got to go through a lot of trouble. Like me. I been through so much, me and my babies, and I get to thinking nobody cares about me. Even Raydell."

Both women focused on the young man who walked just behind Joshua. His hand in the white cast, it might have been comical the way he was imitating the former Marine sergeant. But Liz knew that Joshua had become a role model and a mentor in the community.

"Raydell and me talked," Shauntay whispered. "He said he was sorry for calling me a Hypes queen. But you know . . . I ain't exactly innocent. I did have some things going down with them gangsters, and I can't deny Mo Ded made his moves on me. I thought about jumping off the porch, but I changed my mind. I want to stay clean if I can."

"I hope you will," Liz said, finding her voice with difficulty. The sun was setting, streetlights had begun to glow and she knew the group was now walking right through the center of Hypes turf.

"Raydell is getting his GED," Shauntay continued, "and then he's going to be a cop. Wants to enroll at the police academy and all that. I told him about my job at D'Shondra's Braids. He said he admired me for working hard and taking care of my kids. Anyhow, we back together."

"Together?"

"You know." She covered her mouth with her hand and giggled. "But we ain't doing nothing, because Raydell told me that Sam and Terell said Christian men supposed to stay pure. I could tell them a thing or two about Raydell, and there ain't a drop of purity left in that dog. Me, either, yo. But him and me . . . we decided to be pure anyhow. Pastor S. said God can wash away every bad thing a person did if they just ask Him. Raydell been talking to me about getting married."

"Married?" Liz caught her breath at the idea. She squeezed the young woman's hand. "Shauntay, that would be good."

"Yeah, if Raydell could be like Pastor S., it would. That's the kind of man I want for a husband. Somebody faithful and hardworking. I don't want no more cheaters. You sure got yourself a good one."

Liz had to hold her tongue. How many times could she explain that she and Joshua were not *together?* Not in the sense people assumed.

"You smell that?" Shauntay slowed her pace. "Somebody's cookin' ice. We too close now. Mo Ded ain't gonna like this."

Cooking ice? Liz detected the faint whiff of a familiar odor in the chill air. The putrid, cat-urine smell of methamphetamine. The smell of Mo Ded.

Closing her eyes, she tried to pray as she walked. Impossible. Her heart felt as though it might jump out of her chest. Her knees melted like warm chocolate inside her jeans.

"You and your man staying pure?" Shauntay asked.

For a moment, Liz couldn't reconcile the question with the reality around her. Pure? What could that have to do with the smell of a meth lab, the abandoned buildings, the trash and beer cans in the gutter, the taste of fear on her tongue?

"I didn't think so," the girl said. "He don't look like the type to hold back."

"Wait—yes, we are staying pure," Liz murmured. "Joshua and I don't . . . we don't sleep together, if that's what you're asking. We're like Sam and Raydell and the others at Haven. We're trying to follow Christ's teachings."

"Yeah? That's cool. I never would have thought it. No offense, but none of you is that young no more. I mean, you all been round the block, but you ain't . . ." Shauntay gave a secret smile, as if she found the information delicious and mysterious. "I can't hardly imagine it because you know how it is. People my age, nobody thinks there's anything wrong with—"

Stiffening, she let go of Liz's hand and hugged herself. "It's them."

The group of prayer-walkers came to a sudden halt. The sounds of murmured prayers ceased. Joshua's arms went rigid at his sides.

In the distance, Liz spotted a collection of ragtag young men moving toward them. They hung in the deeply shadowed recesses of buildings, out of the light of streetlamps or neon signs. Gliding as one, they drifted forward.

Then Liz distinguished their leader. A too-large coat hanging from his shoulders, Mo Ded led his pack of gangbangers. Liz imagined the arsenal hidden inside that coat. Her mouth went dry. Her scalp prickled. She reached into her pocket for her phone.

Joshua had told the group that the police would be aware of their route. But as she looked around, Liz saw no sign of a squad car, no evidence that any legal authority would be protecting them.

"We've gone far enough," Joshua said in a low voice. "We made our point here."

"Everyone please turn around now." Sam spoke up from the back of the group where he and Terell had been holding the rear flank. The calm in his voice was forced. "It's time to head back to Haven. Granny and some of the other volunteers have hot cocoa waiting for us."

The uncomfortable silence was followed by a low rumble of dialogue as the group attempted to change direction. Liz caught Joshua's eye for a moment. He was unhappy with the situation.

Pastor Stephen suddenly sprang out into the street. "I must speak with our enemy," he declared in a loud voice. "I must share God's love!"

Before Joshua could stop him, the man started away from the relative safety of the cluster. He waved a hand in the direction of the oncoming gang.

"We come to you in peace!" Stephen called out. "In the name of God, we present ourselves to you!"

A deafening bang silenced him. People screamed and bolted for cover. Liz hung frozen for a moment. Not again! She spotted Joshua on one knee on the pavement. He had knocked Stephen down to avoid the gunfire. Now both men were scrambling to their feet.

Liz searched for an escape route. Intent on her conversation with Shauntay, she hadn't noticed which direction the group had walked. Now she jogged a short distance, tried to follow the crowd. But people had scattered and were vanishing fast. They knew this street, these buildings, the short-cuts to safety.

She swung around and spotted Mo Ded running toward her. Grabbing her phone, she pulled it from her pocket and pressed a button to summon the police. In the distance she heard sirens—someone had beaten her to the call. But the Hypes were close now, moving in.

Liz darted for the shadows. Ran down the side-walk toward a street corner. She turned, searching the night for any sign of Joshua. Unable to find him, she ran again. The sound of feet pounding the sidewalk behind her clenched at her heart. She glanced over her shoulder, saw the glint of green in Mo Ded's eyes, realized she would never make the corner in time.

An Open sign on a storefront beckoned. She shouldered her way inside. A woman cried out in surprise. A man pointed toward a stairwell at the back of the shop.

"Go there!" he shouted. "That way!"

Liz hesitated. Was this a trap? Had Mo Ded planned it ahead of time? Or did people regularly run into this store looking for a place to hide?

Unable to puzzle it out, she obeyed. She threw herself up the steps. Her feet tangled over each other. She caught the handrail. Cold metal. Pulling herself through the darkness, she struggled to breathe.

Rounding a corner, she expected a landing. Instead, she was in a narrow hall. A single low-watt bulb hung from the ceiling. She spotted a window at the far end of the corridor. A metal fire escape.

Doors lined the walkway. Apartments? She saw no numbers.

Now she heard shouting in the store below. Mo Ded's voice, she thought. She reached for a door-knob. It didn't turn. She jiggled it, praying.

Running to the next door, she did the same. Nothing. Locked. All of them.

Footsteps echoed in the stairwell. Liz gasped.

Cried out. Was someone still chasing her? Would she die now? Before she had really begun?

The window at the end of the hall was her only hope. She saw the paint, thick layers caked around the frame. Was the window painted shut? Sealed? Should she break the glass? How?

Crying now, she ran her fingers over the double-hung panes. Her hand found the window latch on the wooden sash. She pressed. It turned!

Bending, she lifted the lower window. A blast of cold air shot down the hall. Sniffling, trying to see through tears, she crawled through the window onto the fire escape. In a fetal ball, she rolled onto a grated landing.

No time to shut the window behind her. She hauled herself to her feet. Black. An alley. No lights.

Feeling for the rail, she wrapped her hand around the chilled iron bar. Her feet somehow found steps. She started down.

Her pulse thrummed in her head. She willed her shoes to silence. Listening for sound overhead, she heard nothing.

Then feet. Someone running down the alley.

She halted, pressed herself against the brick. There was no way out. No way.

Metallic thumps echoed as a dark figure started up the fire escape. She took two steps back toward the window. But Mo Ded would be in the hall. Starting down any moment.

She was caught in the middle. Trapped.

"Liz? Liz, tell me you're up there."

Joshua!

A sob caught in her throat. "It's me."

Chapter Eighteen

He was at her side, catching her up in his arms, holding her tight. Liz buried her face in the crook of Joshua's neck, unable to stop the tears.

"They're gone, babe," he murmured, his hand covering her head, fingers threaded through her hair. "It's over now. Nothing happened. No one got hurt. You're safe."

"Safe?" Drawing back, she hammered her fist on his chest. "You shouldn't have let this happen! We should have stayed at Haven."

"No, it was a good thing after all." He pulled her closer, his body warming her. "You and Pastor Stephen were right. I was wrong."

"How can you say that? They shot at us again."

"That round was fired in fear. Pastor Stephen accomplished more than he intended. Now Mo Ded knows we're not afraid. None of us will back down—he understands that. And he heard the message about love. Peace. If he doesn't already know about the praying, he soon will. It was an eerie thing. Scary, the whole crowd of us walking and praying. Mo Ded is off-kilter. For once, he lost control."

"No, he was on the attack, Joshua. They came after me. Mo Ded could be right there—down in the alley or just around the corner."

"Mo Ded was the first to run. He's the biggest coward of them all. They saw the pastor walking toward them, and someone fired a random shot. A second later they all took off in every direction."

"But I saw Mo Ded coming after me, Joshua! I barely made it into the store."

"He wasn't chasing you. He was running from me."

"You? Were you behind him?" As realization dawned, she sucked down a breath of frigid air. "You were trying to get to me."

"Of course."

As he kissed her gently on the lips, someone shut the window above them. The shop owner whose footsteps she had heard in the stairwell?

"Liz, I won't let anything happen to you," Joshua said. "I love you."

"No, Joshua. You can't love me. Not honestly. You keep saying you're going to Texas, and it isn't possible to say both things at the same time."

"You're going to Africa, and you love me. I know you do."

She looked away. Her acknowledgment came in a whisper. "Yes, Joshua. I do love you."

At her words, he fell silent. The cold night slid dark fingers around them. She shivered and slipped her arms inside his open jacket. Laying her head against his chest, she listened to the even rhythm of his heart. How could the man be so calm? At a time like this, he somehow was relaxed, his hands gentle on her back.

"Liz, come to Texas with me." He spoke the words into her ear. "I'll buy a plane ticket. Fly away with me. Meet my parents. See the house, the office. You'll like the oil fields. They're flat and dry. Nice. Peaceful."

"Nothing like the Hindu Kush," she murmured. "Nothing like the streets of St. Louis. Can you be happy there?"

"Not without you."

Liz squeezed her eyes shut, unable to accept what he was saying. "You'll get over this, Joshua. It was too fast, too crazy. Look at us huddled here in the dark. Nothing has been normal."

"Is that what you're telling yourself? That our love is a knee-jerk reaction to danger? You think what I've told you is some kind of PTSD side effect?"

"I don't know what it is. I've never known anything like this. Anyone like you."

"This is how I am, Liz. This is me. Do you love me or not?"

She lifted her head, trying but unable to make out the features on his face. "I love this man I'm holding . . . this person who battles terrorists and gangsters. This man who's as comfortable in inner-city jungles as he is in foreign countries. But what will you be like in Amarillo? Life there will change you, Joshua. An office. A desk. You'll get comfortable. You'll lose the essence of who you are—that urge to track enemies and take down the evil things in this world. And you know I won't fit."

"But you fit with me. Look how well we fit together."

As she pushed away from him again, a laugh of dismay welled up inside her. "Joshua, I feel at home in this kind of craziness as much as you do. I love these people—my wounded refugees, sad girls like Shauntay clinging to hope, even the angry gangsters who might change their ways. I don't think I can find meaning anywhere else."

"Except in Africa. Ten thousand miles from St. Louis."

She shook her head. "Maybe not, Joshua. You know my struggle. My sleepless nights. Talking to Shauntay on the prayer-walk, I felt her pain. I used to think Africa was where God needed me most. But the need here is just as great. It's different, but the intensity is equal."

"And you're going to fix it all?"

"Don't make fun of me. I have to try."

"I'm not mocking you, Liz. I love you. But Amarillo is a city. It has needy people, too. Why don't you go there with me? We'll drive downtown and try to find the ones who could use our help."

"But in the end, that's not how it would be for us—working with the disadvantaged, trying to make a difference, going where life is hardest. You know it, too. The comfort of *things* would lure us away, Joshua. The swimming pool. The club. That kind of luxury is so easy. I don't want to be tempted."

"So we both suffer? We give each other up? Go separate ways. I never see you again. Do you really want that, Liz? Tell me if you do."

She shuddered and slipped her arms around him again. "No. I want to do whatever God tells me to do."

"Would He put us together and then tear us apart? What purpose could that have? You've been wrestling with your feelings about going to Africa, and I've already surrendered my work for the military. So maybe God wants us someplace new. Together."

"What are you saying, Joshua? You're scaring me."

"Too intense again?" He fell silent, his chest rising and falling as he drew breath. "I want you. That's all I know. I can't ask for promises . . . or give them. But if you'll go with me to Texas, I believe we'll understand what we're supposed to do."

Liz lifted on tiptoe and kissed his cheek. "Take me home. I need to think."

As they started down the fire escape steps, he paused. "I leave Saturday morning. Think fast."

• • •

Liz switched on her laptop and watched as a blue light filled the screen. Too wound up to sleep, she had not even bothered to go to bed.

Earlier that evening, she and Joshua had returned to Haven. Gathered on the indoor basketball court, everyone was drinking hot cocoa and discussing the prayer-walk. Stephen Rudi sat at the edge of the group, Charity curled in a ball on his lap. Mary was still at the hospital with Virtue. Her shift at the cleaning company would start soon. Joshua needed to take Stephen to his son's side and drive Mary to work.

Liz had tried to convince him to let her go to her apartment alone. He refused to hear of it. He bundled the pastor and his daughter into his own car and followed Liz home. She hurried upstairs, thinking how much she missed him already and considering a quick phone call to ask him to come back later that night.

But Shauntay's amazed expression lingered in her thoughts. Liz had promised the young woman that she and Joshua were "staying pure." She didn't want to do anything to make that a lie. It was right to be obedient to Christ's teaching. Agonizing but right.

Wrapped in her robe, Liz ate a sandwich, talked to Molly for a few minutes, touched base with her parents and then stared at the photo album on her sofa. Without knowing exactly why, on an impulse she snatched it up, opened a drawer in her bedroom dresser and shoved the thing to the very back.

There. Take that, Africa.

As she turned away, Liz spotted the jewelry box on the table near her bed. The small painted chest dated back to her childhood, and she recalled the heirloom ring that had come to mind during the gang task force meeting.

Diamonds.

Platinum.

Lifting the lid of the little box, she sifted through a tangle of chains and earrings she rarely wore. Her fingers touched the familiar shape of the ring. She slipped it onto her finger and studied its features under the glow of the lamp. The diamonds glittered, as always. But it was the platinum that intrigued her now.

Bright and shiny, the metal might as well be silver, she thought. Except that it didn't tarnish. Why was platinum so valuable? And why would anyone be trading it on the streets of St. Louis?

Liz put the ring away and returned to her laptop. She scanned through her e-mail, answering a few messages and deleting the rest. Curiosity nagging, she switched to a search engine. After wading through lists of retailers and wholesalers who dealt in platinum, she began to read articles about the precious metal.

Platinum's scarcity on planet Earth had made it more valuable than gold or diamonds, Liz learned.

The commodity was used in jewelry, of course, but it actually had greater significance in industry. More than half the world's output of platinum was assigned to the control of vehicle exhaust emissions. With clean air a global priority, the metal's price was skyrocketing.

Platinum had medical applications, too. Certain implants, anticancer drugs and dental restorations required it. As she digested the flow of information, Liz began to believe that almost every cutting-edge modern industry needed platinum. The rare metal was essential to producers of hard-disk-drive coatings and fiber-optic cables. Fertilizer and aerospace industries had to have it. Platinum even helped household detergents become biodegradable.

If Mo Ded had found a source for the precious metal, she deduced, he could probably peddle it for a bundle of money. But platinum was so uncommon that to find it for sale on the St. Louis black market seemed unthinkable.

As Liz searched the Web for sources of the product, she realized Daniel Ransom had spoken correctly. Most of the world's platinum was mined in two places. South Africa and Russia.

But as the hours passed and Liz dug further, she stumbled on a discovery that chilled her to the core. The newest and potentially most productive platinum mine in the world was located in a struggling, troubled country in central Africa.

Paganda.

Leaning back on her sofa, Liz tried to process the information. Paganda? Little, war-torn, genocidal Paganda? Who had discovered platinum there? Who owned the mine? What had the recent civil war meant to production and export levels?

Shivering uncontrollably, she wrapped her robe tighter and turned her thermostat up a notch. Paganda? Surely Mo Ded didn't have a supplier of Pagandan platinum.

Did he?

Could a refugee have managed to smuggle the metal into the United States? Might that refugee be Stephen Rudi? Surely not. She pictured the pastor at the hospital, his shoulders shaking as he sobbed over his son's injury and his feelings of abandonment by God. She recalled the light in his eyes as he spoke about faith. Shauntay had testified to the man's kindness and warmth.

But people weren't always who they claimed to be. Especially those with a secret agenda.

The thought that Pastor Stephen could be the source of the platinum bothered Liz so much that she went in search of her phone. Should she call Joshua and share her suspicions? It was much too late at night to bother him. And how might he respond to her discovery? It was a crazy notion, connecting the dots between Paganda, Stephen Rudi and Mo Ded. There was no link . . . was there?

Though she felt sure her mental gymnastics were ridiculous, Liz spotted her phone on the kitchen counter. She had almost reached it when the ringtone blasted her. The warbling sound echoed off every tile on the walls and floor. As she snatched up the phone, she nearly dropped it.

She almost didn't bother glancing at the ID. "I was just going to call you."

"I thought so." Joshua sounded wide-awake, curt. "A hunch. Listen, we need to talk."

"Is something wrong?"

"Mary. She wasn't at the hospital. Not at work, either. The woman fled again. A nurse told me that when they were trying to communicate with her about Virtue's condition, Mary got spooked and took off."

"Oh, no."

"I talked to her job supervisor. He fired her. Said he had no choice."

Rubbing her forehead, Liz wandered back into the living room. She couldn't count the times refugees she was trying to assist had lost their jobs for one reason or another. Still, this was serious.

"How is Virtue?" she asked.

"Great. Bouncing back. Kids do that—I saw it in the war. But Stephen is losing it. I'm concerned about his level of agitation."

"Agitation?" Her neck prickled.

"He kept apologizing to me for triggering the gang attack. He blames himself for Mary's problems, too. Feels like everything that's going wrong with the family is his fault."

"That's not true." But even as she said the words, the sickening possibility slid into Liz's stomach. She tried to hold her tongue, but the idea refused to stay put. "Stephen Rudi is a good man . . . at least he seems to be."

"Of course he is, but I have no idea how to fix the Rudis' mess, Liz. I'm leaving, and they're still struggling to get settled and become self-sufficient. Stephen has one child in the hospital and a wife who flees at the first sign of distress. Now he's coming apart fast. He holds himself responsible for the chaos, and nothing I say will change his mind."

"But, Joshua, what if Stephen Rudi really is causing some of these problems in his family? What if he's not exactly the great guy we think he is?"

"Are you kidding me? Stephen has his nose in the Bible all the time. If I need to talk to him, I check his room. He's always up there studying, writing out long notes to himself in his little book. Sermons, I guess."

"Have you read any of his writing?"

"Why would I read someone's private journals? Pastor Stephen's spiritual journey is his own business."

"You didn't have any problem violating Mary Rudi's privacy. It didn't bother you to go digging around in her dress pockets."

He was silent a moment. "Are we going to argue about that again?"

Liz heard the unhappiness in his voice. "I don't want to argue, Joshua. But aren't you curious why Stephen Rudi is so interested in Mo Ded? What's the connection between those two men? It's bothering me that this Pagandan pastor is all fired up about winning a gangbanger to Christ when he has more than enough problems of his own."

She paused long enough for Joshua to respond. When he didn't, she continued. "Why did the Rudi family flee the refugee agency that brought them to America, Joshua? That organization has all their legal documentation and is responsible for their safety and resettlement. It makes no sense to run off to St. Louis. And why did they come to this city, anyway? There was no brother-in-law and no address waiting for them here. Maybe they knew that. Maybe the letter they acted so upset about was really meant to fool *us*. I want to know what that man was thinking when he forced his wife and children onto a bus in Atlanta."

"Those are some serious suspicions, Liz. What are you getting at?"

"Platinum," she said. "And Paganda. I just read something that disturbs me. Joshua, the largest newly discovered reserves of platinum are in Paganda."

Neither spoke. Liz tried to imagine what Joshua was thinking. How would his analytical brain work this new factor into the mysterious equation of Stephen and Mary Rudi? She certainly couldn't piece it together.

"Have you told Ransom about this?" he asked.

"No. I wanted to talk to you first."

"Give me a minute. I'll head over there. It's not a good idea to discuss this by phone."

"You can't come." She swallowed, trying to think how to tell him without sounding silly. Finally, she blurted it out. "I don't trust myself. Not alone with you. Sorry."

When he spoke again, she heard the tenderness in his voice. "My fault. Should have known."

"I wouldn't have given it much thought, but Shauntay reminded me that people are watching us all the time. Our behavior, our actions—they see that, and it matters. She and Raydell are together again. Sam and Terell have been talking to them about abstinence."

"I got in on a little of that the other day. Said I agreed, and I meant it. Doesn't mean it's easy. Good thing we'll be staying at my parents' place in Texas this weekend."

"Joshua, I . . ." Liz couldn't continue.

All at once the idea of fleeing an apartment where she never felt completely safe seemed wonderful. A clean house from top to bottom, inside and out. A shower with full water pressure. No cockroaches. A yard, green grass, landscaping, a swimming pool. Fresh, unpolluted air. Bright, educated adults who spoke the English language well and understood politics, history and art. It would be paradise.

"I bought your ticket online," Joshua said. "The flight leaves early Saturday morning. I'll put you on a plane home if you get there and change your mind."

"Change my mind about what? I haven't agreed to go with you in the first place."

"You need this, Liz. We both do."

She cast her eyes around the apartment, taking in the cracks in the walls and the bars on the windows. What would it be like to step out of this grimy, precarious environment for a few days? How might it feel to be with Joshua in a new place, somewhere calm and bright? Somewhere safe.

"But I keep thinking about Paganda," she said, unwilling to give credence to the truth that she was tempted to leave her home and her work. "What about the platinum and Pastor Stephen? What about Mo Ded and Stephen Rudi? Can there be a connection?"

"Feels remote to me, but you have to wonder."

"The platinum Sergeant Ransom told us about may have been brought in by someone from Paganda. Someone who came here recently. It's possible. Maybe our refugee isn't the man we think he is. Maybe he's doing things we never suspected. Doesn't that worry you?"

"It does. But I'm willing to leave that investigation to Ransom."

"Can you really do that, Joshua? You've worked so hard on all this. And Mo Ded is still on the loose. You said you would bring down the Hypes. You told me you always keep your promises. Can you just let it go?"

"I put the pieces in place for the cops, Liz. I gave them new information on Mo Ded. I stopped the Claymore. And tonight the Hypes went down."

"They'll regroup. You know Mo Ded isn't defeated."

"His armor has chinks, and Ransom knows where they are. Liz, sometimes you have to accept that you've done your job. I walked out of a country where I was deeply involved. I had Afghani friends, favorite restaurants, things I enjoyed. I was comfortable there. My work mattered. It was interesting, and I used my skills. But I left, Liz. You do that when the time comes."

"I can't imagine why."

"Something else calls. You realize you need to pack up and move on. You have other loyalties, other responsibilities. If you've done your work well, it's not a sin to leave."

As he spoke, Liz thought again of the refugees represented by the files on her desk. She saw their faces, their eyes. She felt their hope.

"It feels wrong. For me, anyway." She leaned against the wall, exhaustion overtaking her. "What about the Rudi family, Joshua? How can you abandon them? You just admitted how messed up they are. And you promised to settle them. You're the man who never breaks a vow."

"By Saturday morning, they'll be as settled as they can be. Tomorrow I move them to their new apartment. It's nice, furnished, near the MetroLink line and the school. Stephen has a decent job. I've bought MetroLink passes for the next six months. I talked to Social Services about Mary and her trauma. They agreed to look into the case. Someone will keep tabs on the family and try to get Mary to a counselor. At the least, they'll make sure there's food in the pantry and the kids are safe and well cared for. I'll be in touch, too. If things fall apart, I'll know. Ransom, Sam, Terell—they've all agreed to stay in touch with the Rudis and call me if there's a problem. I can step back in anytime."

"So, it's done? Your responsibility is over?"

"No one has a perfect life, Liz. I can't hand that to the Rudis on a silver platter. I said I would settle them, and I have. My work is complete."

Liz had wandered into her bedroom, and now she curled up on the rumpled comforter. The sadness that had been nagging at her for days welled up in her chest. She didn't want to leave her work, her beautiful refugee families and all they meant to her. But she didn't want to lose Joshua, either. The thought of it tore at her.

"Will you talk to your supervisor tomorrow, Liz?" His voice warmed the aching places inside her. "Will you go with me to Texas?"

Closing her eyes, Liz felt every barrier inside her suddenly collapse. "Yes," she told him. "Yes, I will."

Chapter Nineteen

"A barbecue." Liz looked at Joshua across the table. "We should hold a barbecue picnic and invite the Pagandan community. There aren't many in St. Louis. The outdoor rec area at Haven is perfect, and no one will suspect. It would be natural for us to introduce Stephen Rudi to his countrymen."

The group gathered in the small room at the police station had agreed to keep the current discussion to themselves. Sam Hawke, Terell Roberts and Daniel Ransom had joined Liz and Joshua for the Friday noon meeting. Now they all leaned forward to listen to her idea.

"Paganda is one of the few unregulated producers of platinum in the world," she told them. "The government owns and operates the mine. That means its operation has been unstable during these past few years of civil war. It's possible platinum left the country unreported."

Joshua studied the woman as she outlined her thoughts. As always, the winsome bundle of curls, energy, beauty and intelligence fascinated him.

After she had accepted his offer of a trip to Texas the night before, he went down to the gym to try to work off the buzz of emotion zapping through him. Liz Wallace in Texas. Liz at his home on the ranch in Amarillo.

The idea bemused and excited him at the same time. There were too many "what-ifs" to ponder. Would she like his family? Would they like her? They would love her, of course. But how would he and Liz feel about each other outside the strange world of Haven and the mean streets of St. Louis?

"I contacted Atlanta this morning," Liz was saying. "I talked to a caseworker with the refugee resettlement agency that brought the Rudis to the United States. He told me the Rudis were the only Pagandan family to move out of Georgia this year. All the others have been settled in Atlanta and are accounted for there."

"What about your agency?" Ransom asked. "Could Refugee Hope have brought in someone who had contact with the platinum mine?"

"We haven't resettled anyone from Paganda for a couple of years. This city's Pagandan community is small, but the families are well established. No one has been in trouble with the law, and there's no indication that any of these people could be smuggling contraband into this country—certainly not platinum. To be honest, all our refugees, including the Pagandans, are living just above the poverty level. If any of them were trading a rare metal on the black market, we would see evidence."

"So you think it's possible this new family brought the platinum?" Ransom asked. "Why couldn't it have come from South Africa or Russia? We know those are the major producers."

Liz shot a look at Joshua. Neither wanted to voice their suspicions, but it was no longer wise to remain silent. He cleared his throat.

"Trouble with the Hypes heated up around the time the Rudis appeared on Haven's doorstep," he explained. "You all know I've been tracking the gang's weapons buildup. I learned the infusion of cash and the movement of platinum on the streets coincide with the arrival of the Rudi family. Not long after Stephen Rudi took his job at the restaurant, rumors of the Claymore started buzzing. I didn't put it all together until last night when Liz told me about the connection between Paganda and platinum. I've spent hours thinking through every detail. Though I don't like to admit this, it all fits."

"Hold on," Terell inserted. "I respect your experience, Duff, but you're stepping out on a limb here. You think Stephen Rudi could have brought platinum to St. Louis and started trading it for cash? Why would he do that?"

"Could be a personal thing. He wants to make money. Get rich. The American dream."

“But if you study Paganda’s history,” Liz put in, “you realize he may have a political motivation. Both sides in the conflict have a history of centuries of hatred and slaughter. The power base has gone back and forth many times. Refugees from both sides of the dispute live in Congo, Tanzania, Kenya and other surrounding countries. Stephen Rudi could be using the cash to support a buildup of rebel troops to overthrow the current government.”

Joshua nodded. “He could even be buying arms. We assumed Mo Ded had ordered the Claymore. It might have been Stephen Rudi.”

“I think we have to be careful here,” Ransom said. “We don’t have any definite links. We’re not sure the platinum came from Paganda. We definitely can’t tie it to your little pastor. And by the way, if he’s some kind of evil mastermind, the guy sure has done a great job of covering his tracks. Word on the street about him is nothing but great.”

“That’s true,” Terell said. “People love Pastor S.”

“This morning, talk of his prayer-walk is all over the place. Even in the newspaper—thanks to Hawke’s fiancée and her handy photographer.”

“Ana can’t resist a good story,” Sam said. “It can only help.”

Ransom’s eyebrows lifted a notch. “Maybe so. People are saying the African preacher called down the power of God and sent the Hypes running. I sure hate to see our local hero suddenly transformed into a villain."

Then he shrugged. "But if you can hook him to the Claymore, you know I'm behind you all the way."

"Well, I think Pastor S. is a good man," Terell insisted. "I trust him."

"You trust everyone, T-Rex," Sam said. "That's why we love you, dog."

As Terell gave Sam a playful punch on the arm, Joshua smiled. He had come to feel as much affection for the towering former NBA star as he did for his fellow ex-Marine. Whereas Sam was a warrior like himself, Terell was a bona fide marshmallow. The kids loved him, and he reached them in ways no one else at Haven could.

"So this barbecue?" Joshua asked. "What's your idea, Liz?"

She turned the focus back to Sam and Terell. "If Haven will sponsor a gathering for the Pagandan community at the park, there's naturally going to be a lot of conversation out there. Gossip. Storytelling. People know each other from the refugee camps, and they understand the tribal conflict in a way we never will. With Stephen Rudi and his family mingling among the crowd, I believe Joshua can sniff out the truth."

"Duff is leaving in the morning," Sam said. "And from what I hear, you're going with him."

Joshua saw two pink spots blossom on Liz's

cheeks. She pushed her fingers back through her hair and gave a shrug. "Tonight? Could you pull something together that fast?"

Sam shook his head. "Sorry. We'll have to get a church lined up to donate the food. We'd need some barbecue grills. Not too difficult. Haven has a lot of great partners now. But just contacting the Pagandans in the area is going to take some doing."

"I can handle that," Liz said. "I have enough information to let a few people know. Word will spread fast."

"Weren't these Pagandans among the refugees who were all up in arms about the drive-by?" Ransom asked. "They were calling in to the precinct the next day claiming the gangs are out to get them. What's going to convince these people to show up for a barbecue at the very site where that kid went down?"

"Pastor Stephen," Joshua said. "I know he's our suspect. But he's also our asset. He has a good reputation on the streets, and the Pagandans will respond well to that. They know his boy was shot. They've surely heard he wants to start a church. If they don't know the guy already, they'll want to meet him."

"It's a natural event for Haven to host," Liz said. "Almost expected. No one will suspect what Joshua is up to and he—"

She cut herself off. All eyes turned his way.

Joshua leaned over, elbows on his knees, and laced his fingers. He studied the floor, again weighing options. But in the end, there were none.

"I have to be in Amarillo tomorrow evening," he said finally. "Liz will be with me. Before we leave, she can contact the Pagandans. Ransom, I'll brief you on the latest information I've pulled together. Sam and Terell, if you arrange for the barbecue, I know our friendly local police officer can snoop as well as I could."

"That's your specialty, Duff," Ransom said. "And won't these people be speaking their native language?"

"Not to you." Joshua realized he had some work to do. "I'll spend the afternoon here. Teach you some techniques that work with nationals. Or in this case, imports."

"Refugees," Liz said. She gave him a look he didn't like. The woman was tense about this trip. He knew that. She had asked for—and received—permission to take a week's vacation, but she wouldn't like abandoning the investigation. Especially when it involved the refugee community.

"Well, I think we can pull something together for Sunday evening," Sam told the police officer. "Might as well move on this thing while it's hot. Sounds like you'll be ready to do your detective work if Liz can round up some Pagandans."

"Sunday," she said. "I didn't think it would be

so soon. I guess I thought . . . I hoped I might get back in time to help out."

"Honey, if Duff has his way, you ain't *never* coming back," Terell said. He leaned back in his chair and laughed. "Bye-bye! Been nice knowing you!"

"I only took one week off," she said.

But the others were already standing. The meeting was at an end, and Joshua had work to do. As Sam and Terell headed for the door, Ransom spoke.

"You better work fast," he said. "I don't have a clue how to talk Pagandan, or whatever those people speak."

"Hang on a second," Joshua cut in. He glanced at Liz. Phone to one ear, she was pulling her jacket over her shoulders and hurrying after Sam and Terell.

Would she really go with him? He realized he had no certainty that Liz Wallace was a woman who kept her vows.

The plane began its descent into Amarillo, Texas. Joshua shifted in his seat, again trying to arrange himself more comfortably. First class should offer plenty of legroom, he thought. But his shoulders more than covered the back of the chair, and one knee jutted out into the aisle.

Seated by the window, Liz was a bundle of nerves. Had been the whole flight. Picking her up that morning at her apartment building, he knew right away she was sending him a message to back off. She had packed a carry-on bag, nothing more. On the way to the airport, she phoned her friend Molly, then her parents, then Sam Hawke. In the terminal, she made a beeline for the restroom. Joshua half expected her to vanish like Mary Rudi. Just as their flight was being called, she emerged.

Once inside the plane, she had exclaimed over their seats in the first class cabin. For all his training, Joshua hadn't been able to decipher whether that cry had been one of pleasure or dismay. Liz sat down, buckled her seat belt, put her head back and shut her eyes. Her hands, clutching her purse, were white-knuckled.

"You slept through the food service," he told her when she opened her eyes and looked around. "Airplane food. Shame."

Her brown eyes met his. "I wasn't asleep."

They had barely spoken all morning, and he felt himself getting edgy. "Liz, talk to me. What's going on?"

"I shouldn't be here," she said. "I don't belong in first class."

"You do now. You're with me."

"I didn't get to tell Mrs. Gonzales where I was going. And I don't feel right about leaving the Pagandans in the hands of Sam and Terell. I set up the event, and I should be there. Besides, I hardly know you. I don't know why I'm doing this. It's—"

"Liz." He touched her cheek. "It's me. You know me. You love me. And I love you."

"But it doesn't feel the way it did back in St. Louis. This isn't where we fit."

"You and I fit together anywhere. You'll see."

"No, I mean we don't fit *here.* The airport, the first class cabin, Texas."

As she said the word, the plane's wheels touched down on the tarmac. Tears flooded her eyes.

"I shouldn't have come. I don't know what I was thinking. I *wasn't* thinking! I never do impulsive things like this."

"I always do them." With some effort in the cramped space, he reached around and took her shoulders. "Liz, relax. You can leave anytime you want. But I hope you'll stay."

She pressed her fingertips against the corner of one eye. "I'm sorry, Joshua. You were good to invite me. And I did want to come. But last night I just couldn't—"

"Let me guess. You couldn't sleep? Neither could I. Spent hours in the fitness room. Do you think things like this happen to me all the time, Liz? I never expected to find you in St. Louis. And when I did, I had no idea what to do with you—with my feelings for you. We're in the same place. So, let's go meet my parents. We'll hang out by the pool, have some dinner, visit old friends. Let's give Texas a chance."

As he finished, she nodded. The flight attendant opened the cabin door. People stood and began gathering their belongings. Joshua pushed himself out of his seat and tried to work out the kinks in his legs. Maybe he had overdone the treadmill.

"Prime rib, ma'am? Or would you prefer turkey?" A young man dressed in a tuxedo smiled at Liz. "You can have both if you want."

"Oh . . . turkey. That would be fine. Thank you."

She gripped the edges of her plate as if it might somehow steady her. Nothing in Liz's life had prepared her for this.

The Duff home sprawled across the Amarillo plains like a lazy cougar. Thick adobe walls and saltillo clay tile floors lent an air of comfort to the faded elegance of the old place. Chandeliers hung from the ceilings by massive chains. Furniture upholstered in Mexican and Indian blankets had been carved from pine. Paintings—Western landscapes mostly—hung on the walls. Pottery filled lighted niches.

Liz's room went on and on—with a private bath and sitting area of her own. Her suite opened onto a wide porch, which led to the huge patio that surrounded the swimming pool. For the party, strings of glittering white lights filled the trees and hung in swags from the porch ceiling.

Caterers had arrived while Liz was taking an afternoon nap. She showered and slipped into a dress and heels. By the time she stepped outside, long buffet tables with white skirts stretched endlessly across the patio. Spits turned meat. Barbecue sauce bubbled in pots. Vegetable dishes sat steaming under silver covers. Bread, cheeses, salads of every kind were spread out in a grand array.

And there were people. Lots of people.

Liz had immediately liked Joshua's parents when they met at the airport. His father wore a white Stetson, a blue shirt and bolo tie, jeans and cowboy boots. His mother was elegant and pretty with soft blond hair and pearls at her neck. They embraced their son, admonished him, welcomed him, teased him. They had treated Liz like a queen.

"There you are!" Joshua's father gave a jaunty wave as he crossed to where she stood at the buffet. "You fill up now, honey. We don't want our guests going away hungry."

She laughed. "There's hardly a chance of that."

"Mind if I cut in? Looks like there's room for an old fellow to elbow through." He grabbed a plate and pointed to the prime rib. "Now that's a slab of meat for you, right there. That's from our own stock."

"Killed the fatted calf, did you?" she asked.

He threw back his head and guffawed. "Joshua's

a prodigal son, all right. I thought I'd never get my boy home from the military. Then he stayed so long in St. Louis, we began to wonder if he'd be back at all. Now we understand what was keeping him."

"Oh, it wasn't me." She had forced herself to fill her plate as he talked. The urge to bolt was great, but she kept walking. "Joshua got deeply involved in the work at Haven. Did he tell you about it?"

"The youth center? Yes, great project. Duff-Flannigan is a corporate sponsor, of course. I met Sam Hawke several times. He visited here between deployments. Doesn't surprise me that he went into nonprofit work. I could tell he had a big heart."

"So does your son." Liz glanced over her shoulder at Joshua's father. In the lamplit darkness she was again stricken by the similarities between the two. John Duff was a handsome man. Rugged, strong, imposing. But Elaine Duff had given her second-born child his blue eyes.

"Joshua played a lot of basketball with the kids at Haven, I understand." The older man indicated a table near the pool. They walked together. "He said he taught a few classes in the fitness room and helped build some sort of outdoor recreation area."

"Yes, and it's getting a lot of use." Liz hardly knew what to say. What information had Joshua given his family—and what had he kept secret?

She spotted the man himself across the water. He stood at the center of a group of young women. From the way they were giggling, Liz had a feeling they were not his sisters.

"Oh, don't worry about them," John said, dismissing the women with a flick of his hand. "They've been vying for my boy for years. Known each other since they were kids. Family friends. He used to call those girls 'the bumblebees.' They kept buzzing him, bothering him. Elaine and I speculated half the reason he joined the Marine Corps was to get away from them. Now I suspect they're not much more than gnats drifting around his head. Joshua is all yours."

"I'm not sure about that, Mr. Duff. We haven't known each other long."

"From what he tells me, sounds pretty serious all the same."

"It happened fast."

"Always does with Duffs. We never do anything halfhearted." He pulled back her chair, seated her and then settled into his place nearby. "I met my Elaine one morning, took her out on our first date that evening, married her two weeks later. Her folks weren't too thrilled, but thirty-eight happy years later, I think we've won them over. It's true, a Duff never dawdles in matters of the heart. My grandfather had known my grandmother ten minutes when he asked for her hand. Hope that doesn't scare you, Miss Lizzy."

She smiled at the endearment. “A little. Faithfulness is a Duff tradition I like. Joshua told me he never breaks promises.”

“That’s right,” he said as he chewed. “We’re Irish, you know. Loyal to the bone. Hotheaded. Stubborn. Smart—gotta put that in. And we don’t mess around. We Duffs know what we want. When we want something, we go get it.”

“And you want Joshua to take his place in the family business,” she said. “Director of oil field operations, was it?”

“President. He’ll run that division.” He had stabbed a fork into his prime rib, sawed off a chunk and was dipping it in horseradish sauce.

“Does your son like the oil field?”

“It’s money,” he said. “No other way to put it. Oil is money. It’s what Duffs do. We don’t have *feelings* for the oil patch—we own it. A master-servant relationship. We’re good to the land, but we make it work for us. It serves our family well. Serves others, too. We created a foundation that helps the needy. You’ll get the picture before long. We’ll take you out tomorrow after church. Sunday drive around some of our property.”

She ate a bite of turkey, marveling at the barbecue sauce. Was that another Duff family tradition—like loyalty and stubbornness?

“Is this a secret?” she asked, pointing to the hearty, brick-red liquid that dripped from her meat. “I’d love to give the recipe to the volunteers at Haven. They'd enjoy using it at the Pagandan barbecue tomorrow evening."

"What kind of a barbecue?"

"It's for refugees from Paganda. Joshua didn't mention it? He's probably trying to put it out of his mind. The police were hoping he'd be there to finish the investigation. He worked so hard to get the gang to stop claiming Haven as its turf. I hope they can wrap things up without him."

"You're saying my boy was doing some kind of investigation while he was in St. Louis?"

A knot formed in Liz's stomach. "Didn't he tell you?"

"He said he was helping out at Haven with the fitness room and the basketball. That kind of thing. He met you and wanted time to get to know you better. That's why he stayed in St. Louis as long as he did."

"Because of *me?*"

"Well, he did admit he was enjoying the companionship of a fellow ex-Marine while he was adapting to civilian life." John Duff lowered his voice. "I guess you know Joshua has gone through some harrowing events out there on the battlefield. This isn't the first time he needed a few weeks to get back in the saddle."

"Yes, he told me."

"The last time he came home, Elaine and I could see he was a changed man. He was jumpy, tense, on edge. Like his brain had gotten a little scrambled over there. He did talk to a doc or two on base. Anyhow, it wasn't long before he came out of it. I think it helps him to be here on the ranch with the family. We feed him right, let him rest. He likes to ride his horse, go camping, be alone. Then he's fine."

"That's good."

Liz noticed that Joshua was working his way through the clusters of guests, greeting people and then moving on around the pool. He had spotted her and tipped his chin to signal that he was on his way to her side. Though she had missed him, the thought of their encounter made her nervous.

This Joshua was not the man she had met in St. Louis. Like his father and the other men, he now wore a tailored leather coat, jeans and cowboy boots. He smiled more. Laughed easily. His father was right. Joshua was comfortable at home. He belonged here.

"Now about this investigation you mentioned," John said, drawing Liz's focus. "Tell me more about that."

She wished she could think of an escape. If Joshua hadn't told his family what he'd been doing in St. Louis, maybe he didn't want them to know. But Duff integrity was important, both men had stipulated, and his father deserved at least some information.

"Haven is surrounded by gang territory," she

said. “One group has been trying to take that street. Didn’t he mention the Hypes?”

John Duff’s brow furrowed. “He said he was helping build a basketball court.”

“The new outdoor rec area, right. That’s where the drive-by shooting happened. I saw the whole thing. It was Mo Ded’s gang—the Hypes—who shot that little boy who’s one of the refugees from Paganda. The child is part of the family Joshua offered to help resettle. That was how I met him. You know? The refugee family?”

As she was speaking, she saw confusion and dismay filter across John Duff’s face.

“The Rudi family,” she continued, hesitantly. “They had left their agency and caseworker in Atlanta when they moved to St. Louis. Joshua met them at Haven. Anyway . . . Joshua was a lot of help.”

“I thought he was helping kids in a fitness center.”

“Yes, but you know Joshua.”

As she said it, she suddenly realized that maybe this man did *not* know his son. Not really. Not the way she did.

“So—a child got shot?” John asked.

“He’s going to be all right. Joshua was right there when it happened. Actually, that bullet was meant for . . . for someone else. And . . . it turned out okay.”

As John Duff carved another chunk of prime

rib, Liz searched desperately for a way out of this conversation.

"Your pool must be very nice in the summer," she offered. "I bet it gets hot here."

"Yes, but what was this investigation about? The shooting?"

Liz tried to sound dismissive. "Well, the whole gang situation. Joshua looked into the Hypes problem. He was helping the police put together a plan to take down Mo Ded."

"Mo Ded?" John Duff leaned back in his chair. A frown tugged at the corners of his mouth. "I thought Joshua left that kind of thing behind in Afghanistan. Warlords and investigations and shootings."

She couldn't resist sharing her admiration. "But your son was amazing in St. Louis. He used all his training, all his skills to help us. Mr. Duff, when people hate each other, whether they're fighting over land or power or religion or anything else, it doesn't matter where they live. I wish you could meet my refugees. You'd understand what Joshua was doing. These people have suffered so much. The women come to us, and they're just broken. The children have witnessed things no child should ever see. The men often have wounds that go way beyond obvious physical scars."

"And this is what you do? You help these people find new homes in America?"

"In St. Louis. My refugees would have no idea a

place like this exists. Your home, the pool, the miles of open land. They could never even imagine it."

"Imagine what?" Joshua emerged into the light of the candles on the table. He pulled back a chair and sat. "Dad, are you bragging about your big spread? You'd better not be filling Liz's head with stories about the Duff family and all our shenanigans. A few of your Irish tales, and she'll be running for the hills."

"Your Miss Lizzy is the storyteller tonight. I had no idea what you were up to in St. Louis. Gang shootings, Joshua?"

Both pairs of eyes turned on Liz. One set brown. The other navy-blue.

"I think I may have said too much." Liz scooted back in her chair. "I thought you'd been talking to your family every day, Joshua. I thought they knew. Lest I get caught in the cross fire here, I think I'll go grab some dessert. I saw some pecan pie with my name on it."

Both men rose, a gallant gesture, as she hurried away. Heart hammering, Liz headed for the dessert table. She picked up a plate of pie and a fork and half ran to her room. All she could think about now was going home.

Chapter Twenty

"Liz." Joshua knocked again. "Please talk to me."

The door to her bedroom suite opened, and she stepped out onto the patio. The evening breeze filtered through her hair, lifting the curls and making them dance. He couldn't resist a touch.

"It's okay," he said. "My father and I are fine. It's true, I hadn't told him everything"

"You hadn't told him *anything*. Helping out in the fitness room? Playing basketball with the kids? Joshua, why weren't you honest?"

"I did those things. My dad and mom didn't know the details of what I was doing in Afghanistan. Why would I tell them about St. Louis? That kind of stuff is hard for a parent to hear."

"I'm sorry. I never should have said a word. I stumbled into it because of the barbecue sauce. I was thinking about tomorrow at Haven—the Pagandans and how they would like the taste. I shouldn't have mentioned the gangs. Or Mo Ded."

"Or the drive-by shooting."

"Okay, I blew it." She hugged herself. "Joshua, I've booked a flight. I'm going home tomorrow."

Disbelief flooded through him.

"Tomorrow? You haven't seen our land. The Duff-Flannigan building. We didn't go into Amarillo. There are refugees here, Liz. My mother made some phone calls this afternoon. She found two services that do resettlement work just like in Atlanta and St. Louis. Iraqis and Bosnians are pouring in. And immigrants from down south. Documented, undocumented. It's a crazy place. The need is here."

"But my people are there." Wiping her cheek, she shook her head. "My work is in St. Louis. My Somalis and Burundians and Congolese."

"Your Africans."

"I need to be with my Pagandans tomorrow at that barbecue. If something happens—a drive-by, any kind of problem—I should be with them. They need me, Joshua."

"What about me?" He looked out across the open area around the swimming pool, his welcome-home party still going strong. "I need you, Liz. I love you."

"I love you, too."

Startled at the honest confession, he took her in his arms. "I was afraid you'd changed your mind about me."

"Why do you think I'm such a wreck? I love you so much. Your father. He's wonderful. Your mother is beautiful and kind. All these people welcomed me. They think you hung the moon. So do I, Joshua. But I have to go home."

He wanted to protest. Were a bunch of Pagandans more important than the true love they had found together? But he knew Liz's heart. He understood how she felt, because he felt the same. That craziness, that intense, mind-boggling drama, that crush of people and need and emotion compelled him, too.

"What time do you leave?" he asked.

Holding her, he tried to memorize the curves of her shoulders, the dip of her back, the sweet fragrance of her perfume. He couldn't let her go. It would kill him. But how could he ask her to stay? Stay and be miserable? It would destroy her love for him.

"Noon," she said. "Your father asked me to go to church with the family. And see the oil field."

"I want to take you riding. Show you my favorite places on the ranch. There's a stream. An old abandoned house. A cliff. It's beautiful."

Her arms tightened around him. "I'll visit again, Joshua." She shook her head. "No, I won't. It would be wrong to come and go. To pretend it might work out this way."

"Are you still moving to Africa? Is that what God's telling you?"

"I don't feel certain about that anymore. As I thought about leaving St. Louis, I finally understood how much I need to stay right there. I'm going to talk to my supervisor on Monday to see if I can change some of my responsibilities. I want to be inside the homes. Mary Rudi and those two little children—I see how great their need is, and I have to do what I can. Language, reading, even filling out forms and doing homework with the kids, all of it is so important. Maybe in time, I'll go to Africa. But for now, I have to stay where I am."

"You're in my arms, Liz." He pulled her closer. "That's where you are. Don't you feel how right it is?"

"Yes." Her voice broke. "I do. But not in Texas. It can't be like it was. You'll be working in your big office. President of oil field operations. I don't know what will happen to you—to the man who tracks down Claymore mines. And I really don't know what would happen to us."

He let out a breath. "I have to stay here, Liz. This is my future."

"You made a promise. You're a Duff and Duffs never break vows. Yes, I know that now—even better than I did. It's why I love you. But it makes our love impossible."

She stood on tiptoe and kissed him. Then she backed away. "Let me go, Joshua. Enjoy your party. Give your parents the gift of time, the gift of *you*. They missed you, and they love you so much."

"Come spend the rest of the evening with me."

"Chitchat with the bumblebees?" She smiled at him. "No, I'm going to bed now. I have a long day tomorrow."

Before he could stop her, Liz stepped into her room and shut the door. Alone on the porch, Joshua felt a sudden, boiling, white-hot rage shoot through his veins. Why? Why did it have to be this way? He wanted Liz Wallace. She loved him. They belonged together—even his father had said so.

Afraid of doing something he might regret, Joshua forced the anger into his muscles, filling them, driving him down the porch, through the house, out to the stables. A long ride under the stars. Better than returning to the buffet and the chitchat and the prospect of a long life without the woman he loved.

"Liz?" Ana Burns looked up from a large tub of baked beans. "What are you doing in St. Louis? Sam said you went to Texas with Joshua. I figured the next time we heard from you, we'd be getting a wedding invitation."

Liz tried to find a way to smile. "I thought I should come back. Need some help?"

"We've got it under control. Everyone has been through the line at least once." Her long, dark brown hair tied up in a knot, Ana set the ladle back into the bean pot and wiped her hands on her apron. "I'm surprised how many came this evening. They must have been looking for a reason to get together."

"Always." This time, Liz found her grin. "You have to know Africans the way I do."

Ana wrapped her arm around Liz's shoulders and began walking her away from the crowd of picnickers toward the sidewalk. Darkness was settling over the outdoor recreation area, and the streetlamps were coming on. As planned, Sergeant Ransom and a couple of other detectives were working their way through the crowd on the pretext of good public relations. No doubt Joshua had trained them well.

"All right," Ana said in a low voice. "Let's have the scoop. Why'd you leave your handsome Marine in Amarillo? Didn't like his folks? Found out something you didn't know about the guy? Some big bad secret?"

"No, it was all wonderful." She halted. "Don't make me talk about it, Ana."

"He didn't reject you, did he? It's been a long time since I've seen a man that crazy in love."

"You see a man like that every day."

"True." Ana laughed. "Feels like this wedding will never get here. My mother took over the planning—I finally surrendered to the pressure. She's pouring everything for two daughters' weddings into one."

"How's that?"

"My sister died a few years ago." Her voice was wistful. "This is helping my mom heal. And it gives me time to focus on Sam and Haven. So why did you come back here, Liz? Miss city life?"

"You don't let up, do you?" She surveyed the clusters of happy Pagandans seated on blankets on the ground. "This is where I belong, Ana."

"So does Joshua. Sam can't stop talking about how much help he was. He would have been a great asset to the Haven team."

"Joshua had promises to keep." Liz spotted Charity racing in circles around her father, who was talking to Sergeant Ransom. "I hope the police find out what's going on. I'm sure Sam told you our suspicions."

"And I promised to keep my reporter's nose out of it until they have the whole story. Hard to accept who might be at the root of everything."

Liz studied Pastor Stephen. A broad smile on his face, the man was speaking with his usual fervor. In fact, he looked very much like he was preaching to the police officer.

"Sam agreed to let him lead a short worship time at the end of the picnic for those who want to stay," Ana said. "I hope his wife gets back in time."

"Mary left?" Liz looked around. She could picture the frustration on Joshua's face at yet another disappearance. "Where did she go?"

"Down to the street corner there. I saw her walk away a few minutes ago." Ana studied the empty sidewalk. "I wonder where she went."

"Crowds make her nervous." Liz thought of her resolution to get closer to Mary and the other refugee women. She had done more than enough office duty. It was time to get personally involved.

"Mary lost her job the other day," she told Ana.

"She was working in a crew—all English speakers, several men. I think that must have bothered her."

"Too many people around?"

"That's part of it. She went through a lot in Paganda—her husband and children were killed. Mary was raped."

Ana's face softened. "She can't be comfortable around men. Especially strangers."

"No. I think I'll go see if I can find her. Maybe I'll take Charity with me. Mary doesn't speak much English, but with Charity's help I might be able to talk her into coming back to the picnic. It would be good for her to mingle, maybe even make a friend or two who could help her adjust."

"Listen, if *you* need a friend to help you adjust, I'm right here." Ana gave Liz a brief hug before stepping away. "Well, looks like I need to swap that empty bean pot for a full one. Good to have you back, by the way."

Liz watched the tall woman stride back to the food line. Sam was blessed—Ana Burns could grace the cover of any fashion magazine on the stands. But here she was ladling beans while she waited for her wedding day.

Liz found Charity skipping rope in the circle of light on the sidewalk at the front of Haven. The child spotted her and waved. Dashing over, she did a happy pirouette in front of Liz.

"Charity, will you help me find your mama?" she

asked, kneeling to bring herself to child height. The little girl's English wasn't perfect, but she was learning fast. "Can you help me find Mary?"

Charity's smile faded. "Mary gone."

"Yes, down to the corner. There." Liz pointed. "Come with me. We'll bring her back."

The little girl stared into the distance, her face registering an odd mixture of anger and sadness. Then she turned to look for her father. Liz waved at Pastor Stephen—now talking to two detectives on the gang task force.

"We're going to look for your wife," she called.

"She went that way," he replied, pointing. "The grocery market."

Liz nodded. "I'll bring her home."

She took Charity's hand, and they set off down the block. Her purse locked safely in the trunk of her car, Liz felt relieved to not carry anything. Her morning had begun with loading her travel bag into the Duffs' car. After church and the drive around the oil fields, she had toted that bag through the airport, onto the plane, into a taxi, up her apartment stairs. Now she and Charity swung their clasped hands as they searched the sidewalks for Mary Rudi.

Coming to the corner, Liz paused and looked around. A grocery market? Was that the sort of store to attract the reclusive refugee? Had it become the sanctuary Mary Rudi ran to when her family or her job became too much?

Spotting a little grocery on the next block, Liz saw that it was open late. Mary was probably hiding in there, studying cereal boxes, examining tomatoes. The idea of the small woman in her big glasses and gaudy head scarf trying to loiter unnoticed amused Liz. If Mary were inside the shop, she wouldn't be hard to find.

Liz came to the end of the first block. She tightened her hold on Charity's hand as they waited until the stoplight changed. They stepped down into the street.

At that moment, a large, rusty white car—some ancient vintage Lincoln—pulled out of a nearby parking space. It sped toward them. Surprised, Liz tightened her grip on the child and stepped back. She was halfway onto the sidewalk when the car pulled up in front of them and screeched to a stop. The right passenger doors flew open. Two young men leaped out. One grabbed Liz by the arm, wrestled her down, clamped his hand over her mouth. The other snatched up Charity. The trunk lid flipped open. Liz tried to scream. A third man appeared. Two of them lifted Liz from her feet and tossed her inside. The child tumbled in after her and the lid slammed down.

Darkness. The smell of gasoline and tire rubber. The car gave a lurch, and Liz skidded against the side of the trunk. Her head hit the wheel well. Her elbow jammed into her hip. Charity wailed as the vehicle took off in a blast of exhaust fumes.

Lodged against something hard, Liz sensed the pavement rushing beneath the tires.

Gasping for breath, she reached out to steady herself. She had to find Charity, comfort the child. So obvious who had taken them. Scrawny, nervous kids with purple do-rags tied on their heads. Hypes.

Her urge to berate herself, to scream, to cry—all vanished with the realization that the gangbangers would be headed for Mo Ded.

"Charity?" Liz reached out in the dark, tight space. "Charity, I'm here. Let me hold you."

Whimpering, the little girl edged into Liz's arms. The car turned a corner. Again they rolled, bumping against each other, hitting the inside walls of the trunk.

"Charity, don't be afraid," Liz whispered. "Stay close to me all the time. We can be strong together. Do you understand?"

"It's like me and Virtue in the water barrel," Charity sobbed out. "Pray to God. Pray the way my *baba* does."

"That's good," Liz told her. It would calm them both. "You pray first. Then I'll pray."

As the little girl began speaking in her singsong voice, a plea in the language of her homeland, Liz frantically searched her mind. The Hypes had been watching her, of course. Mo Ded saw her leave the barbecue. He knew what was happening now. He would have a plan.

What did he want? Surely he realized Joshua had gone. Kidnapping Liz and a child would do the man no good. Unless Mo Ded wanted to make some kind of statement. A show of power. Would that mean he intended harm? Or just to scare them?

She thought of her purse. Had she left her phone in the car, too? She needed a weapon. Inside her own car's trunk she carried some potential combat gear. A can of deicer. A jack. A tire iron. A tennis racquet. No telling what else she had tossed in.

As the vehicle slowed, came to a stop, she felt around in the empty space. *Dear God, let me find something. Anything.*

"Amen," Charity said. "Now you."

Liz's hand closed around a shoe. With one arm wrapped around the little girl, she gripped the shoe in her free hand. What kind was it? A sneaker? A boot?

Was there nothing else in this car? Nothing better?

"Now *you,*" Charity repeated. "You pray."

The car surged ahead again. The two in the trunk slid fast, slamming against a wall. Liz stifled a cry of pain. Was there enough air? Would carbon monoxide kill them?

"Please!" Charity squeezed Liz's hand. "Pray to Jesus!"

"Yes, all right." Liz was thinking about cell phones and murder and methamphetamine-crazed gangsters. But she hugged Charity and tried to pray.

"Dear God," she began.

The car slowed. A stoplight? Maybe the police?

"Dear Jesus," the girl corrected.

"Dear Jesus, we ask for your help now. Please help us. Please send someone to—"

The engine roared to life again, revving and sending gas-infused air billowing through rust holes into the trunk. Sirens wailed somewhere—too far, she thought. The car blasted forward. Liz and Charity tumbled, jammed together as the car roared down the street. It swerved. They skidded across the rough carpeted lining of the trunk and slammed against the other side.

"Pray!" Charity shrieked.

"Dear Jesus, please help us now!" Liz cried out. "Oh, God, save us!"

Sirens blared, screaming behind them. Yes, definitely a squad car. Liz kept praying. It was impossible to maintain control of a vehicle at such speeds. Any moment, they would crash. The car took corners, tires screeching, almost lifting from the pavement. Liz fell and rolled and tumbled. She tried to keep her hold on Charity, but the girl rolled and spun out of her arms. They crashed into each other, then came apart again. She lost her grip on the shoe. The child's elbow smashed into her jaw. Her knee hit something soft, and Charity cried out in pain.

The car swerved. And stopped. At impact, the trunk lid popped up.

Someone running. Shouts.

Joshua reached for Liz, caught her, pulled her from the trunk. The car rolled forward again. Liz screamed. As it raced away, she fell into Joshua's arms.

"Charity!" she wailed. The white car veered around a corner and disappeared, the police cruiser in pursuit.

"They have Charity! Joshua, she's still inside!" She covered her face, sinking into his arms. They were alone on the sidewalk, the sirens fading in the distance.

"The trunk lid—it was open. Oh, Joshua, she'll fall out!" She turned and caught his shoulders. "We have to go after them!"

"Liz, breathe." He held her up, his arm at her waist. "Did you see who was driving? Recognize anyone?"

"Hypes," she huffed out. "Purple scarves. Skinny kids. Joshua—what are you doing? You're in Texas."

"I'm here with you now."

"But your father—"

"He sent me, Liz."

She shook her head, feeling sick, confused. "Those creeps got Charity. I let them kidnap that little girl."

"It's not your fault." He began walking, supporting her. "We have to get back to Haven. It's near—can you keep up?"

"Everything hurts. Like being inside a dryer. Tumbling around, bumping into everything."

Her feet tried to match his stride, but she stumbled. He swept her up in his arms. Arm around his neck, she buried her face in his shoulder as he strode. Trying not to cry, trying to pray. *Pray,* Charity had ordered. Pray! And Liz did pray.

"Here we are." Joshua set her down in a chair.

Liz opened her eyes and somehow they were inside Haven. A throng of panicked Pagandans swarmed the place. Pastor Stephen ran up to her.

"My daughter! Where is she? Where have they taken her?"

"Stephen, we need a photograph," Joshua cut in. "Do you have pictures of Charity?"

"Yes, yes! I bring it." He was gone again.

"Liz, drink this." Ana knelt beside her. A cup of cold water. "You're bleeding. Rug burns on your cheek, your elbows and knees. Can I help you?"

"Find that little girl. Oh, Ana!" Liz threw her arms around the caring woman. "This is my fault."

"No, Liz." Joshua spoke with authority. "Mo Ded would have found a way. If not you and Charity, someone else. Maybe Ana or Raydell. Maybe Shauntay. This is a message. He's telling us he's still strong, in control. He won't get away with it."

"Here is my family." Pastor Stephen thrust a

framed photograph into Joshua's hands. "It was the wedding day. See—Charity is there."

"I need to get into the office," Joshua told Liz. People pushed around them, trying to get a look at the picture. "Gotta make photocopies of the girl. The police will put out an Amber Alert once we give them the information."

"I'll make the copy," Ana said. "Sam and Terell are in the office making calls. Give me the portrait. Come with me, Liz. There's a bathroom in the office. We can clean you up."

Joshua helped Liz to her feet and worked her through the throng of Pagandans toward Haven's glass-windowed office. They were almost there when a small elderly woman snatched the photograph from Ana's hand.

"Hold on, there. Gimme that." Joshua reached for the picture. The woman pulled it back, letting out a cry as she stared at the faces.

Throwing back her head, she began to ululate—a shrill, high-pitched, warbling wail. The crowd fell suddenly silent, hanging on the sound. Then they swarmed Liz and the others, grabbing for the photograph, passing it from hand to hand, some screaming out as they saw the picture, others shrieking and beginning to sob. One woman shook her head, writhed a moment, then sank to the gym floor.

"What's going on here? Give me that picture." Joshua waded after it. "We have to make copies of the child. The police need a photo ID. Ma'am, let me—"

"It is her! It is her!" A young woman came at him. Beneath her yellow head scarf, her eyes snapped with fire. "She—in the picture! That is Irene Bangado! Irene Bangado!"

"Who? I need a translator. Pastor Stephen? Where is that guy?"

Liz spotted the man in the swarm. His face wrenched with horror, Stephen Rudi pushed his way toward Joshua.

"Let me have it!" he called out. "It belongs to me. Give me the picture of my family."

"He is married to Irene Bangado. He has brought her among us!" An older woman clamped her hand on Joshua's arm. "You must find her. Find Irene Bangado! Execute her!"

Another roar flowed through the crowd. Liz leaned against Ana, sure she might faint at any moment. The scene around her was surreal, a nightmare. People screaming, women collapsing, a child in the trunk of a speeding car.

Joshua held the photograph now, lifting it over his head. The glass had broken. The frame was falling away.

"Everyone stop!" he bellowed. "Quiet!"

At the command, the shouting and ululating faded to a rumble. He clamped a hand on Stephen Rudi's shoulder. "Tell me what's going on here, man. Make it simple."

"My wife, my Mary." Pastor Stephen trembled as he pointed to the photograph. "They are saying she is not Mary. They believe this is Irene Bangado. The Minister of Women's Health and Family Affairs."

"The Minister of Rape!" someone shouted.

"The Minister of Rape!" The cry went up, a thunderous howl. "Irene Bangado, the Minister of Rape!"

"No!" Tears streamed down Stephen's face as he faced the crowd. "No, it cannot be. Mary was in the camp. She was with us, with our tribe." He turned to Joshua. "She was a widow. I told you this. Her husband and children were killed in the war. The people are wrong. This is not that woman!"

"Yes, she is!" The lady in the yellow head scarf shook her finger at Joshua. "I saw Irene Bangado in person. When I was a little girl, she came to my school. Before the war. She gave prizes. I took first place—my report was on tuberculosis. I remember everything. I know the face of Irene Bangado. That man's wife is the Minister of Rape."

"How dare you say such a thing about her?" Stephen Rudi bellowed. "Look at the woman. The spectacles! The face! No!"

"She hid behind the spectacles and scarf she wore! That was her disguise!" The woman clutched Joshua's arm. "Sir, you must believe me.

This woman authorized the rape and murder of thousands in Paganda. I am one of those women!"

Breathing hard, Joshua turned to Liz. "Irene Bangado?"

"A government minister in Paganda. A top official." Liz touched her cheek. Her fingers came away damp with blood. "Joshua, this doesn't matter now. We have to find Charity. Please call Ransom. Find out what he knows."

"Yes, my child!" Stephen wept. "Please find my daughter!"

Joshua took Liz's hand. "Could she be our connection? The link?"

"That lady is my wife!" Pastor Stephen reached for the photograph in Joshua's hand. "The picture is my family. Mary cannot be that cruel woman."

Despite her pain, Liz had to focus. "Irene Bangado would have access to government property."

"My wife is not Irene Bangado!" Stephen protested. Sweat streaming down his temples mingled with the tears on his cheeks. He grasped Joshua's shirtsleeve. "You must hear this—my wife owns nothing. When I married her, she had nothing, not even a child. She brought nothing to our marriage. Not a cooking pot. Not a comb or a mirror. She had only her clothes in a small plastic sack. I saw those possessions. I brought them in my own bag to America. She is poor, a widow. Please, trust me. Irene Bangado—that demon—

she was a very rich woman when the war came. Mary has no education, no wealth, nothing."

"But she speaks good English," Joshua said.

"My wife has no English."

"Yes—she understands. She knows a lot. Pastor Stephen, when Mary leaves you, where does she go?"

"To the grocery market only. She buys potatoes and cornmeal. Such things as this. Please, you must believe me."

"I believe what you're telling me," Joshua said. "But I want to know more about your wife."

Arm around Liz, he spoke to Ana in a low voice. "Take the picture. Make copies of the girl's face. Get them to the precinct station. Tell Sam and Terell to meet me on the street where the prayer-walk ended. See if they can track down Ransom."

"Where are you going, Joshua?"

"To end this thing."

Chapter Twenty-One

Liz held his hand as they climbed the stairs. The putrid odor drifted in the chill air, nauseating her. It was an abandoned brick building, condemned. The windows had shattered long ago. Some were boarded up, others open to the elements. Spray-painted logos covered walls. Red, green, purple gang signs. Burned-out rooms revealed water damage, trash. Rats scurried, their claws scrabbling across bare wood floors.

Joshua had asked her to wait. Stay behind at Haven. Rest. She refused. Charity was gone because of her. She had taken the child from the safety of her father and the crowd of Pagandans.

Finding the building had not been hard after all. Joshua retraced their steps on the prayer-walk. He pointed out clues—gang signs, purple insignias, the look and smell of each street.

They found the rusted white car in an alley. The trunk stood empty. Joshua's instinct and the acrid scent led them on.

Though still uncertain how Joshua had come to be here—in St. Louis, pulling her from the car trunk, leading her up to Mo Ded's lair—Liz felt a sense of peace.

"In the trunk, I asked God to send help," she whispered. "He sent you."

Joshua nodded, held his finger to his lips. "Up one more flight."

They knew the hallway by the stench. Joshua tucked Liz into a dark corner.

"Someone's cooking meth here," he said. "There will be chemicals. Dangerous, flammable explosives. Mo Ded is probably using. He'll be erratic, unpredictable. I want you to wait here."

"Don't go by yourself. The police are on their way."

"No time. If Charity is inside, she'll be

breathing the chemical cocktail. Or worse. I need to get her out. Ransom is behind me—five minutes at the most. You stay put. I'll be back."

He started down the hall. Liz watched him go and knew she had to follow. Charity would be traumatized. Joshua bashing in the door might terrify her to the point of shock.

Liz left the shadows. Joshua heard her at once. He halted. His face registered dismay, then acceptance.

For a moment, he stood outside the door. Assessing. The thump of music came from inside. A light crept under the transom, spread across the rotten wood floor. People were talking. Low, urgent voices.

Joshua glanced at Liz, then nodded. She pressed herself against the wall. As she watched, the scene seemed to unfold in slow motion. Joshua raised one leg and cocked it. After a moment's pause, he delivered a violent kick that blew the door inward. In the same motion, he stormed the room.

Liz rushed behind him, darting inside as Mary Rudi grabbed Charity, holding her as a shield. Joshua had jumped Mo Ded, was mashing his face into a broken radiator. Two others fled.

Liz started for the child. The gun in Mary's hand stopped her.

"Joshua!"

He was there, too fast for the woman to react.

He chopped her arm, and the weapon flew to the floor. Liz scooped Charity into her arms.

And then Ransom was inside. Officers swarmed the warren of rooms, calling out from the hallways as they searched the building. Mo Ded collected himself from a heap at the base of a wall. Eyes hooded, he shivered and began talking, claiming he was innocent, knew nothing about anything.

"Detroit?" Ransom barked out. "Or did Chicago spawn you, kid?"

"Chi-town." Mo Ded's green eyes flicked toward Liz. "I nearly took this place. Had you running scared, didn't I?"

"Charity," Liz whispered as she cuddled the girl in her arms. "Let's go outside now. I'll take you back to Haven."

"I want my *baba!*" The girl sobbed, rubbing her eyes with little fists. "She is bad! Bad Mary!"

"You both need to get out of here," Joshua said. "We'll get a hazmat crew in here to clean up this mess. The place could blow."

"She is bad!" Charity cried, tiny finger thrust at Mary.

The officer holding the woman's arm prodded her forward. Spectacles smashed on the floor, she glared at the child.

"What's wrong, Mary?" Liz asked. "Or should I call you Irene Bangado?"

"What's this?" she hissed. "Why do you say such a thing?"

"The Pagandans saw your photograph. They recognized you behind your disguise. Your secret is out, Irene."

"Yes, that is my name." Her English flawless, the woman straightened and threw back her shoulders. "Why not address me properly now? But no one can prove the accusations against me. Those things you may have heard. Rumors."

"The cloth!" Charity shouted. "She has little rocks inside the cloth."

A sparkle of chills washed down Liz's arms. "Irene, please remove your scarf."

"Why should I? This is my—"

"Because I said so!" Liz cried, suddenly overcome with anger. She grabbed the brightly colored fabric from the woman's head. As it unwound, countless tiny gray nuggets pattered on the floor.

"Everyone stand back," Joshua ordered. He picked up what looked like a dental filling and rolled it between his thumb and forefinger. Then he handed it to Ransom. "Make sure you gather up all those pellets before the hazmat guys get here. That's the platinum."

Liz was paralyzed, staring at the metal—the death, the rape, the torture rolled up in tiny metallic balls. Irene Bangado had no doubt plotted everything. But the woman even now was ordering the police officers to remove her handcuffs, lamenting her fate, complaining that she was a victim of the gang—not a collaborator.

Aware of the agony the woman had caused, Liz felt her pulse hammer as her anger mounted. Then a warm hand covered her shoulder.

"Come on, girls," Joshua said. Taking Charity from Liz's arms, he headed them toward the door. "Let's get you both home."

Joshua had fallen silent as he drove toward Haven. Charity, beyond exhaustion, had gone to sleep in the backseat. But Liz was fuming.

"That woman must have simply disappeared," she said. "At some point in the chaos, when she realized her political party was losing the civil war, she vanished."

"Wouldn't have been hard," Joshua murmured. "She disguised herself in spectacles and a scarf, which was filled with smuggled platinum. Invented a name and a story. A widow. Kids and husband murdered. Not so unusual, but likely to win sympathy."

Liz shook her head. "Irene Bangado, of all people. She must have gone to the refugee camp on purpose and pretended to be from the dominant tribe there. She probably hid at the fringes until she found a gullible man whose name was already on the resettlement list."

Joshua nodded. "Pastor Stephen heard her heartbreaking tale—a lot like his own—and agreed to marry her and take her to America. Why move to

St. Louis, though? She could have traded her platinum in Atlanta."

"Irene needed to get away from the community of Pagandans in Atlanta where Global Care would have placed the Rudi family. The refugee agency would require her to take English classes with other Pagandans and join those already working at a factory or business. She would need to participate fully with her new neighbors. It wouldn't be long before someone recognized her as Irene Bangado."

"Just like they did at the barbecue tonight." He turned the car onto Haven's street. "She invented a brother, forged a letter, sent it to herself from a false address and talked her husband onto a bus bound for St. Louis. Once they got here, she would have found Mo Ded right away. No wonder she was always disappearing."

A prickle of realization slid down Liz's spine. "That call I got from Mo Ded. His people saw Irene drop your phone when she ran from Duke. He was trying to connect with her but he got me instead."

"They probably started trading within days of her arrival. She needed Mo Ded to move her platinum without drawing suspicion—turning her treasure into cash. He wanted to build and arm his gang. The Claymore could have been ordered by either one. With Ransom tracking it, we'll know soon enough."

The car came to a stop in front of Haven. Joshua

stepped out and gathered the sleeping child in his arms. Liz followed. Ana was carrying a tray of freshly washed silverware when they stepped through Haven's door. Sam, his arms loaded with pans, spotted the new arrivals and passed his fiancée at a trot.

"Got your message," he told Joshua. "Stephen's in the office talking to the police."

"Come here, sugar." With his long legs eating up the basketball court, Terell had passed them both. He reached for the child in Joshua's arms. "Let's go find your *baba.* He misses you."

Charity, wide-awake now, almost leaped across the distance between the two men. Laughing, Terell jogged away. Ana and Sam set the dishes on a table and greeted their friends.

"So, she really is the Minister of Rape?" Ana asked. "Why didn't Stephen recognize her? Or did he know?"

Sam put his arm around her. "Careful what you say, everyone—reporter at work. You could wind up in tomorrow's headline."

"Stop teasing, Sam. This is heavy stuff."

"I have no doubt Mary Rudi is really Irene Bangado," Liz said. "I just can't believe she fooled me."

Joshua shook his head. "She conned everyone, including me."

"You suspected. You told me her behavior was talking to you—shouting at you—but you didn't know what it was saying. And I got upset with you for going through her pockets."

"If I'd found even one pellet of platinum, it would have saved a lot of pain." His arm around Liz tightened. He glanced toward the office. "I'm concerned about Stephen. He had no idea what his wife was up to."

"Clueless," Sam agreed. "In fact, he's still wavering about her. Took out her passport, the marriage certificate, all their documents. Told me he had seen that woman on television, the one they all called the Minister of Rape."

"Irene Bangado," Liz reiterated. "She had been Minister for Women's Health and Family Affairs under the old regime. When our last group of Pagandans came in a couple of years ago, I read about her. Until now, they thought she had escaped justice. She's among the people most feared and despised. She had a son in the military, a high-ranking officer. On the radio and through him, she ordered the rapes."

"To show domination and humiliation," Ana said softly.

"Terror, degradation, power," Liz added. "Irene Bangado also used it to spread the AIDS virus. She made speeches on the radio—ordered rapes staged almost like public performances. She called the enemy dirt, cockroaches. Sometimes women died in the process. And there were child victims, too. Little girls like Charity."

"What will happen to Irene?" Ana asked.

"An international tribunal," Joshua said. "She's a war criminal. She'll be extradited to Paganda to stand trial. The tribunal will decide her fate."

Liz noted movement through the office window, and she saw Stephen emerge into the open area of the basketball court. His daughter in his arms, he covered his eyes with a handkerchief. The police officers and Terell guided him toward the door.

"Pastor Stephen," Joshua said as they approached. "I'll pick you up at the precinct station in a few minutes. We'll drive over to the hospital and visit Virtue. He needs to see his *baba*."

Stephen lifted his head, and Liz saw that his eyes were red-rimmed and swollen. "You will help me?" he murmured. "After what I have done? Bringing that woman here . . . harming my own children . . . Such a fool . . ."

"We've all made mistakes," Joshua told him.

"Mine are many." He gazed at the gym floor. "I was a bad child. I left school, left my home and family. I carried a gun."

"You?" Liz asked. "A gun?"

"I found it one day. I imagined myself a tribal king, a leader of soldiers."

"A warrior?" Joshua asked.

Stephen nodded. "I wanted power and wealth. My father drank. My mother was a seamstress, but we had no money. Then two men murdered my father. I planned revenge. I surely would have died, but one night I heard singing. In a small room, I heard a man tell about God, about His love for me. About Jesus. My life changed because I believed."

"Faith," Liz said.

The flicker of a smile crossed his face. "But when war came, I made more mistakes. I left the city and became a pastor in a small village—so busy with teaching and preaching that I was unprepared. I lost all my family except my son and daughter. Now again, because I was too trusting, I have done this dreadful thing. This . . . this foolish, terrible wrong."

"But you've done a lot that's right," Sam told him. "We need you at Haven, Pastor S. The kids admire you. They trust you."

"Shauntay and the others are looking to you for leadership," Liz agreed. "Pastor Stephen, can you keep your faith?"

He looked at her for a moment. His lips trembled as he held his daughter close. "I am not worthy of the One who died for me. But I shall never cease to proclaim His mercies."

"They're new every morning," Ana said, laying her hand on his arm. "I look forward to hearing your first sermon in St. Louis, Pastor."

"Yeah," the police officer affirmed. "He was preaching at me through most of the barbecue. I'd like to hear the rest of that message sometime."

Stephen blotted his eyes. "I have much to tell," he said. "Very much indeed."

As they left the building, he was still talking—lacking some of his usual enthusiasm, but not much.

"Will Haven take in any more strangers?" Liz asked Sam. "Things haven't gone too smoothly with this bunch."

"Sure we will." Sam smiled at her. "Trouble pretty much goes along with obedience to Christ, doesn't it?"

"Amen to that," Terell told the group. "Listen, I heard the police talking in there. They booked Mo Ded. Real name is Darrell Jones."

"Darrell?" Sam echoed.

"Yeah, our big bad *Mo Ded* had a rap sheet in Chicago," Terell said. "Petty stuff. Problem kid—like most of 'em. His father went to prison for murder. His mother died. Guess he came to St. Louis trying to build a substitute family."

"The Hypes are out of business now," Joshua said. "Darrell Jones will go to prison on weapons charges. Pastor Stephen and I can visit him there. Teach him a better way."

As the group separated for the evening, Joshua and Liz slipped through the front door. They paused for a moment beneath the building's green awning. He slipped his arms around Liz and gently kissed her. For the first time that day, she felt utterly safe.

"You're here," she murmured. "In St. Louis. I still can't believe it. How did you come so fast? You must have been right behind me."

"Did I mention that Duff-Flannigan has its own airport? Small fleet—a couple of helicopters, a Cessna, a Learjet."

Closing her eyes, Liz laid her head on his shoulder. "I truly believed I'd never see you again. But how can this be all right? You broke your vow to your father, Joshua."

"A Duff never breaks a vow. Dad asked to talk to me after you left. Said he wanted to release me from my promise. After your conversation by the pool, he understood things about me he had never known. He gave me his blessing to live in St. Louis and help Sam and Terell run Haven."

She looked up at him. "Then you're staying?"

"I'm moving in. The road ahead won't be easy, Liz." He ran his thumb down the side of her cheek. "But I'm asking if you'll walk it with me . . . as my wife."

Joy welling inside her, Liz nodded. "I promise," she murmured. "And, you know, I always keep my vows. It's a Duff thing."

With a low laugh, he bent and kissed her lips. Above them, the moonlight silvered the doorway to Haven, a beacon of hope in the darkness.

QUESTIONS FOR DISCUSSION

1. What personality traits and interests do Liz and Joshua have in common?

2. What threatens their growing love for each other?

3. The “kill all the enemy” mentality is found worldwide, from armies to street gangs. How has genocide affected history?

4. Does genocide occur in our world today? Where?

5. In the Bible, what does God say about how His people are to treat foreigners and aliens? What did Jesus teach about strangers in *Matthew* 25?

6. Discuss your country’s policies regarding immigrants and refugees. What are your personal beliefs?

7. Liz mentions that young refugees from Africa can become involved in African-American gangs. Why? How similar are these two people groups?

8. Liz and Joshua question God's will for their future. How can you know what He wants of you?

9. By the end of the book, both Liz and Joshua have altered their original life goals. But they feel comfortable about this. Does God ever change His mind?

10. Haven and its volunteers are impacting the community for good. What can you do to make a difference in your neighborhood? In your world?

Center Point Publishing
600 Brooks Road • PO Box 1
Thorndike ME 04986-0001 USA

(207) 568-3717

US & Canada:
1 800 929-9108
www.centerpointlargeprint.com